# Carmichaels

# Carmichaels

TOM GREEN

ARCHWAY
PUBLISHING

Archway Publishing books may be ordered through booksellers or by contacting:

Archway Publishing
1663 Liberty Drive
Bloomington, IN 47403
www.archwaypublishing.com
844-669-3957



Cover illustration by Horst Maria Guilhauman

Interior illustrations by Chris Cooper

Graham's picture by Bubba

Letter by Isaac

ISBN: 978-1-6657-1958-2 (sc)
ISBN: 978-1-6657-1957-5 (hc)
ISBN: 978-1-6657-1959-9 (e)

Library of Congress Control Number: 2022903554

Print information available on the last page.

Archway Publishing rev. date: 03/24/2022

To my son, Graham Green. You will forever live
in the spaces between my heartbeats.
Also, to my friend and partner in fun, Terry Frisk.
Really, really miss ya both.

# Contents

## PART 1



## PART 2

## PART 3

# PART 1

# Frisk

IT WAS AFTER 6:00 P.M., BUT THE SUN WAS STILL UP. I WALKED across the schoolyard, sipping a cold beer from a small brown paper bag. *New York City style*, I thought. Just like discreet drinkers do on those busy streets in the big city.

The elementary school was in the middle of a large postage stamp–style lot. The huge grass schoolyard was surrounded by mature maple trees. The sweet summer smell of grass, trees, and leaves filled the air. I could see Carmichaels' brown front door past the schoolyard corner, on the other side of the street. It was a one-story red-brick building. Carmichaels was flat on top where the peak would be. Then a typical roof dropped down the sides. It was a very long building.

I was anxious but not rushing. Thoughts of kicking ass and shooting pool with Frisk went through my mind as I sipped and walked. My workout earlier today felt great, but I still had an uneasy feeling in my stomach. We had done hip throws earlier at judo practice. Throws are a good way to let someone fly if they attack coming straight in or from above. My middleweight frame was built for this type of defense. It felt so cool, grabbing an attacker by the collar, twisting violently, and taking him over my shoulder and six feet in the air. He would crash hard to the floor while my long, sweat-soaked brown hair lashed across my face. Now that was fun.

But the workout did not shake this feeling of dread that had crept into my mind. The future is a mystery. For that matter, I believe it is a predetermined mystery. The future is already written; unfortunately, we have no idea what it is. A million different things could happen just now, but only one will happen. And that is the one happening right now. Nothing can change that, and as sure as the past is there, written in stone, so too is the future.

Strolling across the grass, sipping cold beer and feeling the can through the paper bag hiding it, I wondered to myself, *What is it I hide?*

It was a hundred yards to the corner. As I walked past the red bricks of the school, wood-framed windows reflected only darkness from inside. If I looked behind me, I would still be able to see my small stucco home. It was the second on the left and directly across the street from the high school. It was a quiet street just now, in a small town. I loved it.

I was also thinking about my pool cue, Falcon. I don't know what type of wood it's made from. I just know it is one fine cue. Frisk sent it to me a few years back while visiting some West Coast friends. I still remember that June day when I got the pick-up-at-post-office notice in the mail. Once it was unwrapped, I had a long black box and when opened, it held the best two-piece pool cue I will ever see in my lifetime.

The note with it said,

> Hi, Tommy. How ya doing? This cue's name is Falcon. Not *the falcon* or *it's a falcon*, just Falcon, and it embodies all birds of prey. Falcon is made from rare West Coast hardwood. I got the cue and a set of nunchakus at the same time. Both were made from the same stick of wood. It is said the sword is the soul of the warrior. So too the cue stick is the soul of the pool player. Let your soul shine through. Enjoy. We should throw a few plants in the ground sometime soon. See you in a few weeks … F.

*Interesting*, I thought to myself. *This is a beautiful cue.* I tried to imagine Falcon being made from one of the hardest trees out there. The West Coast has mountains and valleys riddled with goddamn trees, they say. Hard work and heavy machinery is the only way to get the wood out of the forests and made into something people can use. Well, if this pool cue is anything like Frisk's nunchakus, Falcon should be something rather deadly.

When Frisk finally made it back to town, he told me about Falcon. "I was given Falcon and a set of nunchakus from a kung-fu master I trained with on the coast. Falcon plays excellent. Nice taper, professional style, holding the same diameter several inches up the cue before getting wider to match the joint. Falcon is well balanced and weighs nineteen and a half ounces. The beautiful leather wrap gives Falcon a very personal feel. The tip is an eleven-millimeter diameter and holds the chalk very well with regular roughing. It is a forgiving cue, Tommy. Stay within the limits of the cue ball for English and you will be rewarded. You are ready for Falcon, Tommy. Falcon will be good to you. I love the dark brown design in the butt, with the long, thin, spear-shaped ivory insets in a fleur-de-lis style. To me, this style represented the French medieval social dynasty of those who worked, those who fought, and those who prayed. With this cue, you will be doing all three at the same time."

I was impressed with his knowledge. "Holy God, Frisk, where did you go to college?"

Frisk told me, "Tommy, I wanted you to have this cue. You deserve it." He didn't say why, though.

Frisk is an interesting character, a rather deadly character, in fact. We have been friends for over ten years now. We first met when we were seventeen years old. He was ahead of me by a year in school, but we shared the youthful gene to climb trees, crawl around on building tops, swing from ropes, and stay up all night. We became good friends.

One moonless night, after midnight on an old country road, he told me a little about his past. Our friendship was a few years old at the time. We were smoking blond hash from a small beige skull and drinking cold bottled beer from a cooler full of ice. We had stolen the ice from a local motel hours before. The ice dispenser was around back of the motel and was for the exclusive use of the guests. No attendant was ever on duty at the hours we needed ice, so it was easy to pull around the back and fill a cooler or two with enough ice to last the next ten to twelve hours.

Frisk told me we were smoking this blond hashish in a human skull. "Jesus God Almighty, where did you get this? Are you for fucking real? Did you smuggle this into the country somehow?" I said under my breath yet loud enough to be heard. He just smiled and snickered while biting the tip of his tongue. The hashish was strong and filled my nose and lungs. "If this was a human skull, then I feel lucky to be smoking from it. Yes, it is a rare opportunity indeed," I said as smoke billowed in front of me.

I took another long haul from the skull bong, and the story began. "When I was very young, a baby, I was in Chile with my parents. They were killed, and I was taken." Frisk gave a slight nonchalant stare at the ground. It was a tell, and I instantly knew he had deep feelings for his parents. Light from the dashboard fell upon one half of Frisk's face, lighting it brightly, his strong features clearly visible. The other was half-covered in darkness, hiding a part of him I might never know. Maybe it would help for me to listen closely.

Music played from speakers in the light blue convertible Jeep CJ-5 we were sitting in. The black rag top was down. No one could hear us this far back in the bush. "So, what you are telling me, as it turned out, best you can figure, you were taken as a baby and sold to a family in South America, somewhere in the Medellin area. Just thinking about that is nuts. Man, oh, man." It felt scary. I thought to myself that his situation was not all that uncommon. "Well, Frisk, people go missing every day. Even at this very moment, someone is being taken and will not be coming home tonight." It was scary.

Frisk described it something like this: "I was raised by a powerful cartel. They taught me things, things few people know or will ever know. I learned math and English, but I also studied fighting and agriculture. We trained every day, and we trained to kill. When we weren't doing any of that shit, we would walk the fields of weed. These were the fields the town needed to live on, to survive on. We would guard the fields, and we would grow them. We grew Punta Roja, the best Colombian weed on earth." Frisk had my highest attention level. All of a sudden, for some unknown reason, I was most interested in this weed.

"That sounds very interesting," I said.

"The gringos call this weed Colombian Red," Frisk said by way of translation, and my interest was now ignited.

Mostly everything was fine, but sometimes, unwanted visitors would show up, and it was our job—it was my job—to make sure they didn't come back." There was a relaxed pause. The smoke was tasty, and the beer was godawful cold. It was a great night.

Then he bitched about the weather. "The weather was hot and sticky. We ate lots of lizards and fruits and fish. I actually loved some of it. Then, one day, a German family who were in the area noticed me. They found out I was American and decided to get me out of there. It all happened quickly, and soon I was in Germany. I know the chief of the village was angry, very angry. He did not want to lose me, but what the fuck? I finally had a chance to find out who I really am. They will never find me here. Being a mercenary for those murdering fucks was never on my agenda. I stayed in Germany for a few weeks, where we discovered my parents were from this small town. Shortly thereafter, I made it to the West Coast, then back here to my home."

"How did you figure out your family history? I guess you just started snooping." I was interested to get the whole picture, or at least as much as Frisk knew.

"Did some digging. Eventually, I found out about my parents. They were simple, honest folk. They were hard workers who liked to help people and travel. My dad worked for the local police, he was respected. Mom worked as a pharmacist, dispensing drugs and medicine to the people. Nothing royal or extravagant but people I was and am proud of. They enjoyed traveling—just in the wrong place at the wrong time. It was a good time for baby-napping in South America just then. Probably still is." Frisk did not see any humor in that.

"I never heard about any family from here being killed and their baby missing. Was this covered up?" I had some questions about this one.

Frisk said, "It was a case of nowhere to start. By the time anyone figured out what had happened, it was long over. It was like a dark secret that just died on the vine, so to speak. I did not tell anyone my history, nor who I was, but chose to just settle in and live my life here. Dad was murdered when he tried to fight back. Poncho was one of the cartel leaders looking to buy babies. I was lucky that Poncho was the chief cartel leader. He runs the show down there and gave me a good family and upbringing. He told me he liked me because I would cry, but without tears. He raised me not as a gringo but a son. He knew nothing of my past, nothing."

I wanted to know more about his real parents. "My real dad loved to hunt, fish, play cards, and shoot guns. Mom loved the outdoors, cooking, and sports. I miss them and wish they were here." It was good that Frisk managed to get that level of closure. I was proud of him. I was sympathetic.

"I feel for you man. So that was it. Your parents were basically good local folk who ran up against the most savage bastards on earth. I am truly sorry."

Frisk was OK talking about his past. He put a positive spin to the story. "And you know, I kind of like it here. We met, and that was a good thing." Frisk looked toward me, his face fully in the light now. He glanced downward for a brief moment, smiling. I knew in that instant there was more to be told, just not tonight.

So, God only knows where the real truth lies with this guy, but we have been friends in this small town for a bunch of years now, and man, oh, man, can he fight. I have seen him called to action, and it is not pretty for anyone in front of him.

I was still sucking on my cold beer as I hit the schoolyard corner and started walking on the sidewalk. God, it tasted good. I crossed the street, walking slowly toward Carmichaels.

I loved to play at Carmichaels. It felt right. It was, like, my home-team clubhouse. I felt safe there. It was familiar.

The front door was on the right side. It swung inward, and the washroom was on the left. It was a small one but still big enough to give some speed freak enough room to spread out his gear and do a hit. Not a popular practice, but it was known to happen. A bit farther up, on the left, and just around a small corner, were the lunch counter, pinball machine, and jukebox. Another side entrance was located just beside the bar. Carmichaels was a long, narrow place, enough room for twelve tables, lined up one after the other. Lots of room on the sides to walk by, hang your coat, mark scores, and all that stuff. Maybe roll a joint or two.

The last two tables were full twelve-foot snooker tables. This is where it began for me when I was twelve years old. On many days, I retreated from family and school only to be found at the back of Carmichaels, banging the snooker balls around. I would head to Carmichaels after dinner to hang out. There was an attraction to this pool hall.

I still remember the smell of the place back then, cigarettes, beer, and chuck wagons cooking in the small convection oven. Ah, nothing like a steaming hot chuck wagon—meat and cheese on a toasted hot dog bun smeared with mustard and ketchup to warm your belly. The cloth was a dark green color. It felt soft on my bridge hand when rested upon. My arm and back would get sore from shooting pool balls every night, until closing. My calves would cramp from standing on my toes to make some shots. It was painful. It was not easy, but I played a lot. To get better, I would gamble for small amounts of cash. Sometimes I would lose, but sometimes I would win, and it was the winning that kept me coming back.

It was Johnny who taught me to shoot one ball at a time, over and over. He explained, "For the first few months, you must shoot one ball at a time down the table. That is how I developed my stroke. This is how professionals learn their stroke. They practice every shot, thousands of times, for weeks on end, until they master it, before moving on to the next one." He was so full of life and very inspiring to me with his "and don't forget that it's fucking great to be alive" remarks. He would repeat those words on occasion, expressing his gratitude for life. Johnny was like a brother to me.

Eventually, I learned to play snooker in the spirit of Alex Higgins. He was a world champion player from England and always drank heavily when he played. The only time Alex was not drinking booze was when he was playing snooker. What Stu Unger was to the dark side of poker and cards Alex Higgins was to snooker and pool. As I grew, I learned how to play pool and how to drink. Not so much how to drink, as I never really learned that part. The beer ran constantly during those marathon snooker games. It was intense training and such a wonderful experience to play without fear, to reach such great pleasures from a cue sport. I am sure these emotions were the roots of all my addictions.

In that moment, I imagined a small toast to Alex, bowing my head in reverent honor. I play very little snooker on those tables now. It felt like innocence lost. It was mostly old-timers who seemed to play snooker these days. Maybe someday I'll start again.

Frisk was sitting at the lunch counter, eating his chuck wagon while awaiting another. The ding went off on the small electric oven, telling Johnny it was ready. Frisk remarked eagerly, "The hot-dog-style bun, filled with ham, bologna, and cheese, then cooked until steaming hot, is now ready. Add mustard and ketchup, and I have an incredible meal. All for a cost of forty-five cents," Frisk was reading the "How to Prepare" instructions on the cellophane wrapping.

My beer was done now, so I threw the empty bag and all into the garbage bin by the pinball machine. Sitting on the bar stool beside Frisk, I ordered up a beer. It was cold and frosty, and I started drinking it before saying anything. I guzzled the first half.

I spoke quietly to Frisk. "My thoughts take me to our fields of pot. Multiple fields. Ten thousand shorter Indica plants per hectare, plants that at five feet high, give up two pounds of dried bud each. Don't you know Frisk, these were the same plants grown in the Riff Mountains of Pakistan and Afghanistan."

Frisk spoke. "The trick is to get lots of these plants growing. And this season is off to a great start." He spoke with passion.

Frisk ate while I thought out loud. "Other fields have Sativa and mixed breeds. I have no idea what some of these plants are. Some smaller fields are just for seeds. This year, with Hunter's help, we were going to start harvesting seeds and get our own seed bank going."

Frisk knew about seeds. "There is a lot of cash in just managing seeds for growers, don't you know."

I was anxious to give Frisk the update. "Feeding, harvesting, drying, selling, and spending your money is a lot harder than it sounds. This is a goddamn full-time job. Getting top value for time invested can be a real bastard. Right now, we are in the fertilize and vegetation stage. Grow the plants big. Populate the fields, get the plants out there."

It was the beginning of summer, and the day was getting rather late but only insofar as dusk was coming. My energy was good, high, in fact. "We need to talk." As Frisk finished his chuck wagon and Coke, I finished my mug and ordered a refill. "Play a game or two of eight-ball?" I asked Frisk.

"Sure," he said.

I grabbed Falcon from behind the bar and a set of balls from the stack at the end of the counter. Each set of balls was in its own plastic tray with a cube of chalk. The balls were clean and shiny. I grabbed the top set and started walking toward the back of Carmichaels. "Table nine," I said to Johnny as I walked away. A moment later, the lights came on over table nine.

Frisk grabbed his cue from behind the counter and followed after me. I passed by the tables one by one. Cues racked the walls. Lights were only on over tables in use. I stopped at table nine. The balls were cool to the touch as I dumped them out. They rolled out onto the table, scattering everywhere.

Falcon was in two pieces. I slowly removed the caps protecting the joints and put them in my cue case. The two halves floated together, almost magnetically. It seemed to take a long time, watching the butt and shaft screw together until it was tight. Check the tip for enough chalk, proper shape, and correct roughness. Now, I was ready to play.

The balls were jammed into the rack. Soon they were squared up for a game of eight-ball. I loved eight-ball. It leaves some room for error and run-outs happen for those who can play the game. This made the game exciting for me.

Frisk twisted his cue together. "Ten bucks a set?" A set, in this case, was a run to eleven. The first person to win eleven games wins. It could be called a best out of twenty-one. If the game goes to hill to hill and is tied at ten each, that would be twenty games played, with the deciding game being the twenty-first.

"Sure. Have you seen Lenny around at all these days?" I asked.

"Out fishin', last time I heard, somewhere in the park. He'll be back in a day or two," Frisk told me.

Music started in the jukebox. Someone wanted to hear "Golden Needles and Silver Threads." I enjoyed the song. It was nice and relaxing.

Frisk won the flip and broke the balls. It was a loud break, balls scattered everywhere. The head ball bounced two rails, dropping into the side pocket. Frisk chalked up while circling the table.

He was tall and skinny, maybe six foot one with black hair, a bit short just now and parted in the middle. There was a thin mustache above a happy smile.

His big, round blue eyes were seldom sleepy. His face, a little pudgy from too many beers, held his nearly permanent smile, which relaxed people and instilled confidence. Sometimes, he would walk slowly, appearing meek or frail, but it was an act. He was a strong, wiry motherfucker who could kick a man square in the face twice before he even knew what was happening.

Frisk continued to shoot and talk with a wild sense of humor. "I love to fuck lots of hot chicks. For that matter, I would fuck mostly any chick."

He could drive the pool balls in fast, and he could run racks, one after the other. We probably played rather even, but then we played different styles. We mostly played eight-ball, but sometimes, we played nine-ball, straight pool, one pocket, English billiards, or snooker, if the bet was right.

Frisk had awesome cue-ball control. He hit the cue ball with a snap below its center point, causing it to spin backward toward him after hitting the object ball. The British call this type of cue ball action *screw.* Frisk screwed the cue ball from one end of the table to the other end, as I watched. This shot took but a second or two. And in that brief lull, my mind drifted. In that moment, all I could see were fields of pot.

I spoke to Frisk about where my thoughts had gone. "You know, Frisk, I started smoking pot many years back. No big thing. Then, one summer, after throwing several dozen Mexican pot seeds in the ground and harvesting a homegrown experience, I thought, *Wow, this is easy.* It became obvious there was money in this business. I got bud and trim, learned to make hash, and made a few bucks on the side."

Frisk was there too. "Yeah, the next season was pretty good too. We pulled in fifty pounds of good bud and about ten pounds of hash, if I recall correctly." Actually, Frisk had a lot to do with those early projects being so successful. Frisk was always aware of security. "Privacy is number one. Be vigilant."

I was excited now. "Cool thing was, I found a way to produce good Lebanese-style hashish from the trim and bud. So this season, I said to myself, *What the fuck? I am really going for it this time!* We talked with Lenny and Hunter about our plan for more sites to expand." I praised Frisk too. "Frisk, you seem to have an uncanny knack for this work. I am grateful. Thank you."

Frisk walked and shot. His balls went in one after the other. I commented, "Fuck, you are good. You can move that cue ball to where you need it for the next shot. You got no fear of missing, do you, Frisk?"

When he did miss, he would swear or make pissed-off-looking sneers. Sometimes, he would imagine an opponent in front of him and shoot out a quick lunge punch or throat-grab-type move. "This game is over. Nice shooting." I sounded indifferent. Frisk marked his game and racked the balls for the next game.

Frisk broke, and I began to tell him about the locations. "Lenny has five fields in a valley north of the park at this time. Each field has a good east-to-west vantage and is tilled and planted just as you instructed. Sounds like a trudge just to get there, from what Lenny told me. He said to bring our fishing rods because we get to do some fishing along the route," I mentioned in a low voice.

I lost the next two games. Frisk made some nice long shots. Most impressive. The balls made a hammering sound as they fell directly into the pockets. Then he missed and snagged me with the cue ball against the eight ball, leaving no position. I bridged over the eight ball and called a rail ticky and shot. The cue ball bounced off the side rail directly at my ball, smashing it into the side pocket with a bang. The cue ball rolled softly to the center table. I then proceeded to tear through my balls. The last ball went in.

I racked and continued, "Yeah, we got lots of spots. Each one is out of the way with good sun and good soil. Fuck, Frisk, I tell you, we are going to have something this year, and by all rights, it should go as smooth as Lake Clear on a warm, windless summer night at sunset." I motioned my hand in a slow, horizontal manner, demonstrating a vision of serenity.

"Oh yeah," he said, "we got a bunch of sites we gotta see again soon, and we gotta kill those fucking slugs."

I closed off the conversation. "I agree, we meet in a few days with Hunter and Lenny for some updates. Until then, let's just forget about it for now."

We played on, and I started to get ahead in games. The beer was cold, and I kept drinking. I was getting the load on.

I thought we needed a joint. "Hey, Frisk, have you started to roll a joint yet? There is room on that small side table." It was the one opposite where we broke from. "Use the hash I made last year. The real good stuff, made directly from dried buds."

Frisk was on it. "This stuff is black and moist and well pressed. Yeah, you got this one figured out, Tommy."

Back to playing pool. "This is fucking fun," I said with passion as long shots, bank shots, and combos all went in.

At the hill-to-hill point—that is, the next game wins the match for one of us—we slipped out the back door to burn the joint. There was this five-pound rock outside used to jam the back door open for just this event. We entered the back end of the long driveway between buildings.

Frisk loved drugs. "I love drugs," he said. He was an addict. I was not even sure of all the dope he was on. I think he was hanging out with some crazy types, some rednecks, and sometimes motorcycle gang members. That was fine with me. He also loved fast cars and drinking and drinking while driving fast cars fast.

The joint was great. I was getting really stoned. I began to tell Frisk about breaking up with Holly, this slim British brunette I was seeing. While taking a huge toke, I talked about her. "Holly is a nice gal. She loves to suck cock. She told me many times how her mouth felt like an old shoe from being stuffed full of cock most of the time. I thought that was interesting. Maybe I shouldn't have always made her suck me off twice in a row. I would tell her to imagine the second time was like blowing someone else. I know that's what I was thinking. I guess it went to her head."

Frisk handed me back the joint, telling me in a loud, reassuring voice, "Ah, you're better off without her." Then he pointed out, "She wasn't fit to pick bananas out of trees for monkeys anyway."

As I was now drunk and stoned, his reasoning made perfect sense. "Fuck her," I said, and I walked back inside. Frisk finished the joint and came in seconds behind me.

I broke. It was a dry break. I finished my beer and went up to see Johnny for another cold one. Walking back to the table, I watched Frisk shoot. He was doing great. He was fast and strong. Being tall and skinny, he could reach out onto the table for those long, hard-to-get-at shots. We were practicing, just banging them around, so to speak. He left himself a hard shot and missed. I cleaned up. The beer was going down real good.

I won the set and the ten dollars. "That was fun," I said. "I feel it's best to head down to the pub at the other end of town. It is about fifteen minutes or so, and it would give us time to smoke a few bowls and talk a bit." Frisk concurred with my suggestion. We walked to the front and paid for our table time. Frisk's cowboy boots made a rather unique click with each step. His boots were black and distinctive. They fit him perfectly.

I was thinking, those years in the jungle sure turned Frisk into something unique. I never really asked much about his childhood. He did share on occasion, and tonight would be one of those rare moments. I know it was a lost and difficult time for him to understand. We just let that kind of stuff come out naturally in conversation. I respected Frisk for that.

Carmichaels was coming around as we were heading out. Smoke filled the ceiling, and the fans moved it out the vents. Dave and John Deere were playing on table six. He was called John Deere, or JD for short, because he got caught stealing farm equipment and reselling it. Nice profit at a hundred thousand or more for a machine, but he did five years in jail once the cops caught up to him. So that was not very good and put him at the bottom of the food chain for stupid criminals.

They were both good shooters and loved to play, but I always left with their money. They still played me for small amounts of cash, any time. JD always had something crazy to talk about, how he was going to break someone's knees or burn their house down or start some wild grow operation somewhere with hundreds of plants. He was so full of shit, it was actually sad. I had this guy pegged as an early-graver.

Frisk was waiting. Slowly, I walked toward him, enjoying a total beer buzz. We left together through the side door. It was an immediate turn left, then the hand rails guided us down the short concrete wheelchair-access ramp to the street. We turned left and swung in front of Carmichaels, slowly walking across the front and into the dark. I had something significant to tell Frisk, something that could have been worth millions of dollars to us—or our deaths.

# The Hashish Plan

THE BEER WAS DOING ITS THING. I WAS DRUNK AND GETTING thirsty again. We sat on a bench under a tree to smoke a quick bowl from a small Mayan pipe I smuggled back from Mexico this one time. Pyramid in shape, and only a few inches long, it was handcrafted from indigenous stone.

As we sat and smoked, I verbalized my dollar estimate of the crop. "A thousand pounds of good bud is worth millions, but not all bud is worthy of bringing top price. There are five times that in trim and immature and excess buds. This is where the real value is for us. With thousands of plants, the only practical way to process it for commercial consumption is extracting kief and hot-pressing it into bricks of hashish. The world market has an incredible appetite for good hashish. Trust me, I know what I am talking about."

Frisk was listening. "I am following you, man."

I took a toke and explained further, "I started making hashish many years ago. Once the leaves were cut from the buds and left to dry, I had lots of hash-making material. In fact, about one hundred pounds once it all dried. I was just going to give it to Hunter so he could make oil, but I started to research how Lebanese and Moroccan hashish is made. They use dried weed, hundred-micron fine screens, bins to collect the kief, plastic to cover the bins, and sticks for beating. Kief consists of small crystals called trichomes found on the buds. They give the buds that sugary look when ripe. They also hold the psychoactive and medical properties. These properties are created when burned during smoking."

Frisk was getting the terminology straight. "So, clumps of trichomes are called kief. Where does hashish fit in?" I felt like Frisk was testing me.

"Good question, Frisk. Hashish is different. If the heat is about one hundred Fahrenheit, and the pressure is just enough to break open the trichomes. Then amazing smells, tastes, and colors of hashish can be produced. Trichomes on the plant gives it that sticky touch. That is why plants must be dried and the extraction process performed in cold or freezing conditions. In November, when the days are cooler, the process begins in Lebanon and Morocco. First, the screen is tightened over the bin, weed is placed on top of the screen, and plastic is used to cover the weed. Then they use kids to beat the hell out of it with sticks. Not too fast or hard, as this will damage the trichomes. These kids are the original trichome extractor device and the inspiration for TED, as I like to call it, sort of a code word."

Frisk was trying to be funny but was onto something. Serendipity. "Yeah, like the TED-5700."

I started again, "That was a fast response, and I like it. Very good. Anyway, all the trichomes start to separate from the busted, cooled bud, filter through the screen, and collect in the bins. And presto, they build up at the bottom of the bin inches deep. Make sure the plant material is well dried and frozen, if possible. Moroccan and Lebanese kief is pressed into the world's best hashish and supplies seventy percent of the earth. Let the hashish cool, and presto, it can be smoked within minutes, weeks, or months." I was laughing, but the excitement and passion were coming through.

The pipe was filled again and again because it felt good to me. "Now for the money part. At three thousand a pound—and we have a ton or more than two thousand pounds—that's five to six million dollars. How fucking cool is that, man? We were going to bring in some serious cash, man, oh, man. We will pull in millions if we stick to the plan and ride it out until the spring. Most of the inventory needs to be sold by early next year, anyway. Am I nuts?" I was very excited, my heartbeat going up a few notches. It felt like a nervous uncertainty. It was a gamble of sorts.

Frisk took his toke while putting a match on the packed bowl. The smoke smelled sweet in the air. Frisk was reassuring. "This is going to take a lot of fucking work. And, yup, we are crazy, but maybe worse than you think. There will be risks. I wonder, whose toes we will step on? You are talking about a lot of cash, and this is going to get some attention somewhere, on someone's radar." Frisk saw the bigger picture.

"I agree, but we can't stop now. Let's just keep on going as if nothing was wrong. When the time comes, we sell off the inventory, and that should end that. This really only needs to be a one-shot deal." I gave a slight nod.

Looking back at Frisk, I smiled and began again, "If you liked that plan, you are going to love this part. This is so cool. Wait until you hear this. I got to thinking about this sifting shaker I developed."

"The TED-5700," Frisk said lightly.

"It could be worth millions on the open market for growers and hashish makers everywhere. Nobody has one of these things, so I started writing it up, taking notes, making drawings, sketches, all kinds of design shit." I reached inside my pocket and pulled out a few of the drawings and sketches. Fumbling with papers, I finally unfolded them and tried to present them to Frisk so it made sense. I pointed to grinders and CO2 tanks and screens and multiple cone-shaped bins and a vibrator. Frisk was mildly interested and very stoned as he held another deep toke.

"Fuck you, man," I said with a rage building in my voice. "This is an important invention. I will revolutionize the hashish industry worldwide. The uses are many. Kief can be separated into several qualities instantly from nearly pure kief to various combinations of vegetation and trichome to create wonderful tastes and textures. That is done with multiple bins welded together. Kief can be cold-pressed for later use. The medical industry can use it to accurately reproduce known qualities. There are a lot of medical issues this shit can cure. And the cooking industry will love it for all sorts of consumable products, like drinks, cookies, candies, massage oils, and who knows what else." I pushed Frisk on the arm to reinforce my passion and get his attention.

"So, what the fuck do you call this thing, this TED?" he asked, starting to show more interest as he examined the papers, trying to make sense of the scribbles.

"Technically, it is a continuously operating cannabis trichome extraction machine, but I like to call it the Sifter. I am also going to set up a company called Tom Sift Inc. Get it, eh. "Tom Sift" because I invented it, and it will sift. Plus, it is an amazing way to hide all the fucking money we are going to make. What do you think?" Frisk's eyes narrowed. His breathing slowed. Now I had his attention.

"Maybe franchise the TED-5700 or rent it out. There could be money in it if it works," Frisk said.

I looked directly into his beady little fucking eyes and let the cat out of the bag. "The last thing I wanted to add is that I contacted a patent company called Intellectual Property Guard. They have identified the unique and different parts of the invention to allow for a formal patent application. Imagine that, Frisk. If I were to get a patent on my sifter, then I am really in the money. It has to be worth millions. They are helping me set up the company Tom Sift Inc." Frisk was getting it. "I am fucking serious, man. I will be called the Henry Ford of the hashish business. This is the key to the whole fucking plan, our fucking future, man." My voice was getting loud again. This time, I settled down, and we pondered the moment.

"You are right, Tommy. We need the financial protection from a company like this. It is brilliant." Frisk understood. I let it settle in for a minute before moving on.

I took a moment to thank Frisk for teaching us and all the help to date. "Good thing we have some helpers to split the work up. Lenny is right into it and found most of the sites, but none of it could be possible if not for your fucking help to get this whole thing set up. What you trained us to do was incredible; we can set up fields of pot for miles and miles. I can't thank you enough, and neither can Lenny. You created a fucking monster; he is really into it. Thank you."

Frisk was proud. It showed in his voice and his now wide eyes.

"We've got a world-class grow site, and it's damn near impossible to find if you're not looking. We gotta get out there and see them soon."

I agreed again. "As soon as possible."

I pondered Lenny's involvement, while smoking heavily. Lenny never was one to smoke much dope but he loved money, and he loved to drink. Probably be put in the alcoholic category, but I don't give a shit. He found the spots. He is an invaluable part of the team.

# Bounty Hunter

THE AIR HAD A WARM, SWEET SMELL ABOUT IT—THE SMELL of grass freshly cut and maple trees in full regalia. We walked and talked. Frisk told me how he trained with different weapons. Then he opened up again. "When I got to the southwest coast, we trained hard. I just loved those nunchakus. They saved my life more than once." There was a smirk on his face. His eyes focused somewhere else.

I was OK at martial arts, practicing them mostly for health and some ego-building, but I was no killer. My legs felt light as I walked. Frisk told me a story about this chick who moved into the same dark, grungy apartment building shortly after he did. I gathered this was just before showing up here ten years ago.

He started, "She was a beauty, with a tight body, blonde hair, and tall." Frisk made this twisted look with his face as he explained how hot she was. "I ran into her in the stairs one night. It was an old fucking building. The halls were dark, the doors made of wood. There were only a few apartments per floor. This place must have been ninety years old."

He went on, "So, I meet this chick in the stairs and invite her up to my room. Once I get her up there, I fucked the living shit out of her. I probably fucked her hard for three hours straight. She loved to get pounded from behind." Frisk made a leering grin just the same way I'm sure he did while hammering away on her. "When we were through and she was well fucked, she split back to her place. What I didn't know was that her boyfriend was a fifth dan in tae-kwon-do. I guess he saw her leaving my room and slapped her around until she told him how I had just fucked her senseless. What I also didn't know was that he was from Colombia, from the same goddamn fields I grew up in. And he had an agenda that involved me going back to Colombia.

"So, I am sitting on the couch with track pants on when the doorbell rings. I answer it, and this tall fucker, in good shape, sidekicks me straight in the chest. I go flying onto my coffee table. He grabs me by the wrist and twists me around so I'm facing down, sort of bent at the waist, then kicks me three or four times in the stomach. Then he throws a full-on kick to my head. I went down hard."

"This guy must be good. What happened?" I was wondering about this guy. What was going on?

"It was a few seconds before I came around. I remember this guy telling me how he was going to come back and kill me if I looked at his woman again. He looked around my room like he was checking me out. He stared at my plane ticket from Germany on a shelf, then left." Frisk was not very happy. He was making faces with serious emotion, as if it happened last night instead of ten years ago.

Frisk kept telling the story. "I got up, wiped the blood from my face, and put on the steel-toed shoes I used at work and put my nunchakus in my belt behind my back. The walk down to his room was slow, and once there, I knocked on the door. He answered, but the security chain restricted the opening to a few inches. I punched straight through the door, grabbed him by the throat and pulling him through the door and into the hall. I punched him three times rapidly in the face, and as the motion pushed him back, I did a powerful sidekick, knocking him off his feet and onto the floor. When he stood up, I roundhouse kicked him in the head. He roundhouse kicked me in the shoulder. I pushed him down the hallway with high kicks, low kicks, and spinning kicks until his back crushed into the end wall. We fought down the stairs, punching and kicking each other. I was bleeding, and he was bleeding. His style was familiar and reminiscent of my training days in Colombia. The unique patterns were the same. We fought and rolled into the back alley. It boarded on a huge raging river dumping into the ocean. My hands dropped to my side, and I faced him ten feet away. 'Who are you? What do you want?'" Frisk was painting a dark picture. I guess he never figured anyone would find him.

The killer's response was short. "You left the fields unguarded. You left without warning. That hurt and angered the chief. He will pay for your return to hold you accountable for your treachery, and I will force you back."

"The challenge was now clear, danger imminent. My fists clenched tight, my breathing slowed, and my feet twisted on the ground, ready to attack. We fought, and I kicked him in the ribs. He tried to block the follow-up attack, but I punched him twice to the head. He front-kicked me against a fence. Then he picked up a piece of steel pipe and swung it at my head. He was trying to kill me. I reached behind my back and pulled out my nunchakus, catching the pipe in an X-block, deflecting it to the left, exposing his back to me. He tried to block the axe-kick that was coming at his kidneys, but he was off-balance and weak. This fight had gone on for some fucking time now. He was tough, but I'd had enough of him. My right leg swung straight up, around, and down with tremendous force, my heel crushing into his kidney and spine. It was a brutal kick."

"Holy God, Frisk, wow," was about all I could say.

"I then spun a full circle, letting the nunchakus crack this guy on the back several times. He stood up in time to catch my front roundhouse kick and then a whipping back roundhouse kick with the same leg to his head. He just stood there by the edge on the river bank, bleeding from the ears, and into his kidneys and bowels. He had a few vertebrae chipped, but the nerve damage deadened the pain just then. I stepped back, so there was about fifteen feet between us. Side-stepping forward at him, I cocked my right leg back, not straightening it out until three feet from him and moving fast. My sidekick caught him square in the solar plexus and literally launched this fucker clear off the riverbank into the fast, dark, cold current. His eyes were closed over as he went six feet off the ground and eighty feet off the edge." Frisk breathed deep, almost a sigh.

"He was gone, and that was the last I would ever see of him. The place was dark, and no one was there to see us fight. I went back to my room and stretched out on my bed. The next thing I knew, his woman was lying in bed beside me. Her right eye was swollen. She had a cracked rib and could hardy breathe. I put some ice on her eye, and she put a Band-Aid on my forehead. After thanking me for killing that creep, she told me how they met in South America. She said she was extorted, forced to fuck, then used to bring this killer into the country to search for a guy called Frisk. She said nobody knew where they were yet as he just confirmed today you were the one he was searching for. She would not be complaining or identifying any bodies either. I guess she was free to return to her life, whatever that was."

Frisk tried to explain his thinking to me at the time. "I knew it would be difficult to determine where the body went in exactly. This bounty hunter would be very banged up from the smashing on the rocks. It would look like he fell in anywhere, accidentally, of course. The next day, I packed up and left for this small town. Never heard about it again, and I don't care. Their trail went cold, so to speak."

"You took care of business rather quickly. I felt a little nervous about your story, and it seemed to confirm my earlier feeling of dread, of impending doom." I told Frisk, "I am glad you took care of that creep. Now I know where another body was buried." We laughed together.

Frisk brought it back now with a final word. "The guy was fucked, and his girlfriend was a good fuck." We laughed again.

# Holly

THE JUNE EVENING AIR WAS WARM. IT WAS DARK NOW, BUT streetlights kept the road bright while trees acted like walls against the dark. I could see their shadows lengthen and then end, leaving darkness in the distance. My face was warm from the air. In a minute, we would be at the pub.

Frisk was into drugs, heavy drugs. He ate acid and did needle drugs when he got the right meth. None for me, thanks. Fuck that shit. I stay with the pot and booze. Frisk also loved pot and hash. He sold lots of both and everything else in between. But pussy was highest on his list. Single, married, young, old—he didn't care.

I remember the time he woke up in my room with some Eskimo woman. I was on the couch, and the room reeked. It stunk like dead, rotting fish. That stink you get when fish heads, blood, guts, and scales have been locked in a pail in the garage in the summer heat. The chick looked like she came second in an axe fight. Some ugly scars ran across her face, and she sweated constantly. I think she had gone through a windshield face-first at some time in her recent past. And she weighed in at around two hundred and twenty pounds. Frisk's words on that one were, "It was rough, but I gave her the old Frisk leg, anyway."

The beer was sold along the left side of the pub, and just past the bar were the pool tables. Players put their names on a blackboard and erased them off once they were called to play.

After grabbing beers, we moved toward some empty seats on the far side of the pool table. I drank about half of mine before we sat down. There was nothing like a cold beer, especially when I was already carrying a good buzz.

We watched the pool games. I love watching pool, seeing the balls bouncing around and trying to figure out if the guy shooting was a hustler or just a good shot having some fun. It is important to know the difference. Frisk and I did not plan to win. Well, maybe win a few games, but then fuck off out of here.

The shooter girl was cute, with nice perky tits. Frisk ordered, "Flaming Drambuies to start things off." Soon they were set up, ignited, and hammered back. Frisk commented on the drink. "It was amazing how there was just a faint warm taste in your throat if you did it right." Frisk smirked and flirted with her. Problem was, she fell for it. I was drunk but under control.

I was jealous of Frisk's control. "Frisk, you always seem to be able to handle your booze and dope. I could never figure out how you managed that." Frisk just smirked.

It was semicrowded for a Thursday night. I was getting loose for no good reason. It just felt like the thing to do. I had started now, so there was not much use stopping until I rode this night out to the bitter end.

They were playing doubles now. *Cool*, I thought when our names finally came up to play. The beer went down too fast, so next time, we ordered a jug each.

Frisk was winking at some chick. She was sort of winking and smiling back. Fuck, he had a way with women. I looked closer, and it was Holly at the bar. Frisk motioned to her with his eyes. She got up and came over to our table. The mania was building. I noticed her black, high heels first, then her long, slim legs in white shorts with a tight halter top as my eyes roamed from bottom to top.

Holly watched me check her out, then spoke, "Piece of piss. Rubbish then. I always thought of you as a leg man. Do I drive you wild? Are you going to buy me a splash?" Her British accent made her sexier. She sat between us, and I ordered her a beer.

We played pool and talked. Holly was drunk and having fun.

The guys playing were doing well and had been there since we arrived. They made banks and long rail shots. But they also missed or left themselves out of position. They were good at running out if they had five or fewer balls on the table.

It was finally our chance to play. I jumped up and started to rack the balls. Once racked, I grabbed a cue and took my name off the blackboard. They broke and were running the table but missed an easy shot on the black ball. We had all our balls left on table, and it was my shot. I did love this game. I played slow and lined up the shots. One after the other, the balls went down, until I got to the black. The black sat in front of the first diamond by the back rail, and the cue ball was out in the middle of the table. It really didn't look like I had much of a shot. I called it, "Four banks in the corner." It was actually an easy shot and went almost straight in the pocket. The guys were a little pissed but shook our hands, and we called the next name on the board.

I looked up from my beer to see two Colombians at the table. They had round, tanned faces. The taller one had a small scar under his right eye. Not obvious and not recent. They seemed organized and well-dressed, with a professional demeanor. I said, "You never know what will happen. Every game is a new game." They racked the balls, I broke, and the game began.

I made a few balls, then missed. We were having fun. Sometimes, it is OK to lose a game or two. No problem. Pool is not about winning every game. It is more about winning the right game at the right time. And, sometimes it is good for others to see you lose, so they believe there is a chance of winning. That's what it's all about, thinking you have a chance. We did not talk. I was just tripping out.

The tall one spoke. "Hey, gringo, it is your shot."

"Fuck you," I said, more as a reflex than a planned response. They looked at each other, exchanging the slightest of nods. They had a plan involving bullying specific locals. They believed they were great players and started acting tough, gangster like. I didn't like their attitude. Fuck those guys. I could run fifteen to thirty balls in a row. Not pro but enough to destroy these creeps in short order, and we soon did.

I think they actually believed we just missed our last shot. We could see them struggle to come up with a shot and missed an easy one. "Got yeah now," I said quietly. I felt OK but not like *now I am going to kill you.* I didn't think like that when it was time to win. I just think one shot at a time. Take my time, line it up, and get in the correct footing location from the start. When I did this, my chances of a shot going in and getting to the next ball went way up.

The beer kept going down with ease. I was still at the nice and buzzed stage. "Got the load on," as Lenny liked to say. They had made a difficult shot and left themselves with nothing. Again, they tried a hard shot but missed.

We did some good cut shots, and I made some cool cross sides. The tall guy with the scar was pretty good. Every time it was our shot, he would call us gringos. This was pissing me off. He could run four to seven balls and out, given the chance. Everyone was drunk and partying. Frisk was quietly sitting at the end of the table in the shadows. He watched them.

It was my turn. I approached the table, looking closely at the balls. I planned the next couple of shots. I saw where the eight ball was sitting, half down the long rail and close to it. I made the first shot with position on the second. I played it easy, lined up, and stroked smoothly. A small amount of draw, and I was set up for a side shot, with just the right angle to get to the next ball. And this happened seven times. As each ball went in, I slowly lined up the next shot and made it too. I could see them getting more and more pissed. When I shot the eight ball softly along the rail toward the corner, we all watched it drop. It was a simple straight-in shot, and we won.

I thought we had beaten these guys, but in fact, we were being hustled. They were toying with us. They were feeling out the locals to see who could play and who was a target. Then, we naturally picked it up a bit. I get better and more confident the more I play. A hustler will count on this false sense of security, and strike, win, when it counts the most. Now the game begins as I buckle down and tune in a bit. It is at this time that I try to determine whether I am going to win or get my ass kicked. I try not to get my ass kicked too often.

We went back to drinking. Frisk didn't want to see these guys anymore and fucked off to a different table, where a hot Mexican *chica* was curling her hair with one finger and smiling his way.

The Colombians came over to talk. Holly had been looking their way, smiling and staring.

"Fucking skank," I said under my breath. The chair at the bar was comfortable, and I was relaxing. The booze and the hash calmed my brain. *Yeah, got the load on now,* I thought to myself. These guys were acting cool and dumb, which is a good combo for gals like Holly. One of them smiled and chatted with Holly while the tall one came over and talked to me. *What is happening now?* I wondered.

This guy is in my face, his scar now clearly ugly. He says to me, "Gringo, you are a good player. Let's you and me play some nine-ball." He was moving his hands and arms as he spoke.

"How much yeah wanna play for?" I asked.

"We will make it interesting. Are you scared gringo?" He was inquisitive. He moved a little closer and stared into my eyes, holding my gaze. His scar stood out. It would intimidate the average person, but not me.

"Fuck you," was my snappy retort. There was a tension building between the two of us.

Holly was getting along well with his buddy. Her tanned tits were nicely on display. Her white shorts were twisted, and there was a hot summer evening sweat on her back. "You will come with us, *chica*," the guy said to Holly softly while looking into her eyes. She smiled, bewildered, and said nothing.

All of a sudden, the place became very small and empty, my ears silent to the chatter. These two greasy fucks, Holly, and me all locked together. We set up a rack for nine-ball. Just how much was the bet? He looked at his buddy, who was still talking to Holly and drinking a beer, then looked at me and said in his South American accent, "Hey, gringo, I will put ten thousand against the *chica*."

"What the fuck?" I said. Holly straightened up and looked around. They both got serious.

"If you win, you get ten thousand dollars. Give five thousand to the lovely *chica*, and she will be happy. You lose, and the *chica* comes with us, to our home in Colombia for a short visit, like a vacation."

Holly was drunk and staggered a bit, her mouth half-open. The bet did not sober her up. I smiled, then laughed. "Slut's not worth that much. Why do you want her? What does she have that you want?" There were no answers forthcoming.

Holly gave me a quick leer. I looked at her and tried to read her face. She swayed a bit. Her British accent was clear. "Bugger you. Are you sure you can beat this bloke? Five thousand quid would be great." She swayed some more. "Rubbish. Maybe there are nice beaches down south," Holly slurred as a wad of bills, all hundreds, was laid on the table.

"Holy fuck," I said, looking at Holly.

She eyed the stack. "Perfectly grisly. That looks like ten thousand cash. Shag it. Have at 'er."

"Race to eleven?" I asked.

"OK, gringo."

He moved his left arm about as he spoke. His wrist snapped up, and a coin was flipped. I watched it fly high, rotating many times. It reached the apex, still spinning fast, then began its return to earth. In an instant, the same hand snapped out, catching the coin, and slapped it down on his wrist under the palm. "Heads or tails?" He looked at me again, unflinching.

"Heads," I said. It was a tail. I lost. He won. His break was loud as thunder. Balls went everywhere, and some went in. I took my seat.

It was just me and him now. He won the first two games. He was playing run-out pool. This time he played differently, rolling the cue ball softly from ball to ball. When he missed, it was calculated and on purpose, hiding the cue ball casually behind other balls, leaving me no shot. I tried and missed a ticky shot but didn't leave much. He played very well, making a shot and running out. This made knots in my stomach.

*I will beat this guy straight*, I thought. Un-fucking-fortunately, this guy was a ringer. He was some kind of champion in Colombia. His friend looked at me from across the table and said with a confident grin, "My friend here, Hector, is the nine-ball champion of all Colombia. You cannot beat him." I was quickly beginning to think he was right.

I got some games in, but he took me eleven games to five. Holly's face was something to see. She staggered back, her ass cheeks clinging to her shorts, knees bent a bit, and said with disenchantment in her voice, "A piece of piss then. Wow, perfectly grisly," when the last nine-ball went in and we lost. "This never happened to me before," she slurred.

Looking at Holly, I said, "Never happened to me either. Man, oh, man, sorry about that." I could see her nipples get hard and stand out even more through her top. Her high-heeled shoes wrapped around her legs. She tossed her long brunette hair back and drank heavily from the beer can.

"Bollocks, then. Perfectly grisly. Well, to hell in a handbag." She was catching up to what just happened. "What happened then?" I had no answer for her. She picked up her handbag and moved back a few steps with her new friend. Holly looked at me, smiling, and said optimistically, "Rubbish, then. Probably won't need me brolly down there." I had no idea what the annual rainfall was in Medellin.

Hector, the guy I just lost to, approached with a sickening smirk. "Hey, gringo, thank you for the beautiful *chica*." They were getting ready to leave.

"Fuck off," I told him for the third time. I was sick of his bullshit. My remark angered him. His scared face became serious, like it was just slapped, as he walked away. Hector did not get the last word in, but he was satisfied for the moment.

There was great personal pain in this loss. I was learning a nasty lesson just now. Hector took his pool way more seriously than I did. Next time, I would concentrate on the shot in front of me and not let my ego declare a premature victory. I was humbled, and in that moment, I had a revelation, an awakening. I would find a master pool player to train me. My search had begun.

He was aggressive now, turning back toward me. "OK, gringo, you want a rematch. You have another lovely *chica*, perhaps?" I said nothing, turning my back to him. He became annoyed, but I didn't care. His friend pulled him away, avoiding a scene.

As this was happening, Holly was escorted out the back door by a couple of her new friends. I walked to the door and watched. Last I saw of Holly, she was being handed a beer and loaded into the back seat of their limo. My eyes met Holly's for a brief second. Then she was gone. As they drove away, I noticed the bright red ambassador license plate on the back of the limo. These people were from the consulate and not bound by our laws. *Interesting*, I thought. *They will just fly Holly back home in their private jet, no questions asked.* The engine noise soon disappeared and was replaced by the sound of the warm summer evening breeze blowing in the trees.

# House Party

HOLLY WAS GONE NOW, AND I WAS DRINKING MY FOURTH beer, sitting alone. At one point, I looked over and saw Frisk walking toward me. I could see his cowboy boots, the black shiny ones with cool designs. They were real beauties. Frisk had them shinned up real good. He wore jeans that were tight but still let him stretch. His shirt was white, and he had a black vest on. "Hey, gringo, how are you now?" Frisk said with a near-perfect Spanish accent.

I gave Frisk a dirty look. "I ran five balls and missed. And bam, he ran out. We were done, and they were the new owners of Holly. And she didn't even seem to mind. And fuck them and their gringo and *chica* bullshit," I tried to explain.

Frisk laughed. I was not finding any sympathy in his heart. "I didn't like the looks of those fucks. These guys are out of place," he said, his tone more serious.

I was not sure what to think. Frisk continued, "I am glad you lost. I bet she wanted to go anyway." Without batting an eye and with a smirk, he declared, "Her short pointed nose will be good for shoving up the cracks of those fat men's arses." I lowered my eyes and shook my head slowly.

Frisk was with some dark-haired *chica*, but I didn't really notice. I did cheer up when Frisk looked over at me with one hand on this *chica*'s knee, said, "Well, I guess, she will finally be picking bananas from trees for monkeys, after all." We laughed.

Then he got more serious. "She will tell them about the pot. She does not know everything, but she knows enough to be dangerous. Does she know about the patent? We need to be careful. That's all we can do." I agreed with a slight nod of my head.

I changed the subject. "Turns out some guys are having a party up on the hill with a lot of out-of-town people."

Frisk knew the place. He knew there would be drunken women too. But he had other plans. "Yeah, maybe later," he said, and split with the hot *chica.*

I was now drunker than ever and way past being able to drive. I overheard they had a nice full-size pool table at the party. *Whatever the fuck that means*, I thought to myself.

I lost Frisk but found my way to the party. So far, I was being funny and having a good time playing pool. The pool playing got me in the door, so to speak. However, going down any gambling road was probably a bad idea after what had just happened. Going home and getting laid or just passing out would have been a lot smarter than showing up here drunk.

I started stumbling around their poolroom and talking shit when the alcohol took over. I became obnoxious, tried stupid shots, and missed them. I was drunk. After losing, which I don't remember doing, I stole their chalk holder, the one used to mark the score on the blackboard. It was one of those metal mechanical ones a teacher would use during class. Just push the button on top, and more chalk slides out. This pack of fools' place where I had found myself used pink chalk. Pink is the color of stupidity, and I didn't even know I had stolen it yet. God, alcohol is a great thing.

It was one in the morning, people were having a nice time dancing, talking, and drinking. I stumbled over to the music and found an old record with a picture of a hamburger on the cover. I reached over and hit the open button on the tape player. Abba's "Dancing Queen" was soon replaced by Zappa's "Call Any Vegetable." Frank Zappa, whose music is followed by a semipopular subculture of fans, played his guitar like no one else. It was loud and sounded like something you would hear at your local carnival, at midnight, while standing beside the Zipper. So loud, and the guitars so strong you could barely think.

"Crank some, Frank," I said to no one in particular. Someone gave me a strong hip check. I shuffled, or stumbled, backward several feet. Soon, Abba was happily playing "Fernando" again.

"Fuck, Fernando," is what I said, rather loudly. Next thing I knew, I was in the kitchen, looking for a beer. I had already hammered back four or five so far. Sloppy drunk now but far from passing out. Full of energy and wasted. I tried to pick up some chick. I told her she had beautiful eyes that said, come fuck me. Then I slurred something else. She recoiled in disgust.

It was seconds later when the action started. I was grabbed by two guys and slammed into the wall. They punched me a few times in the guts and head, but I sort of rolled with it, off-balance, awkward. One of the punches caught me rather hard in the jaw. I was knocked down the hallway, toward the front door. Instinctively I rolled with the energy, then tried to get up.

Some guy—I think his name was Al—yelled, "And he stole my chalk holder, too." Now my head was really spinning. I couldn't stand up. I was adrenaline pumped and drunk. *Holy God, fuck me,* I thought.

"Fuck you, bastards," I said with rage as I sucked up a kick to the ribs that launched me through the open doorway. I heard people muttering.

Not too much pain at the moment. Head was spinning again, and all that beer in my stomach sloshed from side to side. The drunken stupidity was now hitting me. I just couldn't get a grip on the situation. Someone was saying they should call me a taxi. Did I phone one earlier? Not sure at the moment. Things going in circles, blood in my mouth, people surrounding me, moving in and out, taking their shots. Some connected, some were blocked. All were thrown with righteous conviction, as if they were somehow doing the right thing. Yeah, like beating the shit out of a single drunk guy. Apparently, that was very good sport in whatever town these assholes came from.

I had managed to get out to the end of the driveway by the road. It was lit by streetlights. Darkness followed quickly behind the telephone poles and bushes. I saw the blackness again when I was grabbed, spun around, and tossed to the ground. I rolled across the asphalt and onto the road. There were several guys surrounding me now. Some were speaking Spanish. The closest guy walked over to me as I got to my knees. I recognized him as one of the punks we were playing earlier. I think he lived here. He was another British piece of work. I was too drunk to make any deeper sense of this situation.

He was going to punch me, but I lunge punched him straight in the nuts. From my position, on my knees, it was the perfect crotch height. He never saw it coming. It didn't feel like hitting much, not like hitting someone in the jaw. I remember it almost like nothing at all, or more like hitting a pillow.

But it worked. He doubled over, moaning in extreme pain. Just then, as I was standing up, a kick caught me in the shoulder. It rolled me farther into the street, causing small stones to become embedded in the palms of my hands. I looked down the street and saw a yellow cab coming up the hill.

I was on the ground and being surrounded. The taxi pulled up right beside me. *Fuck me*, I thought, *could you get any closer?* The taxi was there a moment before the back passenger door opened. *Cool*, I thought. If I can just crawl inside this thing somehow and get the fuck out of here. The group was yelling to stop me from getting into the taxi and moved in to grab me.

TAXI
TAXI

Before I could do anything. I saw a shiny black cowboy boot step out of the taxi and touch the ground beside me. Nothing was said. No words were exchanged. As the first guy reached to grab me, Frisk stood up. He was tall and serious looking. Focused, he was. Frisk's left foot was on the ground beside me. I could see it stiffen as his right foot thrust straight out catching this guy square in the chest. It sent him straight back and down to the ground. Just as Frisk's leg was retracting, a haymaker was thrown at his head. Frisk did a straight punch forward. But it was on the inside of the punch coming at him and three times as fast, sort of a block/attack move.

Frisk's punch caught this guy square on the cheekbone, below his eye. The guy went down hard with a very large hematoma showing up almost instantly. It would be the size of an egg within minutes. He'd be sorry he ever tried that move. It would be a bitter lesson.

The next guy came at Frisk with his own high left punch, and fast too. He was big, over two hundred pounds, and probably played football, but who the fuck cared? I was sitting against the back tire of the cab just now, my head spinning. I felt sick.

Frisk stepped down moving to the left, side-stepping the haymaker, then used a right elbow block and put the guy off balance. Frisk attacked down with a short snap kick behind his left knee. The footballer started to collapse even more to the left side now. Frisk's right arm shot out in a close hanger move, caught him on the chin with his open hand, and grabbed him by the hair. Yanking hard upward now, this guy extended off his one good right leg, going almost straight up. Frisk dropped into a low squat, snapping this guy violently backward and completely over his head. He did some sort of extended backflip over Frisk. Frisk let go of his hair at just the correct moment. The momentum was tremendous. He rolled back onto the driveway and down toward the house. Frisk stood his ground. He settled back into a tall sideways stance.

I crawled into the back seat of the cab, sat up, and gave my head a shake. Behind the driver was the cute *chica* Frisk was sitting with earlier at the bar. She was not looking at me in disgust or questioning my actions in any way. Her attitude seemed one of *let's kick their asses*, because there are bigger plans ahead. We lived by the *never complain, never explain, and just keep on going as if nothing happened* attitude. We watched Frisk through the back window of the taxi.

Frisk stood in the middle of the group now. Some of them fucked off into the house, not wanting any part of this one. Maybe they knew who just got out of the taxi? Maybe they knew of Frisk's legend? Spanish was being spoken.

There were three left. It was a classic defensive move on Frisk's part. He took them one at a time as they came at him. Frisk delivered two real quick punches to the head of the first guy. A hard slap to the face quickly moved him out of the way. The second guy came at him with a long-legged kick. As the kick rose toward Frisk, he delivered a devastating front snap kick at near light speed. The kick coming at Frisk went harmlessly to the side. Before putting his foot down to the ground, Frisk retracted his knee and twisted the foot on the ground from facing forward, to pointing back at the taxi. That meant the kicking leg was now being extended out faster than I could see. It caught this guy again, square in the head, knocking him onto the last guy. Together, they fell to the ground. He completed a magnificent double-kick. The guy that just got kicked was on all fours, sucking for air.

Frisk pointed his finger at the remaining punks, indicating in a back-and-forth motion to fuck off. This party was over, or there would be more pain than it was worth. They backed off into the house. This crowd was not happy. They would not forget who stole their chalk holder from the basement poolroom. They wouldn't forget me or Frisk.

Frisk jumped into the backseat beside his *chica* and instructed the driver, "Get the fuck out of here." He was barely out of breath, laughing and necking with his little honey.

# Carmichaels

"FUCK, TOMMY, WHAT DID YOU SAY TO THOSE PEOPLE? You had them in a fucking frenzy. Lucky, I came looking for you. I need you, man," Frisk said emphatically.

My head was ringing. How long had I been at that fucking party? Who were those people? I don't remember ordering any taxi. Breathing was much better now. "What's up? What time is it?" I asked, trying to be nonchalant about everything over the last five minutes.

"I got a game with those two guys from South America who snagged Holly. They're Colombians and could be trouble, but what the fuck?" Frisk declared. He said it in an upbeat way. He was always a happy kind of guy. My head was still ringing as the taxi continued down the night-time streets. "They got cash and drugs, and I know we can win it. We can beat these guys."

"Yeah, we'll teach them a lesson or two. How much do they have?" I asked sarcastically.

"At least ten grand each, maybe more." Frisk went on, "They want to play doubles for a hundred a game. What do you say, man?"

My brain was sluggish. "I only play eight-ball. No fucking nine-ball."

Frisk had the answer. "That's the game."

I was watching the lamp posts come into view then snap into the blackness as we passed them by. "Frisk, you are making sense. It has been a long, wild night so far, and I haven't been drinking in an hour or so. Hell, I am almost sober and all rested up, you might say. But I look a little rough covered in blood, dirt, scrapes, and ripped clothes. I look like I have been lost in the backwoods for a month." I closed my eyes, enjoying the ride, the moment.

The *chica* with Frisk smelt great, her perfume strong and slutty. She wore a short skirt and had a T-shirt on. Her perky 36D tits filled it out just perfectly. She had long black hair. Her hair was straight, not the curly kind, or at least not tonight. Maybe it was the summer heat. She looked hot. Frisk decided we needed to stop at his place for a few minutes to get cleaned up and get in the right mood for this game.

We pulled up in front of Frisk's place. The taxi waited in the street while we went into his house. It was dark until Frisk turned on the lights. He went to the bathroom and washed his face and hands. He put his vest on the bed and straightened his white shirt. I washed up too and put on a golf shirt I found in a drawer. It was orange and fit me well.

When I came out of the bedroom, Frisk was sitting in a chair at a small desk in a corner of his living room. He opened a drawer and took out a spoon and syringe. He then proceeded to mix up a hit of speed (methamphetamine, that is). It was a white powder as it went into the tablespoon. He added water he got from a glass with the syringe—or fit, as he called it. I watched the white powder dissolve as the water hit it. He mixed it up and then sucked it back into the syringe through a cigarette filter, broken apart moments before. He checked the solution in the needle by holding it straight up and tapping the glass a few times with his finger, much the same way a doctor does. The liquid inside was a pale yellow color.

Then, as Frisk rolled up his shirt sleeve, he looked at his girlfriend and made sounds from the side of his mouth as if he were approaching a chipmunk. His *chica* friend came over and wrapped her hands around Frisk's upper arm. He pumped his arm up and down until a vein popped out. I noticed he had small track lines from previous hits. He tapped the needle tip on the skin and then pushed the sharp tip into his flesh. He drew back the plunger, and blood came into the needle. He then, in one fluid motion, sent the mixture home. As he did so, his little honey let go of his arm. Frisk pulled the needle out and bent his arm forward and up to stop the bleeding.

He sat back on his chair, letting out a huge sigh. It was the meth rush. Your heart beat goes from slow to ramming speed in seconds. As the meth rushes through your lungs, it mixes with air, and you get one hell of a taste in the back of your throat. I know all this secondhand; I have never done needle drugs and have no plans to start anytime soon.

Frisk was sitting completely back in his chair now. His head was back. He breathed another long sigh. His heartbeat must have doubled. He sat forward and said, "Wow." His eyes sort of crossed as he rode out the rush. He started to come back a bit. His pupils were huge, the full size of his eye. The whole process took about five minutes. The round clock on the wall pointed to two-thirty. I looked out the window as I sat in a big, comfy chair. The taxi driver was reading the newspaper while his car idled quietly in the driveway.

Frisk was humming as I questioned him about this game he got me in. I still had a good booze buzz but was on the other side of it now. Things were making sense again. Frisk told me he checked with Johnny, who was having a card game at the front of Carmichaels. He said Johnny told him we were to go in through the back door at three am. We could play on table nine or ten. And there could only be a few of us.

"We play until someone is broke. I don't know for sure how much they have, but I think it's a lot," he said as he slowly cleaned up the needle and spoon. "Here is a sample of their coke. It's direct from Colombia and fourteen percent pure." He handed me a glass vial of white powder.

It was something I could use just now. I had Frisk bust up a line. It was real white, and it shone and twinkled. He took his time chopping the powder into fine lines, obsessed with the cutting process.

I did one small line and felt it almost immediately. My heartbeat went up, I woke up, and my whole body tingled. My nose and throat went numb. *Jesus*, I thought, *this is good stuff.* Just how much of the white death did they have?

My mind switched to cash. I had five thousand on me. So, at a hundred, or so a set to start, we should have been good for some time. Frisk said they met at the bar after I lost Holly. "We played a few games, bouncing back and forth. They like to gamble man," he said. "They were up eight hundred when I suggested we play eight-ball and partners later at Carmichaels. They agreed. And now we're in the right frame of mind."

Frisk looked anxious as he paced back and forth. I tried to talk to him. "I think we are both so stoned and so ready, we aren't sure what to do. But I tell ya, Frisk, now ya got me thinking about the game to come. It's in my mind now too. As a team, we are stronger. We are much better."

Frisk was calmer when he spoke. "My thoughts are on my past, but we are in the moment. Just tripping out, you are right, together, we will kill them." Frisk laughed, and I was reassured he was OK, but I felt the presence of something dark, something hidden.

"These bastards know how to play, but you figure we can beat them?" I asked. "They're real gamblers too? What the fuck are they doing here? I had never heard of any fucking Colombians before." There was no response from anyone. The room was silent. "Do you know these fuckers? Is there something you need to tell me?" I was pushing and showing some rage.

"Never saw these guys before. There is nothing to worry about, that shit is all behind me long ago," Frisk was trying to reassure me.

I mostly felt dread. I felt I was facing an uncertain future. But that also made it exciting, riding a predetermined wave that would collapse into only one reality. We all did another line of coke and walked out to the taxi. We piled in and headed for Carmichaels.

It was five minutes to three when we pulled up. The night air was warm. It filled my lungs and warmed my body. Coke seemed to make me feel cold at times. Just now, I was getting cool rushes, and I was horny and was excited. I had no idea what was in store next. The three of us walked down the side alley toward the back door. I soon saw three young guys and a chick. A little honey, she was. They were Colombian. The guys were medium build, a little fat, actually, except for the taller guy. He was the leader giving orders and speaking mostly in Spanish. The gal was tall, with long, silky black hair. She was athletic. Nice tits in a tight top and beautiful rounded ass cheeks in a pair of short cutoff jeans. She was hot. I overheard them; her name was Catina.

Hector spoke. "It is the gringos."

I said to the guys, "Hi, nice night for some pool, eh." Our names were never exchanged. Looking toward Frisk, I spoke softly. "I only knew the tall guy, Hector, the guy with the scar, the leader of this tribe of misfits. This woman, however, was a true hot *chica*." Frisk was indifferent but recognized I liked her immediately.

She moved toward me and with a low exotic Spanish accent, said, "Hello, my name is Catina."

"Tommy," I said, shaking her hand. It felt warm and soft. "Catina, what a beautiful name you have. Catina means pure, and your heart is full of kindness."

"I love it when you say my name." She smiled ever so sweetly at my flirt. Her eyes were dark and inviting. We lingered a moment in each other's gaze. She was flirting with me, the little slut. *What the fuck?* I thought as we got to work. But then, I thought again, *Was she flirting or hustling, or maybe she just likes me?* Maybe she was not a slut. Maybe she was some kind of cartel leader—I had no idea at this point in time. My cock twinged when I looked at her dark tits and round ass.

We slipped in the back door. Frisk went to the front and checked in with Johnny, who was deep into a late-night card game with Red Ed, Dave, and some other guys. I saw them talk with Frisk, then smile, shake hands and knock knuckles. I watched Frisk grab our cues, a set of balls and head to the back of Carmichaels. He said he gave Johnny a hundred bucks, so we were good until tomorrow sometime.

Carmichaels was dark except for a light way at the front, and now table ten. It gave an eerie feeling, a feeling this spot was reserved for us. There were no early-morning money games starting around here. There were only the select few who would witness this pool challenge. Table ten was the last pro-size table before the two twelve-foot snooker tables that filled the end of the hall. This was a good table, with fast, responsive rails. The pockets were solid, and balls dropped in smoothly.

I was thinking of the home-court advantage as Frisk gave me Falcon. The case was heavy, black, and the texture was fish skin. Laying the box on the end table, I flipped each clasp upwards, the case opened. Falcon lay in a velvet cloth—quiet, comfortable. Picking up the shaft, then the butt, they felt cold and heavy in my hands. I put Falcon together, twisting slowly, watching carefully as the two pieces became one. When the cue was tight, Falcon was alive.

I spoke to the group. "It is eight-ball. Call the pocket and ball only. Make the eight on break, and it comes up. Sewer off the black, and you lose. Frisk and Hector will lag for break. Fouls are ball in hand anywhere on the table, except after a break."

Hector rose to lag with Frisk. His skin was tan colored, face pock-marked from acne and that subtle scar under his right eye. His hair was black, cut over the ear and square at the back. It was an expensive haircut. He was a man of great self-pride.

Hector's stance, and bridge looked good. Frisk won the lag and broke. I was leaning against table nine, farther up, watching Frisk. We bantered back and forth with safeties, then I quickly ran out.

When Hector's partner was shooting and taking his time, I spoke to Frisk. "I wonder if these guys were here because of Don Carmichael's old-time pool connections. Don is well known for working with hustlers and other pool halls, to set up big-time money games, don't ya know. He knows a lot of people in the pool business, including hustlers, gamblers, and politicians. Many times, the backers would not even go on the road with the hustler. They just give their hustler guy a few thousand dollars and point him in a direction. The hustler then goes from pool hall to pool hall playing anyone with more than ten dollars to bet. There is a lot of money in those games, and many thousands could pass hands if your timing was right and you had the guts. I must say, Frisk, that I have concluded these guys are not part of any road map old Don Carmichael had put together."

Frisk spoke. "You are right about two things, Tommy. First, I wonder if Don still backs anyone. Maybe he has hustlers out there right now working for him." He was watching the Colombians carefully. "Second, you are correct, Tommy. These are not hustlers. These are dangerous cartel members from Colombia. Very dangerous. And it is for that reason they will lose tonight. There will be blood." Frisk went silent.

I was chatty. "I do believe these guys are hustlers of sorts and probably killers, and definitely on a different plan. This slimy tribe of misfits is here for something bad, something beyond the law. Now they were in a money game at three in the morning with a couple of locals, a couple of unknowns. Only a fucking hustler would do that, don't ya know. Frisk, I am thinking, what the fuck am I doing?" My heartbeat went up another notch as Frisk stood, a miss brought him to the table. I focused by watching and waiting. Frisk was making one ball at a time, relentless. He played awesome pool. Frisk was also good at making something regularly on break that provided excellent offensive playing.

Catina sat to the side by the door, sipping rye on ice and doing a line every thirty minutes or so. She sat on a tall bar stool at the edge of the darkness but still in the light. A joint was lit, and we shared it together, alone. Questions flowed through my brain, who are these Colombians? Are they any good? Are we being hustled? Will they be good losers if we beat the fuck out of them, and they lose their bankroll? I looked into Catina's eyes, smiling, being playful. She flirted with a sexy wink. A wink that had been practiced before, and that was fine with me. I spoke to Catina. "So mysterious this night." Her eyes met mine. She had no words to say.

We were interrupted by Hector and his partner laughing, as they had just won a game. They were drinking and doing lines of their high-grade coke. Catina declined for the moment. "No, thank you."

We were winning regularly again now and ready for more, "Let's play a thousand a set," I said to Hector. It was Frisk's break.

"One minute," Hector said as he waited outside the back door to finish an important cigarette. It was a dark-papered cigarette with a white ring at the filter. He breathed in that last pull, not vigorously or as if it was the last. He just puffed it into his lungs and slowly blew it out his nose. He threw the butt on the ground, still burning, and came inside.

A low ball went in on the break, but high balls were better, so we took the nine in the side pocket. The cue ball stayed in the middle of the table. Frisk made three more before missing and landing behind a high ball. They were hooked. The short guy shot and made a nice trick shot, then a few more. He missed the last ball and sort of rolled against the long rail near the corner pocket. My ball would need to be side-banked. I checked it out, then hammered it home and went on to run the table and the set. We played on.

I did not think too much. I just breathed, smoked some joints, did a line or two, and played on. They were good, but I knew we were better. They seemed to have good stances and poise, but they missed key shots. We used safety play to wait out slumps and change the flow. The advantage is sometimes measured by the difference between one shot ahead or one behind. We won some and lost some at first, but now we were winning them all. They raised the bet to two thousand a set.

*Fuck me*, I thought again. I hated to lose. This was it. Now was the time. We would either start to lose or clean up. It was up to us, up to the shots we picked and how loose we could stay. I was not sure of the technical things they were doing wrong, but I knew some. Their eyes did not stay level sometimes. Other times, they did not chalk up or would be careless with English. They could win a game or two but not a set. We took them slowly. They seemed to take it OK. They paid up and pulled out more money. This was not backers' money. This was real drug money.

Well, I get better as I play more, and Frisk just plays good all the time. We were up ten thousand or so each by 11:00 a.m. They were getting a little pissed and started yelling at each other in Spanish. Catina sat watching, humming songs to herself. She rolled joints and cut lines. Johnny had split a couple hours earlier. His game was over. We could be here for six more hours if we wanted. Somehow, I knew this party was winding down.

I had been drinking beer and eating chuck wagons for the last couple of hours. Frisk and I continued to shoot very well. They were down, now losing over twenty thousand in total. The tall one tossed a pound of very pure coke onto the table. "It could be cut twice at least," he declared.

Frisk spoke for us. He knew what he was talking about. "This is not any regular drug dealers dope. This is from the source—pure, almost good for you. You want to play for the twenty thousand against your coke, double or nothing? We will play you." Frisk dug deep into his pocket and covered the bet. The cash and coke were put to one side.

I looked at Frisk. "This is it, the moment of truth, all in."

"Sure," Frisk said, enthusiastically and stoned. He loved drugs and winning. He was bouncing the balls well. The meth was doing its thing. He was staying awake and alert. I had been up for about twenty-four hours but still felt fine. My fingers felt a little stiff, sort of puffy at the knuckles but fine.

These Colombian motherfuckers were getting upset, though. It appeared they had spent more than their allowance. Since I hadn't seen them before and probably would never see them again, I was cautious about these guys.

Catina was different. I smiled with her, and we shared back-door tokes. Catina had a beautiful smile, and I told her this: "I love your shoes, Catina. Very nice, and your smile is amazing. Beautiful."

Catina accepted my compliment with a smile and soft, sexy words. "I love to hear you flirt with me." She was fit, about five foot eleven, with perfectly natural, full tits. The straps of her sexy bra were narrow and silk, not that cheap bleached white crap from the dollar store. This bra was worthy of holding those beautiful tits. It had the type of bra clasp I could flip open with the snap of two fingers.

I imagined holding her close to me, kissing her softly, with my right arm holding her tight. I would run my fingers slowly from the base of her ass, up her spine, and when I reached her bra clip, I would nonchalantly wrap my thumb and second finger around the clasp. Then I would softly snap my fingers together, the clasp would open, and her tits would fall free. She would moan softly, feeling her impending nakedness approaching.

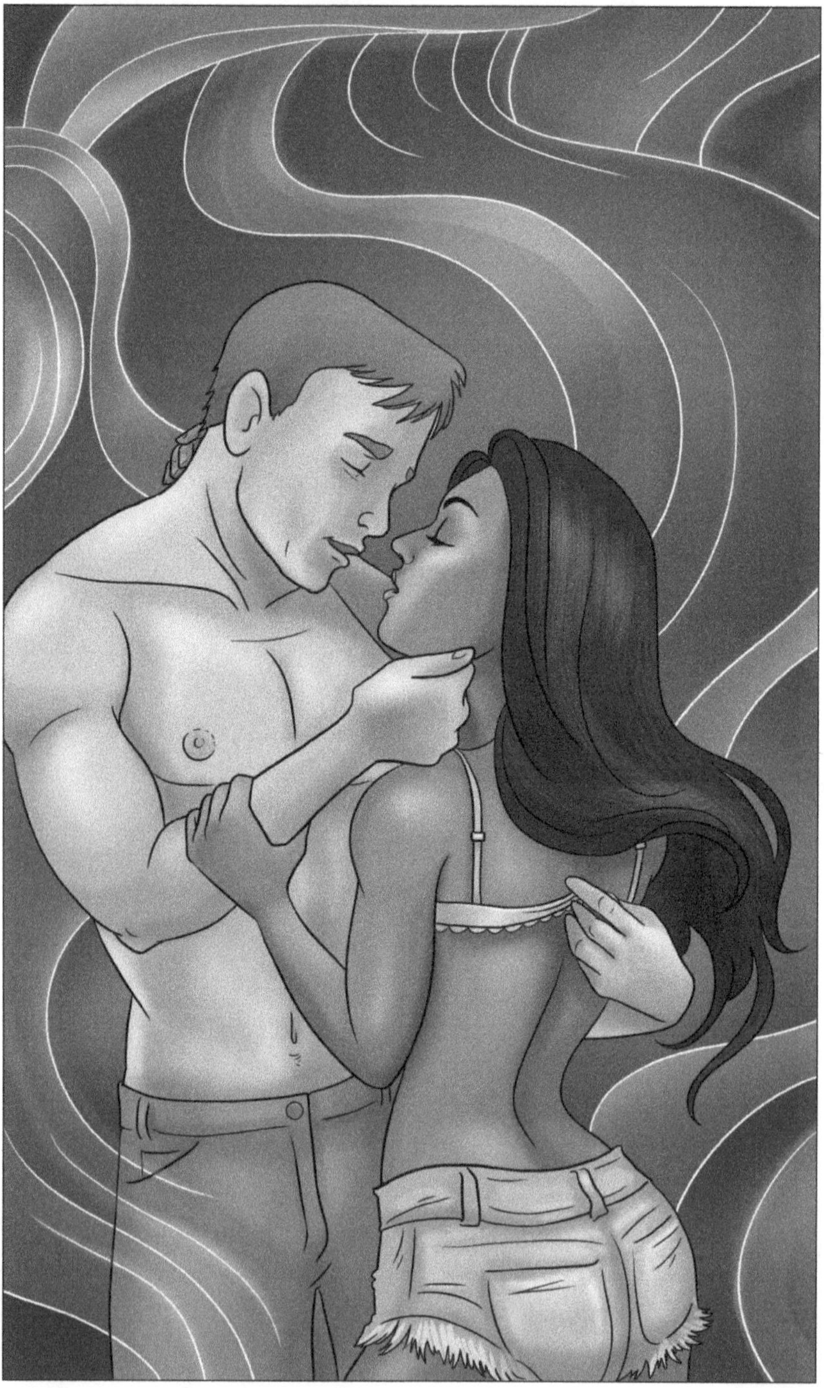

In that instant, I wondered if she knew what I was thinking, and did she share my strong emotion? I believed she did.

She said, "Thank you," and touched my hand. Again, I looked in her eyes. They were dark, narrow, and mysterious. Her exotic body spoke to me, invited me. I was touched by her thoughtfulness.

It was 11:29 in the morning. The Colombians played well but not well enough. As I made the last eight ball on a double cross-side, Frisk reached over and collected the rather large bag of coke and cash, stuffing it into his vest and jacket. The Colombians were not happy. Their little world was now fucked up. They did not plan to lose twenty grand and enough of the white death to kill an elephant.

The tall guy with the scar, known as Hector, stood a few feet in front of me. He was watching, observing, saying nothing. As Frisk waited at the end of the table, bent, ready to take a practice shot the Colombians came up beside him. One was on the left, the other on the right, with his cue in both hands. He was Hector's partner. Everyone was tense, and serious. The other two were yelling at each other in Spanish. Frisk started shooting the cue ball, up and down the length of the table, slowly at first. He was smiling, more a grin.

I spoke loudly, not yelling at them, "You don't know who you are fucking with, you fucking monkeys."

The guy on Frisk's left shouted, "You fucking gringo, you will lose, you fucker, right now." His tone would scare the average person into coronary arrest. He had that South American twang. His silky-smooth shirt lay loose around his chest, hiding his fat belly, just like the others. He was not planning to throw punches. He pulled a long hunting knife from behind his back and began to swing it toward Frisk. Hector and his men were well known for their love of knives to kill, up close and personal.

I stiffened and started to freak out inside. I had moved back to the other end of the table, near the exit. No way were we going to bend now. I would stop them if they bolted, but I had no idea what to do other than that. The knife did not move fast but instead came at a steady pace. The other guy was standing beside Frisk, holding his cue with both hands below the tip and the butt on the floor. It was that waiting-to-shoot pose, but instead, he was blocking Frisk between them. Some sort of attempt to stop him from getting away.

"Yeah, that's fucked up," I said under my breath. Again, an unknown was being presented. Just how tough were these guys? They were hustlers. Maybe they were killers too, maybe just punks trying to push the locals around. Either way, it was not good for them.

Frisk continued to shoot the cue ball down the length of the table and back to himself. They sandwiched him tighter.

Catina was standing behind her chair, staying close to me. Frisk's *chica* was just sitting and watching the Colombians at the far end of the table. She knew they were about to get creamed. I was watching Frisk and noticed he was setting up for a long jump shot. His back hand was near the butt, and he was aiming down on the cue ball. As the knife was being drawn, the Colombian stood tall. He was in the zone, where I watched Frisk shoot at least fifty long-rail jump shots. This is the one where the cue ball is struck very hard straight down the middle of the table. It hits the back rail, and if the rail has enough spring, the cue ball will bounce straight back in the air. If you are fast enough, you can pluck it out of the air as it comes back at you. I have never seen anyone else do this shot. Frisk loved to do it just to catch the cue ball in midair at head height.

"What a buzz," he would say each time he caught it. He placed the cue ball anywhere in the air he wanted. And if the rails were rubbery enough, and these were, he could snap his wrists so hard and so fast and so subtle, you could not see the cue ball launch down the table, hit the back rail, and then spring across the table in the air. And this is exactly what Frisk did. It took about five seconds to mop up these two. Frisk hit the cue ball like before, except at the last second, he snapped the cue stick hard with extreme wrist action.

That guy with the knife was fucked. He never saw it spring off the back rail. He was looking at Frisk when the cue ball cannon-balled him square in the cheekbone, below the eye. The knife hit the floor at about the same time this treacherous motherfucking Colombian did. He was doing the chicken, moaning and bleeding and choking. Catina stayed where she was, her eyes narrow, evaluating. I was looking hard at Frisk.

Before the little dweeb on the left could do anything, Frisk stepped behind and around him, letting go with a high, swinging roundhouse kick aimed at the back of the Colombian's head. Frisk had moved back one giant step just as the cue ball crushed the first punk's face. Standing on his right leg, Frisk's left foot spun three hundred and sixty degrees with grace and accuracy. His foot slapped the back of this treacherous cretin's head. The force was hard, snapping the Colombian's head forward.

Frisk could have kicked this guy three times before he hit the ground, but he only needed once. The roundhouse kick from behind pushed his forehead directly into the tip of the cue. It hit him square in the middle of his head. The cracking of the cue was almost silent, and his head was forced into a ninety-degree angle to his body. Fortunately, his head was very hard, but the resulting force caused the broken tip to rip open his forehead, toward the ear. The gash was about three inches long. The skin split apart, and blood was already soaking his cool, expensive shirt. Frisk completely dominated the situation and was the architect of their misery.

Catina said, "That will be difficult to stitch, even by a good doctor."

I glanced at Catina. She did not look all that upset, maybe even glad on some levels. Tells me she was not a loving girlfriend, at least not to them.

It was now eleven thirty-two in the morning. Catina had seen me watching her. She moved closer. The cue ball actually hit that fucker so square in the side of the head it bounced back onto the table and rolled up to the far end pocket, and dropped in. Frisk's *chica* smirked.

It didn't take long after that. Hector, the other member of the team, moved forward closer to the table and yelled in Spanish to stop fighting, slamming his pool cue across the table, splintering it in half. All of a sudden, forty grand and a pound of high-grade coke seemed cheap. They were not thinking of cash or Catina or anything else at that moment. Hector knew it was life or death and that blood tonight was wrong. Retreat was imminent.

They got up slow, holding their wounds. The guy who got hit with the cue ball must have been seeing orange and white flashes of lightning bolts. Hector helped his two fucked-up buddies. He apologized for their mistake, saying sorry once in English. The other guys were fucked up good, but they would heal.

Frisk spoke in a low, drawn-out tone, bordering between rage and action. "You fucking monkeys, fuck off and don't come back until ya learn some manners." Then, in near-perfect Spanish, Frisk spoke again. "No tears. Your father was a tough man." Hector looked at Frisk differently, something connected in his brain, and then they were gone. In all the action, I did nothing but stand my ground. The wave was upon us quickly, and Frisk knew exactly what to do.

Catina stood beside me, not behind me. I briefly glanced her way, her eyes now wide, not in fear but more like watching an action movie. I felt her independence and knew her inquisitiveness. For her, there was no boredom in this moment. She had discovered a new project, a new lover. Standing closer, Catina whispered in my ear, "May I stay with you for the rest of the day?"

I put my arm around Catina and squeezed her butt. Looking into her eyes, and with an impatient impulse, we kissed, not a wild French kiss but a slow, passionate kiss, with light grinding and eyes closed. When we stopped kissing, I was in love.

This felt like such a strange, intense twist of fate to lose Holly to the same people who had just handed me Catina. How could the universe make this happen? The last day unfolded in such a way, I had to lose one, to gain the other. It felt so strange to me, but I was grateful.

We laughed, and Frisk laughed. After cleaning up a bit, Frisk rolled a of couple fat joints, while Catina cut up thin Medellin size lines. We did them like the addicts we were. Catina was an addict too, addicted to many things. She spoke for me, "I know what I want, but I also know why I want it. Power, respect, leadership, and being ready when called to action. And I am fucking ready." She was drunk and funny.

Together, we smoked the last joint in the back alley. The sun had risen. It was bright and warm. The light summer breeze was incredible. It must have been eighty degrees outside already. Frisk laughed. "I always joked about doing that jump shot on someone but never thought I would get the chance."

I said, "I better practice it sometime."

The coke and cash were split up. *Wow*, I thought, *what the fuck is this worth?* Catina was reading my mind.

"About five thousand an ounce at street level, and what you have can be cut three times. You got a lot of coke there." She smiled a little grin. She knew exactly what was there.

I asked, "Is there anyone else in your family like you, Catina?"

Catina laughed lightly, suggesting there was not. "How you say, 'Just little old me, that's it."

Frisk fucked off to his place with a big smile and a "See ya later."

I brought Catina to my place. It was a slow walk across the schoolyard. We held hands. Catina was soon in my arms while stretched out on the black leather couch in the den. Warm summer air slowly filtered through the screen door. I went to kiss her when she stopped me and spoke with a deep Spanish accent. "I must be honest with you. That man you beat today, his name is Hector, and he is my father. We are here for a short visit to meet a new contact, a woman I only know as Sylvia. She is close to my father and is doing business with him. Hector needs a partner with money, drugs, and political connections. Back home, my family has money and power in a country where force rules, and economics is everything. But we are not that strong here, yet we see much wealth," she said.

Catina had my interest piqued, "Catina, you have just explained a lot, but why tell me?"

"And something even more important ..." She paused to think before continuing. "I think Hector knows your friend—what is his name?—Frisk. The way he looked at him after the fight, like something from the past. Years ago, I remember one of the fighters who tried to follow Frisk after he disappeared. He came to our village and spoke with the Chief and with Hector. This fighter was hurt badly and crippled, but he survived an encounter with that man. Hector was younger then and never met Frisk. He was gone before we went to that village, but the legend never died. Maybe I am wrong, but I wanted you to know."

We fucked, and we made love. We talked, did coke, smoked weed and hash, and ate well for a day and night. We talked about the world, and she told me of travels to different countries. She was an amazing woman, and I thought I was in love. I shared my life and my dream to grow weed and make hash. Catina was in thought.

"You have a vision, Tommy, and I love that about you. I think you are doing some of it now. Growing, as you say, is not easy and needs training, but you have the system figured out. I am impressed."

"Thank you. I did not know if you would understand, but you do." I told her about the hash machine and the patent I was going to get. It all felt natural when talking with Catina. I do not think she really understood what I was saying by the look on her face, much like the look Frisk had when I first told him. With Catina, I did not press the issue and let it slide from there. But she had a deeper understanding of what I was telling her than she let on. She had a poker face.

In those last few hours together, Catina tried to warn me again, "My father is very powerful. These men move drugs and money and usually do not run into someone like you or your friend. The pool game they won, and certainly the game they lost, will not be forgotten by my father. Hector is a pool player and a gambler too. Risk is something he values. Also, I am not sure what he will think when he finds out I am with one of the locals. And not just any local but you, Tommy the pool player with the blue hand from all the chalk you use. You are special because you beat him, and badly, and you have vision and power. Hector is protective of his power and his ego, but do not worry; we will soon leave this place."

I thanked Catina, explaining how grateful I was for her honesty. I told her, "I believe you are someone who can take an idea and make it happen." We shared a high creative force between us, and we were happy.

Finally, Catina staggered out the door after calling a taxi to come get her. She kissed me and whispered in my ear, "I will be holding you in my dreams until we meet again."

And she was gone.

# Hunter and Graham

I AWOKE AT HOME ON THE COUCH. THE PHONE WAS RINGING. IT was ten in the morning. The ringing stopped then started again five minutes later. I was fucked up. Not drunk but well hungover. I was starting to come around. It was bright outside. The sun was shining. It was now thirty minutes later. I answered the phone this time. It was Hunter. He was frantic.

He mumbled on about how the police were circling the street and slowing down as they passed in front of the house. He believed we were busted for sure. "No hope now. The jig is up. Our clone shop was going to be shut down. Lights, plants, bud, seeds including outdoor plants; we are going to make the front page of the paper," he said with despair in this voice.

Hunter's voice was frantic. "I want you to come over and get these plants out of here. You have to do something, man." I was trying to grasp the conversation.

Hunter was a cool kid, a great kid. He was twenty-four years old and weighed in at a hundred and twenty pounds or so. He had a beautiful smile and a great laugh. He was a genuine person. Said he was named after either, the great constellation, Orin the Hunter, or some outlaw journalist. No one knew for sure.

He also loved pot and loved to grow pot. He was my main clone provider and most trusted person, with the keys to the seed and deployment strains. Meaning, what I put in the ground for production had to be approved by Hunter first. This location housed the main female plants and very select male plants. They are being used strictly for seed production. We do not want male plants in with the fields of females. This would cause them to go to seed, vastly reducing the yield. This was the epicenter for our seeds for next year and for further genetic hybrids.

My head was ringing from over drinking at the pub the night before. My ribs were sore from bouncing off a parking meter while staggering to my car, but I recall Frisk drove. I felt like puking. The kitchen was a mess. I really shouldn't cook at three in the morning. The last thing I remember after Frisk dropped me off was stumbling into the house. Now it was today, and the guy doing my clones and holding several huge freshly pollinated mother plants was about to be busted. These plants were five or six feet of ass-kicking indica. This was Himalayan style, outdoor stuff. Every single seed from these mothers would grow into humongous tree-size plants.

Hunter got the seeds with a partner when they worked at the Government Horticultural Engineering Laboratory. It was contract work to research different strains of cannabis for medical use. Many diseases can be stopped in their track with pot, including many cancers. Who would have known? Hunter and his buddy trained for three months in India a few years back. They were studying various cannabis strains that produced the world's best royal hash and cerebral mind-fuck weed. They found it, and now I have it. In fact, I have it all over the goddamn place. And now the cops are closing in.

When I finally got there to figure out what is happening, Hunter had five green garbage bags inside the front door, some empty, and some with plants sticking out, half-covered.

"Wow, man," he said. "Cops drove by a couple of times now. They always slowed down just in front of the house."

"Jesus God Almighty, what the fuck is going on here?" I said.

"Look, I am not going back to jail. Fuck that shit, man," he stated.

"Settle down, Hunter." Then I gave him a pep talk. "I understand you, man, and am proud of the fact you did not flee this immediate area. A lesser person would be in a different town by now, but not you, Hunter. You stand by your passions and convictions, for good or ill, and will defend them to the bitter end. You are my fucking hero, man, don't ya know?" Hunter was listening, accepting but not worrying.

I remember when he was in jail. It was only once, for a few months. He got caught on what I called a Coke for Cops campaign. They set him up by claiming to be his friend and all that shit. He was busted for an eight ball and did six months. I told him, "Be grateful, man, because in some places, you would be either killed or doing twenty years of hard labor. You will be out in four months, and by the way, stop selling dope to cops, OK?"

I went to visit him when I could. The best parts were all the chicks coming by to visit their criminal boyfriends and husbands. They were all hot. Even the ugly ones looked good, but the really hot ones were magnificent.

The day Hunter got out of jail, I picked him up. It was at eight in the morning on a Tuesday. As Hunter was released, I took a bunch of pictures around the area and buildings and Hunter. As it turned out, this was not a good idea. Before we could escape out of the facility, a guard ran out, stopping my truck. He forced me to show him my camera, and then I had to destroy all the pictures I took. Once he was satisfied there were no more pictures, and after he gave me shit, we finally drove out of that fucking place. I truly never want to see it again, even to visit someone. My heart rate was up just from that small encounter.

Then as we were driving back, I handed Hunter an envelope. I explained, "A few days back, I get a phone call and was told to meet a woman outside the local post office an hour before picking you up. I met this lady at the bus stop, where staff members going to work were dropped off. This lady was punctual. Her eyes caught mine. I saw a woman in her late twenties, average height and build. She was wearing a green skirt with a light white sweater, looking just like a regular person going to work and she was. She handed me an envelope, and I knew right away it was full of cash. She asked me to give this to you when you get out. You would know what to do with it." He snapped it quickly from my hand.

He quickly opened the sealed white regular envelope to find several hundred dollars. "What's the cash for?" I said. My heartbeat was starting to go up again. I did not want to get tangled up in prison shit.

"Don't worry about it," he said calmly.

I had to comment on his physique. "I notice you are in good fucking shape. I can see the muscles beneath your shirt are strong and defined," I said, stating the obvious.

Hunter counted out three hundreds from the envelope. He put the three hundred in one pocket and the rest in the other pocket. Hunter gave me directions. "Pull into that shopping mall on the corner over there." I pulled in and stopped close to the entrance.

He picked up a couple forty-ounce bottles of vodka, several cartons of cigarettes, rolling papers, dental floss, two large cans of roll-your-own tobacco, Bic lighters, and a satellite phone. He paid for this from the cash he was given. I think he spent it all.

"Now what the fuck is going on?" was a question that got no response.

Once we had all this shit, he told me, "Head back toward the prison. In a few minutes, I want you to veer off the main road into a small park by a rather wide, fast-moving creek." Once we got there, he had questions. "Do you have the ounce of weed and coke you were supposed to bring too?" I pulled a plastic bag from under my seat and handed it to him. The blood was pounding through the veins in my head. I could feel the throbbing in my forehead and in my chest, going relentlessly.

We grabbed the booze and drugs and cigarettes and satellite phone and started to walk into the bush. Soon we hit a small creek and followed it upstream. There was no real path, just bush and trees and branches. My heart was through the roof. I was surprised I did not pass out. Hunter explained the plan. "So, the plan is to sneak around the back of the prison, then to meet up with some of my buddies, the trusted inmates.

They will be working more or less on their own. I am expected. I am going to deliver all this shit to my buddy and keep a bunch of cash. Not a bad deal, eh?"

I just shook my head. "But then again, who am I to judge you? Just get this done so we can keep on going as if nothing had happened."

Hunter was quiet, focused. "Quit worrying, would ya."

I was worried. "Oh my fucking God. This was way too freaky." We were now crouching and hiding in the bush. The orange shirts of the inmates were visible in the distance through the branches and leaves. I could see the brick corner of the prison building. The barbed wire across the top of the building reflected sunlight, telling the obvious story that it was fucking sharp. This was Hunter's signal. He fucked off to meet his contact and left me there. I wondered how many times he had met someone else from the outside while he was considered a trusted inmate. Too much time was going by. I was getting paranoid. I waited, crouched by the river, trying to make myself small.

I waited a good twenty minutes. It was the longest twenty minutes of my life. I was sure at any moment we were going to get busted, cuffed, and sent directly to jail. Maybe we would be machine-gunned to death right fucking there on the spot and thrown into the creek, face down, bloody and dead. God only knows. The cops would be within their rights if we were caught just now. It would be an ugly scene. Oh, we would be so fucked.

Then Hunter appeared, sneaking quietly along the creek bank and explained, "All is good. It took us an extra bit of time to get the phone working."

"Fucking nuts," I said. "You are fucking nuts," and slapped him on the shoulder and sort of pushed him. Hunter smiled and told me, "Quit worrying, would ya." After that day, I quit worrying about a lot of things.

He fulfilled his commitment to his buddies still inside. They were now grateful to him for pulling off such a gutsy move. Not many inmates actually attain this level of commitment. But that was Hunter. He was committed and stood by his word. Now, these fuckers on the inside could get drunk and stoned and take turns calling their girlfriends. They would hide back in the bush by the river while beating their cocks as they talked dirty to them. I felt like we were doing our bit to keep this part of society sane and to some degree under control. I soon came to realize the guards were in on it. They needed this interaction to keep the underground railroad moving and the inmates calm. I felt privileged, in some strange way, to have been part of this process. Hunter was fine with it. He knew there would be no problems, and there weren't. Once far enough away and feeling safe, we fired up a huge fatty and cracked a beer each.

This memory came and went in a flash. It faded quickly now as reality struck home once again. We were in the kitchen of our pot-growing house, and the cops busting us was imminent.

Just then, Graham, Hunter's brother, stumbled up the stairs from the basement. He was waking up and wanted to know, "What the fuck is going on here?" He was wearing jeans and no shirt or socks. His hair was a mess, and he looked fucked up.

Graham is a tall motherfucker with hazel eyes and long, light brown hair. His body is strong and lean and powerful. His fingers are long and callused heavily on the tips. For a living, he moves steel and plays drums in a heavy metal group. The amount of chicks this guy fucks makes Frisk jealous. He looked like he was working out a lot.

"You look a fucking mess, Graham. What the fuck did you do last night?" I asked him.

Sometimes he gets fucking moody, and bugging him can be a bad idea. I recall driving him onetime to work, and I was playing a country and western tape. It infuriated him, but calmly he turned to me, slowly raising his fist at my face. The knuckles were large, with fingers held tight. Then he said, "Want to see how hard I can hit? That fucking music is shit, and I feel like busting up that tape into pieces and burning it and throwing it in a huge pile of fresh concrete." His long, thin, powerful muscles ran tightly up his arms. I smiled and changed the tape.

Getting a glass of water from the kitchen sink, he told us he was at a party last night on acid. "I was stoned out of my fucking mind and sitting in the corner when this other guy starts freaking me out. He was talking shit, and I thought he was this demon, so I punched him as hard as I could in the head. He went down on the floor and was out cold. I left the party in a blackout. Later I came down a bit but still tripping hard. So I started thinking, maybe I killed him, so a buddy and I went back to the party. The poor fucker was just getting up off the floor. He was shaking his head and moaning while trying to stand up. It was best I just leave before there was a murder." Graham finished the glass of water and had one more. He was a very confident kid with a sweet, honest laugh. There was little fat on his body.

"Jesus Christ, Graham. Good thing you didn't kill that guy," I said, shouting at him.

"Oh well, what the fuck? Many fine bands were formed in jail," was his retort. Then he added something interesting. "I wanted to tell you before, but Frisk has been training me in his crazy martial arts. It is a very special form of combat. He said he learned it in the southern jungle. He felt I was one of the few worthy to learn from him. If he might need backup or a replacement someday, he wanted me to be that person." Graham was proud to be Frisk's student.

POLICE

"Sweet, but we have some bigger problems just now," I replied urgently.

Hunter was listening to his brother ramble on while loading a bong hit. They do their bong hits with tobacco. I always told him, "You shouldn't do bong hits with tobacco. It isn't healthy. That shit will kill you, don't ya know?" I love that kid.

"Get the extra buzz," he always said, laughing and smiling as a cloud of thick, potent, high-altitude Himalayan indica smoke streamed from his nose.

I issued the plan. "OK, we can get the plants in these plastic bags and then start putting them in the back of my truck lying down. Once they are all in, I will cover them with a tarp and make a run for the hills.

"How many plants are there?" Graham asked.

"Twelve in the backyard," I said. "Most are about five feet tall. I got ten clones in the closet, all at eighteen inches and ready for planting. There was still lots of time to get plants in the ground. Every plant could mean a pound or more at harvest time."

By the minute, I was going further out on a limb, loading my truck with all these plants. Graham did seem to remain rather calm, sort of matter-of-fact about it all. He was much like a surgeon, looking at a bleeding patient. Then calmly, with confidence and experience, fixes the problem.

"I hate moving plants, especially hungover and sore and not knowing exactly what happened last night," I said very loudly, but it fell on deaf ears. I was outside digging up the plants. Graham was putting garbage bags over the plants in the hall. We moved them all to my truck. I had backed it down the driveway's slight angle to the house. There was a row of ten-foot-high cedar trees on each side between the houses, extending deep into the backyards. This guaranteed a good level of privacy.

The only house that could really see me moving plants into the truck was one hundred feet opposite on the other side of this residential street. The bay window provided a direct vantage, but the curtains were drawn. Again I spoke out loud to myself. "Little to no chance they would see me and even less chance they would know what I was up to. Just do the work and get out of this place. Stay focused."

My imagination wandered for a moment as I pictured the neighbor asking me what I was up to. "Just the garbage here," I would say to them. "No need for a second glance. Only normal residential garbage here."

Or would the neighbor lose their mind and freak out. "My God, bags of live pot plants. Quick, phone the police and get them here fast. They are trying to escape." Would they think this? Crazy thoughts went through my mind. My blood pressure was going up, but I switched back into the moment again rather quickly. I did not feel any calmer.

"I got two of the plants in garbage bags and into the back of the truck, lying down and tied tight. Move quietly, nothing sudden to attract attention," I told Graham as we passed in the hall.

I was in the backyard again, looking back at Hunter's house. The neighbor on the right has a porch on the second floor overlooking Hunter's backyard. He cannot see the plants. But sure as hell, he would notice something weird and not right if he saw me walking with these huge garbage bags full of something from the garden and these bright green leaves and branches sticking out, especially if he saw me moving quickly up toward the side of the house.

"Just look the other way for twenty minutes," I said out loud while looking nonchalantly in all directions at once. Coast looked clear. The last two pot plants were double bagged and tied. It was a motherfucker getting the bags over the plants. The long branches were difficult to get inside the bag without busting them. I was sweating and felt a little shaky, that diabetic sugardrop feeling.

This is it. I grabbed the last two plants just above the root ball. One plant was in each hand. I left the cover of the garden and moved out onto the back lawn. It was about thirty-five feet to the corner of the house. Every step was a moment in complete exposure. Sweat ran down my face, and it felt like walking through a minefield.

I am sure my brain was recording this event in many more frames per second than normal. Everything seemed to glow that much brighter and was that much crisper to look at. The plants were heavy, and my hands were wet. The plants swayed back and forth inside the bags as I continued my trudge.

It was noon just now. For some reason, I put the plants down and went up the back stairs to get a drink of water. I saw Hunter, and we stopped in front of the kitchen sink. As I ran the tap, I looked out our large kitchen window at the house across the street. All was quiet, just a dull, hot summer day at noon. Then I saw them, just as Hunter said. The cops drove by, slowing down just as they passed our house.

"Fucking hell," I said as my heart skipped a beat. I thought this was it. But how did they find out? The plants were pretty much out of sight. No big traffic in and out, as we were not dealing. Did one of those punk-ass friends of Hunter's rat us out for some tragic and twisted reason? I was always paranoid and loathed some of those freaks.

So now what? Hunter and I looked at each other and thought, *What the fuck? They got us nailed.* I could see them looking at my truck and looking across the street. Their white police car was loaded with sirens and lights and ramming grid and deep thread tires with jet black rims. It slowly drifted by without stopping. I drank my glass of water, trying to look past the cop car as if it were nothing at all.

"Holy old fuck, let's just keep going," Graham said to me.

"Right," I said, and walked with Graham to where I left the plants lying on the ground.

The garbage bags did little to conceal the plant as ninety percent of their volume was above the halfway mark. Grabbing another garbage bag, we stuffed the upper branches into the bag until nothing showed. I told Graham, "Just get them the next fifty feet between houses and into the back of my truck. Once they are lying flat and covered with the tarp, I need to get out of here." Sweat was getting in my eyes, and it stung. "Getting busted would not be good. Police will find leaves and the light system inside with more drug paraphernalia." Everything felt like it was going bad, very bad.

Graham was reassuring. "Chill out, man. You are tripping out. You will be out of here in five minutes." I believed him.

The moment felt surreal. The air was hot. "Fuck me," I said, "this is bullshit. Those fucking kids that show up here from time to time said something. I will hunt every one of them down and kill them." I was tripping out again. Graham shook his head, and we kept moving. The root ball caused a terrible lopsidedness. It caused me to carry them in the middle of the bag, not like conventional garbage bags, which are carried by the end that is tied.

The only clear shot of us now was from the curtain-covered window in the house directly across the street from where we stood in my driveway. I sucked it up and started walking the last few feet to my truck. The narrow alley was opening up and showing more of the street. I was at the tailgate struggling with the plants when out of nowhere came two police cruisers at speed. Lights flashing and sirens wailing. The cop cars slammed on the brakes and skidded to a screeching halt fourteen feet in front of me. Instead of seeing the bay window, I now saw the driver's side of a police car.

After stopping, the lights continued to flash, but the sirens turned off. I froze. My heart stopped. I dropped the bags beside me. I stared at the cop car. As both my arms slowly started to rise in surrender, the driver door burst open. A six-foot full-on geared-up cop with dark sunglasses, a flack jacket, gun, utility belt, flashlight, and shiny boots jumped out. For one brief second, he was staring directly at me. Our eyes met. I was in shock, and this is what the cops wanted. That's how they roll.

They just didn't want me. He continued to move quickly around the front of his cruiser to catch up with his partner. They stormed the front door of the house opposite Hunter's. One cop stood halfway up the driveway while the other pounded on the door. Within seconds, the door swung open. A fat, young punk-ass kid was grabbed and laid out on the lawn face down. Cuffs were slapped on him, and he was up against the cruiser, all in under a minute.

Fucking mother of God, I could feel the blood pound through the veins in my head. It rushed through me as tough questions were being thrown at the neighbor. I quietly reached down, grabbed the garbage bags, and placed them in the back of my truck.

I said to Hunter, who was now standing beside the truck, "Holy fuck. Man, oh, man, am I glad we are moving these plants anyway. This gets lots of heat off of the house." The tarps were tied down, and all was flat and hidden in the back.

Hunter made a good point. " I really didn't want to get busted. You need me for a lot more yet. I am the keeper of the seeds. I know how to grow plants for seed production, and I how to harvest them. And together, we were learning the old-school techniques for making hashish. Yeah, you need me." He was correct.

I told Hunter and Graham, "You are right, Hunter: we all need each other. I will see you guys later."

The cops continued to work on the fat kid. One cop had gone inside the house, and a box of stuff was being sorted on the front lawn. I never did see what it was, but that punk-ass kid across the street was into break-and-enters (B and E's). I wonder what he ripped off from me?

I pulled out of the driveway, turning right onto the street, careful to miss the back end of the police cruiser. I accelerated slowly, pulling away from the house. *Holy God*, I thought, *that was interesting.* I checked the rearview mirror, the flashing lights became smaller and dimmer and fainter, and the whole situation seemed to calm down and fade away. We had gotten away with it. God, I felt sick. It was just some twisted emotional hallucination. "Fuck me," I said out loud.

The orange tarp covering the plants was also visible in the rearview mirror. It was in place and looked good. I meandered through the back streets and onto the main highway. It was uneventful, the way it should have been. I had about twenty miles to go. Then, with a bit of work, I could get them into the ground and be back home before dark. It was a perfect location for the plants. They would rest between short dog trees on a nice southern vantage. I just had to get there first.

I was on the highway just out of town, heading south. Traffic was heavy, bumper-to-bumper for early afternoon, but it was moving along.

When my speed hit fifty miles an hour, with ten miles to go, the unthinkable happened. The orange tarp began to blow loose in the wind. It blew tight against the inside of the tailgate. The green garbage bag holding one of the five-foot plants was coming undone. I could see a branch pull free in the rearview mirror. I was now being tailgated, with no shoulder to pull over. I could see the bag begin to flap faster and higher and harder in the wind. I still had eight miles to go before the turnoff.

Almost immediately, the bag covering the top of the plant blew off. I fucking mean at light speed, literally just flew out of the truck. It hit the car immediately behind me and peeled off their windshield, then caromed to the side of the road. In the rearview mirror, I could see it doing cartwheels and tumbling by the guard rails.

At exactly the same time, the large plant, now exposed to the winds, began a flapping motion. The rush of air over the top of the plant acted as an airfoil and created an area of low pressure. This low pressure caused the plant, like the wing of an airplane, to rise. It started slapping against the truck's floor and then stood straight up in the back of the cab. The plant was lying with its root ball just under my back window. So, as it straightened up, I heard and felt the slap against the cab. My entire back window went pot leaf green.

It stood tall and magnificent and proud and wide. Then, as quickly as the plant stood up, it was knocked down by the force of the wind coming over the top of the truck. The plant then flattened on the floor of the truck. It lay there for about three seconds before starting to oscillate slowly, then faster, then stood straight up again. Branches and leaves entered the cab through the back window. The smell was strong, and the leaves were green and huge.

"Sweet fucking mother of God, this is it," I said out loud. Veins pulsed and pounded, and I could feel the blood in the back of my neck and over my forehead throb rhythmically. My breathing became short. My mouth was dry.

I couldn't pull over because there was no shoulder. I was thinking, *What the fuck do I do?* I was panicking. The car behind me dropped way back. I mean way back. The plant was averaging about one stand up every ten seconds. This was killing me.

*Was there a cop in this procession?* I wondered. There were just minutes to go before the turnoff. Up and down, up and down, the plant went. While it was flat on the bed of the truck, I could see branches from other plants waving and shaking free. *Hang on*, I said to myself over and over. The nearest car was still way back. No cop was pulling me over just now, so that was good. This was hell.

I kept driving down a long steep turn just now. I slowed a bit as the traffic slowed. Had the driver behind me seen the plant and was going to call the police? Did they know it was a pot plant? All I could do was live in this exact moment. It was like waking up in a long free fall. Would I hit the ground at two hundred miles an hour or somehow be saved? I made it down the hill and started slowing for the turn, then pulled into the left turn lane and signaled. The plant stayed low and still on the truck cab floor. The car behind me finally caught up and kept on going as if nothing was wrong. It just kept cruising along, without a glance my way.

"Holy old fucking Jesus on a chairlift," I screamed. No one followed me as I turned and moved off the main road. I was moving slower so the plant didn't jump straight up anymore, but it was still uncovered, and its branches stood tall even from a horizontal position. Still, no one was behind me. I was now turning off to a more secluded and deserted back road. Finally, the side road taking me up toward the plants appeared. It was very secluded. I backed into a small spot. The plants were moved out of the truck and under some cover. It was now mid afternoon. No one was around for miles. My grow show at this spot was still on the other side of some very sharp thorn bushes. There would be pain and blood getting through that gatekeeper, but I was at my destination. What a journey. You might say I was finally safe. I felt like firing up a joint. I felt as if I had just passed my math final. A person gets to experience big ups and downs in this pot-cultivating business, and the last three hours was a ride on the jagged edge.

*Fuck this*, I thought. I'd been fucking around there too long. It was getting late again, and I was hungry, tired, and sick. I needed a beer. I must have had some sickness, I thought.

Once back home, I called Hunter. I told him everything about the drive in detail, ending happily with, "The plants made it into a cozy spot with lots of sun and water, and are safe from bugs, slugs, thugs, and cops. What a messed up situation. Did we do all that for nothing? What was that cop shit really all about?" I said, trying to be funny and figure out what really happened today.

Hunter was still freaked out. "Fuck this shit, man. It was haunting. They did their shit with that punk bastard, but I noticed they would look our way every so often, so I started watching them. At one point, I saw a cop looking this way while talking on his radio. Then, later in the day, there was an unmarked car drive-by. You know what I mean, the midsize car, with dark windows and black tires, the scary kind. It drove by slow, but this time, they were looking at us. It was like a fucking horror movie." He went on, "Well, let's look at the positive side. We got those plants out of the house, and I got the closet cleaned. It was a mess. Good timing from that perspective. It's washed and ready to go again."

"What the fuck? There will be *no* again. Good fucking work getting the place clean. Let's keep it that way. These cops freak me out. We got no protection. We are at the mercy of those fucks. So here's the deal: we are done with that place. Next week, we do one more good cleaning, then give notice. It's time to get you the fuck out of there. Get a newspaper and start looking for a new place, maybe one in the country we can buy and own the land."

Hunter agreed and was very matter-of-fact when he suggested, "Why not take Lenny up on that offer for that land he wants to sell. And he does have that panic room he uses for a cold cellar in his basement. I told you a hundred times we could start to store our seeds there, and it's fucking safe."

I knew exactly what Hunter was saying and what we were going to do. "Holy God, you are right. First, I secure our own land and build a home. Lenny has ten acres near Lake Clear for sale, with access to hundreds of miles of bushland and fields. I was highly compelled to close this deal now more than ever with Lenny. Second, we will set up a safe place for our seeds. Lenny's panic room in his basement is perfect. You are right. The low temperature and humidity make it a natural for a seed bank. And no one is going to bother Lenny. Yes, it is safe and out of the way. I want you to begin the necessary work to make this happen—and quickly."

"You buy the land, and I will get the seed bank going," was Hunter's short summary.

I wanted to share some news I received. "Here is something else. Guess what I got today in the mail?" I was excited and Hunter was lost. "I got my goddamn patent pending for the Sifter. Imagine that: I am first to hit the patent office with a continuously operating hash-making machine that is unique and about to be very much in demand. I will be the holder of the patent, and I have Tom Sift Inc., set up and operating. Neat, eh?"

"No shit. Good work." Hunter did not fully comprehend the significance of the patent and company yet.

My last comment was about Graham. "I didn't know Frisk was training Graham. That is interesting. I never knew Frisk to train anyone. I wonder who else he is training?"

Hunter was getting tired. "Might be good to have more security as things move forward. Graham is the perfect choice. I wonder where Frisk learned to fight like that? Anyway, I gotta go. Getting tired." I added, "We could still get clones from my gorilla grow if you can stand the thorn bushes."

"Fuck that, you idiot thorn boy. You are crazy for getting so torn up each time you see those plants for more clones. Most should be pollinated by now. Just a matter of waiting for harvest."

"That's the plan. So fuck you, go find a place to live." I hung up, then got a week's rest.

# Lenny

I COULD PLAY POOL FOR HOURS AND HOURS—TEN, TWELVE, AND longer sometimes. It was three in the afternoon. A few beers, a couple of side door joints, and life at Carmichaels was good. Then I heard someone yelling at me.

"Jesus Christ, Tommy, what in the fuck are you doing now?" I heard in a rolling voice. It was Lenny.

"Just practicing. Where ya been?" I asked.

"Been fishin' in the park. Let's play some eight-ball, then fuck off to the lake," he growled, putting a brown paper bag full of beers on the counter. He snagged a can and flipped open the tab.

Lenny is a big guy—six feet, two inches tall and two hundred and fifty pounds, with a large beer belly. He has big bones and a receding hairline. Tattoos run up and down both arms, making him look like a merchant sailor, but he was no sailor. He was a fisherman and a gambler. He has more fishing shit than anyone I know. Flies, spinners, deep-water stuff, freshwater stuff, fish finders, boats, rods, reels—you name it, he had it, or he didn't want it.

One time, when I questioned his desire to buy all this shit, he said to me, "Fuck you, Tommy." That made sense. Only Lenny knows when he has had enough.

He is the type of guy who would have lunch at a restaurant, then steal the salt and pepper shakers, knives, forks, and a ketchup bottle. When driving back home, Lenny would throw most of it out the window of his truck. It was funny to see a saltshaker bounce off the highway, followed by a "fuck you" as the pepper shaker was tossed out next.

"Jesus God Almighty," I said when I saw what happened. "Are you fucking crazy? You could kill someone, or at least cause a fucking serious accident. What the fuck?"

Lenny just did his low sort of grunt and kept on driving.

He was a guy who truly did not give a shit about anyone or anything. Whatever worked for Lenny was as good as it got. I guess the twenty-five years he spent in New York City was a big influence on him because most of the people there were crazy. Truly, it was the crazy leading the crazy.

Lenny was shooting good pool just now. His shots were going in. The beer he opened foamed and spilled a bit. He started sucking on the beer before guzzling the whole motherfucker in thirty seconds. "That's how we do it in New York, don't ya know. Gitting the big load on now," he declared. His eyebrows were long and thick, moving up and down together as one when he talked. He threw the can in the garbage and opened another beer before breaking the next rack.

We played a race to five for twenty bucks. Lenny, being a big guy, still played smoothly. He did not appear awkward, he picked his shots quickly, and he was smart, very smart. He mostly used a closed bridge. He was able to get the cue ball where he wanted it. He made bank shots and nice draw shots. We didn't talk much more. We just hammered back a few beers and shot pool.

He would sip on his beer awhile, then guzzle the rest of it. Lenny smoked about ten cigarettes, throwing the finished butts on the floor. He would light a cigarette and not smoke it. Instead, it smoldered away in the ashtray. Sometimes, the ash would be just about as long as the cigarette itself. He would then knock it off and take a drag, at the same time giving a short moan or type of growl. It was something he did when he was thinking.

When I made a good shot, he would acknowledge it. "Jingling Jesus, Tommy, good shootin'." Then a low uhmmm, with his mouth shut and using his back teeth. "Man, oh, man," could be heard under his breath occasionally.

Soon, it was three to nothing for Lenny. Then it was four to three for Lenny. Then it was over. I lost. I did try. I hate to lose. I would have beaten him if I could. I didn't like it, but I paid him the twenty.

"It's time to fucking go, Tommy, don't you know," Lenny told me. Then I paid for the table, drank up the last of the beer, put Falcon away, and followed after Lenny.

We bailed out of Carmichaels and jumped into his red quarter-ton truck and headed out of town. After picking up Hunter and Frisk, we stopped at a fried chicken joint for a few snack boxes to go. While we were waiting, we had an ice cream cone each. The lady serving us was rather overweight but seemed happy. She wore an apron covered with previous ice cream stains. It was tied at the front.

Once Lenny had his cone, he looked at the woman and said in a rather inquisitive tone, "I bet you are one sour-tasting woman to lick." Looking directly at her, he put the whole scoop of ice cream and half the cone in his mouth. He used his tongue to lick as much as possible and then pulled it out of his mouth, still licking it. He grinned.

She looked at Lenny, standing her ground, and said, "You don't know just how sour I really am." She stared Lenny right in the eyes. After a brief moment in time, they both laughed.

Lenny smiled and leered at her, agreeing. "Well, Jingling Jesus, is that right?" He continued to take big licks of his cone.

Soon we were on the road again and slowly driving out of town. Lenny devoured his chicken as if he hadn't eaten in a week. When he was done, he took the box, the chicken parts, and everything else and threw it out the window and onto the street, then rolled the window back up slowly.

"That's how we do it in the big fucking city, don't you know, Tommy," he said. Then he threw out the napkins and little coleslaw cup.

I enjoyed the slow cruise through the residential area on the outskirts of town while the lunch boxes bounced off the road behind us, then blew away in the wind. It was weird. There should be a law against that. I said nothing.

The car behind Lenny started to beep his horn relentlessly. Lenny went into a rage, cursing, swearing, and breathing faster. The car approached to pass us but slowed to give Lenny the finger. He was screaming at Lenny while waving the finger. "You fucking retard, asshole." The guy seemed to repeat himself.

At that point, Lenny was frantic and began rolling down his window while yelling and waving his fist, his eyes wide with rage and focused on the mouthy driver beside him. Lenny was not looking at the road. He was in his element. He loved the attention. The guy driving, who thought he was going to teach this garbage-throwing retard a lesson, was wrong. His expression changed from anger to concern, then a new level of deeper shock as he realized Lenny was a big guy, scary looking, and pissed off. It all happened very quickly.

Lenny began coughing loudly, hacked up a huge green phlegm ball, and spat directly at the car opposite us while screaming at the top of lungs, "Fuck you, you fucking cocksucker." Unfortunately, Lenny had rolled his window only halfway down when he spat on the car. The yelling while trying to spit caused a malfunction with his plan. Spit went everywhere. The driver recoiled in shock and disgust, then went instantly wide-eyed. A large portion of saliva had hit his car directly on the passenger window and stuck, partially blocking his view of Lenny, but a lot splattered on the inside of Lenny's window too, while some rebounded on his shirt and pants.

I yelled, "Holy God, Lenny, what the fuck are you doing? We could be arrested. Let's get the hell out of here, OK?" We accelerated quickly ahead of this guy, leaving him far behind.

Lenny never wiped it off and went back to driving. The mania had passed. Lenny now offered valuable insight and a life lesson. Lenny looked directly at me. "Fuck that guy, Tommy. Just keep on going in life. Keep on going as if nothing had happened." Lenny was looking at the highway now, thinking. I understood. I was as indifferent as Lenny was.

Lenny was like a dad to me. At one point in the drive, I told Lenny, "Everything you do makes perfect sense to me, Lenny, and is completely justified. In fact, Lenny, you are setting the pace. I love ya, man. I learn a lot from you. Thank you." He was deep in thought, but he heard me. We drove on toward the lake. Lenny was not a fast driver.

Hunter was sitting in the back, drinking and telling us about how he is going to go to Africa around Christmas to check out some fields for seed generation. "If this goes according to plan, I'll have enough seeds to take care of the entire world." He had a vision, and he was making it happen.

Frisk was quietly enjoying the ride. With eyes closed, he spoke. "I am completely buzzed."

*I am sure he is*, I thought.

Hunter started to tell us about JD. "As it turns out, this guy is a big loser. He managed to bang his head while out mountain biking. Fuck me, wait until you hear this. They had to get a helicopter to get him off the trail. He has some kind of brain damage and was in the hospital for a few weeks. He's been drooling all over himself and does spastic and retarded movements most of the time. JD left the hospital confined to a wheelchair and is still majorly fucked up. He was at home and started fighting with his girlfriend about something stupid. So the neighbors called the cops. When the cops got there, he was told to stand up so they could search him and the wheelchair. But he couldn't stand and became very aggressive against the police, so they Tasered him with fifty thousand volts from their new energy weapons. Zapped him right senseless until he pissed and shit himself."

"Holy God," was all I could say.

"He was blown right out of the wheelchair and onto the floor, where he curled up into the fetal position. His heart stopped, and they had to call the paramedics to revive him. JD wasn't long at the hospital before the cops became anxious, decided to yank the intravenous tubes from his arms, and dragged him off to jail."

Hunter was laughing and smiling. I told him, "I think you like telling this story."

"When he got out of jail, he was pushing his wheelchair down Main Street, where he ran into some guys that hated him. An argument ensued. JD stabbed one guy in the heart, almost killing him. The rest of the guys knocked JD out of his wheelchair and proceeded to kick the living shit out of him. He had a bunch of seizures, and white froth poured from his mouth. The cops sent him back to jail. Now he is out again and waiting to go on trial for attempted murder."

Frisk still had his eyes closed and said, "He always was fucked up, always something wrong. He just threatened people in a bad way. Someone will slit his throat someday before kicking him in the face."

I responded to Frisk and Hunter, "Interesting prophecy, Frisk. Jesus Christ, Hunter, what kind of loser is that guy?"

Laughing again, Hunter finished the story. "So, he was at home waiting to be sentenced and decided to get a bunch of coke with a buddy.

I guess their welfare checks came in at the same time. So they got an eight ball of coke and took off in their car. They pulled over and snorted a good half gram each, maybe more. By the way, they were drunk as hell too. JD started driving them about. JD has no idea how long they were driving before noticing his buddy wasn't moving, so he pulled over and had enough wits about him to know he was dead. Fucking dead, man. He didn't want to get caught with a body in his car, so he decided to drive back to this guy's house and drop him off. He dragged this poor dead fucker's corpse back into his house and sat him up in his chair."

Hunter went on, "What JD didn't know was the neighbor saw all this and called the cops. The cops got there, and he was questioned again. As it turns out, the coke he bought was actually heroin. A rather common mistake, apparently. His buddy had a big allergy to opiates, so a direct snort of over a half gram up and killed him."

I was curious, "Why didn't JD die too?"

Hunter had a really good answer to that question. "They figured the only reason JD didn't die was his high drug tolerance and the adrenaline rush he got when first realizing his buddy was dead. That rush from the adrenal gland probably saved his life. At emergency wards everywhere, doctors dressed in blue gowns, white rubber gloves, and powder-blue paper shoe covers soaked in blood are shooting adrenaline directly to the hearts of opiate overdose victims as we speak. So this time, the cops are keeping him in jail, but I am sure he will be out soon enough. He has a way of just coasting along." Hunter thought, *Coasting is a good thing.*

All I could say was, "Wow, but keep in mind coasting implies going downhill, sometimes quickly." We drove on in silence.

Twilight was imminent, and Lenny's home was close. The sun was moving toward the western horizon. The sky was red. Shortly, Lenny started to drive up a side road to visit Calvin. "Motherfucker owes me money, and I am going to collect, don't ya know."

Calvin lived at the end of a short dirt driveway. Lenny pulled up in front of Calvin's front door. His house was in the typical back country style. Reminded me of a place made from sheet plywood with an outhouse on the front lawn. Calvin had a few kids and a big, fat wife. He was average height yet stocky, with short red hair. He loved to drink whiskey. Probably owed Lenny money from gambling.

Lenny got out of his truck and immediately started yelling for Calvin, "I am calling you out, you fucker. Get out here, you bastard. I am calling you out now." He said it again and slapped the hood of his truck, giving it a good crack. I could hear the low growl coming from Lenny. The emotion was raw and seething. He lit a cigarette when the porch light came on but never took a drag. I got out of the truck and came over to stand with Lenny. He had wide eyes, and there was spit on his lip.

Calvin came staggering out, screaming at Lenny, "What the fuck are you doing, you fucking maniac?" As he approached, Lenny leaned out and slapped him square on the right side of the head and ear with his large open cupped hand. Calvin stopped dead in his tracks and didn't say a thing. I am sure his head was ringing. I immediately thought of the old proverb, "What is the sound of one hand clapping?" I think Calvin just found out the answer to that one.

Lenny looked directly at Calvin and told him, "My mother always said people you like need a good slap in the ears every once in a while." Calvin was shaking his head, trying to regain his senses. It was sort of funny. Lenny laughed, and they walked to the porch. Calvin went inside, coming out a couple minutes later with a wad of twenties. "That's better, you fucking old cocksucker." Lenny threw the half-finished cigarette he presently had going on the front lawn, letting it burn, and lit up another.

While we stood in a momentary uncomfortable silence, Calvin spoke. "Let me offer you gentlemen a drink." So we went inside for a short visit.

His place was very nice inside, despite the outside appearance. We sat at the kitchen table while Calvin poured each of us a water glass half full of rye whiskey. It was God awful, but we drank it anyway. Calvin's girlfriend came in from the living room. She was not a fat chick at all. I got her mixed up with someone else. She was in good shape, very beautiful, with long black hair.

Frisk and Hunter waited in the truck. It was running, and they listened to rock music while smoking a joint. It was a ballad about a captain sailing and being far from home, Frisk said to himself but out load, "I am your captain."

Lenny was relaxed and a bit giddy now, "Jesus Christ, Calvin, we gotta get some fishing at Shaving Lake next week. The trout are fucking biting." Everyone agreed. We finished our drinks, and Lenny butted his cigarette on the floor. Just threw it down and stepped on it. No one said anything when we got up to leave. Calvin's wife got up too and Lenny went to give her a big hug. Lenny took notice of her.

Lenny was tall and heavyset, and she was much shorter. He walked over, putting one arm around her, and said in a sneering, outrageous tone, "Isn't this a nice woman." She smiled. Then Lenny stepped it up, looking directly at Calvin. "Holy old God, if you could only get killed in a car accident somehow, I would take her over for you. I'd have a beautiful little twenty-one-year-old honey here. I'd lick behind her kneecaps every night, don't ya know."

He sneered and squeezed his arm a little tighter around her. Lenny looked at her, then at Calvin, and stood tall. We all laughed and moved toward the door. Then Lenny looked back at Calvin and asked, "Does she have any hair on her belly? Some women have the odd hair, don't you know." Calvin sort of laughed, uncertain what to say to that. I laughed, but Lenny got serious, his attention switching back to our mission. "Let's fucking go, Tommy." We left Calvin's house.

In no time, we were at Lenny's. It is safe to say, Lenny collects lots of shit. His house is a repository of artifacts from his life. Fishing gear, videos, pictures, china cabinet full of beautiful ornaments, and two deep freezers full of fish and deer meat. Guns on the walls, fish finders, and fishing gear were strewn everywhere. A wall-mounted TV with a pirate satellite dish took up the corner with the pool table. A small grow op was in the attic. A huge finished basement was full of tools, motors, bear traps, and minnow traps. In one corner of the basement, near the cold cellar, was my shaker, the working prototype ready to be called into action. Lenny was instrumental in making this machine a reality. The basement could be accessed from the inside his home and from a small outside entrance with a rather large padlock on it.

As I finally hit the couch and was passing out, I could hear Lenny yelling at his wife, "Jesus Christ, Bridget, where are my fucking boots?" I was out.

# Field Trip

WE WERE UP AT FOUR. IT WAS STILL NIGHT. THE STARS were bright in the sky. The great constellation Orion the Hunter was magnificent, towering over us. I was standing beside Frisk, having a piss, while the truck warmed up. He said to me, "I don't have goals. I just take things day by day."

"Yeah, today will be a field trip sort of day," I replied, watching the sky. We finished pissing, grabbed a coffee with a shot of whiskey, lots of beer, weed, and music and jumped into Lenny's truck. It was warm and comfortable inside. Lenny was last. Eventually, he jumped in smoking a cigarette, carrying a coffee and drinking a beer.

Frisk spoke. "We are on our way to see some of the best pot fields in the world. It is about eight weeks before harvest time." A north road, then a series of old logging roads, brought us to a small parking area. We parked and got out. The sun was up, and it was warm for late August.

After walking into the bush for about twenty minutes, we came by a small creek and culvert dumping into a rather large lake. Lenny wanted to get some minnows from the minnow trap he left here last week. Apparently, we were going to do some fishing along the way. Hunter had his pack with a hundred or more plants in small tubes, ready for planting in the fields we were about to see. These clones were short now but would flower beautiful purple and red buds. As the older plants matured, these plants would grow beside them. Within a couple of months, there would be nearly two tons of pot.

I had my fishing rod in hand and rubber boots on my feet. I was still on the coffee. Frisk was being silly and serious at the same time. He was having a beer. I felt good.

Lenny pulled up the trap from about four feet under the water. As he pulled it out, I said, "Something is not exactly right. There are more than minnows in that trap. Fuck me, there is a four-foot water snake in there too. It looks dead." It was all upside down and twisted. A minnow tail stuck out from its mouth.

Lenny commented, "This bastard struggled to get itself out of this one, but he was fucked. He was doomed. That would be the last minnow he would eat."

Lenny reached into the trap, pulled out the snake, removed the minnow from its jaws, and threw it at me, laughing and cursing at the same time. He was the only person I knew who could show both emotions simultaneously.

The snake hit the ground and rolled over, not moving. It was a long one, with brown, green, and black stripes. We got a couple hundred minnows in our pail and started to leave. Just then, the snake came to life. I was beside the fucker when its eyes and mouth went wide. It squirmed and untwisted, falling quickly into the classic snake attack position. Its head was held high, fanged jaws opened wide, seething, spitting, and snapping. The snake had gone crazy. It scared the hell out of me. Frisk stepped back, just staring at the snake.

The old water moccasin went to strike at me as Lenny's foot stepped on it. He picked it up and in one motion, twisted its head right around and then around again. He threw the snake into the trees. Flipping around branches, it finally became hung up in one of them, truly lifeless this time. "Motherfucker won't be eating any more of my fucking minnows. Fuck him, don't ya know." Lenny laughed and smirked and said, "Scared you, did it, Tommy? Maybe you're getting a little soft in the head from sucking on that hash pipe all the time." He lit a cigarette. His attention quickly went back to getting on the water and getting our lines wet. I just shook my head. I would hate to think he was right.

We fished for about an hour or so before drifting into a small cove. We pulled the boat behind a natural barrier of leaves and branches. This boat was well hidden. The water was warm and calm. Walking was not a trudge through sharp patches of thorns. It was a short walk to a magnificent view of rolling hills, with fields of pot going for miles. Frisk spoke. "We are in God's country." We hiked between beautiful pot plants, some well over eight feet high. These fields represented some of the best this earth has to offer.

Lenny was a serious operator. I could tell this from the work he put into this project. He also saw the cash reward and was fearless of capture. We walked into patches of pot. Not patches but small fields, separated by trees or low brush.

Hunter was ecstatic. He lectured as we walked the fields. "This is fucking beautiful, Lenny, just fucking beautiful. I love the way you used the burnt wood to fertilize the soil. You can see how those plants are a little greener than others because of the fertilizer difference." Lenny had made piles of fertilizer from burnt trees hit by lightning and natural compost.

Frisk trained us how to grow weed. He would tell us, "Indica and Sativa plants are spread over both the south and west vantage points. Height varies with elevation. The lower fields being eight or more feet high and have a longer season to mature. The plants higher up the mountainside will only reach five feet high. We will harvest from the higher to the lower elevations. Nature is doing its thing.

One of the main rules with these Sativa dominant strain is to make sure they vegetate for at least three months. Otherwise, the potency can drop. Lenny did well with the holes for the plants, three feet by three feet by two feet deep—perfect. Simple nutrients in the soil should be enough, but we must try to keep the soil pH around seven and no more. Now another very important part to growing: there must be enough mycorrhiza fungus, or myco fungi. Lenny has been adding cow manure, so that should help. The few seeds we have from Colombia are heirlooms and are growing excellent in these conditions. Heirloom means they have been around from an earlier era. Some have been growing for hundreds of years in one place and are know as a landrace."

Hunter jumped in, "Basically an open-pollinated phenotype that is old. We like to call ourselves 'old-world cultivators,' and these are a 'long inbred line."

I spoke my thought. "Nature is always in charge, but it sure helps to have an expert to guide us."

Frisk leaned over to me and said, "Tommy, these fields, these valleys, are very similar in elevation and temperature to where I grew up. What I am saying is that we could grow Punta Roja."

I said, "Yes, I agree, Colombian Red, but how can we get the million seeds we will require?" Frisk just shrugged his shoulders. We laughed silently together before continuing on.

Lenny guided us through the different fields. There were small dug-outs every few hundred feet. "I had small pits dug for harvest time. We can do the sorting and drying under these tents."

It was good work, and I told Lenny, "Nice work, man. You were definitely paying attention to Frisk's lessons. Wow."

Hunter was freaking out. "Look at this! There are many different phenol types here. Some are fruitier, and the leaves are pointier. The leaves on these are different, less pointy with a longer inter-node and stronger branches. The better ones have thick red veins. These are the transmission highways." Hunter explained what we had here. "Some have the pine smell, some are more minty, and some are woody. The aroma is so intense. You can smell it in the mountains. These fields remind me of the Riff Mountains in the Indian Himalayas. Riff means Valley of the Devils. This marijuana is so complex, it is incredible."

Hunter had us remove the males from most fields. "The males are being removed at the right time. I have one field that has gone to seed with numerous varieties and is protected by numerous thorn bushes. Tommy is handling that field specifically. This will produce many times what we will need for next year. We can sell seeds too. Don't worry, I know what to do with this stuff." Hunter reassured us his plan would supply growers from South America to Eastern Africa, with enough seed for their fields. Many will be used in the higher altitudes.

"Hunter, you should test these in our seed bank laboratory over at Lenny's," I said.

Hunter was ahead of us. "I have some samples already. Let's hand rub some hash. It should be fun. You start by gently rubbing your hands on the outside of a large bud. As the resin collects, make it into a ball. The ball grows and grows as you collect more and more, and you get the best hash."

It took about an hour or so, but we ended up with some superior balls of hand-rubbed hashish. They were dark, soft, creamy, and when smoked, oh so nice. We learned something that afternoon. Hunter was thanked by all.

We spent the night partying and watching the stars and the familiar patterns they make drift slowly across the sky. The stars were bright and magnificent. The plants were such a wonder to see at night too. Frisk just loved it and told us stories about being in the South American pot fields. He was at home in this remote valley.

The night was hot. Dope was growing everywhere. This was no-man's-land, hundreds of miles of forest, valleys, and lakes covering a vast stretch of this great country. There was no chance of this area being found. It was too vast a wilderness. No one would be coming by.

Frisk stood tall on top of an old stump struck by lightning. His arms raised, an incredibly bright universe his backdrop, he formally named this valley, "We need to name this place, Tommy. I formally declare this valley to be eternally known as the Great Valley of Lenny, after its founder and creator. It is a rather complex system of mountains, hills, and valleys. I toast . to you Lenny and your new namesake, Valley of Lenny." We all toasted to Val Lenny.

"Brilliant, Frisk, just fucking brilliant. Great idea." Frisk surprised me, and I wished for a brief moment it was my idea.

In the morning, we had a quiet breakfast. The fields were bathed in sunshine from early morning until late evening. This little valley, now known as Val Lenny, was just perfect. We packed up and headed back to town. We had seen what we needed to. Val Lenny was vast and healthy and would produce hashish for many generations to come.

We slowly floated back in Lenny's boat, fishing and smoking and drinking. The actual fields were soon lost and out of sight. The countryside and the general direction of the valley were all that remained. It was night now, and we were heading home. Everyone was quiet, reflecting on the world-class project we had just witnessed. Sometimes we could drink and smoke and still be resolved, still be somber if not sober.

I loaded the cooler into the back of my truck, close to the cab's back window. This was for easy access to the cold beer, inside the cooler. It was dark when Hunter, Frisk, and I left Lenny's place for home. The beer was very cold. We drove for twenty miles on dirt roads before pulling onto the highway. No sooner was I at road speed than Frisk fired up a giant hash joint. It smelled so good; it tasted so good. I drove the speed limit back home. I drove like a champ.

# PART 2

# Road Players

IT WAS EARLY OCTOBER NOW, HARVEST TIME. A COOL BREEZE blew through Carmichaels. Old Don sat in his wheelchair with his blanket over him. He was counting his money while Johnny served customers.

Johnny was his manager. He looked after Carmichaels in all ways, from handyman to bouncer. Johnny made sure Carmichaels was run with the family spirit in mind. He kept the place clean, no riffraff, and the games were friendly. Johnny was an excellent pool shot and a gambler. He learned to play snooker while in the air force. In fact, Johnny helped teach me when I started playing pool. I remember learning the open bridges first while developing my stroke. Later, he showed me the closed finger wrap bridge. It felt so cool to do that bridge. I think it's still cool today.

I was sitting at Carmichaels little lunch counter and feeling much better. It was one in the afternoon, and I was on my third chuck wagon. The side door was closed, and people were playing pool. It was bright outside. The harvest would begin soon—tomorrow.

"Fucking alcohol can take a lot out of a guy," I said to Johnny while working on my fourth cup of coffee. I ordered a beer and finished the last tasty bite of my chuck wagon. I spun around on the small round swivel stool to face the tables and jukebox. The stool was bolted to the floor, just like the other five. It was change of seasons, and the shadows were cool. I sat in a cool shadow. I watched someone put a quarter in the jukebox. He selected some songs. "Jumpin' Jack Flash" came on.

Old Don spoke to me. He was reminiscing. "I was a big wig in the billiards world back in the day and knew many people. After a bad accident, I ended up in this wheelchair, instantly retired. Carmichaels was designed and built by me. It was my retirement strategy, a dream come true, and I love it." He lived just across the street. It is just a straight push of the wheelchair, down his special access ramp from his house, across the street, and up the side ramp into Carmichaels. That was pretty much his life, back and forth.

He only gave me one piece of advice, and it was a good one, "Tommy, you don't need to win every game, but *never* miss the money ball." I thought that was good. Never miss the money ball. Those were words to live by.

Most of the people I played back then left me in horrible safeties, virtually impossible to make a shot or even hit my ball. I suffered, but I won a few too.

I had been at Carmichaels for twenty minutes. "Goddamn, those chuck wagons are good," I said, now facing back at Johnny.

Suddenly, Johnny started telling me about this big guy who came in earlier that morning. "Holy God, Tommy, you should have seen this guy. He called himself the Kid, and he was big, two hundred and fifty pounds if he was ounce. He ate five chuck wagons and drank three Cokes, holy God."

"He figured out those chuck wagons were the best pretty quick, eh?" I said to Johnny.

Johnny sat and told me the story. "Yeah, he started getting friendly with Lenny. They started gambling by flipping coins for ten bucks. They had a way of laughing together. The Kid was a real gas. Then they were gambling on sports games on TV. Lenny won another fifty or seventy-five. They had fun, and the big guy didn't seem to mind losing a hundred or so. Lenny was happy to win it. The Kid asked Lenny to shoot some pool. The Kid didn't really care what game. That should have been the tip-off, but Lenny missed it or didn't care. They grabbed some balls and set up on table two. They played nine-ball. The bet was ten bucks a game to start."

I asked about the bet. "That sounds cheap."

Johnny went on, "Lenny broke first and ran out. That was the last rack he won for a while. Maybe the Kid was a bit nervous of Lenny, or maybe he just wanted to make an example of someone. Either way, he went to town on him. He made long shots and banks. He could get out of any safety Lenny put him in. Lenny was outclassed. Lenny lost a hundred dollars pretty quick and then lost another nine before quitting."

I recalled seeing Lenny after that encounter. "He was not happy. He had bad things to say about this, Kid," I said, looking down the length of Carmichaels.

Johnny continued, "Lenny fucked off shortly after that. The Kid hung around and played more guys. He picked up a few more hundred, then left as happy as when he got here. That guy was a pro, probably put onto us by one of Don's old connections." Johnny looked over at Don, smiling and taunting him.

Don was done counting his money for the moment. Looking up, he said, "Yeah, my old connections did not forget about me too quickly. I remember the last big gun that came through here last year. He was definitely being obvious as to why he was here—he was a road player."

I was drinking a nice cold beer, and God, it tasted great. I drank half of it in two gulps. The bubbles and froth backed up my nose and filled my lungs. I coughed as I spoke. "Can I order another chuck wagon with mustard and ketchup?" I asked Johnny. He nodded and put another one in the oven. "God fucking almighty, these are good. I remembered that road player. His name was Edie, the Italian hustler."

Don recalled that night at Carmichaels for us when Edie, the road player, showed up. "I remember he was Italian with a black mustache and hair. The girls thought he was cute. He showed up here after dinner. He did the same sort of thing as the Kid, betting on anything. When he got here, he started drinking and betting on tennis balls. I recall his words. "I bet anyone here I can throw a tennis ball the furthest in one pitch." I was impressed and would have taken that bet, but he never got around to it."

I interjected, "He was drunk when he showed up. However, this smooth-talking Sicilian was a professional. He was out of our league. He could shoot them one after the other without a problem for days." I smirked, then said, "Remember Red? Around three hours into his hustle, he noticed that local gal, Red, at the bar drinking beer and listening to the jukebox. She also played some pinball. That little honey is a gorgeous redhead. Tall, voluptuous, striking features, a beautiful laugh, and narrow, fun-loving eyes. This was not her usual hangout, as I recall."

Johnny remembered Red too. "She was depressed and looking for something different to do for a couple hours. Her brother, who was a serious alcoholic and drug addict, had shown up dead a month earlier. They found him in a hotel room. It was a couple of hookers who called it in. He had them over and sort of partied out—all the way out, room temperature out, dead. Turned out to be an overdose of cocaine and speed, administered by needle."

I spoke softly from experience. "I did lots of drinking with that guy. Addiction can be strong in some people. What a waste. Poor Red found out a few weeks ago, but I didn't want to say anything about it. Just keep on going as if nothing had happened. Don't get me wrong; my heart is truly with her." We all agreed to that one.

Don began again, "I watched Edie play and shoot his mouth off. He was hitting on Red. He bought her drinks, and they talked about anything she wanted to. He made her laugh and generally feel good while full-on flirting."

I jumped in, "She did not mind, as I recall, and I don't care; she was not on my Christmas card list. I am just indifferent, but I could see how she would be attracted to him—young, in shape, confident, and horny. He was all these things."

Don continued, "This Italian, who called himself Edie, was taking immediate advantage of those suckers who were anxious to play him. I knew he was working the room. Everyone just sort of paid their money and took their chances at beating him. I must say, it was fun to watch this guy run the racks. Once he got set up, he just kept putting the cue ball in the right place. If he got out of line, he could make a tough slice or leave a sickening safety. Red had moved over beside him. Both of them were drunk now. Each was being motivated for their own reasons. He wanted to get the money and get laid. She was forgetting her deceased brother. Both were achieving their goal."

I was impressed by Edie and told Don. "He said, 'Never a doubt' a lot. It became taking on the pro time, and we all did it, including Red. It started with Edie rubbing up against her, then kissing her, then drinking more. Edie's routine was polished, I must admit. His game did slump a bit, but he was so good it didn't matter. The way I figured it, every game was a new game, and sometimes, these guys would fail. They would malfunction, or some unforeseen thing would fuck up their karma. One of the best parts about Edie: he was funny, telling tales of other games and adventures on the road. I personally thought it was all true and actually believed his shit. It sounded like fun. It got me excited."

Marching on, he won another six hundred dollars, as well as two beers. Edie was staggering and slurring somewhat but still in control. He was very much in control. It was midnight, and I was playing this guy at two hundred a rack. Fuck me he was good, but I did beat him once or twice. It felt good and I remembered that feeling. It was emotional. I saw him waver. He could lose.

He went for a piss at one point between games, with Red following him quietly into the can. It was a shitty washroom, but it had some size. They were in there twenty minutes. I knew Red had coke. When they came back from the can, there was white dust under her nose. She wiped it away once back at the table.

When the last ball dropped, my eyes opened a little wider. My heartbeat went up as he took my cash. Even though the money didn't matter, my hand shook a bit. I was not happy about this defeat. My voice slightly raised, I gave him my thoughts: "Won't be bleeding anymore to you tonight. But thanks—it was fun. I gotta say, you taught me a few things."

I shook his hand for an extra second while looking him in the eyes. I was truly thankful, and I think he knew it. I liked the way he held the bridge hand close to the cue ball or a short bridge. The way he held the cue tip in front of the cue ball and how he only took a very short backstroke before striking was key to his success. He was happy to oblige. I promised myself I would find a way to get better at this game. A quest had begun. I looked over toward the side door and saw Frisk wandering in.

He looked cold and pale but smiled when he saw me. He had been partying, selling hash and not sleeping. He ordered two chuck wagons and sat down. Frisk ate his meal quickly. Blood returned to his face and head. He threw his elbows back, declaring he was fit and ready for action. Frisk had a weird luck about him. The Italian played on table two.

Frisk said, "I'll give you a try. Say two hundred a game, a race to five? Someone could win a thousand dollars if they won all the games."

For some reason, Frisk ran out or left a good safety and won the set. It looked like a hustle, but Frisk was OK with it. He had the beginners luck ticket going for him. He was having beer and fries. The more he ate, the better he got. My friend Frisk had spirit. He was in the zone.

Red was smiling while smoking a cigarette and drinking her beer. It was good to see her smile.

Balls rattled then dropped and were soon racked again. Energy was good at Carmichaels at midnight. They played on. For some reason, Frisk was beating this guy. Edie came here to steal from us, but Frisk was actually up. That was the hustle. This was how it was done. Frisk was in the jaws of the trap. Red rubbed against Edie and they kissed. She was actually distracting him. His game was down. They played on and bets went up. Soon they were playing for four thousand dollars.

The last set was a race to nine. The game started with Red's new boyfriend, breaking and winning the first three games. Frisk was standing, smoking a cigarette, and waiting. He was laughing and cracking jokes. He knew he was out classed, but was not prepared to lose either. He had energy, raw energy, not just drug-fueled brains. Well, that too. But the little Italian had spirit. Red was a railbird; she was just a sweater, an observer like the rest of us.

Nine-ball is interesting, in that you hit the lowest ball number on the table first as hard as you can, and anything going in counts. It is not a call-pocket game. Flukes and slop count. The nine just has to fall to win. I remember how Frisk worked like hell to get it five games to Edie's six. Frisk was behind by one game and being hustled. They were making side bets. This crazy wop was ready to strike like a cat ready to pounce. He was in the zone. He suggested the bet be raised another thousand.

Frisk agreed, saying, "In for a penny, in for a pound."

Frisk was about to lose. Once he missed, there would be virtually no chance of getting to the table again. He would be meatballs. It was Frisk's break, with four games to go. Fate works in strange and mysterious ways and seldom at the time of anyone's bidding. He hammered the cue ball full on into the rack. Balls went everywhere. They rattled, and the nine was hit from behind by the red seven ball. The nine rolled straight into the side pocket. It was now six games each.

The balls were racked. Frisk stood in the same place. Lining up square, behind the cue ball, he struck, grinning the whole time. The force was incredible. The nine rolled and bounced and went into an end pocket. Now Frisk was leading seven games to six.

He broke again. I said, "Holy old fuck" when the cue ball hit the rack dead on, bounced straight back, and stopped dead in the middle of the table. The spin was tremendous. The cue ball immediately began to move toward the rack again. The nine was sitting still, having not moved at all when the rack spit apart, and took the near full hit of the cue ball. The cue ball hit the nine at a forty-two-degree angle, which, by chance, was the exact angle needed to send it into the end pocket.

It was eight games to six. Frisk was on the hill. Edie was restless. She kissed him, but he was distant. He was preoccupied. He knew he could still win if only a shot would come his way. Frisk needed one more win. *Impossible* was my thought. Frisk laughed and swung hard for the fourth time in a row. Again, balls moved and rolled. The nine stayed right in the middle of the rack again as every other ball scattered at speed. Balls moved fast, some more than others. The seven hit the side pocket point and fired straight back toward the rack. It missed every ball, bounced off the long rail, then off the short rail, and came up behind the nine.

"Wow, holy God," I said loudly in unison with the other rail birds. I remember standing up to watch history to witness a tale in the making. It unfolded in slow motion. This Italian hustler and the lonely redhead were silent. His eyes were wide, hers closed.

The red seven cracked the yellow-and-white nine ball, dead on from behind and directly toward the side pocket. Suddenly, and out of nowhere, the three ball was rolling toward a collision with the nine. Just when I thought the three would hit the nine ball away from the pocket, it slowed. As if by some mysterious and unseen force, it stopped. Divine intervention, I am sure. The nine rolled past the three and up to the lip of the side pocket, waited, and then dropped in. Frisk won. He actually beat this Italian hustler five games straight. Frisk laughed, shook his hand, grabbed the money, and split. Hard to believe, but it did happen that way.

The not-so-happy Edie kept saying, "Who would believe this? Who would fucking believe that just happened? Never a doubt. Never a doubt." *Fuck* was said—a lot. Holding the cue at the tip with both hands, he leaned in and pushed down. The cue bowed in the middle, and in another second, it snapped.

Wood went in different directions. His face changed quickly, like someone who had just tripped on the curb of the street, and was snapped back to reality. He took the cue apart and threw the broken shaft in the garbage. There was a release in his actions. He turned around and laughed and finished his drink. He talked and drank some more, with the few of us who were left. He partied with his new friends.

Don finished the story. "Apparently, he never got a chance to throw a tennis ball half way across town. Nor did he get the cash that night, but Edie did get the chick, and he did have a great party."

I had the vision of them leaving. "The last I remember, those two were staggering off together into the cold, dark night." We all laughed together.

Johnny remembered it well too. "That was rather fun to watch."

Don spoke. "I am proud. Carmichaels is still on the road players' radar. It is all I hoped it would be," he said with a contented grin on this face.

I said to Johnny and Don, "Never a doubt, never a doubt." The next day, I was meeting Frisk, Lenny, and Hunter. It was harvest time. "Well, I gotta head home and get some rest. Cheers, gentlemen," I said, and I left.

# Harvest Time

I REMEMBER THE DAY WE LEFT FOR THE HARVEST. WE WERE SITting at my place, shooting the shit and drinking. The back porch was soaking up the sun and placed perfectly for a sunny fall day, like today. Frisk and I had just snorted a few lines and were actually thinking about food. Frisk suggested, "A little lunch maybe, Tommy?"

I was making a cold soup. It was very nice on a hot day. It was probably a little hotter where we were sitting, beside my house and just below the Juliet balcony. Birds fluttered and swept the air above us. It was truly a marvelous day. Hunter was facing the sun with his eyes closed. The neighbor's eleven-year-old daughter, Sam, was over for lunch. Our backyards share a short fence. Sam is a very pleasant gal and had been a bit reserved lately. Sipping her cold soup, she spoke about a tragedy in her soft ladylike voice. "My dog, Scotty, was playing outside two days ago and got killed. Scotty was a car chaser. That black little mutt sure had spirit. He could run a mile a minute and bark like old hell." Sam was one to speak her mind, much like her mom. She continued, "So, the other day, Scotty was running after a truck, but the truck driver slammed on the brakes. My poor Scotty didn't have a chance. He hit the back wheel with a vengeance, finally achieving his goal, finally catching the tire. Mom said, 'He died happy.'" I was thinking, this logic, this form of condolence, did not really sit well with this poor kid, but she was happy enough at the moment.

While sitting outside on the deck, unbeknownst to us, a drama was unfolding above. Our young neighbor friend was relaxed and enjoying her soup when a small bird, no older than two weeks, was about to lose its place in the nest. This nest was on the top of the railing surrounding the Juliet balcony, about twenty feet directly above the table where we sat.

This poor, weak little baby bird stood on the edge of its nest, fluttered, and fell. Being so recently hatched, it was incapable of flight and went straight down into Sam's soup, just as she was taking a big spoonful. It landed square in the bowl and did a very short death flop. It was brown, and its small beak wide open and pointing straight up in the air. One wing was under the body, which was in the middle of the bowl, and the other wing was stretched out and hung over the side. The lifeless carcass was covered in soup and noodles. It was an ugly fucking site.

The soup had splashed all over the table and Sam's clothes. At first, there was shock in her eyes, then panic. She screamed and began to cry and yell, "Get it off. Get it off. Why me? Why? Why? Get it the fuck out of here." She recoiled from the table but hit the wall and was pinned in. Struggling savagely, she was soon free from behind the table and stood in front of the mess, looking at the soup and dead bird. "Why me?" was all Sam said.

Frisk looked at the situation, smirking, saying nothing.

It all happened rather quickly from there. The bird was dead. It took up most of the bowl and was totally disgusting. It was lifeless. I grabbed the bowl and threw the whole mess out in the far corner of the yard, by the fence. The bird slid into the tall grass, and that was the last I had to deal with that one. *Why me?* I thought. Eventually, we all calmed down, and Sam split for home.

"Enough fucking around," I said. "This is going to be a lot of work, so let's get to it. Get the fucking picture?" We loaded up our packs and hit the road to Val Lenny.

The trip was enjoyable. We were ready for a month's work. It would be an adventure for sure. When we got to the fields, the sun was on the plants. The buds were huge and fresh and beautiful and full. We set up camp and rested. We rested until it was night. The sun slowly went down on the fields, and then we began.

Once the harvest began, there was no stopping it. Plants were trimmed while still in the ground. All the leaves were saved and dried. Plants were cut and hung in the makeshift tents and ditches Lenny had created earlier in the season. We were well out off the beaten path, so to speak, and feeling relaxed, with no pressure. The days of work were enjoyable and felt very rewarding. Soon, pounds and pounds of commercial quality buds were drying before being vacuum-sealed and sold.

Trim was gathered in large bags and brought to a small hunting camp we had on beautiful Lake Clear, where Lenny lived. We packed that cottage with bud and trim and set up a hashish manufacturing factory. Once the pot was dry enough, the sifting began, and soon, pounds of hashish were stacked up. It was beautiful to make and to see. The Sifter worked wonderfully. The grinding and freezing with the shaking and multiple bins was brilliant. Just keep feeding in the weed and keep collecting multiple grades of hash near instantly. The continuous operation was incredible, brilliant.

We used Lenny's boats to move the weed and hashish. Many pounds were sold right from the start. It was instant cash in hand. Frisk was selling many pounds to this guy Nailer. Frisk described Nailer when I asked about him, "Nailer is a gangster—past the fringe, dangerous—but he has cash."

I had a question. "So, who does he sell to?"

Frisk spoke with caution. "He is selling to some heavy contacts, people who deal internationally for distribution. He is selling to people who are moving the hashish out of the country," he said with a hint of concern in his voice.

I felt excited. "Wow, we are becoming famous, but Nailer sounds like he is a true criminal." Nailer sounded a bit too fucked up for my liking, but maybe someday, we would meet.

Lenny sold lots of both weed and hashish to the Native Indians. He got along very well with the local tribes and was considered part of the clan. In fact, Lenny had Indian status and could purchase any item without tax, but it was not always like that. He was jealous of the local Indians, who could hunt deer at night using salt blocks and night scopes, without fear of prosecution. Or the fact they could use nets to catch fish at any time of year. Lenny always had this goal to buy his cigarettes without paying tax too. Lenny wanted to be part of the Indian culture so badly.

This is how Lenny explained what happened. "The way I figured it, Tommy, since they were all basically alcoholics and hunters. Anytime I would visit the Chief, I would drop off a forty-ouncer of strong whiskey and a ten-pound trout, or a few pounds of deer meat. They appreciated it very much, and over the years, we became good friends."

So, one day, Lenny went for it. "I told the Indian chief my father was not my real father. In fact, what happened was my mother was raped by a number of natives years ago, while her husband was away, working in the bush. I am, in fact, the offspring of that unholy indigenous bonding. And since my real father is an Indian, this makes me half Indian, which is more than enough to be considered eligible for Indian status."

I confirmed what he was telling me. "So, the Indian chief agreed with your crazy suggestion?"

Lenny nodded. "So, the papers were signed and submitted to the government. Within four weeks, I received my status card in the mail. The first thing I did with my new status was to buy a carton of tax-free smokes and a tank of gasoline." He grinned from ear to ear, proud of his accomplishment.

Lenny was my hero. "And what an accomplishment it is, Lenny, as I know of no other human being not only to think up that crazy shit but to actually pull it off. You are a god."

He was happy and proud. Not everyone felt that way, and he had been shunned in some circles for years. But do you think Lenny cared?

I only asked him about it once. "So, what does everyone think about your status? Your family must be pissed."

His response convinced me to not worry about this one. "I don't give a motherfucking shit what people think. If they don't like it, they can fuck right off. I will burn their fucking house to the ground at midnight." He was starting to froth at the mouth.

Then he calmed down and spoke sincerely. "You know what I will do to people who fuck me over, Tommy? I will drive the highway until I find a dead raccoon or dog, then stop and wipe some saliva from its tongue and shit and blood from its rotting carcass. Then, when these fuckers are over for coffee sometime, I will wipe the inside of their coffee cups with the saliva and shit." Lenny was making faces and being gesticulating as if he were doing the process just now. He continued, "Then, later, after the fucker drinks that coffee, he will be frothing white foam from the mouth and howling at the moon. That spit from roadkill has some sort of germ in it to make a person crazy. It will drive the fucker insane, don't ya know." Lenny talked like he was giving a lecture and was getting louder.

I nodded my head up and down. "It sounds like the only right thing to do." I was proud for him. It sounded OK with me.

Hunter had a prosperous experience with the fields used to generate seeds. He would have enough to supply many small villages. These operations would be around football field size, most under canopies and camouflage. It was a wonderful thing to see Hunter so happy and smiling. I felt warm inside.

As each field was finished, we ensured it was clean, pulling the old plants and spreading the roots all about. This made for a more uniform soil mixture next year. The area was racked and lightly fertilized. Before the weather turned bad, all the fields were harvested, cleaned, and prepped for next year. We could tell the weather was going to turn bad soon, as the nights were dark and cold and frost was in the air. Some of the last plants we brought in were purple and gold and red in color. We had hundreds of pounds of weed like this.

I would be busy shaking and sifting bud for the next few weeks with the newly designed sifting machine. This sifter had four bins with 100-micron holes, the first three for trichomes. The last bin had no screen, its only function being to catch all the busted-up plant material. This material could be sold for cooking or THC production or could be used in multiple joint-rolling devices. The colder air was better for the sifting. The little particles did not float in the air, as the sifter is hermetically sealed. These trichomes, this kief, would be packed into cellophane bags and pressed into half-pound bricks. So far, I had over two hundred pounds pressed and ready for transit to various dealers. That was a lot of goddamn pressing. The sifting machine did what it was designed to do, extracting trichomes quickly and completely. It was amazing to see the different qualities being separated at the same time into each bin—the purest first, then top-grade commercial hashish, and finally a third-grade commercial variety. The machine is pure genius. It would be worth millions when sold commercially via Tom Sift Inc. I would eventually sift almost two tons of kief of various grades.

Lenny and Hunter were paid out first. Frisk and I agreed to make our cash over the winter. Our return on investment was larger but took longer to collect. Lenny counted his money and made plans for Vegas. Me, I just wanted to rest and stay low this year. It had already been exciting enough. Maybe travel in a year or two.

# The Kid

IT WAS COLD TONIGHT. FINISHING THE HARVEST AND PRESSING a ton of hashish got me excited. I stared at the bubbles in my beer when the side door to Carmichaels blew open and this rather large guy, with a goatee and very short hair cut, a brush cut, came in. This was the guy who had slammed Lenny earlier this month. He was carrying a black cue case. I guess he figured he would show up and play anyone who wanted to try their luck. He was alone, and I got the impression he was on the return trip home.

The Kid took off his coat then sat on the stool next to mine. He looked stoned, with dark rings under his eyes. We introduced ourselves, and I half rose when we shook hands. His left hand had a blue tinge to it from pool chalk. "The Blue Hand," I said out loud.

Smiling, he said to me, "Never heard that one before. I like it: the Blue Hand. Thank you, but please just call me the Kid." We sat back down.

"Then you are here for the chuck wagons too." We both laughed.

He grabbed some balls and went to table two. It seemed to be the table of choice for these hustlers. It was near the front so people could see them play and want to try a game. It was like a form of advertising. He poured them out and started shooting balls around. He missed a few. He made some. Then the Kid looked at me and asked, "Do you want to play a few games, Tommy?"

"Sure. Ten bucks a game," I said, and I grabbed Falcon.

"Let's make it twenty," he replied while racking. We lagged for break.

The Kid won and got up to break. He had come all chatty and shit, but now he was quiet and focused. All his moves were second nature.

He put chalk on by looking at the tip closely and brushing the chalk cube around the tip. He did it like a woman putting on lipstick. He stroked the top half of the shaft by moving his bridge hand and fingers quickly up and down along its length. I had never seen anyone do it as vigorously or as often as he did. Sometimes, his hand would come off the end to help round the tip. When he broke, his whole body went into it. He leaned way out onto the table as the balls scattered and the cue was pulled off to the side. It was quite a thing to see.

I was thinking how I felt a deep level of respect for the Kid. I liked him and wanted to learn from him. We had just met, but in some way, I felt like a student who was ready and the teacher appeared. Was this the end of my search? Had I finally found someone to truly help me?

I would not beat this guy. Every dollar lost to him, I rationalized, was tuition for lessons. I watched and learned. At this point, the Kid thought he was hustling me, but I was donating my cash just to watch him play.

He ran racks slowly, with rhythm and grace. He was studying which side of each object ball he needed to be on for each subsequent shot. He would hit the cue hall firm, the stroke short and direct. His dark eyes were level, watching the cue ball. Easy shot or hard shot, they all went in. It seemed most shots were hit with the same speed and the cue ball rolled thru the middle of the table a lot.

His strong New York accent made him all the more likable. He was very polite. We played and talked. I asked him questions, and he answered them in detail. When I was down enough, I pulled out to let him try the next victim. We shook hands, and I said, "Don't worry, Kid. The Blue Hand will be back," lifting up my now blue shade of palm and fingers. We laughed together.

The Kid played many matches that night. I watched from my position by table four. Even if freezing outside, we still snuck out the back door for a joint. It wasn't too long before we were dragging the Kid along too. He could handle his weed and hash. I let the Kid know about my self-training program. I wanted him to know. I wanted to learn more about playing and winning. "I want to learn everything I can from you, Kid," I said during a long toke. I added, "By the way, I grew this weed and made this hashish." I pulled out a two-ounce chunk. The Kid was most impressed.

He held the chunk, sniffing it and bouncing it in his hand. He smiled—no, grinned, then smirked. He asked in his New York twang, "Want to play some eight-ball for that?" He smiled at me, thinking I would say no.

"Sure do. We can chat later," I replied. The night was clear, and stars shone through, bright in the cold sky. The Kid went back inside to play. I stayed out for a few more minutes to finish the joint and contemplate what I was doing. It felt like a moment to seize. I felt a burning in my stomach that told me to do something, to ask for help.

I went back inside and watched the Kid play pool for half the night. After midnight is when most hustlers start work. The Kid was a god. His skill was talking to the opponent while continually increasing the bet. I am sure I got better just watching him.

I watched as Frisk gave it a try. He was crushed under the spell of the Kid. I had a desire to see how he would do without giving too much warning. At five hundred for a race to nine, Frisk thought he had a chance. Not a hope in hell was the real answer. The Kid played around at first. When it looked like Frisk was getting serious, the Kid laid a six-pack on him, then three more. Frisk had that happen to him three times. I couldn't believe it, but Frisk lost twenty-seven fucking games straight. Oh, he got some shots, but no real advantage went his way.

After Frisk's last game, we took the Kid out the back door and smoked a few beauty hash joints. The Kid played on with even deeper focus. He had energy, lots of energy. Playing and winning was full-on reality for this guy. You could see it in his eyes. They sparkled and grew wide with each new game. He played until there was no more money or people to play. He was up six or seven thousand, easy. Everyone loved the Kid. They all seemed OK with losing, even Frisk, but I was not sure about Lenny. He was not happy. He did not like the Kid.

I was the only one with ulterior motives. I wanted to learn from the Kid. When he played, everything he did was designed to give him an edge. I could see this and planned to emulate those moves. Others just missed it or didn't care that much, but I did. It was almost four in the morning. The place was quiet. The Kid and I ate two chuck wagons each, drank Cokes, and talked.

I go to the point. "Look, Kid, I know you are out of here tomorrow, and we will probably never see each other again, so, what do ya say I give you a bunch of cash and a few bricks of hashish and we go back to table nine and you train me for the next seven hours? I learn fast, and what I don't get, I can work on later."

"Ya, let's do it," he said. The Kid was awesome, pumping his arm in the air as he had so many times earlier this night. He ordered another chuck wagon with mustard and ketchup, and we headed to the back. He told stories about experiences with different shots and how he learned them. Usually, it was after losing to someone gracious enough to show him the winning shots.

We went over stance, grip, aim, and stroke. He told me, "Stop the cue tip at the cue ball to ensure proper contact position. This will ensure accuracy." His hands helped form my elbow and wrist into a straight line with my cue, back foot, and dominant eye. He encouraged me. "You must shoot a few thousand single-ball shots while working on your new stroke. This is the key to getting your stroke, to becoming a strong player."

It was true. Johnny had me doing this so many years before. He made me shoot one ball after another to get the stroke ingrained in my conscious. I worked on all the natural bank shots, one ball at a time, for days. I was a fool to not realize I needed to do this more often.

He had a good way to picture the cue ball. "I suggest imagining the cue ball like the face of a clock. We will practice hitting each different hour and half hour. This teaches English, speed control, and cue-ball placement. This method will change your world. Always try to bring the cue ball thru the center of the table. If you do this it is impossible to sink the cue ball in a side or corner pocket" He explained the half ball hit where the cue ball strikes half the object ball. He put the object ball near the end pocket and took the cue ball to the center of the table. He had me stroke the cue straight until the tip struck the face of the cue ball at one o'clock. Next, I watched where the cue ball rebounds after hitting the object ball.

"Strict practice going around the clock hundreds of times and making sure the object ball goes into the pocket and the cue ball goes thru center table, will guarantee success. You will become unstoppable. This will move you into the big times," is what he said, over and over.

I reiterated what he told me so far. "So, the trick is to take the time and shoot hundreds of the same style shots before moving on. This practice will give me a confidence to shot after shot in a row. This is how the old masters did it, many repetitions of the same shot, until it was second nature. Ya know, they do it like this in many sports, golf, karate, and billiards too—nice."

The Kid continued, "Go to one o'clock on the cue ball and shoot another hundred shots." He stressed control. "Be mindful of where the cue ball ends up. The point of this exercise is to learn cue ball control. Set them up again and shoot at two o'clock on the cue ball face. Every position sends the cue ball to a slightly different location on the table. It is critical to know the different cue ball positions. In run-out pool, it is essential to avoid scratching the cue ball in a pocket. Master these patterns so you know exactly where the cue ball will end up every time. Picture these shots in your mind. Move past the words you tell yourself. Visualize." Pool was all about visualizing the balls in action. Eventually, a mastery of cue-ball control will begin to happen.

"Your aiming will become automatic when you can visualize these shots. You must see the shots in your mind. You must work through the boredom, the pain, and if you actually do this, you will become a champion. You must work these exercises eight hours a day for at least a month. Do not play anyone. No playing at all. No tournaments, gambling, or friendly games while you're going through this. The danger is you will go back to shooting with your old bad habits. It is like an intestinal cleanse. You must free the bad and then build on the good. If you want to develop a smooth, straight, reliable stroke, well, this is it."

"Jesus. Holy God," I said.

"Trust me totally." He gave a short, low laugh under his breath, daring me, taunting me. "Do this, and you will get good, real good. It will work." He went through each clock number, showing me where the cue ball would land. He did each shot many times, and so did I.

I watched carefully how he did everything—how he leveled his eyes and head, how he would raise and lower his head up and down like a periscope. The Kid did this bobbing action until he was lined up. Each time, he stared out the pocket and object ball. He knew where it would hit, where to aim, and where the cue ball would end up within inches.

He showed me which side of the pocket to aim at when applying English and demonstrated the errors people make. He would take a few long practice stokes when lining up. His final stroke, short and directly through the point on the cue ball he was aiming at. "This is a near foolproof way to be consistent. Just take a shorter backstroke. Slow and very controlled," was his advice.

The Kid commented again, "Sometimes, the best stroke is a very short backstroke with a longer follow-through. We call this stroke the barroom stroke. It is the one to use in sports bars and on smaller tables for sure, and it is so effective on big tables too." Balls go in with that special sound they make when the whole thing is done just right.

When he made a good shot, he would act enthusiastic, as if finding a hundred dollars. This was a shark technique too. Your opponent would be thrown off, his adrenaline would flow more, and he'd be apt to miss. Sometimes, the Kid would do the arm-pump thing and go, "Yeah, yeah." He told me about the left and right sides of the brain. He described how asking your opponent a simple question and having him speak will destroy his concentration because it stops visualization. He went on, "One side of your brain is for visualizing, and the other is used to learn the steps. Today, we practice the steps, and soon you will be visualizing the shots." We smoked a few joints before continuing the training.

There were some great eight-ball and nine-ball racking secrets he shared. "I should take this information to the grave, but no, I want people to know this stuff. I will show you bank and kick-shot systems that just work," and he did.

Many times, he pumped his bridge hand quickly from the tip of the shaft to just about the joint before shooting. This is something many players do, but not the way the Kid does it. He would rub the shaft quickly up and down through his bridge fingers, sometimes pulling the shaft out of his bridge. He did this to help smooth out the edge of the tip itself. "It makes the shaft and tip smooth and warm," he said. "It also loosens up the arm, getting the blood going to the important parts of the body, including the bridge fingers. This focuses my thoughts and is part of my routine. It is absolutely imperative you develop a routine and stick to it every time. But this motion does annoy people sometimes and is a good sharking move."

I commented, "I was thinking about golfers. They do the same routine every time too."

The Kid explained sharking versus hustling. "A shark is a player who seldom misses and will do anything to throw you off, for even one shot. The shark is obvious and different from the hustler. Hustling is an excellent player. More likely than not, he is a professional level player who tricks people by not playing his best. They are tricked into making huge bets and then, wham, the hustler turns it on; he gets the cash, and you are left standing with your dick in your hand." This is a very important lesson.

I had a question: "So, how do I beat the hustler, the shark?" I thought this was a good question.

The Kid had an answer. "I agree, Tommy, that is a very good question. You don't see sharking or hustling on TV, but in my world—in our world—it is part of the game. I am always on the lookout for the hustler. The sharks were OK, and I always beat them. To beat a hustler—that is, the guy who is a shark but can hide his skills—I must first recognize the hustler and then step it up, show some speed, and stay ahead of him the whole time. You have to out hustle a hustler." The Kid was watching me, helping to ensure that my stance and bridge were repeatable.

We worked on very specialized position shots. One used draw to pull the cue ball off an object ball, bouncing it off two long rails and back to the far end. He called it a zinger shot. It taught proper aim, and stroke. I learned all over again to use draw, from short to long distances. And, ways to use English, to twist the cue ball off various rails, and back. He called it "doubling and tripling the rail." But mostly, he taught stroking the cue ball in the center with follow, stop, or draw.

"Very interesting," I told him, watching and taking notes. I was actually getting the hang of it. The Kid made me shoot these shots over and over. We worked jump shots and practiced stopping the cue on the backstroke, just a momentary thing, then snap forward. This worked well. Speed control started to come as a result of my smooth stroke.

The Kid was just talking to me. "There are still the challenges between playing for fun and playing for a thousand bucks. Knowing you can make the shot and following a focused routine means your odds go way up on each shot. Plan shots and games from start to finish, and most importantly, finish to start. You must always be aware of how you will finish up the last few balls. You must see this pattern in your mind every time."

"I am having fun," I said, and we were having fun. I could tell the Kid absolutely loved this.

We played nine-ball with ball-in-hand after break. The Kid told me lessons he learned while on the road and playing for cash. "The weak will try to take down the strong, but it will not happen to you. If all rules are the same for each player, the stronger one will dominate. Winning money at pool is gambling. To be good at gambling, understand that you must enjoy gambling for the sake of gambling. Not everyone has this gene. Gambling has its own rewards, whether win, lose, or draw. You need to get a buzz from coin-flipping for a buck, guessing if the next license plate to drive by will end in an even or odd number, or will the next gumball from the penny machine be red or green."

I talked with him about my feelings. "I am starting to see that you have to go past the money, no matter how much it was or whose money it was. Sometimes I will win; sometimes I will lose. I need to develop a second sense for it, just like shooting these pool shots over and over. I must gamble repeatedly. I must never be afraid but, in fact, embrace it, welcome it. If I actually get to this point, then I will start to win. I will become a winner. Winning will take on a new meaning, a new freedom." I was tripping out somewhat, but this was the point the Kid was making.

"Don't be afraid. When you miss, put it behind you quickly. Clear your mind, stop the emotional connection. On your next shot, get back to doing the job of winning, the job of running the table," the Kid said with deep passion. We played on, and I was grateful for the secrets from the master.

I was getting it. "Yeah, I get it. Just keep on going as if nothing had happened. It's all about the run-out. I get it." The Kid smiled.

It was two in the afternoon when people showed up again. The Kid was most gracious, giving his time to me. We walked out to his car, where I paid him cash and a few bricks of my best hashish. He tucked the hash into a small pocket in a golf bag he had won somewhere on the road. The cash went directly into his pocket. It was so worth it. We shook hands.

The Kid noticed my right hand was covered in chalk. My bridge hand was blue from chalking my cue tip for the last ten hours. He smirked, calling me the "Blue Hand." That will be your pool handle. I am called the Kid, and you shall be the Blue Hand." The Kid gave me one last lesson to ponder. "When you are cornered, when *they* are getting close, when it's all on the line, remember your training. Let the Blue Hand assassinate the enemy, severely and publicly. If you need me, just ask, and I will be with you, Tommy. Keep the faith, boys."

He smiled and drove away. I appreciated his calm. He has a way of not worrying. I like that, as I too had found a way to relax thanks to Hunter. The ability to not worry about things gave me new freedom. I had moved to a new level in my pool game. I became less distracted during those critical moments between aiming and shooting. *Interesting*, I thought, embracing my new confidence.

It was four in the afternoon. I practiced what I learned that night, over and over. I felt comfortable being the Blue Hand. Having the Kid bestow the name upon me gave it credibility. When I told Johnny about my time with the Kid and the Blue Hand, he smiled and agreed. It became permanent.

Frisk was at the front playing the pinball machine and running up a good score. I stopped beside him while I rested for a moment. He knew I was practicing and heard my story about the Blue Hand, but I changed the subject. I told Frisk about a phone call from Shanelle. "I am meeting an old girlfriend, Shanelle, on Tuesday in the city. She has been bugging me to get together and left a message suggesting she wants to buy some weed. Said she had forty thousand to spend." Frisk smirked, advising like a doctor. "Make sure she is well fucked by the time you leave. Enough of the small talk. I gotta fuck off," he said, leaving quickly after the pinball machine went TILT.

I finally went home. As I lay in bed, looking at the ceiling, I began banking balls across the walls and ceiling. All I could see were pool balls. All I could hear were the clang and click of racks breaking and balls smashing together. I did long shots, with and without English. Sleep came easy, a sleep that was deep, restful, and rewarding.

# Shanelle

SHANELLE HAD LEFT SEVERAL MESSAGES, WANTING TO GET together. I mostly ignored them because harvesting fields of weed takes a few weeks. She persisted. She was offering to meet at a hotel in the city. We were old pros at this one. A bunch of wine, party, and fuck and drink. Sometime during these drunken fuck binges, she would remember to call her boyfriend, explaining how she was tied up somewhere and would probably not be home for a while. Poor shmoe bought into it every time. Not much he could do, anyway. Shanelle was the other side of bad.

Shanelle was a tall, drop-dead gorgeous California gal with a super twat. Her exotic blue eyes would reflect her ever-changing moods. Her hair was always beach blonde and bouncy. Some days, Shanelle was a real golden-hair surprise. Her light blonde pussy, with just a thin covering of short, curly hairs laying upon bleached white skin, looked very sexy. The short landing strip stopped before her clit. The rest of her pussy was always clean shaven to flaunt those beautiful lips. I loved to lick up and down gently, suck softly, and fuck for hours on this one. But I was literally so busy lately with this pot harvest and hash-making business, I forgot about her. Shame on me. Well, Shanelle didn't forget about me.

She called in the middle of the week, sounding inviting, semidrunk, and wanting to get together somewhere. "I am going to bring a friend with forty thousand dollars, for hash and weed," Shanelle said. "A friend in the community wants to score, so I told him about you."

"What a gal you are. The timing is great. I have excellent weed and lots of hashish. Two grades of hash: one is rare, top-of-the-class black. The other, a good commercial brown," I said. She was passing on the information.

*Wow*, I thought. *This is neat-o.*

"When do you want to meet?" I asked.

"How about tonight?" she suggested with her soft, inviting voice.

It was one in the afternoon. I thought, how interesting. I could book a place, pick up the dope, head to the city, and see her for dinner. "It's a deal, Shanelle. I'll call you shortly with the place we can get together at. You bring the wine; I'll bring the rest," I told her.

I knew she would have the cash, no problem. We swap money, dope, and then some body fluids for a few hours. She gets drunk, and I get to cum a lot. Then, adios.

So the next thing I know, I am checked into a not-bad hotel with a good view, sitting in a chair by myself, cutting up a line, when a knock comes to the door. Shanelle is there, looking hot as usual. She is wearing a nice white skirt and blue blouse. The top few buttons were undone. A gold chain hung freely around her neck, and many freckles stretched across her chest, like God's little kisses. She had small diamond-stud earrings on. Her bushy blonde hair was everywhere. Her eyes, narrow and inviting, had black eye shadow, perfectly applied. *Those bedroom eyes*, I thought. She also seemed to have a freshly fucked look about her. She was pulling her small red travel bag by the extended handle. Behind her was this thirty-year-old black guy. A rather large guy.

"This is Raff. He is new around here and a good friend," Shanelle said.

Looking Shanelle up and down, I greeted them. "Nice to see you both."

"What the fuck? Are you going to let us in," she asked.

"Right this way," I said, showing them into the main living area. There was a table, a large couch, and a TV.

We shook hands. Raff was strong and black but seemed cool. He had a strange-sounding banter, somewhat hard to place, maybe South

American. And his stature was upright and methodical, almost like Frisk. We sat and talked for a moment. I asked him about the accent and where he was from. He laughed, happy to share. "Grew up in the jungle, mon. Way down south, way down. It was beautiful. Grew weed for a living with my brothers and sisters. I have traveled and made many friends. I like this big city. Maybe someday I will come visit you in your small town." He was trying to build trust. I wondered if he was fishing for something or just knew more than he was letting on.

"I always wanted to travel below the equator. Maybe someday we can visit some of those fields together. A friend of mine, Hunter, would love to grow vast fields of pot and bring back millions of seeds" was my initial gut reaction to what he said. I also thought, *I know someone else who matches your background too*, but I said nothing about that. "Enough of the small talk. Let's get to work," I said enthusiastically.

I pulled out the weed while Shanelle put four bottles of red wine in the fridge. Raff was opening one of the pounds and checking out the buds. All nice and tight, compact. The colors were green, and red, and purple. I was thinking the brown paper bag method to facilitate drying worked well for final curing.

He was twisting a joint while Shanelle poured us a glass of wine each. It was sweet and tasted oh so good, like fudge to a diabetic. Shanelle sat down, and Raff lit the joint. White smoke rolled from the end and into the air. No unnecessary additives. *Well flushed*, as we say in the trade. Shanelle did not partake, being the alcoholic she was, saying it hurt her lungs to smoke dope. She sat on the edge of her chair beside the couch, as chatty as usual. She was asking questions about how things were going, how were my girlfriends doing, and she gave me shit for not seeing her sooner.

Raff checked out each pound, making sure it was genuine bud and hashish. He then had Shanelle flip open her red travel suitcase. She threw it on the bed, letting out a short breath as the bag bounced on the mattress. She unzipped the top. Raff reached over the case, pulling out a set of old-school triple beam scales, the type stolen directly from grade-ten science class.

I noticed the muscles in Raff's arms. They were long and bulging and strong. This guy probably did time somewhere, or he just worked out a lot.

Shanelle sat back down on the chair. This time, she sat back a little further and her skirt pulled up a few inches. Her legs began to spread naturally, and I could see her white panties, pulled tight against her twat. Shanelle knew she was here for a fucking. She was horny. It was in her eyes and mouth and hips and the way she drank. Not that romantic flirting-type sips, more like guzzle a glass, then refill from the bottle in front of her and then drink more. She smiled at me.

Raff weighed out enough pounds of weed to satisfy that part of his budget. For knowing Shanelle, I gave him an extra two pounds of the good stuff. He was grateful. As I brought out the hashish, Raff asked me if Shanelle had told me how they met.

I looked at Shanelle, thinking only that she told me she needed money, and getting her friend some good weed at a good price would help her. *Fucking Jesus*, I thought. *Here we go again, always something with this woman*. But I could not stall her any longer. My interest was piqued.

So Raff looks at Shanelle and said in a telling, asking tone, "Yeah, like to gamble don't ya?" Then, looking at me, "She managed to lose ten thousand of her own money first. Then we got hooked up at the blackjack tables. I had some friends with cash, so I got her another twenty thousand. And guess what—she lost it too, didn't ya, my little gal?"

Shanelle just looked at me, all rather matter-of-fact about the whole thing. "I fucked up," she stated. "I went too far with the wrong people."

*Mother of God*, I thought to myself. I knew this hot California beach babe was a flirt, liked to fuck, but gave poor blowjobs. She was a party girl, so I didn't know what to think when Raff reached over, putting his rather large hand on Shanelle's knee. He looked at her again. "That's when we started to become real good friends. As you know, she is as cute as a button and will do whatever she is told. You tell him the rest, Shanelle."

She hammered back about half the glass of wine, then refilled it. "At first, Raff and I were just friends. He said he could lend me some money until I got going again. He told me he could get up to forty thousand from his East Indian friend. You know how I hate those smelly bastards. But when we met this guy, he was tall and dark and cute, more Persian in race. When I was being handed the money, the terms were clear. Begin payments in thirty days. And payment meant ten thousand at first, then five thousand a month, for the next eight months. That was ten thousand in profit and seemed reasonable. If I didn't pay them back on time, my first job would be to service the entire Shriner's pack of motherfuckers. He laughed and said they would be in town for their parade in about five weeks. You know, the ones that drive around on those small motorcycles."

Shanelle continued, "He says to me, 'How would you like to fuck three hundred drunken bastards with big hard cocks and half their girlfriends?' He circled close, rubbing up against me, whispering in my ear, 'Event lasts a few weeks. It will take about that long, maybe a bit more to cover this loan. They'll fuck and suck that sweet cunt of yours into hamburger.' Told me I could bring in thousands of dollars. It would be the start of a great love affair, and he squeezed my pussy, right through my jeans, while stroking two fingers between my legs. He smiled when I pushed back against his hand, showing off the natural slut in me."

I looked at Shanelle and told her, "I bet your twat twinged when you heard those terms?"

Raff said, slowly and drawn out, "Yeah, it twinged a lot," and laughed. "She blew the cash, and missed the payments, didn't ya, sweetie?" He pulled on her knee and her legs spread even more, and oh so naturally. Shanelle turned to look at me, and I saw those killer bedroom eyes, reflecting a changing mood. She had that come-over-here-and-fuck-me look.

Raff continued to check out the hashish, weighing each piece and marking its weight and quality. I had, by his estimation, twenty pounds of top-quality and five pounds of commercial grade, which was just perfect. We smoked a big joint of the black hash. Even though Shanelle didn't smoke, she got stoned, I am sure of that.

Raff noticed I was cutting up a few lines when they arrived. He said, "Let's do a line."

"You bet," I said, reaching over to grab the plate I had the lines busted out on. Raff reached into his pocket, pulling out a bag of coke to mix with mine.

"But let's finish business first," I said, implying I wanted my cash.

"Yeah, fuck ya, mon," Raff replied. Shanelle stood up and removed a large envelope from the suitcase. It was underneath a flimsy nightie.

How fucking long was that going to stay on her, I wondered, and I laughed to myself.

Then for the extra, he threw in another grand. "Here. For the extras, I return the favor," he said.

He counted out forty grand, then resumed chopping up the lines. She began again, "So, I blew the cash, blew off the payment schedule, and have since blown half the Shriners in America. I am a good little worker. They dropped me off at one of their friend's special places, with a spare room. It was a nice room. It had a nice big bed and a hot tub and mirrors and wall-to-wall video coverage. Then they started sending the troops over. I fucked and sucked, swallowing gallons of cum rather happily. I drained a lot of balls." Raff laughed while Shanelle swallowed hard.

"Wow, that is a wild story," I said. "You make my cock hard when I think of you with a lineup of guys, about to blow hot, sticky cum down your tight throat or up your spread-open pussy lips." Looking at Shanelle, I asked her, "So, what it is like to suck cock all day?" I wondered for a very brief instant about Holly and how her day might be going.

Shanelle said, "I still got the taste of their cocks and cum in my mouth. The guys were mostly all good to me and just wanted to get their cocks off, one way or the other. I did suck a lot of pussy too. Raff said I made him money." I shared a half glass toast of red wine with Shanelle. She did the refilling.

Raff smiled, becoming more serious, more pimp-like. "Since then, she has been fucking me and all my friends and whoever else I find that wants to pay."

Raff handed me a rolled-up hundred, and I did the first line. Coke seemed to start slow with me. Then my heartbeat jumps up, and within ten minutes, I am getting a buzz. I usually get real horny at this point. I handed the bill to Raff, and he hit back twice what I did. I did not expect Shanelle to do any, as she always complained about her small nose and how it didn't work well snorting anything. She was going to the fridge to open more wine. I was thirsty, and Raff was now drinking a little more heavily.

Laughing quietly as if going over something in his mind, he said, "She is on the long term fuck plan." He handed Shanelle the rolled-up hundred and told her, "It's your turn to do a line, sweetie." Without hesitation, she seemed to fall into the routine. Like a dog following orders from the master, she bent forward at the waist. Shanelle slowed as our heads and faces passed, her eyes reflecting submission without any misunderstanding, before burying her face in the plate.

I could see her beautiful perky tits hanging inside her blouse. Then I noticed one of the tits being smothered by her blouse. It was Raff reaching over, groping Shanelle with one of those big black hands of his. She finished the line and straightened up. Raff told her to take off her blouse and skirt. She stood, slowly dancing, and obediently began stripping. There was no shyness in her response. Looking both of us in the eyes, she danced and stripped. She was beautiful as ever, maybe more so.

She got on her knees when Raff stood up and pulled off his shirt. Shanelle undid his jeans, and while stuffing his cock in her mouth, he encouraged me to join in. Seconds later, we were sharing a joint while Shanelle sucked both our cocks. Her tight mouth felt just fucking great. While she sucked and slurped, our cocks got long and hard.

I was some buzzing now, with wine, pot, hash, coke, and this cute slut babe sucking to beat the band. I looked down and could see saliva streaming out of all parts of her mouth and down onto her pointy tits. Her perfect tits were white with perky pink nipples. She had the tits of an eighteen-year-old, the kind of tits people pay good money to suck and cum on. Her legs were spread, and the little landing strip of pubic hair trim looked just perfect. I watched as she moved between cocks.

"Very good," I said. "No hesitation this time, Shanelle. No forcing my cock between your lips before slowly fucking your mouth for an hour or so as you lay half passed out on a mattress somewhere. I am sure, many times your only recollection the next day was the strong taste of cum in your mouth and a sore neck."

She spoke briefly. "Yes, that was something we did numerous times in the past." Then it was back to work on our cocks.

Sharing the hash joint, Raff expressed obvious satisfaction with my work in much the same way I was in satisfaction of his work with Shanelle. We moved to the couch, and Shanelle waddled over on her knees. She used one finger to wipe her chin and then sucked that finger all the way into her mouth.

*Fucking God*, I thought, *what did they do to this woman?* The thought just made my cock harder and more swollen. She slurped and licked. She sucked Raff's big black balls one at a time in her mouth. She always kept one hand on each of our cocks. Her knees were apart. I could see her pink pussy lips spread open and wet. Her smooth, tight freckled skin rubbed on my legs. Her tits rubbed and flattened on Raff's legs. Occasionally, Shanelle would rub her twat quickly and hard as if it were itchy. I am sure it was itchy.

I couldn't take it anymore. As Shanelle wrapped her mouth around my stiff cock once more, I felt her throat open, and my cock pushed in, toward her stomach. My cock was fucking her throat. I am sure Shanelle knew she was in for a mouthful of hot cum. She seemed, in a subtle way, to brace herself, and my cock unleashed. I started to pour cum in her throat. The first few shots went straight into her stomach. She hardly flinched at all, her gag reflex nonexistent. My cock slipped out of her throat and into her mouth. She squeezed tighter with her lips.

Raff saw I was cumming. He made pigtails from her long blonde hair and helped fuck her mouth faster and faster on my cock. His cock got stiffer too and seemed to bounce straight up. Shanelle's mouth was now full of cum. She swallowed some. The rest blew out the sides of her lips onto my balls and down her chin onto her stomach. Her sleek narrow eyes were closing and opening. Raff held her head down for another few minutes on my cock. This time she choked and squirmed a bit. As he let her head up, her mouth slipped off my hard cock. Then with her face covered in slimy, sticky, salty cum, Shanelle moved over a bit to square up in front of us again.

Raff stretched out and Shanelle went back to work on his cock. "So, it was going to be one of those nights," I said to Shanelle. As my cock started to get hard again, we slipped into a sixty-nine with me on top. Shanelle's mouth slipped off his cock and onto mine.

Shanelle grabbed me by the back of the head, forcing my tongue and face deep into her crotch. I licked mouthfuls of her cum down my throat. Her hands were in my hair, and my head was being moved up and down forcefully. I was being guided. I sucked and licked and used my tongue. When I was pulled away, my face looked like a honey-dipped doughnut, all glistening and shiny.

Sperm leaked from my cock and was covering more and more of the inside of Shanelle's mouth with each long, sucking stroke. Shanelle was swallowing sperm and semen.

I felt my cock slip out of her mouth. Shanelle stood up and spread her legs over Raff's cock. She pushed and rubbed his cock against her beautiful pussy until it slid up to the hilt inside her. Her pussy was flat against his groin. Then Shanelle pulled off his cock. The head of his black cock rested for a moment at the opening of her pussy, her swollen pink lips spread naturally open.

His cock soon disappeared into her. She rode him like she has so many times in the past. She took it to the hilt, over and over, often stopping with his cock fully in her to grind her crotch hard onto his. Her clit and the nerves running up the inside of her pussy lips were rubbed vigorously, back and forth on his pelvis. Her twat came hard, contracting tightly around his black cock. Shanelle didn't squirt, but ejaculation drained from her twat onto his crotch.

When Shanelle finally came enough, she slid off his cock, cum draining from her pussy, and began sucking his cock again. Her throat was immediately hit with a very hot, salty gob of cum. It reminded Shanelle of swallowing egg whites, and it kept on cumming. Raff's cock was very stiff and slippery as cum repeatedly shot into her mouth. It was salty and ran in long gobs down her throat. Shanelle's lips were stretched tight around his cock head as cum pushed out the sides of her mouth. She swallowed what she could by natural gag action.

Every part of her mouth was coated with Raff's cum. In an instant, hot, salty cum was forced down her throat and up her sinus and out her nose. Shanelle could feel the long strings of cum running down her throat and into her stomach. The rest of his cum rolled off her lips and drained from her nose. Sloppy, hot cum slid off Shanelle's face, onto his cock and balls. Her head slid up Raff's shaft. Her lips were pulled further apart as the head of his cock slipped from her mouth. Shanelle gulped air. The head of Raff's cock rubbed against her face and nose and lips and eyes.

Raff pushed Shanelle's head back onto his cock and told her, "Suck hard and drain my balls into your mouth and stomach, the way men tell you to, over and over." Shanelle was not bitter, just really horny. She loved to be fucked. She reached with her other hand and squeezed Raff's big, black hanging balls tightly. One more load was forced into her mouth before taking a short break for some chain-smoking and wine guzzling.

The rest of the night went something along those lines. In particular, the part where Raff wanted to play egg timer. Raff found a three-minute egg timer in the kitchen. He instructed Shanelle, "To get on the small coffee table, on all fours." He then told me, "Set the timer for full. Then, while one of us fucks her in her sweet California slit, the other fucks her mouth. Every time the timer goes off, we switch positions. Every three minutes, we pull out of Shanelle, move to the other end of her, and start pumping our cocks into that part of her body. The game is to be the first to cum in her twat or mouth. Sound like fun?"

"I'll try anything a few times, and this sounds like fun, but what's next?" I was excited. Raff and I had fun for some time with that one. We laughed and smoked more joints.

At one point, we set Shanelle up on the edge of the bed on her back legs up in the air in the universal gesture of greeting and took turns fucking her, pounding her pussy hard. What we found out was that if we blew nose tokes at her, forcing her to cough hard, her pussy muscles tightened up real strong with each cough. I mean, a real tight contraction around the hard cock in her at the time. She would buck and squirm trying to breathe, and we would just grind cock into her and hold on for the ride.

She never really complained about what we did to her body. We laughed and blew load after load between her legs and made her hoarse from the smoking and coughing. She must have been very stoned. *What the fuck now?* I thought to myself. Raff sort of passed out, and Shanelle fucked me in a reverse cowgirl position, just lying on the bed, snuggling. My cock, buried deep inside Shanelle, my stomach rubbing her back. I squeezed her tits from behind, rolling her nipples ever so softly between my fingers. Holding her tightly above this aroused an erogenous zone, and Shanelle moaned softly. We made love together.

I kissed Shanelle's neck and ears. Her eyes rolled back in her head while she moaned softly. Her back arched against my stomach, and she grabbed to bedposts, forcing her pussy to take my cock as deep as it could go into her. I would hold her tight, my fingers spread across her stomach and belly button while grinding her in a slow tantric manner.

A simple tantric mantra of counting stokes into her warm body from one to five, over and over again, allowed me to stay up that beautiful blonde pussy for an hour or so. I finally filled her with what cum was left in my balls.

When I started cumming, I could feel her pussy muscles contract at the same time, pulling cum from me. "I think I love you," I said quietly in Shanelle's ear. She was so good, controlling the muscles in her groin at will. "What a woman, holy God, milking my cock with your pussy at will," I said, kissing her neck before passing out.

When Raff came too, he packed up his stuff and told Shanelle, "Get dressed. It's time to go." She staggered around, getting most of her stuff together and packing it into her red suitcase. Shanelle put on her blouse and skirt without panties and stood before me. A totally satisfied look was in her eyes. We shared a smile. At least I fulfilled Frisk's request, making sure she was well fucked.

My money was safe, all forty thousand or so. It was seven in the morning. *Fuck me*, I thought, *now what?* Raff and I did a line. He told Shanelle to do one too. She did so without hesitation. We wandered to the hotel door. Shanelle gave me a hug and a kiss with lips that were chapped and dry. Her mouth and breath tasted strongly of cum. Now I know what she meant about having the taste of cum in her mouth for a month. It was going to be a lot longer than that for her, was my thought.

After our lips separated, I wished them both a good day, then nonchalantly said, "Cheers. Have a great day. I gotta head back and see my buddy Frisk."

Shanelle continued walking toward the elevator, but Raff stopped, turned, and looked at me when he heard the name Frisk. It seemed to conjure up a secret memory. His eyes gave him away. They were distant. "I know that name. Who is this Frisk?" Raff inquired.

I dodged the question, saying, "Just an old buddy. No one you would know."

But Raff knew more. "I know of a man named Frisk. In the fields, they spoke of a man by that name, and the people knew to stay clear of him or die. He would guard his village fields with a deadly passion. He was in our fields with his chief, trading seeds and equipment when we met. He trained us for a short while. Not sure how he got so deadly, but he was, and I learned from him. Then his escape and the anger it caused. It was a brave soul to go up against the man called Frisk. I should like to meet your friend someday."

A moment of truth was being realized. Yes, this was the same man.

Shanelle was singing in a low voice, over and over, "Tell my baby I'll be back by November, back by November." I heard the elevator arrive, and they were gone.

"I look forward to it." This fell on deaf ears, so I went into my hotel room. My interest was piqued. Could Frisk know Raff? I would be sure to ask next time we meet.

I am sure at some point, Shanelle paid her debt in full. And Raff, I am sure, just said, "Yeah, thank you very much Shanelle sweetie, your dept is no more. You are free to return back to her life."

*Not!* Once you were in, you were in for life.

# Nailer

IT HAD BEEN A FEW WEEKS SINCE I'D SEEN FRISK LAST. A LOT HAD happened. Frisk wore his boots and black vest, with a white shirt, the cuffs rolled back. He was clean-shaven. Carmichaels was quiet just now. The balls were rolling good for both of us. It was a good time to talk.

"Been making money from this guy, Nailer. The crazy motherfucker I told you about. I really mean it: he's a real criminal." Frisk was being honest. "He has been moving some of the hash for me. He also has some real good grit—speed, that is," he said, smiling like he had just finished a Christmas dinner.

"On to more important things," I started with a laugh. "Frisk, I got a question for ya. Not sure what you are going to say, but here goes. I met up with Shanelle a few days back—you know, that gal from the city I know. Interesting adventure that was. She introduced me to a great new contact. This guy with her dropped forty thousand."

I took a breath, having a quick flashback. I got to the point, "The guy she brought, who was doing the deal, is a big black guy, Raff. Raff said, he grew up in South America tending pot fields. Sound familiar? When I briefly mentioned your name, he knew you. I didn't say anything more to him. So what's up? Do you know this guy? Who is he?"

"Interesting. Raff, ya I know him. I can't fucking believe you ran into him, I wonder how that happened. I knew him for a short while. Sometimes, I would travel about the mountain side with my Chief, helping our neighbors while trading for more seeds. Raff was one of those neighbors. He is strong, and smart, and a good guy." Frisk stopped for a moment, glancing downward, he was thinking about the past. "Raff wanted to travel, as I recall. He was going north, and probably went through Mexico before getting here. Maybe he knows our Colombian friends? Maybe he knows Catina?" I was indifferent, but did consider the possibility as very real.

I looked at Frisk showing approval with a smile, and nod, "It is the universe who is bringing us all together. So you know Raff, and you have trained him, interesting. Graham said you were training him too. We can use more help and you picked, very probably, the two best choices on earth to learn your skills. I know you want to keep this under wraps, so I won't mention it to anyone. How about I get Raff and you in touch. Maybe they can help us if you work with him and Graham together?" Frisk nodded acceptance as he finished up a game, winning easily. It was so much fun to watch someone run out the balls and win.

Now I was hopeful, "Well, if Raff can move as much dope as I think he can, and if he wants to consider joining our team, then I want him. Seamed to me he was running as an independent. At this level it's best a few of us stick together as a tight team. What do you think?" We knocked knuckles in silent agreement. The light was full in Frisk's face, he smiled a little smile. He read into my eyes, he knew my thoughts at that moment.

"You are thinking I will go to Colombia someday, to visit the fields again." Frisk was speaking my thoughts. "I got no plans at this time to leave here for that place," Frisk said, in such a way I got the feeling he didn't want to dwell on that thought. But he was right, I just had a brief feeling he would return to his first home someday soon.

It was time to change the subject, "So, tell me about this gangster, Nailer. The guy selling our hash?"

"Yeah, he has connections with heavy people, man," Frisk said softly. His game was on, and he rolled through the racks.

"I should meet him sometime, he sounds interesting," I suggested, feeling attracted to something about that situation.

"Right, good idea, I am heading over there shortly, but we won't tell him you're the guy on this one. Is that cool? Don't tell him too much, OK?" Frisk cautioned.

Interesting, I thought. "Not to worry." I said.

After finishing up a few games, Frisk gave Nailer a call. He came back to the table looking all serious and shit. He was looking gangster. He was getting in character. We paid and left.

The wind was getting cold. "Snow is in the air; going to be a tough winter," I said, but he didn't answer. We turned down the last street before the Main drag. We walked toward the back of an apartment building. A long, outside staircase got us up to Nailer's apartment. Frisk knocked on the door, and we went in.

Nailer was sitting in a chair, at the kitchen table. There was a glass of water in front of him, and a spoon beside it. He was bald, rather heavy set, and tall, but not quite as tall as Frisk. He spoke with a heavy gangster voice. "Right on, man. Dig it. Cool. Dig it, man." Everything had man, at the end. Not in a hippy way, but in a tough way. We shook hands, and I sat at the table. Frisk sat between me and Nailer.

Frisk introduced me as, a friend. We talked briefly. Nailer thought I was cool, and accepted me at that level. This place had a strong, clinical smell, like a dentist had worked out of here previously. I don't know why I noticed the smell, but I did. It was strong.

Nailer began talking to Frisk, "Loved the hash. It was easy to move, man. I have connections, and we can move that stuff," he said, speaking with a deep tone, like he had been punched in the throat. Frisk was handed five thousand dollars, covering off several pounds of hash.

Next, Nailer brought out an ounce of top quality speed, or meth. He had a syringe, and filled it with the hit of mixed up speed from the spoon in front of him. Frisk rolled up his sleeve, while pumping his arm to get the veins to stand out. Nailer grabbed Frisk's upper arm with his left hand and squeezed. With his right hand, he tapped on the skin, found a vein, and hit Frisk up. Frisk got the rush.

Nailer had this upper lip issue from a birth defect. His face looked like it had been hit with a crowbar and bones were crushed. Then some doctor with a spoon like tool and who really didn't give shit about this guy pried the bones under his eye back into place. They didn't heal all that well. He was an ugly guy. Nailer did look like a gangster, no he was a gangster. He cleaned the spoon, and syringe before mixing another hit. This time he looked over at me "You want a hit, man?"

Frisk had moved over to a large lazy boy chair. He was squatting on his toes, on the chair. Breathing deep, he kept saying, "Wow," over and over.

And for no good reason at all, I said, "What the fuck?" moving over to where Frisk had just sat. It was time to take the ride. I had a short-sleeve shirt on.

"Right on man. Cool," was the slur from Nailer. He showed me where to squeeze on my upper arm to make the veins pop out. I pumped my arm as he drew the speed out of the spoon and into the syringe through a cigarette filter. Nailer tapped the needle and looked at my veins. He picked the large, healthy one in the middle. He brought the needle point to the skin. The needle tip was small and sharp.

It was scary, like those final moments before takeoff in a commercial jet at night in the middle of an ice storm. You are on board, strapped into your seat, no way out. This was it. Go for it. I could feel engines revving up in my mind. Then I felt its sharpness. Nailer tapped the syringe. It pricked as it went in. It penetrated me. The mixture was a light yellowish color. Nailer flagged it by drawing blood into the syringe. This made sure the needle was in a vein. It was. The blood sank quickly once inside the syringe. I watched as he pushed the plunger, and it went slowly into my arm.

The rush was incredible. My heart rate skyrocketed as the speed went through my veins. My heart immediately sent this blood to my lungs for rejuvenation. As that happened, I got the second part of the rush. There was a strong taste of meth in my mouth. It was deep and came from way inside me. Its taste was inviting. The needle was pulled from me, and I bent my arm up.

"Oh fuck," I said, and I sat still. My eyes rolled back in my head, and my brain instantly went from zero to near light speed.

Nailer said in his low drawl, "Cool, man. You are fucking cool." I was stoned. The speed buzz is glorious; you are the king. I was singing in my mind. My body and brain were alive. The rush lasted forever. Then, somewhere, it began to slow down to something manageable. I can see the allure to riding that fucker out, holding on and surviving. For me, it didn't slow down to much below the absolute maximum.

"Wow," I said without thinking. Now I know what Frisk was going through. It was incredible to see it from this side of the fence. To do a hit and ride your brain into overdrive is not for everyone, but that day, it was for me. I lived. I survived take off and was now flying high.

Frisk and I soon came down enough to talk some more with Nailer. I was a babbling king. We talked about dope and money, and I acted as if I were someone I was not. I was on top of the world.

I could see Nailer was a thief and a crook and a dope peddler. God only knew how many people he had killed. He certainly appeared to be tough enough. He had guns with him. Frisk was already hooked, and now we both were.

This was the dragon I would chase for the next couple of months. I was addicted almost instantaneously to this drug and to the needle. It was powerful, and I was powerless. It was a new demon. I didn't care at all that I was on a one-way trip to self-destruction, not one bit. Ignorance was bliss.

When we left, I took a quarter ounce of meth and a couple of syringes. I was ripped to the tits. All night, I lay in bed, not hallucinating but speed-rushing. My heart was going a mile, a minute. There was no way I was going to sleep. It was strange, spending a night where watching pool balls bounce off the walls and ceiling for hours was the only thing to do.

Once I came down, later the next day, I thought I would try this myself. I got out all the paraphernalia and began the process of mixing a hit. It didn't take me long to have the syringe filled and the needle tip resting on my vein. It was just below where Nailer hit me up. My fingers were sweaty, and the fit slid between my fingers. Now the needle's tip was in me, and I did it. I hit myself up. It worked; I was stoned again. It was almost the same level of buzz. I sat there in happy bliss.

I soon started to dress like Frisk and talk like Nailer. I wore long-sleeved shirts and said, "Hey, ya got any good grit on ya, man?" with the cool banter of a tough guy. I became something I was not. I was not tough at all.

But I also found the green light in my mind to start my pool training. No playing against anyone for a while. I enjoyed shooting one ball at a time, down the rails, for a couple of hours. Just sitting at the back of Carmichaels, grinding my teeth night and day while working on my game and shot patterns. This was my new world.

They call it grit because speed makes you constantly grind your teeth, as if you have small pieces of sand, or grit, between them. It was true.

Within weeks, my consumption of grit was up to three hits a day. I was fucked. At the local pharmacy, I was buying boxes of needles and plastic syringes for diabetic use twice a week. The pharmacist must have thought I had a bad sugar problem. I had a problem all right, but sugar wasn't it. Some of the needle tips were designed bent, so I started to use this style. They had boxes of fits on shelves out in the open. It wasn't long before I was stealing them and trading them to Nailer for more speed. I would pay for two boxes and steal five under my long green winter jacket. Eventually, the pharmacy moved all the needles behind the counter.

When the needle tips became dull, I was shown how to sharpen them on the rough striking surface on a book of matches. Gently file the barb off the needle tip, and it was ready to go again. This seemed to make the tip sharp again. It was a cool part of the process to eliminate the barb before it tore your vein open and you bled to death. Sometimes a barb rip will become infected, and then you have a real problem on your hands.

A few people at Carmichaels figured out I was fucked up on something just by looking at me. I was skinny, pale, talking weird, and overall looking stupid while playing pool for hours by myself. But booze and drugs are good when you don't want to hear those things. I was not listening yet. One guy asked me, "Why do you need those drugs? They are not good for you."

I got pissed off and told him, "Go fuck yourself, man." That ended that conversation. I was developing a couple of nice track lines. That is a callused narrow single track lying on top of a vein, usually with one end fresh. Still open waiting for the next hit to be laid just below the last one, carrying on the track and leaving evidence of dangerous drug use.

Maybe I just wanted some danger in my life, a need to revolt. I was not sure why or against whom. I just had to do it. Why would I risk exposing a million-dollar hash trade for an ounce of speed? It made no sense. But I was hooked.

I was at Nailer's place one afternoon and about to do a hit. Every time we did a hit with Nailer, he had to do the injection. He looked at my arm in wonder and asked, "Have you been cutting yourself with a razor, man?" before laying the next spike in the line. My arm looked like a pin cushion from my own missed attempts at self-injection and the many successful ones. I had a few track lines by now. They were ugly, but they looked cool to me.

It was full-on winter now, and I was sweating. "Holy God, we are ahead a million and a half. Wow," I said out loud. That much money warmed me up. I still had some inventory, but I was very happy. This was a retirement in itself. I felt secure.

Lenny was in Vegas, gambling. Hunter was in Morocco, setting up a gargantuan field for seed harvest in August. Frisk and I had become the keepers of the keys, holding the fort and running Tom Sift Inc., at full steam. That meant looking after the cash as product went out. Product meant pounds and pounds of hashish and several franchises using the now famous TED-5700. It also involved Frisk training Graham not just to be a crazy fighter but to show a passion for the fields. That was the true goal, while martial arts were just a means to that end.

Well, I can tell you more than the passion fires were burning. My veins and brain were slow cooking. One starts to know they are addicted when they hate being stoned but hate being straight too. There becomes a clear distinction between worlds. They are different and both intolerable. In that moment, I became aware one world must go. Since death by needle is not an option, the answer became obvious: I must stop using needles and speed as soon as I can. Once there is any doubt, there is no doubt. The seed was planted. Now I had to wait for something to break. Recovery had begun.

I was spending quiet nights at Carmichaels playing pool by myself.

I would practice the clock system for hours. I played straight pool and could run forty balls in a row. That was not too bad. I worked nine-ball run-out patterns with ball in hand. I would practice the same shot over and over and over until it was automatic, until it was mastered.

Eventually, I played other hustlers and night owls when they showed up. I could win a thousand bucks in a night. Some nights, I wanted to lose. I needed to know that feeling. I hated the feeling of losing.

I learned to play a game called one pocket. Here, you pick one of the end pockets while your opponent gets the other end pocket beside it. The objective is to get eight balls in your pocket before the other guy sinks eight in his pocket. I liked this and won many games.

I was starting to gamble a lot more, betting on sports and hitting the casinos when I got a chance. I learned to love keno. I never lost money at keno when playing my two lucky numbers, three and fifty-seven. In my mind, it was all training. I was training myself not to sweat under pressure. My life had become part of this gamble. My thoughts took me places. When would it end? Where was the high watermark? When would it break and roll back? When would I understand? When would my character have enough discipline to avoid the wrong gambles? I needed to make a few more mistakes first.

I was in the phone booth across the street from Nailer's apartment, calling to see if it was OK to stop by. He had not bought any hashish for a few weeks, instead talking tough about this one big deal he wanted to do. He reminded me of JD.

Nailer was fucked up. He was acting hyper and crazy, probably some sort of psychosis from doing speed for too long. He told me, "I have an infrared scope with laser sighting on a high-powered rifle, trained straight at you. I could kill you right now if I wanted." Then he laughed and told me, "Come ahead up."

I thought, *You fucking moron.*

I told him, "Be right there." I felt as if I were working for Nailer.

His place always had this strange antiseptic smell. Maybe they just washed the bathroom with strong disinfectant, or maybe they were cooking the meth right there in the other room. Who the fuck knows? I did a small hit. I felt nervous. The rush was quick and over fast. The taste was there but stale.

Nailer looked at me with his ugly, unsmiling face and started to tell me about this plan he had to make a bunch of cash. "I've been scoping out the hardware store down the street, man. They have lots of guns and ammo just sitting in a huge showcase. I need you to wait inside the store until after they close. You are small and can hide somewhere easily. They don't have any alarms. Then a few hours after they lock up and all staff have left, you come out and let me in. I want to steal all the guns they have, including the ammo." This did not sound like a plan for me.

I said to Nailer in my own tough voice, "The gun racks are out in the open, as I recall. Everything was there. A few hockey bags, and we could clean the place out." I knew this was wrong. This was not going to happen. This was a bottom I was not going to reach, but what would happen next?

"We could make twenty grand, man. You could make some serious cash, man, and some good fucking grit." My head was ringing.

Frisk was there. I don't think he gave a shit about Nailer's fucked-up plan. He was way too smart for that shit. Frisk would never be there if that deal ever went down. He had his cowboy boots on and a tight thin sweater. He was getting skinnier and looked pale. I wondered for a brief moment, *Is he* OK. *Is he sick?*

"Fucking Christ," I said. "This is wrong for me, man. This is not my plan. You fuckers don't care about me." I had pushed this one to where I wanted it. Any further, and I would be in too great of danger. I knew in my heart of hearts it would soon end. I felt a calm come over me.

I went on, "For all I know, you are planning to get me busted and take the rap." This was the bottom I was looking for. This party was soon to be over. I told Nailer, "I will think about it and let you know later." I moved toward the door.

"Yeah, we gotta set this up soon, man," Nailer said.

Frisk was leaving too. We got ready to split, and I picked up an eight ball of grit, saying, "Get back to ya later, man," as we left.

I talked to Frisk as we walked down by the river. "Nailer does not know I am the owner, energy, and glue behind the hashish deals. Then again, I do not know who he is involved with either. There are things I didn't know—nor do I care to know—and I sort of feel the need to not know. This is over my head and out of my league. The only way to keep on going in this world is to leave guys like Nailer dead in their tracks behind you. There is no fucking way on earth I am going to hide in a hardware store to steal their guns. I found my line in the sand."

Frisk asked, "Anything else?"

"My next problem is Raff. He called, sounded all business and wanted to meet, said he was in town and wanted to pick up more weed. I feel our next encounter will be much different from the first. He sounded different." Frisk was in his own world, he heard me, but knew much more.

# Raff

IT WAS AROUND MIDNIGHT. FRISK AND I WERE STILL WALKING the back streets after leaving Nailer's. I was cold and talking about quitting speed and missing Catina. I told Frisk, "I have been thinking of Catina. Oh ya, I do not want to end up dead like Red's fucked-up brother." Frisk was still in his own world but listening to me. "I am missing the taste of her lips and holding her. My nights with her were bewitched. I have a feeling I will see her again soon. I also have a feeling those Colombians bastards are back in town, if even for just a day or two. It was strange, Raff calling just now."

We were now walking across the schoolyard toward Carmichaels and close to a corner where tennis was played. The air was cool. There was no moon to be seen, but it was still bright.

"They want revenge, pure and simple. It is a matter of honor," Frisk said. "Raff has figured out who I am, and more importantly, where I am. We were friends then, but I believe he will try to stop us if he is still trying to collect any type of reward."

The courtyard was big, basketball in one corner of the schoolyard and tennis courts in this corner. I would walk past these every day on the way to Carmichaels. The light from the tennis court made it bright just now. No games were being played. The courts were empty, no nets assembled. The timer must be defective, broken and stuck in the "on" position.

I saw Catina. She was standing by the corner, against the wall, waiting for me in the shadows. We stopped. Then I continued to her.

Frisk waiting where he was, looking about. We hugged and kissed with the same passion, moving into the light. She was warm, unlike the night air. There was love between us. I asked, "Why are you here and now?"

"I am in town for a day only and by myself. My father is not here. I wanted to see you." She moved closer with a shyness I did not know. "I need to warn you, the Colombians are coming for you, for your friend." Catina feared my response.

Frisk was pissed, saying with conviction, "These guys think they are going to get revenge. Did they not learn the first time?"

"How do they know so much?" I said. Her eyes told the story. She was not alone. I immediately believed she was feeding information back to Hector regarding our whereabouts and our operation. "Did you tell Hector about my patent?"

She spoke in a quiet voice. "Last time, my father was here to do business with people in this place, with Sylvia. The trouble was not expected. To protect themselves, it was said Frisk attacked and stole from them. They are threatened by your weed and hashish operation. They said you are causing trouble, a war. Hector discovered Frisk is the man the Chief was looking for by accident. It was, how you say, a fluke. I told the truth, that you played fair, that you had no intention of a war. I said you did not even care and did not know about them until they acted first. I told my father his men were deceitful. My father took poorly to being challenged. His men said I went with you for many days. They confused Hector with lies. I did not want trouble. You are someone I miss. I told my father this. He was calmer but no less the enthused with you." In fact, Hector was plotting against Tommy. A fire raged inside him and was building stronger.

There was the promise of a fight in the air. I wanted answers, "I believed you betrayed me, told them everything." My eyes showed it. "Did you tell me everything? Did you tell Hector about my patent and the company Tom Sift Inc. that I am behind, and the money it is laundering. This is a desirable piece in a complicated plan, should a foreign cartel want to set up business here. It just donned on me what I have created. So what is next Catina?"

"No, I am in danger too," she said, sounding worried. "I did not betray you. I love you. There is more you do not know. A thug by the name of Nailer is causing trouble in this area, and word is you and Frisk are with him. I know this is not true, but be careful."

Catina told me more. "And the girl, Holly, she was helpful, telling about your operation. Holly is very friendly and is working for Hector. She did not know a lot but enough to convince us you were the right person behind the rather huge pot-growing and distribution, the one who appeared from nowhere with so much hashish. This hashish of yours is respected and craved by the users. But Hector wants a part of it. He sees the money being made, and when he found out it was you who told him to fuck off, and Frisk was working with you, he wanted revenge. He was very angry with you."

Catina went deeper, "However, there is another agenda, held by Hector, and it is to force you to turn over your patent to him. So they want to attack you, to intimidate you. Hector will use the bounty hunter to attack you. This was where Holly helped. They asked her about your habits, your likes and dislikes. They know you walk across this schoolyard every night and day to get to Carmichaels. They knew you are OK at pool—not a pro, more lucky than skillful. That was how Holly described you. I do not think she knows the new Tommy, does she?" Catina moved closer.

I chuckled and said, "Well, she knows me a bit, Catina. You are not telling me everything, and I am OK with that, but I wonder if Holly was targeted because she knew me. I thought it was random, but maybe they were already onto me. Anyway, I don't fucking care. I can only deal with this moment in time. But maybe I will see Holly again sometime."

Catina looked at me, saying softly, "I so love it when you say my name. Hector had other ideas for Holly. It was not you, Tommy." Then she tied it all together. "It was threats from Nailer against Sylvia, when

Hector became worried. We can only wait until he acts and then defend ourselves," but I could tell there was more.

I looked at Catina, my eyes asking, *What else?* But we were both silent. I started to understand Catina was Hector's second-in-command. She knew the business inside out. She could run a cartel.

Behind us was nothing but shadows and alleys. There was cruelty in the air. "What now?" I asked. Catina did not want this, I could tell by the way she began to squeeze my hand tighter and tighter.

Frisk was building a rage. He told us, "Stay fucking back, stay against the wall. Trust me; I know what I am doing." He was alert. There would be action soon. I stood tall, watching, waiting. Then they attacked.

Two sleek assassins came at us from the dark, knives drawn. A punch to my head made me step back, but I did not go down. I twisted, protecting Catina, and side-kicking the Colombian fucker out toward Frisk.

Knives pulled, they went for Frisk, two against one. We would be next. Their knives were more like short swords, held high, glittering and threatening. Frisk once told me, "Fundamental arts render weapons unnecessary and a hindrance as well."

"What the fuck do you want?" is what I yelled at them.

Only a few words were said, "We want to take you with us, and we want to kill Frisk." They looked at me first, then at Frisk. I knew they wanted the patent, but before I could ask any questions, Frisk answered with violence.

Frisk spun and leapt, dodging and attacking. A knife caressed his cheek; it was too close. They stepped back. Their attack was coordinated and focused. This time, a front kick sent the first guy straight back. An elbow block and straight punch sent the other guy in the opposite direction. Frisk was between them, like wheat before the scythe.

They squared off for the final time. The one in front raised his blade to attack while the other rushed from behind, also raising his blade high. Frisk moved, dropping quickly, long arms reaching out to grab the lapels of each attacker, and pulled them violently together.

They cut on nothing but themselves. Their wounds were too much, the cuts too deep. They could not continue. It was over. Their master was before them.

Once again, assassins were taught a lesson in violence and would not attack again this night. Frisk looked at me as a car raced at speed then slammed on the brakes, screeching to a stop. These two guys hobbled rather quickly into the vehicle. As it sped away, Frisk recognized the driver as the killer who had tried to force him back to Colombia years ago. He had survived that kick into the river, but his injuries would plague him the rest of his life. He was left a gimp, with only partial use of his legs and arms. Tonight's assassins also failed to extract revenge on Frisk.

No sooner were they gone than a familiar face appeared. "Well done, Frisk. Well executed." It was Raff. He had been watching, observing, evaluating. "You have not lost your skill." I was surprised to see Raff. It was a different Raff. He held a long wooden pole in his strong, callused hands. His arms, rippling with tough muscles, pushed on his tight t-shirt. He knew there would be trouble, that blood would be spilt.

Frisk spun to face Raff and said, "It has been many years. What a strange twist of fate that we should meet here, and tonight."

Raff, who was muscle for Hector, said, "Hector wants you two out of the way. Fucking with his daughter, putting his men in the hospital, and fucking with his business were all bad ideas. And this patent you have, Tommy, has him very interested." The wooden staff stood beside Raff. He began again, now walking and circling slowly. "Hector figures you are going to damage his business and his reputation. He sent me to convince you otherwise." He planned to cripple us or kill Frisk and force me to turn over my patent to Hector. But Raff had underestimated Frisk.

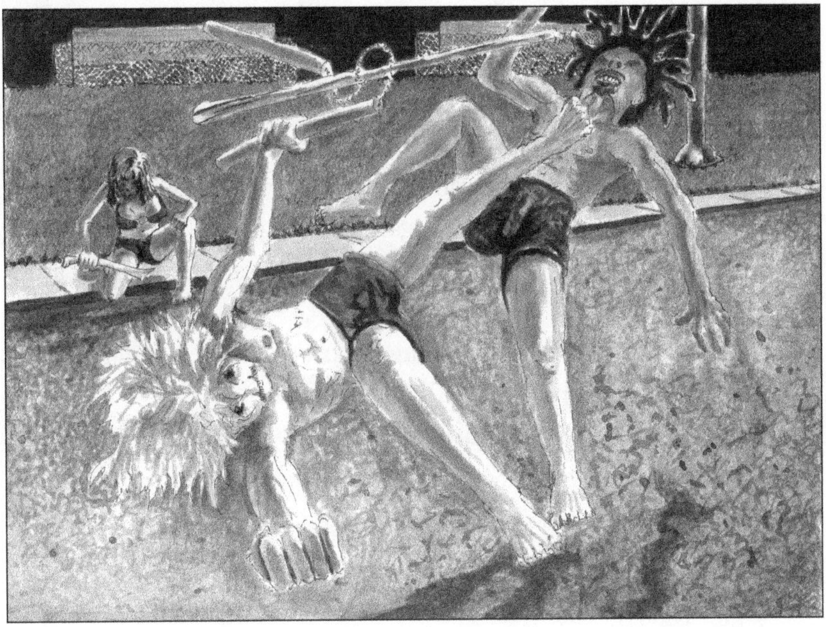

Catina looked toward Frisk and Raff, trying to explain, "My father is evil. Money and power are not things he wants to lose. Hector is not here. He does not understand Tommy did not start this. Tommy is *not* with Nailer. I do not know what to do." Turning to me, she pleaded, "I've come to you, Tommy. Please help." Asking for help is the first step to recovery. We have taken the first step. There was a sense of surrender in her eyes. I trusted her again.

All of a sudden, things started to make better sense. It was wise of me to end my time with Nailer when I did. I knew then, his plan would not end well. My gut feeling, my intuition, saved me again. Both Catina and I shared strong intuition and self-preservation.

Frisk believed her too. "I believe you, but there is more to this fucking story."

Raff did not believe her. He was being paid to believe a lie. He still knew there was a problem. "Frisk is wanted by Hector's boss for desertion, and you have something of great value to Hector."

I spoke up. "I really do not have a lot of time for question-and-answer, Raff." Catina was stiff as a board, frozen.

Frisk circled, slowly unbuttoning and removing his jacket, then throwing it across the court. He stepped back falling into a low crouch. Raff stood in front of him, snapping the staff forward, pointing at Frisk. Frisk pulled his nunchakus and began spinning them very quickly. It was impressive to see the patterns he went through at such speed. Catina looked afraid this time.

Raff and Frisk had trudged through many challenges, and it brought them together. Now a lie might kill one of them.

Words were not spoken during combat; it was a sign of weakness. Raff jumped high in the air, spinning to deflect a nunchaku with his staff. He twirled and kicked; Frisk blocked and attacked. Both warriors showed muscles highly trained from birth.

The nunchaku's zing echoed off the school walls. Raff struck well, Frisk recoiled, and both warriors missed their targets. Frisk stepped around the staff, smashing Raff many times, nunchucks spinning like a propeller on a light airplane. He was hurt. Raff's next attack was slow, and the nunchakus spun quickly around the end of the pole, snagging it. Frisk twisted and pulled the long wooden pole from Raff's weakening hands, tossing both weapons to the ground. The moment held the action, fists, and feet traded pain. Frisk had a rage stronger than Raff's. Raff realized he could not win. His eyes lost hope.

Frisk had spun Raff and was setting him up for a powerful kick that would cause serious damage, and Raff would not recover. In that brief moment, as Raff prepared himself for an attack he could not defend, his mind became calm, surrendering to his master, to Frisk.

Then Catina came forward. "Stop!"

As Frisk stepped forward to attack, Catina screamed, "Stop," and just then, the lights to the tennis court went out, and a thunk was heard. The timer had kicked off, dropping us into darkness for a brief moment before the night lights came on. We were lit by street lamps, and night lights.

Frisk hesitated, the rage contained.

Catina picked up a knife from the first attackers, then stood tall, holding the blade high above her head, its razor-sharp edge bright while the rest stood in darkness. Then she plunged it into her shoulder. Skin parted easily, and it ran red with her blood. This was a very sharp blade. "Stop," she said again.

Her voice now was weary, not urgent. "You are fools. You are full of pride and greed. You are not making sense. There is no reason to fight. I told Hector of your operation, of the money being made. There was no threat to Hector. He knew little of your operation. Nailer is the problem. He is threatened by Frisk going direct to the Colombians, directly to Sylvia. Nailer is considering an attack on Hector's connection Sylvia and probably you too, and that could be very bad for him. That is all anyone knows. The truth was twisted to suit Hector, and Raff was lied to. Raff did not know you were kicking the fucking shit out of Hector's boys in defense. He did not know all the history. They had framed you guys. It was too late. And that bounty hunter looking for Frisk is a fucking mess."

I ran forward to her, uncertain. The knife was on the ground. I took her arm, examining the wound, flesh parted and bleeding. I said, "It is only a flesh wound. Not to worry. Cover it quickly."

The rage was released. Calm was restored. The nunchakus were put away.

Raff stood over Catina, now realizing she was correct. He said with conviction in his voice, "A mistake has been made. Frisk is not the problem. He would never attack Sylvia in the spirit suggested. I know Tommy is not the problem either, so what the fuck? Hector lied to me, that bastard. He really hates you Tommy. Hector made Tommy and Frisk into something they are not. Now he wants what Tommy has."

Frisk looked toward Tommy, now fully comprehending the situation. Raff was sincere, reaching an arm to help Catina, giving her wound direct pressure. In that moment, lies were revealed, and trust was restored. We had become friends with Raff.

We gathered in the near dark. I laughed and said, "Frisk could fight these fucks all night and day, but that wasn't going to solve this problem. It must be fixed on a higher level. Hector needs to understand we can help him or someone is going to die. I will find a way to change Hector's mind should he ever show up here again or should I ever go to Medellin."

Raff added more about what those first Colombians had said when they were beaten. "They painted a picture of a new family rising to take over the drug business. What a fucking laugh. It was just Frisk and Tommy and some fucker with a bag of seeds. It was a college project gone nuclear. But then there is the Sifter. Your fucking hashish machine, now, is a stroke of brilliance. The rewards from owning this device far outweighs just one or two fields of weed. This could be beyond comprehension. People will kill to own this patent." I think he was tripping out, but he could be right, it could be more trouble than it is worth.

Catina explained exactly what I must do, "You must prove to Hector you can bring him more power and money in this area of the country, and protect his interests. He wants this region. This is how you will win him over."

Frisk pointed out who reports to whom. "Poncho runs the show. Hector must be careful too. Don't ever forget that. Any peace must start with Poncho."

"Well, we do have the best team on earth," I said. "We can grow on a scale few people can complete with. I just want to grow weed, make hash, and just generally keep on going. I think I can explain that much to Hector."

We stood together in that corner of the schoolyard, Frisk, Catina, and Raff. There was a meeting of minds, an alliance forming. We stood together. Raff reassured us, "This is a battle I will not fight for Hector. It is pointless to fight against Frisk for the wrong reasons. I will only fight with him." We knocked knuckles, and Raff was gone, for now.

Catina talked further. "The fighting attracts attention. The cartels do not need problems. There was a question of trust. You need to explain to Hector in person. He doesn't respect you, has no reason to. All he knows is that Frisk's a deserter and you beat him at pool. He has your girlfriend, and you told him to fuck off, which pissed him off. If you could do something to earn his respect, that might help. Otherwise, he will take over your operation, steal your patent, and you would be lucky to be allowed even to live on the streets."

"What if I beat him at pool?" I said.

She didn't know I had been practicing. Catina said, "That is unlikely one on one. He is national champion. But perhaps, if you were to hold your own against him, it might help. We must try something, and I can't think of anything else." I held Catina close to me. She held onto me, "I must go now." We kissed. There was trust and magic in her eyes. Then she disappeared into the night.

# Death in the Dark

WE MADE IT TO CARMICHAELS, AND HAD A FEW QUIET games of pool. "What the fuck are we doing, Frisk?" I asked.

"Nailer is setting up a rather large hash deal with me. He wants a hundred pounds or more to move to his connection. Something doesn't sit well. I am concerned." Frisk was pacing about. "Nailer's connections were Raff and Sylvia, and we might be getting close to dealing directly with them. This worries the piece-of-shit bastard. He thinks we are going to take his business. Stupid fuck doesn't realize we *are* the business. I think we are going to get killed on this one."

I was sarcastic, "No, ya think so? It makes no sense what you say. Maybe you're right." I paused, then said, "I trust your instincts. You're right." My naivety showed for a moment, and I apologized. "I misjudged how far Nailer would go. That will not happen again." Frisk and I knocked knuckles, and I was grateful we had that little chat. I slept well that night, knowing I was on a hit list.

I did one more hit the next day. As I mixed the chunky, white powder with water, I knew it would be wrong. The hit was strong and clean. This was good shit. When I pulled the needle from my arm, I knew it was over. That was the last spoonful of grit I would ever do. I was stoned, and I smoked a joint anyway. I got paranoid. I became fearful. The pot was acting like medicine. It made me feel like I never wanted to do that shit again. The paranoia heightened my instincts, warning me. I listened. I took what was left and flushed it down the toilet. I took the fits, busted them into little pieces, and threw them in the garbage.

I yelled at the universe, begging to be heard. "Help me take this out of my life. Please take this evil addiction away. I don't want this shit in my life anymore. Please help me." The universe listened and I felt better almost instantly, the black hole of misery evaporating. There was a new presence about me, I did not feel so alone. Some call it a spiritual awakening.

And so began my journey out from under a dark and dangerous cloud. I went to Carmichaels that fateful day and played pool until tired. I went home and slept until dinner the next day. Frisk and I shared a late-night Chinese feast. We munched out to the maximum. Once we were full, I began to tell Frisk about stopping meth completely, "I am off the speed for good. Way to dangerous, and ending up like Nailer is not going to happen. I feel better already. It was weird Frisk, I asked the universe for help out loud and I got it." I was being honest.

Frisk was honest too. "I usually know when to back off. Hate to complain about being tired, but I am wiped out all the time. It may be too late. I am sick."

I was half-honest. "You do look pale," I said. His eyes were yellow.

Frisk explained more. "I went to emergency today, and they said I was sick. The doctor told me to get lots of rest and immediately start taking this medicine he gave me. I need to rehab and heal in Mount Saint Patrick for a few weeks. I will drop by when I get feeling better." I wished him luck and he left. I lost track of Frisk for a few weeks after that talk.

I started working out more. Within a couple of weeks, I was doing better. I could only hope my friend was resting and healing too.

I heard my friend was sick from a dirty needle he shared with someone last year. Sure glad I missed that day of partying, as I was feeling fine. I heard he had something called yellow jaundice. I figured he just needed a bit of time to rest and get better. I really did not understand the implications of what he had done to himself. *Could a dirty needle really kill someone?*

I tried to send a small amount of white stuff Frisk's way when I heard he was hurting. But the package never made it. That was probably a good thing. I might have killed him with the white death. The universe had intervened.

When Frisk got back, he was looking better. We joked, "I won't be swapping underwear with you any time soon. You look on the other side of it now."

He spoke from the heart. "I am done with that shit."

I wondered if Frisk was still keeping the door open. "You are looking a lot better. Stay off that shit from now on. OK. Glad to have you back to your old self. I am grateful."

It was a damp, cold Monday night at the end of February when Nailer called me about the gun deal. I told him, "I am out, man," but he argued, threatening me with violence. I finally thundered before hanging up, "Sorry, can't do it, man. I got other things happening. Just get someone else. Maybe JD will do it." Nailer was pissed. He wanted the guns. It was part of his plan.

The next day, Frisk walked into Carmichaels, where I was practicing and we had a short talk. Frisk started, "I met with Nailer, and he wants five hundred pounds of hashish. The plan is to meet Friday night at three in the morning, fifty-seven miles from here on a back road. I know the place. We could make a half-million dollars in one deal."

I had to ask. "Why out so far?"

Frisk had the answer. "Nailer said it was closer to his connections and another bullshit job he has going."

Friday night was cold, and it was soon early Saturday morning. Frisk and I were driving in my truck, loaded with a thousand bricks of hashish, about five hundred pounds. I questioned our actions. "I wonder if we really believe we are about to pick up a half-million dollars?"

Frisk was serious, very serious. "Be strong. Be vigilant. When it starts, you will know what to do."

The snow was crunchy under the wheels of my truck. We drove for an hour down snowy back roads, finally approaching a tree-shrouded cul-de-sac.

"Why the fuck am I out here in the middle of fucking nowhere?" I said.

"To make five hundred grand in one shot," Frisk said with suspicion in his tone while looking around, checking the area. "We are in a corner. Our backs are against the wall, so to speak." He added, "But that's a good thing." I noticed we were talking more normal lately, not the heavy gangster banter.

The hashish was in the back of my truck, covered with a dark green tarp. It was hunter green. We had used a few old one-piece pool cues along the sides and a couple of old tires to hold the tarp down.

The snowbanks were a couple of feet high. There was a natural ditch just at the end of the cul-de-sac. I was approaching too quickly. Frisk began laughing, then spoke loudly, "Watch out or we will drive right off the fucking road." I jammed the emergency brakes, pulling hard on the steering wheel. The truck did an immediate hundred and eighty-degree power turn, spinning on a dime. We felt the g-force on our bodies, but it wore off quickly as we came to rest, pointing in the other direction. I turned the headlights out.

Opening a beer each and cranking the tunes, Frisk chatted. "Lenny will be back in a few weeks. We can start growing again and get this season going. Hunter will be back soon too, with enough seeds to grow tens of thousands of plants."

"Holy God, it's a lot of work," I said.

Frisk agreed. "Maybe we should just do this every second year."

Before I could answer, we saw lights slowly coming up the road toward us. It was a medium-size K car. As the car pulled up, it was JD behind the wheel, and Nailer in the passenger seat. JD's long face, with that ever-stunned retarded look, was nearly as ugly as Nailer's.

I looked at Frisk, saying, "Well, Nailer picked a perfect partner. Between them, they don't add up to much."

Frisk added in his own way, "Both those fucking pieces of festering roadkill should be eliminated forever."

It was nearly three in the morning now. The moon was full, a gleaming, unbiased observer. I knew Nailer was dangerous, so I breathed deeply in anticipation.

"Let me handle this," Frisk said. "Just follow my lead. If they are going to try anything, it will be very soon."

We got out of the truck and walked to the back. JD had their car on an angle to us the headlights pointed at the hash. Nailer walked the long way around, going by the trunk and up the other side of the car. He just looked at me and said nothing. Walking over to Frisk, and in a raspy tone, he asked, "Got the fucking hash, man?" He had not changed.

"Got the cash?" Frisk asked.

"Yeah, man," came the reply. JD was standing by the trunk of his car. We walked to the back and pulled the pool cues from the sides of the tarp. I pulled the tarp off, revealing a very large plastic box. Reaching inside, I pulled out a few of the half-pound bricks and threw one at Nailer. He gave it a look and a sniff.

"Over five hundred pounds in here," I said. Nailer walked with Frisk toward the back of the car. The trunk was open now. I jumped over the side of the truck and walked toward the open trunk. There were four brand new hockey bags, packed full of stolen guns, laying tightly beside each other. Nailer unzipped one and reached inside. Moonlight lit the gun barrels. My heartbeat went up. There was no cash.

The trunk was full of guns. They had ripped off the hardware store after all, probably within the last couple of hours. Nailer pulled out a Glock handgun and pointed it at me. I spoke to him. "So, this was how it will go down. You stealing guns and hash. Then killing us, selling it to Sylvia, and walking away with all the cash. You fucking loser, you didn't figure out I was the brains and producer of what has become a very lucrative hashish business with legitimate connections in Tom Sift. You have no idea who Frisk really is or his history, do you? Nailer, you are one fucked-up asshole," I said, and he was very dangerous as well.

With a loaded pistol at my head, I laughed at JD. "JD, you stupid fucking asshole. How the fuck did you get involved with this slime bucket, you fucking idiot?" I looked at Frisk. He had a small grin on his face. He was calm inside. He knew something.

Nailer instructed JD and me to move the hashish into their car. Next, Nailer told me to get over by my truck. Frisk was just waiting, not moving much with a gun at his chest. Nailer was bragging about how smooth it went, "Yeah, motherfucker. Man, we cleaned out that stupid fucking hardware store. We got away scot-free. They won't know until morning, and we'll be long gone, man." Then he got deadly serious. "Now, I want the hash, man. You guys got too close to my contacts for your own fucking good, man. You are fucking with my plans. I'm go-anna kill you two fucks and end this."

I spat at Nailer. "Fuck you, Nailer. You never did have the buy money, did you? You planned to kill us and deal directly with Sylvia, or some other cartel fuckers all along, didn't you?" When Nailer was nonresponsive, I added something my father would sometimes say, "Nailer, you have a head the very same as a fucking nail." Nailer's rage was building.

JD was by the trunk, looking at the large amount of hashish. He knew it was worth the effort to kill us for it. He was in, and he said so. "Nailer is going to waste you fuckers for five hundred pounds of hashish, and three quarters of a million, or more in cash from his buyer. Not to mention hockey bags full of guns." I quickly thought, and God only knows what else. "That is well worth killing you two. Nice haul, eh." Nailer raised the gun. Frisk stepped back two steps, out of reach.

It would end here tonight. We were all within twenty feet of each other. Nailer followed Frisk's sudden, purposeful motion, pointing the gun toward him at the same time. I was six feet from Nailer. He had murder in his eyes, his lips pulled tight. It was the closest I have seen him come to smile since the time he gave me my first hit.

He held the handgun straight out and turned so the handle was horizontal. Maybe it felt cool, more gangster like, to hold it that way. He didn't expect my kick to be so fast. The snap kick went straight up, under Nailer's gun elbow. His arm snapped at the elbow, bending downward in an unnatural position. The gun dropped to the ground. Nailer would never smile again. Frisk moved in with a sidekick, laying him flat against the back fender. He came at Frisk again and was side kicked back into the truck.

I approached JD quickly. He turned to meet me, stepping off his back fender, leaping high in the air. He tried to come down on me with a hammer punch to the head. I twisted at just the right moment, his hammer punch missing me. I caught him in midair with the judo hip throw I practiced diligently so many times in the past. Now we moved together as his energy came with me. I grabbed his lapel and threw my rear leg up high, all the while twisting violently down. JD went into the ground hard. I rolled off and stood up. When he tried to roll over, I grabbed him and stood him up.

I threw a devastating straight punch to his jaw, then punched him again hard in the mouth, cracking his nose and upper teeth. He fell backwards into the trunk, dazed, sitting up with legs dangling over the license plate.

He was slumped forward and struggling. Reaching up, I grabbed the trunk hood and slammed it violently into the back of his head, neck, and shoulders. It took a few tries, but he finally folded forward in half, his chest flat against his thighs. There was crunching and groaning. I continued to slam the trunk with extreme force each time, while yelling, "JD, you are an asshole. You fucking asshole." His breathing was laborious, his face beet red.

I looked over to see Frisk roundhouse Nailer in the face. His head spun. He was going down. Nailer's nose was now broken too. He rolled on the ground, standing up by the tailgate.

I grabbed JD, pulling him from the trunk. Another spin and hip throw, straight up and straight down to the ground. He hit hard again. No breath was in his body. It had been knocked out of him. He could not get his breath back. He couldn't move. In one swift motion, I stood up and came straight down with a punch to the heart. I hit it square on, rupturing the main aorta from the heart wall. No shot of adrenaline would cure this problem. He knew he was dying on a frozen moonlit back road. This was not his plan.

His chest felt hot. Blood filled the cavity surrounding the lungs, collapsing them. The last breath of air was being forced out. He tried to cough, but only muscle spasms engulfed him. He died just then.

I looked up, and Nailer was at the back of the truck. His left arm snapped, his right arm holding him up.

Frisk approached Nailer. Moonlight reflected off Frisk's face revealing chiselled focus. Frisk was alert. I could see his breath. It was slow and controlled as he approached, creeping forward slowly. Nailer saw one of the pool cues holding the tarp and, in one swift motion, drew it from the truck, swinging hard and fast at Frisk.

Frisk tried to block, by moving his head back, but the cue tip caught him just across the check. A blue streak appeared below his eye. Frisk stopped. He was stunned for a moment, then swore, "Fuck you, asshole."

In that moment, I moved toward Nailer. Nailer thrust the cue at Frisk, catching him square in the chest. Frisk anticipated the attack and was moving backward but not fast enough. Nailer brought the cue back and swung once more, hitting Frisk in the side of the head again. Frisk was stunned while Nailer dealt with his pain. His chest was sprained, his arm broke, his nose broke, but he had a momentary advantage. He leaned on the cue. It was his support, his *alia*.

Nailer had another gun behind his back and was reaching for it. He was not rushing, resting briefly against the truck. The pool cue was supporting his broken left side. He pulled a six-shot pistol from his belt. Frisk was still standing. I was still unnoticed by Nailer. He pointed the gun at the ground to undo the safety. I heard it click. He raised the gun.

He stepped forward, struggling with the gun. He had momentum, but he was still weak. I approached quickly, kicking at him again. He moved fast, faster than I thought possible. I slipped and went down hard. Nailer swung the gun toward me, his back now toward Frisk. In an instant, Frisk snapped back to life. His recovery was incredible. He was an Olympian, a hero standing strong, focused and well trained. Looking directly at Nailer as he would an object ball—and not any object ball but the one that would close the night out and game over—he attacked.

Frisk screamed loud, startling Nailer. He threw a beautiful sidekick straight to the back of Nailer's head. Nailer never really saw it coming. He never really got the gun aimed at me either. The pool cue, cuddled in Nailer's arm, bounced forward when Frisk yelled. The sidekick hit Nailer hard, forcing his head forward and down, the tip of the cue catching him directly in the right eyeball. The force was incredible. The eyeball squished, and the brain was penetrated straight through. The cue tip hit the back of the skull from the inside. The skull gave way, and a cue tip appeared out the back.

Nailer collapsed. The cue slowly slid through his brains and skull. He got hung up for a few brief moments, all slumped over, the twitching finally knocking him off balance. He was dead before hitting the ground. Blood was sparse. Once the heart stops, blood has a tendency to stay in the body.

Frisk retracted his leg after holding it there for a second. The sidekick would have been judged as perfect form. He brought the leg down and helped me up.

"Fucking Jesus God almighty, what the fuck was that?" I screamed.

Frisk actually laughed. "Hey, man, I would go on a Break and Enter with you, anytime, Tommy." We both laughed.

I walked toward Nailer. "Well, your little fucking plan didn't work, did it, you fucking shithead?" I spit on him as I kicked his face. "Now you're dead motherfucker, and I am alive."

We moved the hashish and hockey bags of weapons to my truck. The moon had moved, and the shadows were facing the other way. Clouds began to cover the sky. It felt just a little colder. Frisk noticed it too and said, "Moisture in the air makes it cooler, but this will help." He pulled out a case of unopened bottles of southern whiskey from the back of the K-car. There was a picture of a wild turkey on the labels. Cracking one open each, we took long hits, simultaneously laughing and coughing, water coming to our eyes. On occasion, we had to restrain ourselves from puking.

We also found ten pounds of pure meth, ready for sale, and fifty thousand in cash. Frisk broke the cue off with a snap kick just above Nailer's dead nose. The cue made a quiet crack. We threw the bodies in the front seat of their car along with the piece of broken cue.

Taking a couple gallons of gasoline from my four-gallon plastic emergency reserve carboy, I threw it across the bodies. We pushed the car up to the edge of the ditch, lining it up with the edge.

I smoked a cigar size joint of hash and kept hammering back the whiskey. I was drunk now, awake, alive. After finishing my joint, I tossed the burning roach through the half-open front window. The gas ignited almost instantaneously, with a loud *swoosh*. There was too much gasoline. A couple of gallons was insane. It only needed a cup or two. "Holy God, what the fuck," I yelped, my hair frying at the ends, the stink sickening. I recoiled back, twisting around away from the flames and the giant engulfing fireball. The whiskey was warmed in the bottle.

We jumped into my truck, and while slamming whiskey, we drove straight into the flaming car's back bumper, easily pushing it over the snowy berm. The K car rolled down the small bank, coming to rest in a natural grave. The flames caught on, engulfing the car within seconds. That was the end of those two bastards. The world would be a safer place now.

As we turned the truck around, a set of lights appeared directly in front us. "Fuck me, what now? Who the fuck could be here? Who knew we were here? It's not cops, cause there ain't no colored lights." I put the truck in park. We got out, whiskey bottles still in hand, and faced the lights. Doors opened, and people got out.

# Sylvia

"WELL, CONGRATULATIONS, BOYS. GOOD WORK," Sylvia said, walking toward us. Her steps, long and deliberate like a woman wearing high heels, would take. Sylvia stepped out of the headlights. A bodyguard was not far away, still in the bright light. She reached out, shaking Frisk's hand, then mine, before walking over to look at the burning car. It was still completely on fire. First, the windshield exploded loudly, then the back windows. Nobody jumped or flinched when they popped. She walked over to my truck observing all the guns, hashish, meth, and a case of whiskey. Reaching into the case Sylvia pulled her own bottle of whiskey, twisted it open and took a long swig.

Sylvia was a drop-dead gorgeous Russian woman. She came from a royal family and was very wealthy. She was well educated in politics and economics. She spoke four languages, had many worldly experiences, and slept with a gun under her pillow—excellent credentials to do the will of an international criminal cartel. Her political connections allowed her to move freely, in obscurity, without fear. These are some of the reasons why Sylvia ended up in charge.

I scoped her out. Sylvia was six feet tall and athletic, with large, full breasts. She was drop-dead beautiful. Her long hair had dark-red curls, streaked with various tones, but was quickly tucked under her white mink fur hat. She wore a light blue down-filled jacket, which would keep her warm to minus fifty. Her perfume was strong and alluring and not cheap. She was world-class.

I had to speak first. "Sylvie, what in the name of baby Jesus are you doing here?" I staggered back a step. Frisk was steady beside me, quietly observing the unfolding events.

Sylvia has a strong, friendly charisma. She invited us to sit in her warm four-door truck to discuss a few things. Happy to oblige, we jumped in the back. Her driver was a very bushy-haired guy, with a pale, thin white face but smiling. His hair was the big, black Afro style. He reminded me of Frisk in some peculiar way, and he looked like one of the original freak brothers. Sylvia did a quick introduction. "Guys, this is Bob, my driver. Bob this is Tommy and Frisk." Bob nodded, remaining out of our conversation, focusing on the steering wheel.

Taking a swig of whiskey, she told her story. "I was to meet Nailer down the road, twenty miles from here in an hour. He was going to sell me five hundred pounds of hashish, some guns, and a large amount of methamphetamine. He never showed up. Do you know anything about that?"

*One step at a time*, I thought.

Frisk was very matter-of-fact about the past twenty minutes. "We were selling the hash to Nailer. He got greedy and tried to kill us. He died instead." Sylvia's genuine leather seats were hot. They had heaters in them, and that was cool.

Another small swig and Sylvia began again, "I saw Nailer come up this way and followed. We watched you guys take care of those two. I must say, I am very impressed. He was our connection to your product and more, but I am happy that motherfucking criminal is off this earth. He became a big threat when he started to believe the voices in his head. He was—how you say?—self-destructing, and you took care of my problem. For that, I thank you both." The Russian accent was becoming more evident now. She went on, "My contact tells me you two grow all the weed and make all the hash in this area. Tom Sift Inc., a company you own, is the front for your profits, and best of all, the crown jewel: you have a machine to produce quality hashish almost instantly. Ah, but you not only have the Sifter, you hold the patent on this device. That is very impressive. I understand you are making a lot of money."""

"So, you knew everything about our business." Frisk did not say anything. My thought was she found out through the Colombians from Catina. "Frisk, you were right when you said we would step on someone's toes, and Hector was that someone."

The Russian accent switched to Russian flirting. "And you, Frisk, mister deserter person. Your presence here is causing a little problem. It appears your past has caught up to you. A crippled bounty hunter who is old, but his memory is still fresh. And that you beat and threw him into the river was not forgotten." Sylvia laughed a little laugh. "He should have died then, but alas, he pursues you with a personal vengeance. And then you two beat Hector at Carmichaels and told him to fuck off. He leads a Colombian cartel with lots of drugs and money. He is a ruthless businessman. He is one of my clients, so to speak. His men have only recently began working in this area. They got the shit kicked out of themselves in that pool match, and they are sore losers, very sore. It took a doctor some time to put them back together." We all laughed. I was correct: she has a very strong connection with Hector. On one last serious note. Sylvia made her point. "This is becoming dangerous for the community and dangerous for business. They think you want some sort of war. They will send someone again."

I wanted to know more. "What else do you know?"

Sylvia's face was turned toward us, fully lit on one side. The other was dark, but every so often a reflection of flames changed the hues of that side of her face, ever so slightly. "I met with the mayor, and she is not happy about this brewing conflict. She is trusting me to get a lot of the hard drugs Nailer was making and selling out of her town."

Frisk jumped in, saying sarcastically, "But there is an appetite for pure Colombian cocaine."

Sylvia remained focused, undeterred. "We are the type of people who need to be out of sight and out of mind, as the mayor put it. Maximum deniability. So long as we run a quiet show, no problem. You are part of a much bigger organization now by supplying drugs to us directly, and fortunately, you do not need to know anything more about our business. But know my decisions are swift and decisive." She was now very serious, very much at work explaining reality. "If I sense disloyalty or weakness, I will snuff it out." She demonstrated by snapping closed her fist in front of our faces. Kentucky whiskey warmed Sylvia's throat as she took a long haul.

Best I could figure, this level of drug dealing is exactly what Frisk was trying to avoid, yet the universe would not let him go. I smiled. "Appears to me you have the divine right to rule. It's in your blood. You were born with it. Nice speech, very poetic, threatening but in a good way."

The Russian accent was sexy. "We are never free of ourselves, but we are free to find our own destinies. You two need to find your destiny to be complete." Moving closer to us, she said in a slow, deliberate way, my heart began to speed up being this close to Sylvia, "Find your fucking destinies and find it soon before you are both destroyed by it."

Frisk was sarcastic, nearly laughing. "Yeah, terrifying yet inspirational at the same time. Where the fuck do you get your information, from rumor and small children?" In that moment, it became obvious to Frisk and me what must be done. Sylvia made us realize it. We must go to Colombia. We had to face this mess and fix it. I looked at Frisk. He looked at me, and we nodded acceptance.

It started to snow lightly, and the fire raged on in the distance. Both Frisk and I swallowed hard. We put everything we had on the table. It was all in at this point. I looked at Sylvia and said, "I want five hundred grand. You get to save two hundred and fifty thousand. For that, you get all the hashish, all the guns, and ten pounds of speed, and fuck, yes, we will fix these problems. Just tell us where to find Hector.

Frisk responded, "Trust us. We know what we are doing."

Then I asked for the cash, "I do trust you have the cash here?"

Sylvia smiled and shook my hand. "Deal," she said, handing me a midsize, red steel toolbox. I put it on my lap and opened it up. There were piles of cash inside. Then Sylvia quantified the total. "That is one half-million dollars." She was looking us up and down, checking us out. Was she getting drunk? I pondered her desires.

I said, "OK, what's next?" and closed it.

We sipped whiskey while Sylvia explained more of what we were dealing with. "These guys are hustlers in their country. Drug-dealing, thieving extortionists who gamble at pool." Frisk never batted an eye. I was not scared either. Sylvia looked at Frisk, smiling. "Women hate indecisive men. You two are very much in control. I like that."

She softened a bit. Maybe it was the whiskey. "You gotta have a lot of nerve to stay in this business. Do you boys have the nerve?" Sylvia put a hand of Frisk's knee.

"We got this far, but I am not interested in taking on the Colombian cartels. They are crazy motherfuckers," I said, making an ugly fucking face. "They would mow us down in the street, with fully automatic weapons if they wanted to."

Sylvia straightened in her seat and was serious again. "This is a very big deal for him to be a cartel leader here in a foreign country. He is playing for keeps. Hector wants to take you out, humiliate the gringo for insulting him, telling them to fuck off in public, fucking his daughter, and fucking with his drug trade, all in the last six fucking months. You guys made a lot of fucking money in a rather short time. That is concerning. There is more. Your friend Holly, the *chica*, she is not safe, I cannot tell you anymore, but she is in danger."

I replied, "I didn't think telling that creep to fuck off was a big deal. I guess it was after all. What about Holly?" There was more to be said, but Sylvia did not know the answers.

Frisk stopped her. "Hector seldom comes this way. I don't think he travels much at all. I have no fear of dealing with Hector, wherever he is."

"It is true. His trips here are rare, but the violence is growing." Sylvia confirmed the observation. "That is why you two must go to him."

I looked at Sylvia, politely thanking her for everything while suggesting someday we will meet again. "This party is over. I truly look forward to the next time we meet. It is time to move on."

Sylvia was gracious. "That was all I needed to hear. Beware, Tommy. Temptation will always be knocking on your door."

We got out of her vehicle, and a rush of cold air took my breath away.

I soon adjusted. The hashish, guns, and speed took several minutes to change vehicles. We kept all the cash.

Sylvia said, "Good work, and good luck."

By now, the car was not burning as intensely. This concerned me. I threw the two old tires on the burning rubble. It jumped back to life, and I felt better. This car would burn into nothing.

Sylvia told us, "Fuck off out of here. Once the flames die down, I will ensure this grave is covered with rock and dirt. It will be the next fucking ice age before anyone uncovers these two cocksuckers." I took Sylvia's hand in mine, shaking it again.

We drove the long road out of that place. The flames soon disappeared behind us. No music played, so I talked with Frisk. "You know, Frisk, it is said sound can only travel a few miles. So guess we are safe." Looking about, I said, "There's not one fucking person for miles in any fucking direction. Just the chance meeting of three parties, all masters of their own domain. Now there are two." I was sounding self-righteous, almost funny, while waving the whiskey bottle with my free hand.

Frisk agreed. "Sylvia is the right person to be working with. We need each other. There will be a cartel leader appointed to rule this area, to work with Sylvia. Sure looks like Hector is that guy, so we better find a way to get along." He stretched out, relaxing. Frisk believed in this partnership. It was necessary.

The whiskey was soon gone. Hanging my arm out the driver's window, I flung the empty bottle over the top of the cab and into the dark marshes. The front of the truck skidded and swerved when I did that. I steered it back onto the road, and we kept on going as if nothing had happened. We opened a beer each.

"Fuck Nailer and JD, those thieving bastards," Frisk said.

"To hell with them. They had no honor," I said. "It will be a long time before anyone finds that mess."

It was snowing heavily now. The flakes were large in the headlights, but the windshield wipers kept the vision clear. Our tracks disappeared quickly behind us. I drove slowly. I drove for the conditions. "We stick to hash, and I don't want to hear about anything else once we get this problem fixed," I said, with a tone of leadership and finality.

Frisk was upbeat, adding positive energy to the night. "God hates a coward. I am Siegfried, and I have tasted the blood of the dragon. I can read the minds of my enemies, and they will fall before me." His fist waved and cut the air in a slow, stubborn motion. His voice was strong and believing. Life was frozen for a moment in time. I saw a snapshot of a hero who was too large for life.

I added, "Right fucking on, man. We are the godly people, and we are right and justified in our actions."

By the time we got back to town, we had a meeting of minds. "Don't worry, Tommy. Everything will be OK."

I was confident now. "I believe you, Frisk. It will all work out." I dropped Frisk off and made it back home in one piece. In the morning, snow was piled three feet deep in my driveway. I was worried about Holly. I was coming and began to pack for sunnier and much warmer places.

# PART 3

# Colombia

"THE ONLY GOOD THING ABOUT AIRPLANES IS GETTING off one," I told Lenny, who was sitting beside me in first class. Being over six feet tall and probably two hundred and twenty pounds, Lenny took up most of the middle seat, but he still had room to stretch out. Frisk had the aisle seat.

We were stopped on the final taxi before making a short right turn onto the main runway. At that point, the captain would hit the gas, smoothly accelerate down the runway, and take off. The jet instead began engine thrust with full brakes applied while stopped and not on the runway yet, a brake stand of sorts in a commercial jet airliner while waiting to taxi onto the runway. The engines were getting louder and louder. Suddenly, the brakes released. The jet lunged forward, then, skidding sideways, turned onto the main runway at speed. At this point, the powerful engines were engaged one hundred percent, the sound now loud in the cabin. I was pushed back into my seat, and my stomach relaxed. Acceleration was rapid. Wheels rolled, the plane bouncing, trying to become airborne. Then we were up. We gained distance from the ground quickly.

Frisk leaned over toward Lenny and me while looking out the window, remaking, "Fighter-pilot takeoff. Love it when the captain does that. Must have been a short runway. Needed every inch of it." I was just happy to be flying and watch home quickly disappear behind us.

It was a no-smoking flight, but Lenny lit one up anyway. The smell carried everywhere. Within moments, the stewardess had it extinguished. Lenny barked, calling her an old pie-sucker and an old moccasin. She was stunned, caught by surprise by Lenny's rage. Tears began welling in her eyes. Lenny bent forward and said loudly to her, "Jesus Christ, I just lost my wife to some unpronounceable disease. She is dead, and I am under a lot of stress, can't ya see." Lenny threw the half-smoked cigarette on the floor of the jet and stomped it under his left foot. She brought beer and whiskey shots for the three of us. That calmed the situation for the moment.

"Holy God, Lenny, you would lie about anything. Bridget is fine and at home." What else could I say?

Lenny pulled out his deck of cards. "Well, thank you, Tommy. I was just getting her tuned up." He immediately began flipping over cards, one at a time, and counting quietly to himself, "Plus one, plus two, plus three, plus two, plus three, plus four, plus three, plus two." He was counting cards with the high-low system. "When playing blackjack, the first step is to learn your basic strategy. That is, knowing which cards to play depending on what you have and what the dealer has showing up. When more smaller cards are out of the deck, the advantage is for the player, and if more high cards are out of the deck, the advantage is for the dealer. Counting cards tells you the imbalance between high cards and low cards."

I was curious. "So, Lenny, does that card-counting work?"

Lenny talked while counting, "Yes, it does. It helps to know how to adjust basic strategy depending on the up cards, but that is not all. There is something else of equal importance no one ever talks about. Everyone has heard of counting cards at blackjack, but they have never heard of shuffle tracking."

"What the fuck is shuffle tracking?" Frisk's interest was now piqued. The plane continued to cruise along effortlessly.

Lenny could explain it. "It is knowing exactly where the cards are in the deck. In particular, the advantage player will know the pre-cards before they come up. An ace or high card or another card they are looking for is tracked during the shuffling process. When these pre-cards start to turn up, then the card they want is soon to appear. Basically, shuffle tracking allows a person to know when certain cards are likely to appear. Shuffle tracking with card-counting makes a player very dangerous to a casino. This player knows exactly when to make crazy big bets and will very likely win. Then, if this player can get a trend going, he can win a lot of money—a lot. He becomes an advantage player. This is based on mathematical models done by super mainframe computers playing millions of hands, over and over, to find the patterns." Lenny kept on counting. I looked out the window until asleep.

It was a long and uneventful night flight. We would arrive in Medellin, Colombia, by early dawn.

The engines slowed as we left cruising altitude and the plane began to descend. We were high above the clouds, and the ground was dark and yet to be discernible. Dozing in and out, I marveled at the absolute wonder of the universe. I was grateful to live in a time of such cool ways to travel. A ding went off in the cabin, indicating the plane was now descending through ten thousand feet. We broke through the clouds, and all I could see for miles and miles was jungle bathed in morning twilight, those few minutes as darkness is devoured by light, as shadows start small, stretch long, and then disappear. The sun was a dark orange ball on the distant horizon. A few clouds sat calmly on each side. Green trees spread in all directions. Narrow winding rivers snaked beneath the foliage. Smoke rose in slim stacks fairly often from what I presumed to be small villages or travelers.

The sun was just coming up, but I felt wide awake. Frisk and Lenny were up too, drinking coffee, eating muffins, and looking out the window with me.

"Cartels. Cartels and their drug factories—cocaine. Many tons of white death are being made beneath us at this moment," Frisk enlightened us as he peered deep into the jungle, past the jungle, with knowing eyes. He has seen the violence, the death, the worst being what he didn't say. The worry on his face and in his eyes told of a real danger. He knew this trip should be quick.

I was sort of picking up on that feeling. "I figure this should be a quick trip, right, like we planned, maybe a week max."

"Jesus Christ, Tommy," Lenny began. "The way I figure it, Sylvia helps to manage drugs, cash, and God only knows what else for cartels. The cartels need her to be strong, to have a presence in our backyard. We might have to kill Hector if he won't talk sense, but the fucker needs us." The coffee was going down good, so we all asked for cognac shots instead of milk. Lenny knew the deal. "Tommy, you gotta see this Hector fucker and get him on board. The fields of weed, your machine, the patent, Tom Sift Inc., maybe get your little honey back, the one with the nice tits. There is too much at stake. He needs you. And we need the Colombian Red seeds, and we need peace. That is what we gotta get, Tommy. He wants to get his honor back. Play him some fucking pool, gain his confidence, get him on our side somehow. Kiss his monkey ass," he said, laughing and snickering at the same time. Lenny had that figured about right.

He looked at Frisk. "And you, Frisk, you gotta kill that fucker chasing you for good this time and get freedom with your chief. If you talk with Poncho, you can make a peace. Tell him, 'Closure on the past will open doors in the future.' We are helping but in a different part of the world. You must get us to those fields so we can check the plants and get the seeds we need." Lenny surprised me sometimes. He was really smart.

Frisk intervened again, "Get a grip, Lenny. Hector and the Chief are insatiable. We must make them an offer, an offer that will work for all of us, like a business plan. The problem is, it will take everything to get them to even consider a union. It will not be obvious to the Chief and Hector at first." Frisk explained more about dealing with Hector. "First, you must beat him, but he must feel like he got a game. You need to dance with this man. Hector is a top Colombian nine-ball player, but you're better. Play him a game of freeze-out—that is, the winner is declared when either opponent is ten games ahead or whatever number you decide. That would give him a good challenge. Consider that, Tommy."

I have come here to his home, my fear mostly fueled by the fact that I was on the bubble. It was going to be up to me to end this one. To help make the peace through an assassination of sorts to stop Hector. History will justify the vigilante, I thought.

We approached Medellin Colombia. *Wow*, I thought. I could feel the heat radiating from the city through the fuselage. It was hot below. The city was enormous, spread out for miles. Luckily for us, we were transferring immediately to a smaller plane to get us very deep into the jungle.

The speaker crackled and came alive. The captain began in Spanish, soon repeating his message in English. With a very deep Spanish accent, almost singing, he said, "Welcome to Medellin, Colombia. As your captain, I want to remind you, the safest part of your journey is now over. Be careful driving home," and the microphone clicked, off. *Interesting prophecy*, I thought.

The transfer was quick from a jet to a plane. In fact it was a Fokker-50 twin-propeller plane. Soon we were in the air again. Light turbulence felt good. It empowered me. I was bonding with the new environment. The vision of jungle in all directions was becoming familiar. We drank beer constantly for the last hour of the flight. It was cold and refreshing with every guzzle. Lenny drank two for each one I drank. He is a big guy. Frisk savored his, choosing to sip and drink slowly. Lenny was now going on about wanting to go fishing, catch some big sharks, shooting them from the boat before gutting and throwing the mangled carcass back into the ocean. Eventually, we touched down on a gravel runway. It was bumpy, and the plane stopped quickly. I felt lost. This was way out of my comfort zone but right in the middle of Frisks.

The hot air pushed on me as I stepped from the plane and walked down the short staircase. Lenny and Frisk were in front of me. I had all I needed in my carry-on bag—shorts, shirts, socks, Falcon. All three of us sweated profusely; we had that in common. As we gathered our luggage, music played rather quietly in the background. It was from a legend. I caught part of the lyrics. "She looked at him with those soft eyes, so innocent and blue. He knew right there he was too far from home, too far from home." Yes, that is how I felt, too far from home.

# La Villa

WE STOOD OUTSIDE THIS SMALL AIRPORT SURROUNDED by dense jungle. It was hot outside. I had just bought a six-pack of bottled beer for each of us from the bar. This particular bar was basically a tent of sorts, with a rather nice setup inside. A very pleasant young lady worked the cash, selling mostly beer, liquor, and a few other things, like cigarettes, newspapers, and books. We all wore shorts, button-up silk shirts (hanging out), running shoes, hats, and dark sunglasses. The shirts had a pocket on the right side. Lenny had a pack of smokes tucked in his. After a brief walk, we were lying on the grass in the small park across from the airport terminal entrance. We were being forced to wait until the next rental car was returned. The rental place was out of vehicles for a couple hours.

I was just looking down the long dirt road into this little airport, constantly sipping beer and watching a small trail of dust approaching. In a couple of minutes, a dark red—no, dusty dark red convertible—Chevrolet Impala appeared. The Chevy parked just a few feet past us, half on the lawn, half on the road. It was an old model with the top down. The rear turning lights had three small circular lights on each side. Around the key lock on the trunk was a balloon-shaped design. The license plate was between the turning lights. Other than that, rather plain white leather interior.

The Impala caused a small dust cloud. It just settled in the area. Frisk looked at the car. "Looks like a beat-up old red whale to me." A blonde was driving, from what I could tell, with spiked hair and dark sunglasses. She got out and walked slowly toward us. Holy God, it was Holly. My heart stopped. She was as hot as the last time I had seen her—short Levis shorts, halter top, skin tanned native brown. Holly pulled her dark sunglasses down over her nose, exposing beautiful blue eyes. She smelled wonderful. Nice perfume.

"Hello, Tommy. Well, that was a piece of piss, but I am happy to see you." Holly was referring my poor pool playing, which landed her here, and gave me a brief hug, her British accent still sexy.

"Love your hair, nice. So good to see you, Holly. You look beautiful," I said, standing quickly, looking into her eyes, searching for answers.

"Well, holy old fuck. Look who it is, your little sweetie, Tommy. By God, Tommy, you did good with this young honey," Lenny said, drinking long from the tall beer bottle with one hand, a cigarette burning between two fingers on the other hand. We were all happy to see a familiar face. It was hugs all around. Then we loaded our stuff into the trunk and jumped into the red whale.

Holly sat in the driver seat. I was beside her. The other two were in the back seat. She spun to greet us, but before saying anything, she leaned over and kissed me full on the lips. Holly's passion was strong, closing her eyes, holding the moment before slowing falling back into her seat.

A British accent explained, "Hector told me to pick up some gringo's at the airport. Said it was some old friends. He laughed, then said Sylvia had called. She told him Tommy and Frisk were coming here. And good to see you too, Lenny. Hector wants to meet in a few days and have a chat, to play some pool, but for now, you can stay with us at our little home away from home."

We were all feeling drunk and more relaxed. Holly took us to a beautiful Spanish-style villa. Many cabins, hotels with casinos, homes, and shops help make up the place. We were staying at a small gated community where Holly lived with other friends and workers. Hector ran this whole setup and much more.

"Jesus God Almighty, what have you got us into. Tommy, I gotta go play some blackjack, don't ya know," said Lenny after he saw the casinos. While waiting to see the fields, Lenny was hoping to play some cards, some blackjack at the local casino. That was his big goal.

Frisk did not say anything at first. He knew where he was and where he had to go. For now, it was stay cool and be vigilant. Then he spoke. "Hector is powerful, but the man he works for has even more power. That is my chief, Poncho. Soon, we will need to leave here for his villa. We will be back in a few days. Then Tommy can play some pool and we can think about getting out of here."

Frisk was calm, looking about nonchalantly, not just looking but checking the area. Then he warned us about something I never really thought about. "It is not the cartels we should fear but the police. They can raid at any time, and when they figure out who we are, out of place, they might stop by and ask questions. Plus, it gives them a good reason to harass Hector and maybe try to bust him, depending on their mood. Good idea to do some gambling. It will help us blend in for the short time we are here."

The day was getting late, and I was tired. We all had our own bachelor-style suite, ground floor, small private yard, very nice of Hector. I stretched out and fell asleep. Frisk stayed in his room for now, meditating, stretching, planning. Lenny unpacked, showered, and hit the casino.

Lenny was showered, clean-shaven, and smelling good as he walked down the ancient stone street. "I am ready," he said loudly, walking into one of several casinos on this strip.

A difference in air pressure felt cool and refreshing. Lenny enjoyed air conditioning. It was a casino—large, loud, lots of security and lots of slot machines. Lenny checked out the different table games, having no time for the slots. After a few minutes, he sat down at an empty table, just Lenny and the dealer. Lenny was doing some quick thinking. One on one. This is the best scenario, as a player will play the maximum number of games and play multiple hands at the same time.

It was a six-deck shoe, where the cut card was placed near the rear. The dealer shuffled after each shoe. There were no automatic shufflers.

This helps with shuffle tracking because the dealers all follow a set shuffling routine. Lenny, being an advantage player, studied these patterns like a pool player knows every clock-pattern shot. All this worked in Lenny's favor. Even a slight imbalance in the odds to favor the player could be devastating to the casino. The lion approached the sheep, a shadow fell upon this casino.

"Good evening, ma'am. You look very nice tonight." Lenny was always complimentary—well, most of the time, anyway. He pulled out a large bankroll of hundred-dollar bills. In fact, he had twenty-five thousand with him.

She said, in Spanish and English, "Changing one thousand."

The cash was pushed into the money box, and Lenny was handed his chips. The table's minimum bet was one hundred. The maximum bet, ten thousand. The game started immediately from a new shoe. Lenny was now in a card game.

"Place your bets." Lenny put down two hundred-dollar bets, in two spots. Six cards were dealt, four up for Lenny, one up for the dealer, one down. Lenny had twelve and eighteen against a dealer's two. Lenny hit the first hand for a nine to get twenty-one. He stayed on the second hand. The dealer flipped her card over. It was a ten, for twelve. She flipped another ten for twenty-two and a bust. Lenny won both hands.

Lenny screamed, "Jesus Christ, holy God. Thank you, Jesus."

There were strong religious overtones in this part of the world, lots of crosses and baby Jesus effigies, most of them with a serious tan. The count was negative three. Lenny doubled the bets and played again, a blackjack and a nineteen. Dealer lost again. The games went in Lenny's favor, and he quickly ran up the chips. The count dropped to minus fourteen. Usually, this is bad for betting, and a player must be careful.

Lenny played his basic strategy correctly for a low count. The dealer complimented him, "Very good play, *senor*. You know your game. You are very lucky tonight." She continued to shuffle the cards and talk while Lenny studied the card patterns.

Lenny was very forthcoming. "I recognize I am in a trend. I am going to win games if I follow my plan. I can't lose." She laughed too, not realizing he was right. She would continue to lose.

Lenny made several blackjacks and many double-downs and splits to collect heavily. If this had been a pool game, Lenny would have been considered in dead stroke. He amazed the dealer and others as he predicted cards' appearance with uncanny accuracy. The last shoe he played was classic. The count went up fast to twenty, the dream of a card-counter. Lenny went for it, making maximum table bets from a number of positions. It got the casino's attention, and they were tracking him, but it was too late. The damage was done. He played quietly, humming and hawing every so often. He did not drink much but smoked constantly. That should have been the tip off for the casino, but they missed it. His playing and betting pattern with shuffle tracking threw off the pit bosses from thinking he was card counting. They were confused and a step behind as Lenny won with both high and low counts. He just appeared very lucky.

At the end of it all, Lenny was up over one hundred and ninety thousand dollars and had met a few new friends. He had a keen sense of when to quit. Soon he cashed out to his credit card and went over to one of those new friends for a nightcap. Later, he got to his villa safely, then passed out for a deep, restful sleep.

It was after midnight local time. I had slept for six or so hours and waking up slowly. The shower was hot and refreshing. I hung my arms from the shower nozzle, stretching, relaxing, when I felt the hands on my back. I was startled, turning around quickly, catching Holly as she slipped into the shower with me. Her wet, hot body pressed against mine. Our mouths kissed deeply. We showered together, slowly washing and caressing each other. No words were spoken.

We toweled down. Holly went into the bedroom while I opened the bathroom window. A nice breeze drifted into the suite. When I went into the bedroom, Holly was lying flat on her stomach, arms reaching out long in front of her. She was beautiful. Her long legs slightly spread. Her body was completely tanned, no tan lines. *Nice*, I thought, *sexy*. Coming up behind her, I kissed her back, stroked her, and massaged the strong muscles in her shoulders. Soft moans came in muffled spurts, her face buried in the mattress.

She was totally relaxed. I knelt by her feet, admiring the beautiful lady spread out before me. The long legs slightly spread, her hips tilted naturally upwards, and her pussy shaved, exposing her narrow slit. Grabbing her ankles, spreading her legs a bit more, I began kissing those legs upwards until my tongue was tickling her ass and running the narrow gap between pussy lips. Her moaning deepened. Those hips pushed into my face. I licked deeper and longer, from the tip of her clit, up the slit, across her ass, to the base of her spine and back again. The taste was sweet and felt sticky and warm. I continued licking her from behind for some time. I stretched out on my stomach too, burying my face in her ass. Sometimes, my head would be still as she humped her hips against my face. Her pussy was swollen and hot. She was becoming restless.

Climbing on top of Holly, my stiff cock easily slipped into her. Holly pushed, and my cock was in to the hilt. She fucked me slowly and sometimes quickly while I stretched out on top of her. The room lights were off. Light from the villa held our bodies in shadow. I pulled back, and she got on her knees. Holly's back ached, blonde head deep in the mattress, ass raised high in the air. I began fucking Holly from behind. Her pussy was perfect on my cock, holding me firmly. She stopped to ask something. "Shag me hard, then pull out of me quickly, then back into me. My pussy will cum longer and more powerful with your cock being pulled quickly and completely out of me, then back in to the hilt, then out again fast. This type of fucking will drive me wild. I have something for you too. When you think you are going to cum, I want you to wiggle your toes. Do that a lot. For some reason, wiggling your toes when fucking me will slow down your orgasm. It will stop you from cumming. Give it a try."

Her ass reached higher and higher as I fucked her relentlessly, relaxing my legs by wiggling my toes until she came in uncontrolled spasms from deep inside her groin. Finally, Holly slid off my cock, moaning, well satisfied for the moment.

"Wiggling my toes definitely worked. I wonder where you learned that one. And by the way, what the fuck have you done to your hair? Last time I saw you, you were a brunette."

I rolled over and faced Holly but was a little premature with the questions. Her eyes were still rolling in her head, her body experiencing small orgasmic quivers. I had certainly learned something about a woman's pussy in that moment. The withdrawing of my cock from deep inside her to outside, emphasizing the last few inches, making that part as quick as possible, drove Holly wild with desire. Sort of the opposite of a pounding her twat. Instead, the force was on the way out. I was hitting a much more sensitive part of her body with that style of stroke. She was still cumming.

Her arms encircled my neck. Her lips fell upon mine. Holly slowly came back. "Bleeding nice to see you, Tommy. Thank you." Her eyes closed, and her head rested on my shoulder. "Check the small table by the bed. I brought you a present."

"What could this be?" I feigned naivety. On the coffee table was a bag with white powder, a bag of weed, and a bottle of local whiskey with some water glasses.

Holly laughed. "Got that at the local boot sale." We spent the next twenty minutes cutting slits, or very narrow lines, of the best cocaine on earth. The small line of coke before me briefly reminded me of Holly as she lay on her stomach, legs spread open, that narrow slit between her legs. I was still horny, thinking about how sexy her pussy was from behind.

We did the lines. Then she teased me with the bag of weed. "Guess what's in here?"

I reviewed the weed, "Let's see now. This weed you brought is dark red in color, the odor sweet, a tinge of mountain pine lingering in my nostrils. Holly, you have given me Colombian Red, or Colombian Rojo Haze, or as the locals like to say, Punta Roja."

Soon I rolled a slim New-York-City joint. I told Holly about this style of joint. "This skinny style of joint rolling was taught to me by my near brother and great friend, Johnny, back at Carmichaels. He would warn me, if I ever went to New York City, they have extremely powerful weed there. In fact, so powerful you must roll very skinny joints, or you will get too stoned."

Holly was already stoned and said, "Ohh, will I be praying to baby Jesus to come down?" smiling and laughing and moving her arms about.

We smoked deeply, enjoying each exquisite toke. Blowing a small smoke ring I said to Holly with acceptance, "This was the prize we have sought, the holy grail of weed."

Holly now gave me a lesson on Colombian Rojo. Speaking slowly, passion in her eyes, she began, "This is the Sativa strain of weed you have been searching for. The plant is red by its genetics and will turn dark red when left for a late harvest at the lower elevations. The longer the buds stay on the plant, the bigger, redder, and stickier they become. This only happens at the lower elevations. Colombian Rojo grows very large, the yields are in the pounds from each plant and must be planted properly. Frisk knows how to grow this strain very well. This is a different type of Sativa. It does not make a person paranoid or anxious. But instead, it is a more intense cerebral stone, and the effect is long-lasting. It is perfect for morning or daytime smoking. This is the plant you want to put in your fields, Tommy. The trichomes are approximately 100 microns in length, longer and thicker than other weed and therefore well suited for hashish production. How is that for an update?"

I told Holly what I was thinking. "I am thinking you were listening when I would ramble on about my plans to grow Sativa genetics and manufacture hashish. Incredible. I love ya."

I was reveling in her description of exactly what I had been searching for. "Thank you, Holly. Thank you." I moved on, "So, how have you been, Holly?" Holly began to fill in the last few months.

"I like when you say my name." Interesting, Catina said the same thing. Then came the answer: "The men here never call me by my name. They never call me Holly. It is just *chica* or the girl."

"Holly, you are experiencing cultural differences." I tried to express empathy. "I do understand the *chica* thing, but I would not practice cultural expropriation myself."

Holly understood it was not personal. She went on, "Bollocks. Guess what this cartel had in mind for me. Get this." The British accent was now strong and sexy. I kissed her lips. We each took shots of whiskey indigenous to this area. It was strong. "They are extortionist, and I was recruited to be part of this particular group. Hector wanted me for this job from the first time he saw me at the pub. What he didn't know was the amount I know about your projects, as you called them, a bonus for him. Well, your projects went from small scale to international in a couple of years. Good work, Tommy, and yes, I told him most everything I knew. What did I care? I had no idea the drama you and Frisk created. They never told me anything, and I had no reason to ask. I was gone before any of the shit happened, remember?" Sarcasm was evident in her tone, but she was still friendly.

"It just sort of happened." I was not good trying to explain the obvious.

"We are fucking extortionists. We force unfortunates who come here and party too much, lose too much money gambling, or happen to be in the wrong place at the wrong time. We fuck them and subject them to violence until a blackmail ransom is paid. We film lots of it, take pictures, and start sending them to family and friends if they refuse to pay up. More regularly, the ransom is not paid fast enough, sometimes taking several days. At that point, if no payment came about, they are sold, and we move on. Wives and husbands are forced to watch each other fuck for hours, sometimes days. Drug addiction begins from the start. We force them to drink heavily, snort cocaine, and smoke and inject heroin. The women just collapse once that starts, not much resistance at all. She will do whatever we say, especially after being kept awake for days and days."

I commented, "Sounds very dangerous." I could see now why Sylvia was worried about Holly.

"Yeah. No feeling on earth more freaky than walking down the hallway in a hotel somewhere knowing you are going there to fuck a stranger. And not just fuck some guy but to extort a family. People now on the hook for a hundred thousand or more must pay, or else the blackmail continues, then violence. The person is soon lost, and they become meat being used until we were done with them. Before my first job, I was told to change my hair. They wanted blonde and spiked like this, so this is what I did. Like it? They said we were there to get money and embarrass and intimidate the people. That was our part. They were always checking out couples or men or women who were out of place, who could be preyed upon, who had money. Once the cartel knew there was money to be had, they moved in on them. Usually, a heavy would enter their hotel room and explain the situation they were now involved in. They were told to find a large sum of money and have it deposited into a certain bank account. Very simple, actually. Not one person or couple ever paid up immediately. At that point, myself and a couple of the men would show up."

"Yeah, take that long walk down a dark and lonesome hotel hallway somewhere." I was being understanding. "Please, go on."

"My first extortion experience was with a young couple who were slow to pay. We were demanding seventy-five thousand dollars. Ashley, the woman, was very beautiful. She had long, straight blonde hair, cut with short bangs, the long locks curled for a special occasion. Ashley was about five feet, eleven inches, long legs, wearing very sexy strap-on high heels. Her body was athletic and nicely tanned. She wore a medium-length skirt, summer blouse, and bra. Her eye shadow was a dark purple. The man was OK, in good shape and dressed formally. I thought, maybe they were at a wedding. They were frantic and scared. He was stripped naked, tied to a chair but with enough slack in his arms to move them about somewhat. He was given heavy drugs and whiskey until wired for sound. Then we put him sitting in front of the bed and went to work on his hot wife. The cameras were rolling, and the party began."

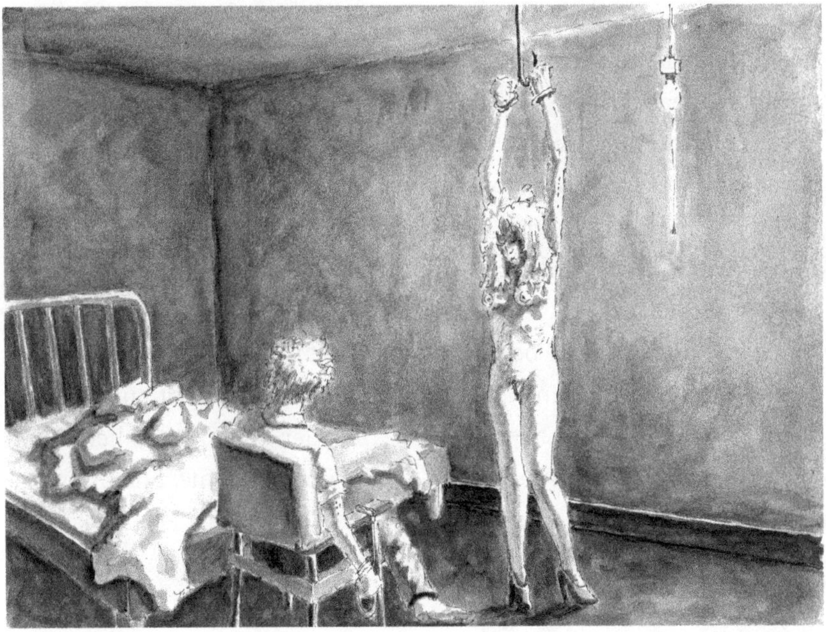

Holly went on, "Ashley was forced to drink whiskey and snort coke until she was stunned stupid. When she still resisted, we stood her up in front of everyone and handcuffed her hands over her head from a small hook in the ceiling. She was hung perfect, totally stretched out when limp, her high heels just touching the floor. Her toes pointed down, pushing her hips forward. It was a sexy picture.

"In front of her husband, I ripped open her blouse, pulled her tits from her expensive brassiere, and began the face and tit slapping. We slapped her face and tits for an hour, until long after her begging us to stop had fallen silent. Her dark-colored eyes watered, and she cried. The handcuffs bit into her wrists. The slaps were loud, each leaving a red welt on her face or tit. The sting hurt to Ashley's core, sometimes taking her breath away. Her tight bra held her exposed tits firmly in place for the beating, her nipples erect. We all took turns slapping her. I sometimes slapped Ashley as hard as I could in the face. Her head spun, blonde hair following with the force. My hand hurt. Then I would slap her with my other hand, and her head and hair would snap the other way. It was fun to do that five or six times in a row, leaving her dizzy. Sort of rang her clock. Her ears must have been ringing as many slaps got Ashley in the side of the head.

"Sometimes she would yelp, sometimes moan. Her blonde hair, sweet face, and six-pack stomach was soaked from sweat, tears, and drool. The men were impressed when she began to moan, 'Thank you' and 'I love you,' as she dangled from the ceiling, the cute curls in hair now gone.

"The poor husband begged us to stop, but we didn't. His fear got us more excited. Clips and buttons were undone, her skirt pulled down and off. When she was begging us to fuck her, we stripped her naked while hanging there and slapped her tits one at a time. She hung her head watching, yelping from the sting of each attack. Her legs spread, her pussy swollen. I pulled up a chair and put one of her legs on each side of my head and licked Ashley's pussy for a long time. It was a comfortable position for me, she just dangled there, moaning, cumming, submitting to my tongue and fingers. We all partied hard with lots of whiskey and cocaine. I licked from her tailbone to her belly button. The husband had this very stiff cock in his hands. I too stripped, showing off my tits and pussy. I would suck his cock and balls while his wife watched him cum in my mouth. She just hung there leering as I rode him reverse cowgirl, my pussy wet, his cock up to the balls inside me. I necked with him, and he told me he loved me in front of his wife. I came a lot fucking him in front of her." Holly was getting horny recalling the experience.

"Finally, we took her down and forced her to walk—no, strut—to the bed in her high heels, where we all took turns fucking the living hell out of his woman for a long time. Her husband watched just feet from the raw fucking she was taking. We laughed at him as he jerked his cock, watching her fuck relentlessly."

"We fucked her long and hard. We fucked her unconscious and then conscious. It was funny to see the weak look on her red face when she would wake to find her legs up in the air, and a big black guy stuffing his large cock into her body, over and over. And then to realize the situation she was in, and then to realize it was not the same person fucking and groping her as when she passed out."

"Who are you?" she would moan, arms stretched out over her head, loosely holding the bedposts, her body sloshing about with each new thrust into her.

Holly liked this woman. "I would sleep with her, holding her close to me, my tits on her back and kissing her neck. We would awaken, and I would spread my legs over her face, her tongue always finding my small round clit and sucking it endlessly. Ashley became very good at eating my pussy while waiting for payment. The men got very hard cocks watching me play with Ashley."

"Soon, the men took her and put her on top of one of those cocks, her ass and pussy spread open. All the poor husband could see was his wife's ass, legs spread wide across a man's hips, her pussy wrapped tight around a cock fucking her over and over until his cum ran down her legs. This gave the husband a raging hard-on. At first, he did not want to jerk himself off as the slack allowed him to grab his cock. That did not last long. Soon he was beating his cock faster than his wife was being fucked.

After he came the first time, he was upset and guilty, but he soon got hard again. We flipped his wife around reverse-cowgirl style so she could watch him jerk off while he watched her spread-open cum-soaked twat fuck. She was made to rotate just her hips, to use just her pussy to fuck each cock while rubbing her body against each new lover, one arm around his neck, holding him close, like a professional whore will do. Ashley's red and swollen tits were molested constantly all the while being French kissed and sucking a man's tongue. Each new lover had a cock that would fuck her pussy or asshole deep, balls deep, until he came. Ashley's body was full of fresh cum, sperm, and spit. Her mind was gone." Holly sounded indifferent at the moment.

Holly described more. "Sometimes, I would suck the husband's cock but not let him cum. We were nasty. At one point, when Ashley was unconscious, they gave her a tongue piercing, and I gave her a tattoo on her back. The tattoo was the outline of a single-angle wing. It started just inches above the crack of her ass and ended bellow her shoulder blades. It needed a lot more work, but it was large and permanent. Her husband begged us again to stop. When she woke up, there was a brand-new piercing and stud in her tongue. It was a nice pink one to match the eye shadow we put on her too. Her back was itchy. She didn't know she was sporting a rather promiscuous tramp stamp, and we didn't tell her. The heroin we gave her deadened a lot of the pain."

"Ashley freaked out about the tongue piercing when she tried to talk. She just stuttered and mumbled, trying to speak with a rather large stud in her tongue. I remember Ashley sitting in the middle of the bed, legs crossed, babbling and crying again. Her hands touching her face and tongue softly, tears fell in her straight matted hair. But Ashley submitted quickly to more whiskey and dope. Soon the piercing was put to good use. She happily blew everyone in the room, including me and her husband. She really could roll that stud across my clit and ever so sweetly between my pussy lips. And when she stuck her tongue and piercing inside my pussy I came all over her face, oh so many times." Holly was getting hot again.

"Eventually, the fun ended, and the family paid up. We packed up their stuff, drove them to the airport, and wished them well. Ashley needed a wheelchair to get her into the airport, as she could barely walk or talk from the fucking and serious heroin addiction. They were grateful, however, to be alive and getting the hell out of this place. Which brings me to us."

"Well, holy God, and here I thought you were relaxing in the sun, having a nice vacation." I knew as much about her existence after we split up as she knew about mine. "I must ask, though, Holly, it felt to me you enjoyed your work, and that is OK." I was trying to be supportive.

Turns out, it was not Holly's cup of tea. "Bleeding rubbish. Bollocks to that trash. As you would say, the party is over. Time to move on." It was true. She did know me. "Shag it and tell me, how are you going to make it up to me, then?" Holly was searching for a hero. She needed to win this time. She needed to get out of here. The heat was rising. I needed to win for her.

I was reassuring. "Do not worry, Holly. You will be coming with us when we leave here. Bring whatever you want, including a passport, if you have it, and be ready to bail out on short notice. I am here to settle things with Hector and Frisk with his boss, Poncho." We hugged each other, enjoying the wonderful buzz from two very powerful drugs. The front door bell chimed quietly. Someone was at the door. Putting on a shirt, I answered it.

It was Catina. "Good evening, Tommy. I missed you." She threw her arms around my neck and kissed me. I kissed her, then stepped back. She was with someone. A tall local gringo. He just smiled. "This is my—how you say?—special friend. This gringo, his name is Jose." No, I was not having another Shanelle experience, but I did invite them into my suite, into my bedroom. Holly sat up in bed, a sheet over her hips, the rest of her naked. They all knew each other. They were friends.

I found more glasses. Soon, we all shared a strong drink. Then it came back to me. "I am pissed at you for telling Hector about my invention and the patent to the point where he thinks he wants it, but he is wrong."

Catina could see it in my face. She knew I was upset. "Yes, it was me, as you know, but I did not fully realize what I was saying. At first, I was bragging for you. Then the truth was realized about your invention. The mood changed from indifference to very high interest to obsession. Hector is crazy about this thing. For that, I am sorry. I never meant to have that happen, for him to hate you, but it did."

What could I say? "It was inevitable, Holly. I realize it was not your fault. That makes sense, just as we spoke about last time in the schoolyard. It was you who told Hector about my invention. The patent spoke for itself. Once someone figured out its value and how it could change the world, it became very desirable. I am sure it was accidental enthusiasm, much the same way when I shared it with you. I know you told Hector everything, yet somehow, you remain indifferent."

She tried to explain her attitude. "I do not feel guilty. It was an unintentional mistake, and it is over." She demonstrated leadership, and I understood. That part was done with.

"From there, Poncho found out and told that old bounty hunter where to find you. The bounty hunter was very enthused. I know Poncho will be happy to see Frisk." Catina just confirmed what was obvious, the fact we must see Poncho. I was leering at Catina, and thinking she still wanted to fuck me.

"She still wants to fuck you Tommy." Holly laughed, she was empathetic while looking at Catina. She knew the feeling exactly of saying the wrong thing and getting Tommy further down the wrong road. "This is truly a case of 'if you don't know where you are going, any road will get you there.' It was true: us two women had no idea where we were going, and it got us there, to the same place and rather quickly. To a place where Hector believes you are a dangerous, rouge individual who wants a war. It could not be further from the truth. That is rather interesting." Holly said that rather simply and with insight.

The light was dim. We all shared more whiskey and smoke and narrow lines of very powerful cocaine. Holly and Catina took over. It was not complicated. We all stretched out on the same large bed. The women faced each other. I watched Catina fuck, and she watched me fuck Holly. It was poetic and restful. Then the women would switch, and I would be with Catina, watching Holly. The drugs, the women, the warm South American breeze rubbing gently on our skin, and most of all, the pale light of a small town with many secrets, touched all our faces. Jose and I lay on our backs as the women fucked each of us, sometimes on top, sometimes backwards, switching partners, gently playing, doing what they loved, what we loved.

Eventually, we all fell asleep with the women facing each other in the center of the bed. I was with Holly, my stomach on her back, my arms hugging her from behind. Catina was being held the same by Jose. My left hand rested on Holly's breast, her heart beating slowly beneath my fingers, then resting for that ever-so-fraction of a second before beating again. I felt love, and now I understood where love lived. Love lives in the spaces between heartbeats. I fell asleep holding Holly while looking into Catina's eyes.

# Poncho

MY DOOR WAS BEING POUNDED ON. IT WAS FRISK. I TOLD him to "Fuck off, come back in an hour." He came back in twenty minutes. By then, we were up. Holly served coffee and toast while talking about the universe and how the ego drives the individual. It was from some book she was reading between extortions. I laughed to myself. Holly left us the Impala for a couple of days. She knew we had work to do. The doorbell rang again. As Frisk and Lenny were coming in the front door, the rest of the tribe left through the back door.

Frisk was anxious to meet Poncho again. He was confident he could reason with him. We all loved the red whale and loaded it up with beer, whiskey, coke, Colombian weed, and several sandwiches we bought at a local deli. We were ready, and Frisk knew the way. He knew the road to take. Frisk drove slowly at first, then picked up the pace as we moved into the countryside. We enjoyed the ride, Frisk now driving just about as fast as he could, Lenny and I sitting in the back, drinking constantly, admiring the rolling mountains. Sometimes the road became bumpy. Sometimes it felt nonexistent, we pushed on at high speed. The road was long, but the drugs were better.

Lenny stated the obvious. "Man, oh man, boys, this is where Frisk confronts his boss, where we confront his boss. It will be a meeting of minds, a contract on a higher level, on an eternal level, don't ya know."

Frisk spoke up. "You are right, Lenny. We have to set it straight with Poncho first. Then we can move to the next issue. That is the order of the universe." Then he referenced the philosophical truths. "The universe will unfold one layer at a time as we roll through the infinite number of moments strung together, called reality. God exists in the ether between thoughts." He was being deeply philosophical.

It was mid afternoon when we came to a village. This was not a tourist resort like Hector was running. The fields in the distance hills turned to a lighter shade of green. My heartbeat went up. We were in the fields now, and Frisk was home. "Looks like you are home, Frisk. How does it feel?" He looked a little anxious. The car slowed.

Pulling the red whale over to the side of the road. Frisk formalized our plan. "This is it. Poncho lives very close. Those fields you see in the distance are just the beginning. They go for many miles in all directions past the horizon. That was my job—to grow and to protect." We all laughed at that pun. "You, Tommy, and Lenny are here because we are the team. Together we are doing this in the mountains and valleys in your backyard, in Val Lenny." Lenny smoked cigarettes and drank constantly. I just drank constantly. Frisk was looking around, taking it all in, reflecting, remembering, rationalizing his life.

*I must be shrewd.*

He went on again, "We have somehow managed to get ourselves to this production level, and it drew attention to us, to me. I feel responsible somewhat for this mess, but fuck it, here we are. I do not believe Poncho will kill us. He would have done that by now. No, he wants to meet me, to meet us and try to figure out or confirm what he presently knows. Like many things in life, Tommy, we must face our worst nightmares to end their existence." I was following what he said, relaxing, breathing, letting the universe unfold before me. Frisk detached for a moment, sinking into his seat behind the wheel, just looking at the countryside, truly enjoying this moment in time and space. We were all enjoying what was happening for several minutes.

Frisk had a bottle of whiskey and passed it to Lenny. "It is time for whiskey, boys, my favorite. You can only get it here in Colombia."

Lenny cracked the bottle and filled our water glasses mostly full. We each took a huge swig. Our eyes watered, throats burning. Lenny commented, "Jingling Jesus, Holy God, that is good whiskey," taking another hit.

I sat back in my seat watching Frisk cut up some lines. We did our share before sitting back again. My brain twisted, and I felt sick for a moment. Sweat ran down my forehead. Lenny was smoking and looking at the clouds. "Oh, the smell of the rush," I said out loud. My heartbeat had doubled in the last minute.

Frisk added, "Be grateful to be doing the best cocaine on earth." My brain caught up to my heart, and I was stoned. The car started. Frisk was taking us to Poncho.

The gate was large, but it was the armed guards—and armed with machine guns—that got my attention. And not a couple guards but several. They stared at us. Frisk laid on the horn. The sound, loud and piercing, caused them to step back a pace. Then the gates opened, and we entered in silence. Men wearing camouflage and army fatigues could be spotted across the landscape. It was late afternoon. At two thousand feet above sea level, the cool air mixed with a rare warm breeze, causing light fog to fill the area. It just sat there, much like the mercenaries, watching, waiting, hoping for the best.

Frisk drove slowly up a long crescent-style driveway. We approached from the right, slowly turning toward the left. The red whale pulled over in front of the house and stopped. The house was a mansion. Armed men sat and walked about in the distance. A nice Colombian lady approached, then greeted us, "Good afternoon, *senor*." Poncho knew we were coming. The three of us causally walked into Poncho's home. We entered under a large half-circle brick archway. The stone was all beautiful reds, greens, and blues.

I said to Frisk, "It's tall enough to ride a horse in here." There were crucifixes and holy pictures throughout. "A very religious-looking place." We walked past the foyer onto a large and vacant outdoor patio area. It sported a brick barbeque, and in the far end was a pool and hot tub. Beyond that, mountains filled the landscape. We sat in comfy armchairs under a beautiful Colombian sky. Drinks were already served. Lenny smoked constantly, saying nothing, instead observing and learning. Frisk waited.

From inside his home, Poncho began speaking in Spanish. "Today, you stand on a razor blade Frisk. You were like a son to me. I raised you as my own. Others have died for lesser sins." He walked toward us. Sweat on his blemished, marked face was dabbed dry by a small handkerchief he carried. The age in his face reflected experience, wisdom, and strength. His silk shirt was open, exposing his hairy chest. Many gold chains hung about his neck. Long dark pants covered his legs, and he wore black loafers on his feet, supporting an athletic two-hundred-pound frame. A slim gold watch was on this left wrist, a gold chain on the other.

Frisk was humble. His was a different plan, one of direct confrontation. "I could not hope to beat you, Poncho. Therefore, I knew I must come back here to see you again, to explain, to ask forgiveness." Frisk threw himself at the mercy of Poncho.

Poncho walked toward Lenny and me. We both stood immediately, acting solemn as if at church and the pope had shown up. He shook our hands, then moved toward Frisk. As we stared at each other, a tension was building. We were all at the mercy of Poncho. Poncho walked toward Frisk, looking him up and down, admiring the man he had become. "You have been missed, my friend. How have you been?" They shook hands and embraced each other.

Frisk responded, "It has been difficult, lonely sometimes, but I am OK. When I left, it was all so fast. I never meant to hurt anyone. I was young, well trained, and powerful. I wanted to know my past, who I was. Those people offered me a chance to do that, so I acted." He was cut short by Poncho.

Poncho had his own feelings. "Stop. I know more than you think. The threat of force is never as good as force itself. Threats never bothered you because you are the force. We had little idea at first where you went. We did figure out it was the German couple. We went to Germany, but it was too late. You had left for the West Coast. That was all the information we got from them before they died. It was tragic. That was where a bounty hunter was sent to try and find you. He did a very good job. He used one of the women extorted by Hector to get into the country." Poncho was laughing, somewhat akin to Sylvia when she talked about the same guy. "However, he completely underestimated you, Frisk. You nearly killed him. For not dying, he is cursed to ever hunt you down, to kill you."

Frisk told the truth. "I was trying to kill him. Never expected I would be found again either. How was I to know I would run into you?" Frisk was now talking to Poncho. "Poncho, you live in a world of madness and nonsense. I cannot live like that. I needed to find out who I am, what I was meant to be. I am grateful to understand much more today. We can offer you so much more. I brought my partners Tommy and Lenny with me. I am sorry. It was like the Greek tragedies we studied. We are living the dream. All was going very well like the hero flying closer to the sun. Then it begins to go bad. The signs are missed, mistakes are made, disaster imminent. I saw the signs and averted disaster by leaving you, and I hope to have averted disaster by coming back."

I leaned over to Lenny and said, "Nicely said, Frisk."

Lenny quietly responded. "Jesus Christ, Tommy, he was fucking well educated, don't you know."

Poncho spoke, "After we lost contact with you on the West Coast, things settled down. We mourned our loss and moved on. Soon we forgot about you, but I secretly wondered where you were, how you were doing. We never expected to see you again. Nearly killing the man who went after you certainly confirmed he had the right person. The guy who found you was one of the best, and he was no challenge to you. I was impressed and happy you beat him. You earned your release—how you say?—graduation. But you left the fields unguarded. You left your post, and those crimes warrant serious punishment."

Frisk said quietly, almost under his breath in Spanish, "Closing doors on the past will open new ones in the future." He was thinking what Lenny had said on the flight here.

Poncho already knew the answers and the outcome. "As you once said to me, it is not what you want but what you are going to get. Careful what you desire for. I too wanted you to find yourself to evolve into the man you are today. Yes, the son had to leave home to finish the training. I did not expect it to happen as it did. However, you are complete. So be it. You have embraced the universe." Poncho expressed acceptance with his arms and face, then closure.

Frisk relaxed, telling our story. "Today, it is different. I am training Tommy and Lenny to operate large fields. I am training Graham and Raff to protect those fields, but we are not in competition with you. I would never have guessed who was behind all this, but we can work together. I have come here to make peace, to ask to work again but in my true home. There is much to do in that part of the world to benefit you." Then, in perfect Spanish, Frisk told Poncho again, this time with conviction, "Closure on the past will open doors in the future. We are helping but in a different part of the world. We are only strong together. I have my home now, and we want to share with you all that will help you."

He switched back to English. "Tommy and Lenny have brought much to the table for you and without prejudice. There was no malice toward you. They did not even know who you were. It was after meeting Hector and Sylvia and killing Nailer that we knew we must make peace, to ask forgiveness from you. We can do the job for you. We can work with Sylvia, let her be our contact, and we will honor your flag." Frisk and Poncho shared a moment of silence. Again acceptance and commitment were exchanged. It was over.

Poncho turned and walked about the patio, talking with Frisk. Lenny and I sat watching, drinking. After a short time, they walked our way. Then Poncho began, "Your instincts still serve you well. Killing that fool Nailer was needed, and you too, Tommy, killed without hesitation. Sylvia told me of your fight and how Frisk hung him off the end of a pool cue." Poncho laughed again, then became serious, "I am proud of you, Frisk. I am also the Chief—powerful, respected, and feared. Respect is earned. I have earned my respect, and you have earned yours. For that, I respect you, Frisk, but I do not fear you."

Lenny looked at me with relief and a big grin. "Good thing we passed the job interview. Otherwise, we would be dead." I just nodded.

Poncho was reasonable. "I see the bigger value. I understand how important it is to stay friends in business. I agree, we clear the air. Now that you are at peace, we are at peace. Tommy and Lenny have truth and honor in their hearts. You have come here as one. If I were to kill Frisk for his sin, I would kill everyone. Coming here proves you want change, you embrace challenge. My challenge is the extension, the creation, of a new cartel in your homeland. We must all work together or face terrible consequences."

Frisk waited, then looking at Tommy spoke, "I knew Poncho would want to claim our territory, to extend a family there." I nodded with acceptance while looking at Poncho.

Poncho spoke of my challenge. “First, Tommy must clear the air with Hector. You have things he would like. You have a patent worth many dollars, honor, and a woman. He is a very jealous man.” Poncho was being sincere and laughing lightly, moving his arms about. “I cannot decide that future. I will only support the outcome. If you two like pool so much, then pool it is. Play the games of your choice at your leisure. When it is over, both sides must agree, and the final peace will be had. It must be clear: the objective is to grow our business, to extend my cartels. Soon, a new cartel will be born. It is so.” An order was given.

“So be it.” Lenny spoke up loudly, startling us, half drunk. A cigarette was burning to the end between his fingers without being smoked, the ash nearly as long as the original cigarette. He just let it burn away. Poncho looked at Lenny, then at the cigarette ash, before resuming. I shook my head and looked back toward Poncho.

Poncho refocused, walking and moving his arms about, talking with his hands. “Once that is done, I will personally grant you the eternal license to grow weed and produce hashish in your region, forever. I will ensure you receive many hundred pounds of the finest Punta Roja to your doorstep at your home. There will be enough seeds to start an incredible operation. You must manage the seed production from there. Further, you must train new guardians and captains to grow weed and produce hashish. To honor my flag, as you have done, with Tommy and Lenny and your team. Your work will soon rival the Beqaa Valley in Lebanon and Riff mountains of Morocco.” This was the job description. It was his vision, and it was our vision.

I spoke to Poncho. “You are truly happy to see Frisk again, aren’t you?” Poncho gave the slightest of nods in agreement.

Frisk understood very well. He spoke to us all. “Poncho, my father, taught me to never show weakness. My father taught me to do or die. Guns before food. We have to take what we want in this world, and if it does not exist, we create it. Tommy has a machine of great value and worth. He is a genius. Together we are stronger when we all do the part we were born to do." Frisk walked, then stood behind us. Poncho saw us together as a powerful team.

Sitting at the table, glasses of whiskey were poured. Poncho gave us one more lesson. "If you want to deal drugs, have no gun battles in your house. I will make sure your bounty hunter is told to give up his quest, his revenge." We laughed and toasted to eternal peace.

Frisk spoke of his personal interest with this problem, "And if he defies you? If he continues to track me, to follow his rage? I am not worried, but I do want this point to be very clear."

"If he defies me, you do what you do best. If there is a next time, it is up to you to ensure it is the final time." Poncho was talking business. Frisk was given an order just then.

Poncho looked at me and paused, waiting. I spoke. "Hector is next on the list. This battle could be a show-stopper for me, but I must win for my dignity. I must now prove I can live and operate at the level of Hector, in a world where violence could erupt at any time."

Poncho spoke to me. "It is up to Tommy to make the final peace." It was an order.

My response was short and honest. "I will not fail to correct this problem. Nor will I lose my honor."

Poncho smiled. "So, this is your team. I am happy to welcome you to my home. *Mon casa su casa.*"

He shook Lenny's hand. When he shook my hand, it was with a new confidence. We locked eyes. I felt his power. His strength was my strength. Turning toward Frisk, he spoke. "Enjoy a night in the fields, a night at your old home. Then, tomorrow, it will be time to go to your new home, to get back to work."

A light lunch was shared. More drinks and a relaxing couple of hours finished up our visit. Frisk looked confident, a higher level of life trust reached. Frisk's energy shifted. He was now anxious to take us on a tour of the fields. "It is time to go. Thank you, and we will meet again soon." Poncho understood. Hands were shaken, and we departed.

Soon we were back in the red whale driving slowly uphill, toward the mountains, toward the fields. Lenny was giggling and getting the load on. "I am right there with you, Lenny."

After driving until dark, parking, and hiking for two hours, I finally spoke to Frisk. "I know we are in a huge field of pot plants, the sound of wild animals is unnerving. And by the way, what the fuck are we doing?" The darkness hid a perspective on the scale of the operation.

Frisk knew the way but had to comment. "Trust me, I know what I am doing." It was very late when we walked up to a spot with a small yurt. A fire was started. We smoked and drank under a clear, moonless night. It was dark. Only the stars and the unfamiliar patterns they made brightened our faces. The sound of wild animals big and small surrounded us. There was no easy escape just now.

Frisk was laughing. "This is one of my old rest spots. There are many over the long distance these valleys reach out into. It was out there I met Raff and others too." We all sat in silence.

Frisk commented on the meeting. "The time with Poncho was not long but most valuable. Then again, he knew everything about us from Hector and others. He knew I would come here. That was his true goal, to get me here, to meet me again. He was able to weigh the stories, decide for himself, and act accordingly. Poncho is worthy of being the chief, the boss. He shared the divine insight with Sylvia. His blood was royal."

I waited for a pause, then spoke, not wanting to interrupt Frisk. "I could buy into that. Just make sure we get the job done. Follow the orders given today."

Lenny got his two cents in. "Snappin' arseholes, Frisk. That fucked piece of shit chasing you will not stop. He might even go after Poncho for trying to get him to end his pursuit. He is a fucking reptile, and you gotta kill that snake. Uhmm, man on man. Twist the fuckers head clean motherfucking off." Lenny had a way with words.

"Wake me when the coffee is on." I finally stretched out on a soft foam mat. The strong odor of fresh weed filled my nose, and I was asleep.

When I awoke, it was raining. A light beating on the roof. I lay there relaxing, listening. Birds were chirping. Small animals hustled about.

My nose filled with the wonderful full-bodied aroma of Colombian Rojo and Colombian Gold plants nearing maturity, as well as coffee brewing. I stood, stretching inside the slowly brightening yurt. Then the rain stopped.

Outside now, Frisk was making coffee, and I soon joined in. The yurt was on a small ledge overlooking an ever-widening valley. The sun, rising in the east, was a bright orange ball. I had to say something. "Weed is everywhere. It goes for fifty miles in all directions. Hunter would die to see this. Someday, I am sure he will." I then looked closer at the plants. "These stalks are anywhere from four feet high to over eight feet high. All healthy female plants with buds developing according to plan A. I am very happy to be here. Lenny, you look at home as much as Frisk does. You guys feel safe, don't ya?" They smiled and drank their coffee.

The sunrise was memorable. Stretching my back again, hands on hips, looking up toward the sky, I saw the vapor trail from a jet airline heading into Medellin. Yelling at Frisk, I asked him, "Hey, Frisk, I wonder, do they see the smoke from our fire? Do curious passengers know it is fields of weed to supply the world's need for hashish, just miles below them?"

Frisk spoke naturally. "Few would know the truth or want to know the truth. It is too dangerous."

I laughed. "And yet, here we are, sleeping and having coffee in the middle of it all. I wonder if spy satellites are taking our pictures just now." I strained to look deeper into the sky.

We spent the day wondering, enjoying, recording, and learning. We saw water systems that supplied thousands of plants. Frisk showed us how the males were separated for seed production. "Picking the right seeds, with the right phenol type, is beyond critical. You must look closely at the fields for the greener color; longer, skinnier leaves, with pine and fruity aromas. These are the signs indicating premium plants, and therefore, hopefully seeds too. Seed production in the operation, is as equal in importance, as making the fully mature, seedless females. In order to propagate the species from season to season, it is absolutely imperative many tens of thousands of viable seeds be produced."

Frisk showed us boxes of glass jars, and hundreds of canvas bags in nice, neat piles, used to store seeds from the ripe plants. "Seeds must be healthy and properly stored until next season. Each bag will hold about twenty pounds of seeds and is kept in a cool, dark place. The next season, we plant until the fields are full and trade the remainder for different, healthy seeds or other things we might need. It is your basic barter system—nothing complicated."

Frisk was giving us a short lesson about plants at different elevations. "These plants we see here, in the valleys, are mostly Punta Roja, as the locals call them. They are exactly what we want for our fields, the prize, Colombian Red. These plants will take longer to mature, and the warmer valleys are conducive to excellent harvests. Plants at higher altitudes in the mountains mature earlier in the season."

This was already evident by bigger, fuller buds as we walked uphill. "These are Colombia Gold plants. The later in the season they are harvested, the deeper the gold color becomes. These plants make excellent brown Lebanese-style hashish. The options are vast. Some plants were making seeds." We pushed these buds between our fingers to find large, healthy brown seeds forming. These were the ones we wanted. Lenny took extensive notes on the fields, location, variety, and harvest time.

Lenny had a lot of notes. He had what he needed. "Well, boys, I got what I needed. Soon time to get the fuck out of here." The day was getting on.

Frisk took one last look around, his heart heavy. "I know who I am. I know it is OK to leave, to return with you, Tommy. I have found my home, and it is not here." Soon, we were in the red whale making a high-speed run back to Villa Hector.

Once back, it was time to relax. Holly was waiting. We shared strong whiskey and thin lines again. Holly spoke of her conversation with Hector earlier today. "I talked with Hector, and the bloke wants to see us tomorrow, around noon, at a local pool hall. It is a small place in a busy part of town. He should feel safe from Old Bill there. Bloody hell, it is an outside place and very public. You will see tomorrow." Holly and I slept well together. We awoke rested. It would be a big day.

# Nine-Ball

THIS WOULD BE OUR LAST DAY HERE, HAVING CHECKED OUT of Hotel Hector earlier. Holly had parked the red whale on a side street. It was safe. We had all our luggage locked in the trunk. Frisk and Lenny went shopping. Holly walked with me up the alley and onto the street, if it could be called that.

Talk about outside now. This place is a slaughterhouse. The street was dirt, hard-packed dirt. Many different shops sold cloth, spices, tofu, snakes, and God-only-knows what else on both sides of the street. Chickens and roosters roamed freely, making loud noises randomly. Hector could feel safe here, as it was his hometown. The poolroom consisted of four professional nine-foot tables under a large tent structure. Dirt floor, open in the front allowed people wearing sandals, shorts, and muscle shirts to play pool or bet on the games openly. We would play at the back.

The ice cream cone I was eating melted quicker than expected, running down my chin before staining my new shirt right in the middle. Chuckling, I thought about the Kid—his look, his laugh, his confidence. The Kid was with me in spirit, a vision of his presence now clear in my mind. I was sitting at a small square table near the back of this rural pool hall. I imagined the Kid sitting with me discussing strategy to beat Hector.

There was nothing special or obvious about this wood table I was sitting at, just a square bar table with burnt cigarette tracks and sturdy enough to support many bottles of beer. A person could dance on this table. It was a bright, hot day. Dogs found shade under parked cars and chairs. A rather ugly woman was window shopping in the street. For a moment, our gazes locked. Her face was long. Wrinkles and small scars reflected a difficult life. She broke our stare but continued looking into the poolroom as her trudge resumed.

The cone finished now so I waved at the female bartender and ordered a local beer by sign language. She brought it over with all the elegance of a woman who had not been fucked in a year. I was checking her out. This was a well-built woman and probably well fucked, despite my previous thought. She is short and tough looking, athletic and very sexy. Spiky black hair, cut square at the back, matched her long rectangular head. Her face sported black square-rim glasses, beneath them a stone-cold stare. Her eyes were wide. Purple eye shadow complemented the sweet smell of lilacs that filled my nose as she approached. It was her pheromones. This was a stern bitch who held all the power.

Her name tag read, "Anna."

"That bitch you watch has a face that has been dragged through forty miles of gravel road. Your beer, one dollar." Her voice low and raspy from chain-smoking cigarettes. Elegant tattoos ran up and down her lean muscular arms and across her back. She looked at home here, confirming my thoughts that Anna should be working in this shitty little poolroom, serving scum-sucking maggots all day. This was the highlight of her life. It was her calling.

Her comment about the ugly window shopper made me laugh. "That was a good one. Nice." I was friendly and honest when I said, "Love your eyes, Anna. Sexy. Tell me, what do you do to stay in such great shape?"

She looked like she wanted to beat me with a bicycle chain, but that was just her way. We shared a smile as I paid her. "Thank you," I said, giving a good tip. She left wiggling her hot ass, the smell of lilac lingering in the air.

As Anna left the table, Hector arrived, Catina just behind him. I knew Hector by the small scar under his right eye. I smiled. He was deadly serious and looking as ugly as ever, scars and all. A tan leather case tucked under Hector's left arm held his cue. Catina wore a teal dress—light, summery. I motioned for them to pull up a chair but remained sitting as they sat down. It was a sign of disrespect or defiance, a challenge. We were all silent. Catina appeared indifferent, as if she wanted to be somewhere else.

I spoke directly at Hector. "You brought Catina to try and weaken me, to confuse me, to gain an edge. It will not work." He knew I was not afraid of him. I poured my beer into the tall chilled glass that came with it.

Hector spoke. "So you think you are good gringo, tough. Well, fuck you, Tommy. I will finish you," Hector said directly to my face.

I spoke from the heart. "You will not beat me—of that, I am sure. The threat of violence is never as strong as violence itself, which roughly means your words are harmless to me and you will soon feel my wrath." Hector's expression showed a hint of worry. I continued with renewed confidence, "I surprised you. Not many men stand up to you. Nor do they have a chance to beat you. My nerves are steady, and my stomach is calm."

Chickens and roosters continued to run free in the street, clucking constantly. Hector wanted to meet in a public spot, a place where we were all safe. "Look, Hector, all I want is what is mine. First, I want Holly back. Enough of your lease on her pussy. You are doomed with that extortion scheme; it could even be your downfall. The hashish business and the fields and the hash machine are mine. And, yes, you can fuck off. I will not kiss your monkey ass." We sat at this small table at the back of the pool hall tent. Some people were up front, but they left us alone. Some of those people carried guns to protect Hector and the rest of us.

Lenny returned from his walkabout, moving to the back where Holly and Frisk were now sitting quietly. He was tall. His nearly bald head looked good with a clean-shaven face. His belt buckled on the left side and not the front, like everyone else I know. The belt held his black pants. He wore a light shirt and a white jacket. The jacket was loose and very casual. I noticed he had been wearing it for the last day or two. He ordered beer and shots for everyone, then lit up a smoke and sat at our table. "How's the games going boys? Sitting at the back in case we have to make a quick exit, eh?" He was right. We laughed and drank up.

Hector was direct. "Don't push me, you fuck, you. I will take everything you have. I will not stop. Even if you beat me, I will still win." He hated Tommy. Catina was smiling inside, proud of Tommy for being so direct and standing his ground, like a rock, against Hector.

I was ready. "Enough. It is time. Let's you and me play some pool, Hector." The Kid was with me now, evaluating the surroundings, providing confidence.

Frisk stood beside me as I took Falcon from the case and began the slow ritual, twisting the shaft with the butt to make one solid piece. I was curious and questioned Frisk, "I have always wondered, Frisk, why did you get me Falcon?"

Frisk knew the answer. "Falcon is my gift to you. I got you Falcon for this exact moment in time, when you to begin the winning, to take back what is yours and forever own your life. Falcon is part of you and part of me. My strength will be your strength. Your soul lives in Falcon, the soul of the warrior. Falcon is a bird of prey. There is no question as to who will win. Kill him. Squash the maggot."

I had to let Frisk know how I felt. "Nice pep talk Frisk. From the heart, I thank you. I am proud of you, Frisk, and grateful for our friendship."

Hector agreed to play for Holly once more. "OK, I will play you for the *chica* to warm up. We play a race to seven. If you win, she goes with you." We racked. I won the lag and prepared to break.

The Kid spoke in my ear. "The key to pool playing is your stance. You must step on this cats tail. Only let him think he is winning for a short time, then chip away. A rock is stubborn and strong. Be that rock, Tommy."

I broke, ran a couple of balls, and then missed but left the table safe. Hector tried a wild shot and missed, and I ran out. I ran out again and again. Shortly, I was seven games up, and it was over.

Hector laughed sarcastically. "So, you practice. I am sad the *chica* is going back, that she will be leaving our little family."

Holly quietly watched the games for her ass, gaining confidence with each win. A smirk, then a smile, crossed her face when I won. "Perfectly grisly and shag, you motherfucker. That wrong was just corrected."

"Never a doubt," I said, looking over at Holly, who did two shots in a row. I thought how winning Holly back would be one less thing for me to hide.

Catina showed emotion. She was happy for Holly and more so for me. Hector was embarrassed by Catina's rejection. Rage reeked from his every fiber as he walked toward her, raising his hand. Hector delivered a calculated and deliberate slap to the side of her head. It caught her full across the face, making a loud slapping noise. Catina's head moved with the slap, then returned back to face us under her own power. She grinned, speaking in Spanish. "Beauty knows no pain."

Violence was part of her life. It stung for a moment. Then it was gone. Frisk stiffened in his seat. Lenny let out a low hum for a few seconds, then drank long from the bottle. Hector stepped back, laughing. Catina decided that was enough and left the poolroom. Hector was more glad than sorry she was gone. She had served her purpose. It didn't work.

Looking at Hector, I said, "You and me play a game of freeze-out. You know what that means, eh? We play until someone is, say, twenty games ahead. The champion will have surfaced. Are you afraid?"

Hector thought, then responded as if he had been waiting for this question, "OK, my friend, I will play you a freeze-out. We will play for your dignity and honor." Leaning forward, Hector was serious, a rage boiling. "But we play for the hashish machine, your patent, and Tom Sift. We play for your life."

I spoke a truth. "You know we met with Poncho, but did you know he left this conflict to us to fight it out on a pool table. Best man takes all."

Hector spoke softly, "Fuck Poncho and fuck you."

I tried to set some boundaries. "And when you lose, this war is over. The patent and the machine remain mine. We work together to grow our business and profits and to honor our common flag. You stop that fucker chasing Frisk. Finally, you make sure we have safe passage for all the Punta Rojo seeds and Colombian weed we need or want. And when we have hundreds of pounds of world-class hashish ready for consumption, you get first pick at everything we have. You will be a cartel leader in my world."

"Do not misunderstand me, Tommy. I want your machine, the patent, and I want you dead."

I responded, "Hector, we seem to have a communication problem."

Hector sat across from me, angry. Leaning toward me, he spoke softly. "I have killed many people with knives. Up close, I watch them die slowly."

I responded with sarcasm, "Yeah, I know. Their screams could be heard blocks away before dying a slow horrible death. You believe beating me at the table will be like knifing me in the back. You think you can beat me again and take everything. You think he can scare me. Well, you are wrong, Hector. You have underestimated your opponent."

Frisk looked into Hector's eyes, then made a strong fist with his left hand. Hector backed off.

It was a small group watching the games. Everyone realized the true stakes in quiet reverence while rail bets went about freely.

Twilight had come and gone. It was dark outside. I held my own as we ran racks from noon past midnight. Our freeze-out was a stalemate so far, but relentless side betting was adding up. We played back and forth, neither of us giving an advantage. I felt like I could win but the universe had other plans this day. We had been playing for sixteen hours, and the clock read four in the morning. I noticed the tent had a few different observers. These guys were not gambling but watching. It was a style of watching Frisk would do when on yellow alert. Their faces were lean, strong, and chiseled. They were watching and waiting. I was hoping for the best.

Fueled by world-class cocaine, we played many games in the morning darkness without a winner. Neither Hector nor myself were ready to call it quits. Eventually, it started to feel brighter. The darkness was losing strength. Sunrise was upon us.

Hector had stayed too long in one place. His plan was to win and be gone by now, but it was not working out that way. Hector was in imminent danger. He was seen by informants, or maybe it was Catina who ratted him out, but someone told the police where to find him.

Frisk knew the police would confront Hector sometime soon. He explained quietly, "Poncho told me when we talked together alone, the police are looking for Hector. They believe he is behind that fucked-up extortion and drug ring. The police are pissed at him. The extortion ring was well known to police. They know about the British blonde, Holly. Some of those victims complained pretty hard. Others were just glad to be alive. At first, the police were not interested. They took bribe money and looked the other way, but eventually a good thing runs out of steam. Hector didn't give a shit. He was on a suicide mission with all those involved. Everyone was being used on both sides. Poncho told me Holly was not safe. Her time is up."

It all happened very quickly, a moment similar to the day I moved the pot plants, except this time, the police were out for us. This time, they came fully geared up with automatic weapons. Hector's men reacted fast, drawing their weapons as police cars approached from both sides of the street. They wanted Hector for questioning but would take him dead if they had to.

Fully geared up police with hats, black shorts, brown shirts, black guns, holsters strapped across their chests loaded with bullets, they approached, telling everyone, "Get down. This is a raid." Hector's men stood their ground, firing over their heads. Hector's name was being said loudly from a handheld loudspeaker.

Frisk was calm. "Don't worry. I have a plan. The cops are not coming in from the rear, only the front." He had this figured out the second he showed up here.

Just then, shots were fired our way. The force of one bullet vibrating the air strongly enough we felt its close presence. We dove behind this square table. It was very thick, and I felt safe. Another shot, and the table moved, but the bullet did not go through. So there was something special about this table after all. It stopped bullets.

"Too close, Frisk. Way too close. Let's get the fuck outa here." Panic was obvious in my voice. Then another shot and return fire. A smoke bomb went off. The police thought Hector was at the front of the poolroom, and this confused them for a moment. Burning orange tracer shots were being fired from police machine guns. One tracer hit the pool table we were playing on. Balls scattered and the tracer stuck in the cloth by the side pocket.

"Holy old sweet mother of Jesus. Holy God," Lenny said as flames started near a side pocket, then grew. Within seconds, the cloth was on fire, the table nearly engulfed. "Fuck me. Burnt the cloth right off the goddamn table. Man, oh, man." Lenny was frantic, not panicking but disparate to defend himself. "Fuck this shit. Fuck you cocksuckers." Lenny reached with opposite hands under his jacket. He was wearing a double shoulder holster. Nearly instantly, Lenny held a serious-looking Glock-style pistol in each hand. Lenny had a grin that told me he felt safe, like being at home.

I screamed at him, "You crazy fucker, where the fuck did you get those guns?" The only answer was more bullets. Lenny poked up his head and began firing shots from both pistols into the smoke. Blue flames extended a foot past the barrel ends as bullets exited.

"I have never seen anything like this before," I said out loud and to no one in particular. As fast as I had Falcon taken apart and returned to the case, so too had Hector protected his cue.

Anna, the lifer bartender, came forth with a shotgun, held at hip level. She had crazy eyes. Her mouth frothing and spitting as she yelled repeatedly in Spanish, "Lick my nuts, you fuckers. Die." Anna fired blast after blast toward the police, each new shot shaking me to the core. Anna moved toward the front, firing as she went, then disappeared into the smoke and flames. Now I know what she did to keep in shape.

Frisk knew the way out, the escape route. Lenny and Frisk had checked out the neighborhood and where the escape route would be located. “Fun is fun. Time to fucking go,” Frisk said.

Hector’s heavily armed men quickly guarded him. In slow motion, with guns blazing in all directions, we made our move. Through the smoke and fire from the now fully engulfed poolroom, we made it to the back door. Once through the back door, it opened to a narrow alley. It was dark. The stench of rotting garbage was overwhelming. The buildings were tall, with many windows, each supporting an air conditioner turned to maximum. We were on a direct path away from the police, quickly leading to a busy street.

Lenny walked out backward, shooting wildly into the flames, smoke and figures inside. A bullet screamed over his head, and that was enough. His long legs carried him to the street quickly, the pistols returned to the concealed holsters under his arms. Holly and I were grateful to be still alive.

Hector was next out the back door. Anna and his men were holding the police at bay, causing confusion and allowing his escape.

"Fucking great to be alive," I said to Holly.

Holly showed remarkable insight. "Don't you mean fucking *grateful* to be alive?"

This was a moment of truth, and I let Holly and the universe know. "I do appreciate the difference. Thank you, universe."

We ran to a street crowded with people and cars. Hector and I looked at each other. We had but a moment before heading in different directions. I said to him, "Come to my home. Come to Carmichaels when you are ready. Fuck this nine-ball shit. We will finish this with straight pool, a true test of character."

Hector snapped at me. "We shall finish this one way or the other." Hector made good his escape.

Holly knew the way. In no time, we were on a back road, heading away from this fucked-up town. Holly had a plan. A small plane was waiting to get us back to Medellin, a plane on a landing strip few people knew about. This was a private airstrip with portable lights. The trip to the air strip was not long. Once there, the plane turned out to be a Cessna, perfect for a quick exit. Our luggage fit in the back easily.

Holly was protective of her carry-on bag, so I asked, "What's with your carry-on bag? Got something special in there?"

Holly kept her carry-on bag across her shoulder at most times. Leaning over, she opened a corner of the bag showing me the contents. It was stuffed with cash, mostly hundred-dollar bills in neat stacks. "There are over two hundred thousand dollars inside, my share of a job that brought in millions, a job that is now over. Praise the Lord. Amen."

"God bless you," I said, being biblical.

Lenny immediately spoke up, partially singing the prayer. "And with you too." A common response at mass in a Catholic church. Lenny blessed us all with the sign of the cross.

I took the moment to question Lenny. "Where the fuck did you get those pistols? Holy God, that was crazy. Thank God you had them, or we might have been killed."

Lenny responded with confidence, "It's not thank God. It's thank *gun*." He tapped the weapons under his jacket. "Got them from a new friend I met playing blackjack the first night we were here. He played blackjack too. We went to his place and had a few drinks after winning. He sold me the shoulder holster and guns. I got lots of bullets and clips for a good price. Great defense weapon, don't you know, Tommy. Most people here are gangsters, Tommy, like a land of vampires. Scary. They all feed off each other." Lenny made a low humming sound while pulling his lips straight back. His shoulder were straight and square. His arms were folded as he smoked, then held the cigarette while his arms were crossed. He starred at me, saying nothing.

I was proud of Lenny. "Good work, Lenny. By the way, nice jacket too. I knew you would be armed somehow. Never a doubt."

Lenny was laughing with his arms still folded. Smoke curled in front of his face as the ash grew longer. "He sold jackets to go with the shoulder holsters. What a deal. Even had one my size."

Take off was smooth and fast. Looking at Holly, I said, "As I sometimes like to say, it was great when it all began. Now I am glad this party is over." There were tears in her eyes and only blue skies ahead. We were both glad.

The flights and connections were uneventful. Eventually, we were all back home and grateful to be safe. Finally in bed, I had one repeating thought: *The battle is not over. It is not complete. A fire is still burning.*

# Uncle Cid

"I'D RATHER SUCK A NIGGER'S DIRTY COCK THAN PLAY THAT guy again." Lenny's rage came out quick at the mention of the Kid.

I was not sure what to say. "Holy God, Lenny. A minute ago, you were fine." Lenny had not changed. Those were his comments when I suggested playing the Kid again.

Then he made a low, growling "Uhmmmmr," sound.

Lenny had left for Vegas after returning from Colombia, he still had the gambling bug. Now Lenny had been back a few days, when Frisk and I saw him leaving Carmichaels. Not wanting to upset Lenny further, I dropped the subject, but I was thinking how the Kid had changed my game.

He calmed quickly, refocusing, and said, "So, boys. How did my winter share of the cash turn out?"

I said, "Give me a week, and I will drop it off."

Lenny was happy with that, "Thank you, boys. Come see me next week for a few drinks, and we will talk about your new home." He got into his small red half-ton truck, lit up a cigarette, opened a beer, and started the half-hour drive home to his place at Lake Clear.

Frisk and I went ahead into Carmichaels to play some pool and talk. "Frisk, I have a problem, and only you can help me," I said, walking past the washroom.

Playing pool with Frisk at the back of Carmichaels was relaxing, but it was not enough. "Frisk, I need something more. I feel dead-ended. A lot has happened, and my mind feels stuck. It feels full. I know I can beat

Hector. That is not the problem. I feel like my mind has some blockages. Not my brain but my mind, like my thoughts can't get through to me."

Frisk responded like he knew what he was talking about, like a guru, experienced. "It is your chakras. They are blocked. There are seven chakras in the body. They represent different parts of a person, like the mind, guilt, sex, fear. The goal of mastering your chakras is to gain balance within yourself. They are like pools of swirling energy within your body. The key is how they are connected—by streams or rivers of cosmic energy. If there is nothing to interfere with the energy, it will flow free and clear, but things fall from our lives and into the river, slowing or blocking the connections between chakras. When these emotional blocks are removed, the energy flows again. So, when the connections get blocked up, we get stuck, but I can help."

My interest was piqued. "So, do I need to sit in the mountains with a guru for a few months or years, sipping banana and beet juice until I hallucinate myself straight? Does that even make sense?" It did to Frisk. He was about to educate me, to guide me.

Frisk taught me about chakras. "What could take months or even years, I am about to help you with in a day, but first, let me explain a few things about chakras. The first is the earth chakra, or fear chakra. You must face your fears and surrender to them. Second, water chakra deals with pleasure and is blocked by guilt. Discover what you blame yourself for, and forgive yourself. Third is the fire chakra, located in the stomach, which deals with will power. It is blocked by shame and disappointments in yourself. You must have discipline to release your failures. The fourth chakra is located in the heart and deals with love. It is blocked by grief. Face all your grief and all your loss. Only then will new loves appear.

The fifth chakra in the chain is the sound chakra, located in the throat. It deals with truth and is blocked by the lies we tell ourselves. Do not lie about your own nature. Accept your character. Light energy is sixth and deals with insight. It is located in the center of the forehead and is blocked by the illusion of separation. Many things are one and the same; everything is connected. You must open your mind to see that all the elements of the universe are connected. We are all one, but live as if divided.

The last chakra is the thought chakra, located at the crown of the head. It deals with pure cosmic energy, and is blocked by your earthly attachments. Meditate on what attaches you to this world, and let them go, down the river. It is the only way to let the pure cosmic energy from the universe flow in and through. You must learn to surrender. To master yourself, you must open all the chakras. This is only attained through deep meditation, self-introspective, and surrender."

I was catching on. "Yeah, I can see how that makes a lot of sense. I can also see how it could take a few years. Well, Frisk, at this point, I am open to just about any suggestion. What did you have in mind?" I was laughing yet feeling defeated.

Frisk had a plan. "I can help you get your chakras cleared in a weekend. But know this, Tommy: it is very dangerous and could drive you insane before it is over." Reaching into his pocket, he pulled out a small piece of tin foil folded into a square. He was showing me something I never saw before. When unfolded there were several small orange pills in the shape of tiny barrels.

"How could something that small hurt someone?" I questioned Frisk.

Frisk explained, "This is LSD, man, orange double-barrel acid, man. The heaviest of psychedelics, to be exact. On the street it is called 'Uncle Cid."

I commented on its size and color, "It looks like the center lead from an orange HB pencil. They are round and cut to look like small barrels. Can this really clear out my blocked chakras?"

"Oh, fuck yeah," Frisk said. "You better block out twenty-four hours and have someone with you who is straight. This is powerful shit, man." He grinned as he looked at me. He was unknowingly biting the tip of his tongue at the side of his mouth. "Look, Tommy, I am going to let you in on a secret about LSD. It is one of those things that is public knowledge but never talked about." Frisk was looking around and over his shoulder, as if someone were listening. "You know that thing they are calling the computer. Well, get this. The guy who invented it would take LSD in the morning, then meditate on the electrical circuitry designs. While 'peaking' on LSD, he could see which direction the electrons would flow under various designs, and guess what? He saw the working model during a hallucination. Once the LSD wore off, he was able to build the circuits, putting them together as he hallucinated it, and sure enough, success. He was credited with the discovery of the first working computer. Imagine that. Heard he got a Nobel award for that one, and few people know he was on LSD to make it happen. Cool, eh!"

I thought I understood. "So you are saying, Frisk, I must take LSD, then meditate on these seven chakras, trying to understand what they mean to me. Then to unblock them, I must come face to face with a series of inner demons and flawed character values. Only then will my mind become unblocked and I'll get my energy and vision back. You are saying all my answers are within this small, orange pill? Interesting, Frisk. Very interesting."

Frisk was serious for a minute. "Tommy, this will take you places you may not want to go. And it will change you. After taking this LSD, you 'will' be different. So …"

I talked with Frisk before deciding. "This is what I need. I need to take some LSD. I have been trying hard to find my path, to accept myself, but I am lost. A mental break is in order because I believe you. My chakras are blocked. A lot has happened in the last year, especially the last month, don't ya know. I am sure this is the break I need before playing the most important pool game of my life. There is no stopping it now, Frisk. Soon, Hector will return, and I must face him."

Frisk wanted to know, "Do you think you can handle all that?" A short pause, then "What's it going to be?"

"Holy God," I said. "What the fuck? Give me two hits. I'll do them Friday night." I paid Frisk ten bucks, and he dropped two hits in my hand. I wrapped them in tin foil from a cigarette pack and put them in my jacket pocket.

"Keep them in the fridge," he added. "I did some last week, and this is going to blow your mind. Don't forget to meditate on what I told you. Start tonight. Become familiar with your goal."

I humbly asked Frisk, "How do I know if I am getting off? I never did LSD before. This is going to be interesting."

"You will know when you start to see traces." He waved his hand in front of his face slowly. "It will start to look like your fingers are leaving a blur in front of you. After that, hang on." He had a big grin on his face.

It was the last Friday in April. I'd had a good dinner in my new home and felt full. Quietly sitting in a dark corner of my living room, I went over the chakras in my mind—what blocks them and what it will take to clear them. I had no answers at this time. I left home with the Uncle Cid in my pocket. It was a nice, cool night, maybe around freezing, and not much wind as I drove into town. Soon I found myself sitting at Carmichaels, having a beer. The beer was cold, but strangely, not refreshing. I felt, for a brief moment, the true power of alcohol and where it could take me when abused. That was not a good thing. The moment vanished when Dave sat down beside me.

Dave, a good friend, was now sitting with me. He is an excellent musician, earning a good living playing and teaching music. He is one of those gifted individuals—bright, good energy. Dave likes a good party now and then but has not done many drugs. He does smoke dope when he can afford it.

It is weird, the mood you can find people in sometimes. Or maybe I was just a bad influence. Regardless, I looked over at Dave and was brutally honest. "Dave, look, I got these two hits of orange double-barrel acid here. I was going to eat both, but then I thought maybe that would be too much. So what do you say? Want to try some LSD tonight, Dave, some extremely high powered acid, Uncle Cid? Like right now." I pulled out the tin foil, discretely showing Dave the two hits. They were small, round, and bright orange.

"Rather small, don't you think?" Dave said. "Maybe you got ripped off?"

"Well, let's find out," I said. It was now eight o'clock on this fateful Friday night. I picked out one of the bright orange barrels. When I put it in my mouth, it was hard, like a small rock. I crunched it in my teeth, and it broke into a few smaller pieces. Everything mixed with saliva, and I swallowed. Dave was looking at me as the LSD settled into my stomach. "It's too late for me. How about you?"

In that moment, Dave saw what I did and took the other hit. He looked at it, I am sure marveling at the smallness and brightness. He placed it on the tip of his tongue and swallowed it whole. It was gone. We spun around on our stools and said, almost together, "Now what?"

"Wait for the traces to start," I said, reiterating what Frisk told me.

We chatted about local politics. Dave said, "I was reading about the mayor. She is going to eliminate dangerous drugs on our streets. She said, 'Pot should be available through your doctor for medical reasons, and the rest of the people can buy it at grocery stores, like wine and whiskey. This would create jobs and slow down a lot of drug problems.' She is right, and as usual, ahead of her time."

I was cynical. "Yeah, well, when it comes to drugs and crime, there is always a small select few who have special privileges. That odd group who just seem to dodge around shit, who never get caught or have their names in the paper. They are the open secrets."

We talked about the local underworld. Dave enlightened me. "This town has a secret. There is a place in society, just below where most people live. It is alive and lucrative. In our little town, I hear it is run by a Russian woman, Sylvia. She is a well-kept secret. Heard she was an Olympian, winning medals in gymnastics. I saw her once at a late-night restaurant. A very beautiful woman, tall and full-figured. Her eyes were long and narrow. Her dark red hair flowed with easy curls throughout. She had high cheek bones and full, pouting lips. Her teeth were white and straight. She spoke near-perfect English. Her arms and legs were strong like steel bands yet feminine. Apparently, she was very tough and very business smart, with degrees from some European university. I heard she was, like, a forensic financial engineer. She has her finger in everything going on here." We joked about how she must be the muscle for the mayor. "Weird shit. Who knows?" Dave said. On that, we agreed.

It was eight-thirty now, and we were still sitting and talking.

Everything felt fine. I was in control. I remember saying to Dave, "Let's go outside for a walk."

"Sure, sounds like a good idea."

We threw on our coats and split out the side door. It was not too cold out as we began walking down a back street with no particular direction in mind. The residential street was lined with tall lampposts every five hundred feet, leaving bright footprints under them. Darkness was the backdrop for the homes.

My breathing began to feel like I could taste it. I stopped. Dave stopped too. We had not been talking. Suddenly, I noticed the footprint from the streetlamp behind me, getting brighter and moving toward me, like a car coming up behind me. The lights were getting brighter, and the sound of the car came closer. It was a blue-shifted Doppler effect, getting louder and higher pitched as it approached. When I turned quickly to see what was happening, everything was all in place, with nothing moving. I turned back to Dave and immediately saw the lights from behind getting brighter and louder and closer again, but upon turning around, all was normal.

The cool April air was not warmed by the street lights. I felt safe under that lamp until the curtains closed shut in a house across the street. A woman had looked at me from that window. Words slurred and rolled from my mind and mouth. "She has seen me, and I have seen her." My fingers made long traces in front of my face, and I followed those traces with distracted interest.

I moved forward, away from the lamp. It seemed to fall away behind me. Soon, I was the dark. The outline was a woman in flames, her hair short, glasses, tattoos. Was it her? Was it the girl who invades my dreams? She who comes to me on a beach and we make love on the sand, under a purple and red sky. The ocean swells, and we disappear beneath the warm waves, then surface in a dream. I feel her lips on mine while the sweet smell of lilacs fills the air. The smell was strong, but was it real?

What was it that made me walk this street tonight? What force ensured I took this route and stopped beneath that lamp as it danced and teased me? Why did I look up at just that moment in time and space and peer into her window? I was tall and wide in my mind. Things had become very different from normal.

My heart raced. The hair on my neck straightened. My steps were predetermined, and my will was not mine. Now the night air blew soft and almost warm on my face, as if a sauna mist had come upon me. I breathed in that warmth, and I was inflated. Like a balloon inflating, then deflating, my mind and vision were moving in steep waves. My perspective was in motion. But what did it mean?

I was radiating within myself. I looked at Dave, his face red and gray and black and moving. His eyes were wide, and his pupils huge. Dave began laughing. We babbled about hair and grass, and nothing made sense, and everything made sense. All was beautiful. Colors were alive. The buildings were crisp and shiny. Each breath was alive in me, and I could taste it. I stared at myself in a mirror, marveling at the act of reflection. My face was flushed red, and my pupils were wide, fully dilated.

We met some people, but communication was not possible. I knew they were people. They just came out of the darkness. They spoke to us. Their words were like repeated echoes from a microphone and speaker system set up to close. "Hello-o-o-o … there-ere-ere-ere," with delays. It was like an old time movie reel skipping. We tried to answer, making no sense. Words came out, but not in any order humans could understand. I could feel my words, but only idiocy was heard. I saw my arms moving and tracing, and I had to leave. I said something like, "Theuu grassss is blue," grabbed Dave, and floated away.

We had just graduated from pot to the world of psychedelics. We were high, peaking. My brain crackled hard. Everywhere we went was an adventure. Colors, psychological primary colors, and lights, fading to dim, then flaring bright, were so beautiful. My body experienced bouncing and vibrating at a low frequency. We laughed, enjoying the simplicity of things. It was amazing we could walk or stand, and for a while, we could not. I got lost in a corner and could not get out. Things came and went, making no sense and sometimes making perfect sense. I stood there in silence when a fear came over me. I realized I was stoned but not drunk.

The earth was not solid, and I was afraid, scared of alcohol. In my mind, a fear of drunkenness and loss of control was boiling, rising, sinking, over and over. I had to let it go. I would not be a slave to the loss of control. The rising and falling continued until I screamed out to the universe, "Take this from me, please …"

Something awakened in me, and I let the fear go, into the river, and it was gone. I had opened my first chakra. I felt free of my deepest fear, but I had to ask for the release out loud. We continued wondering. Dave was in his own world, separate from anything else he ever knew.

It was four in the morning, and we had been peaking now for six hours. The chakras seemed to pop in and out, or more like pictures sliding across a slow action movie screen. Then it hit me with the force of a rocket lifting off. Killing was a problem. The guilt was strong and stuck on me. The guilt of murdering JD was a problem, worse than expected. I did not want to kill him. I did not want to kill anyone, but I did. Ripples of silver spread across the ground. Ants were crawling, doing their thing. How simple it is to kill an ant and not worry. I have feelings, but I am also strong enough to defend myself. I must defend myself. It is my nature. I let it go into the river and float away. Another chakra was open.

My thoughts were focusing on my character, who I really was. Who was I? Denial, lies, wants, and needs were emotions to confuse my mind. The worst type of lie is the one I tell myself. Why would I lie to myself? What was the value? Wait, it was the voice in my head, but I am the voice in my head. My heartbeat quickened. Confusion reigned. My mind was coming apart, not knowing who was speaking. Suddenly, a loud noise attacked me. It was only in my mind. There was no real sound, but it shocked me.

*Henceforth, I will not lie about my character to myself or anyone. I accept my shortcomings and will not lie about who I am, what my character really is.*

The lying went into the river, and was washed away. My sound chakra was open and running clear.

The morning twilight had begun, things were crisp and moving and alive. The reds were at the bottom and then orange and yellow and green. Blues and reds painted the sky and horizon in swirls and twists. The swirls of colors melted into each other. The colors represented different chakras. My mind was assimilating what Frisk had told me earlier this week, on a level I might never understand, no matter how many years spent in the mountains, with my own personal guru. LSD was my guru, my mental guide, and my connection to the universe. I felt many releases and waves of energy. I could feel and see positive and negative energy all around me. This was the energy used to make the pool shots. It was not me. It was the universe.

My mind swam in the morning air. I could see and feel waves and ripples in my life. Synapses in my brain were becoming brighter with each new firing. New synapse paths were being created and began firing. I started to focus on specific thoughts and started to see and feel things differently from before. There was a new understanding developing in my mind.

Somewhere along the line, Dave and I split up. I was calm while walking in a small park. I sat on a bench, meditating on my failures. Mostly, my mind focused on my personal failure to look after myself. Somehow, I felt like I let myself down, I was starting to freak out. I wanted to go home, but could not. I had no idea what was going on, when a friend, I only knew as, Jimbo appeared. His smile, wide, then thin, then wide again. A beard covering his face crawled, and moved in blotches, and patches. He is about my height, but his size was changing to that seen in a fun house mirror. I was very stoned, totally fucked, and Jimbo knew it. I could not figure out what he was saying, except for one half sentence: "not looking after yourself …"

Jimbo had triggered my next chakra. It was open and raw. All I could feel was the shame and disappointment of countless fuckups. Then Jimbo spoke again, and I only understood one word—"discipline"—but my mind was working on a new level.

I screamed, "Yes!" That was all I could say. The answer was discipline. My will power was returning as I let my personal failures fall into the river. I was in trouble, and Jimbo was my savior at this moment in time and space. The universe put Jimbo in my path to awaken this chakra and to save me from a total acid meltdown. He was also a Sherpa, as he led me to my home by the school. Jimbo was a hero. Then he was gone.

Managing to make it upstairs to my bedroom, I played a new record Johnny had given me a couple of weeks earlier. He said to me, "They are just another semipopular subculture band from Los Angeles." I listened with my headphones on. The music played loud and in stereo, different sounds blasting from each speaker. Stretching out on my bed, the deep personal introspective continued.

The music from the band was amazing, incredible, audio echoes rolling through the canyons in my mind. I took leave from my body for a velvety land, skies without clouds, sparkling stars, and seas filled with shining jewels. Colors were so clear and bright. The ceiling was moving, patterns flowing into each other, then spiraling in all directions. I was absolutely free.

My breathing led to meditating. It was separate from my thoughts, then it was one. I was experiencing the chakra associated with separation. Things that I thought were separate were actually one. Fields of weed in Colombia and Val Lenny were not separate but the same. My breathing was the gateway to meditation. New synapses formed, and in that moment, it became clear: there was no more illusion of separation, and I let that fall into the river. The reward, insight, intuitively knowing what to do. During the storm of hallucinations, a calmness came over me. I had matured.

The hallucinations worsened. Darkness and colors all flowed together. I began to rise up and up, further and further. I was walking upwards, above the earth, looking down on the dark blue and silvery planet. All my earthly attachments were below me. Faces of my women came and went. Pool games I won and the ones I lost appeared and disappeared, bricks of hashish and the sifter all below me. Strange I did not see or feel Frisk. He was strangely absent. The cosmic energy of the universe was all around me, flowing in and out. There was an aura of grief, of loss in this universe, slowly mixing with the chakra of pure cosmic energy. I needed to separate them but could not.

I lay there for five hours, hallucinating, thinking, feeling the cosmic energy soak my body and brain. It was afternoon when the cosmic energy faded, the hallucinations receded, and reality locked in again. I was coming down. Colors that were alive and sparkling bright became regular again, but it was gradual. My brain stayed hot, cooking in the stoned mode until evening. Finally, my thoughts became my own again, and I screamed, "No. not yet. I have not mastered myself. There is still a grief to release and a love to embrace," but the universe had spoken. My final answer would lie elsewhere.

I saw my phone. I felt I knew how to use it but would not, even if I had to. I was hungry. I ate toast and drank juice but could not taste much. Looking in the mirror, my face was still red and flushed. My pupils were not large anymore, I felt disappointed, then relieved, then free. My body was tired. My brain was cooling. It felt good, I was down, but I was different, changed.

I lay down on my bed with headphones on. The record player was queued to play a number of records for a few hours. I fell asleep listening to music. I woke up listening to music. It was just after midnight. I was into another day now. It was Sunday. I felt fucked up. I was not sleepy but felt dead tired. This was the time to partake in the "kind" weed. The joint I smoked was smooth and refreshing, and it took me to a different place. It was a gentler place, where I could rest. Amazing music played in my ears. I was in love. I lay in bed, looking at the ceiling when The Kid's face appeared. He had a serious look about him as if playing for a million dollars. This time, I could see pool balls moving. The corner shots, long shots, and the bank shots. Each time I would feel the cue ball roll through the center of the table avoiding any scratch. The Kid's face showed approval in shadows and paint. Many bank shots played out naturally in front of me. I felt them and controlled them with the English in my mind. This deep introspective experience was changing me. I felt different in how I looked at things, clearer in my thoughts more confident after seeing The Kid. I drifted off to a deep sleep, not waking until late the next afternoon.

"Fuck me, Frisk. Where did you get that stuff?" I asked when I finally got to Carmichaels again. Frisk looked yellow around the checks. I didn't think too much about it.

We were playing eight-ball. I tried to explain my LSD trip and how I felt I was different, how my chakras had been opened. "Holy God, Frisk, I was taken places, and I have been changed. Heavy shit, Frisk. I am dead serious. A lot of chakras were opened, and I felt the cosmic energy flow, and I was changed. I do get it now Frisk. I understand so much more. Thank you. Fuck me Frisk, I am still seeing traces." I moved my hand in front of my face.

He laughed, coughing, totally empathizing with my story. "Don't worry. There is no more of that shit around. Probably won't be any more either. You got the last of it."

I started to believe this was a good thing. Acid is some powerful shit.

Frisk played slowly. He looked sick. Frisk had a message for me. "Hector will come next month. He will come soon to challenge you. I am tired, Tommy. I feel weak." Then he mentioned how training with Graham and Raff was going well. "Those two I am training, they have learned much. They are powerful. They have the gene for violence, almost ready to graduate." Obvious pride in his voice. Frisk encouraged me to work out and keep limber too. Then he stopped, looking into the distance. He became pale.

"Frisk, you don't look good. Do you need a doctor?" Frisk looked sick, as if he needed to be in a hospital. Then he collapsed.

# Inevitable Defeat

IT WAS NOT A GOOD DAY. I WOULD TALK TO MY FRIEND FOR THE last time tonight. I would cry for someone in my life, and it would feel good. I was once told, "For every passing, there is a giving." Could there ever be a giving from the passing of someone so close? What could I possibly learn from this?

Before I left to be with my friend, I stood looking out over Lake Clear, grieving. Its waves relentless, like the sadness in the spaces between my heartbeats. They were endless, almost infinite from my little viewpoint, sitting on my front porch. It felt surreal and euphoric, but I was sober. I could not be here impaired. I was needed to be with my friend. The great bell was tolling. I would follow my intuition and gut feeling. I will honor my friend and our lives with better choices. And it was possible.

My friend Frisk made a bad choice some time ago. A needle was passed around that had an evil disease in it. Frisk got stung with that bad dart. It made him sick, and he had to go away to rest. It cut Frisk down. He got weaker. It put him on the edge, but he was always hopeful. Hope is such a tricky emotion because it comes with dreams. To hope is to dream. Sometimes when dreams fail, hope will fail. Sometimes. It is not a luxury to have hope. Hope is something I freely give myself. To dream is the root of my self-confidence. It is tough because sometimes, when hope starts, it does not stop until there is nothing left to hope or dream for. Hope is always in the future.

I hope for Frisk. He came here with hope. He moved here to the West

Coast, where I stand just now. He moved here to enjoy the ocean and the healthy clean air and the mountains. His love and passion for the mountains ran deep. His earliest memories were in the mountains. He knew the sight of long rolling green hills, rich with vegetation and life, oh so well. Those young days were spent running free, eating, exercising, and training his mind and body. Enjoying the days free of the stresses he would come to know later in life. And those mountains were a home to him. He owned those fields. He would stand his ground as if he were rooted to it. He would stand tall.

In these final days, we talked a lot in his room. We would sit, looking out the window, pondering life. A room with dark cherry floors and windows covered by heavy curtains to keep the sun out. His bed could be tilted in several directions at the touch of a button. We talked about our past, our adventures, and our women. We talked about the gift of Falcon and how our spirits were connected. Sometimes, we talked about the life lessons we learned, what we would do again and what we would never do again. I especially thanked Frisk for the lesson of the seven chakras.

I learned from Frisk, and some lessons were severe. We were unconditional friends, and we did not judge each other. We stood by each other. We shared an unconditional love. But he was strong in mind and in body, and so was I. The most important lessons ran through my mind, and I heard Frisk saying, "You got to always keep your head up. Always look for the signs, as they are all around us. Follow your gut feeling, Tommy, and never worry, never complain. Walk tall, kick ass, love music and never forget that you come from a long line of fierce truth seekers, lovers and warriors. Trust me, I know what I am talking about."

Fierce truth-seeker, lover and warrior seemed to define Frisk. He did not bullshit, he loved life, and he would fight to the bitter end. And he would fight for what was right. As crazy as he was, Frisk always had a respect for life and a willingness to share. He had a passion to help. Yet his judgments were swift and final. Maybe this is what those people saw in him so many years ago.

I had entered the hospice through a side door. It closed slowly and on its own authority. The place smelled bleach clean and shone bright. I slowly walked the empty halls of the first floor toward Frisk's room.

I was with my friend now, holding his hand, looking into his soft eyes. He was sick, quiet, with a pale look. "Well, Frisk, my friend, I know these are very tough times, and I am here to share these moments when you need a friend. I think of you often during the day and try to imagine you laughing, talking, enjoying the sun and the beauty of the land."

Frisk's eyes were closed. His thin hand was in mine. I continued, "I am very proud of you, Frisk. From here, it seems like a person could look east, and see the rest of the world spin by. It seems to me I can see all my life, the good things, the successes and failures—all that makes us who we are. And on those days, when I think of you, I think of the times we've had. Those really were the best times of our lives. We had fun, did what we wanted, traveled, partied, and basically lived our lives like dolphins—free, truly free, to come and go as we dared.

But the ocean swelled, things became complicated, and responsibility caught up with us. It was the high watermark, where life was pushed to the limit. Then the fever broke and rolled back. But the spirit of the dolphin never left us. You know, Frisk, I think that is the quality about you I admire the most: being free and responsible at the same time. You are able to balance that so well."

Frisk was calm, eyes closed, his hand in mine.

"But now, as you face this difficult time, I want you to know I am with you. It is also difficult for me, but you are in my heart and my dreams. And when you look to the east, look for the high watermark, and with special eyes, you will see that spot where you took control of your life and became the person you are today. Be proud of yourself, Frisk. You are such a special person.

And wherever I go in life, I want you to know you will be part of me. A part of you will live on in me. You will be with me always." I was not leaving my friend.

I held his hand, kissed his cheek, stroked his hair, and smiled. Frisk smiled and gave me a weak thumbs-up. "Stay with me, Tommy. I am waiting, waiting for the miracle to happen," he mouthed. His head was raised high with pillows. A smirk appeared upon his face. It was the eternal smirk. Suddenly, his hand was still in mine. He was still.

I felt the air become quiet. The room was dark, and in that moment, I stood before a moonless snowy night. My mind lost focus, or focused on some other place. Nothing existed. I saw a dark mountainside through the snow storm dream. The snow fell straight down. There was no wind to touch this mountain. A guitar started to play in the distance. The notes were long and pronounced. The sound was a soft, soothing guitar strum. On occasion it would strike strong, then relax into near nothing, before starting again. The imaginary guitar solo guided the transition. The song was a gift. This moment belonged to the universe, to this solo, to Frisk. To understand it, would be like trying to grow watermelons in Easter hay.

I could feel cool air deep in my lungs. In that snowy moment, my eyes peered into the night. I saw darkness, filled with flakes of white everywhere. A gentle brush touched my cheek then moved up, to dance with the snowflakes. Those special snowflakes, so very lucky to be touched, would move and waggle against the landscape. The gentle brush moved on and up against the blackness and into the sky, to touch the stars. In that moment, I breathed again, and my friend was gone.

The drive home to Lake Clear was long. I cried for Frisk, and it felt good. It was a revelation, an awakening. Love has not been lost so much as it will be reborn in a new form. In that moment, I felt control and awareness over my actions, and it felt good. There was a release from my loss and my tears, in the notes of a guitar solo. I would miss my friend, yet he would always be with me. I embraced this moment, this gift.

# Hector

CARMICHAELS WAS CLOSED THIS SATURDAY NIGHT. THE lights were out on all tables except table eight.

I was apoplectic with Graham while sitting at Carmichaels' bar. "So, this is how it will end. In a small town pool hall, on the third last table, on a rainy Saturday night in May. If Hector wants to play me pool for my life and those of my friends, he knows where to find me—Carmichaels. Come on over. We will get in a game."

Graham recited a teaching from Frisk. "The rule was, war isn't over until both sides say so."

I was impressed. "Very poetic, but will Hector say it is over when I beat him? Is that other guy pissed at Poncho for not letting him kill Frisk when he was alive? Did he transfer his rage to Poncho? That is the question I think about. I think that is what you are trying to say, Graham."

Graham knew it was a waiting game. "There are no answers just now, yet to be revealed," he said. "Hector is here in this country, with access to many resources. Five million in cash is not unreasonable. He wants to take your money, your business, and fuck you up, but don't worry; I have a good feeling about this game. You have one chance, Tommy, to calm this down for everyone. He has a rage, and very little can stop it, but Tommy, listen to this: I know you can beat him, so let's beat him good. You two will play for your machine and your future, but there will also be large betting going on the side, on the rails. This is where we can really take him down. If you are that good, then play it out, drag it out to the bitter end, and we will take his money." Graham knew exactly what to do. Interesting, I thought, Frisk was right: Graham had the gene for this work. Johnny walked back to talk with me, with us. Red Ed was with him. Ed was looking good, giving us a smile and a nod.

Johnny explained what he knew. "Sylvie stopped by the other day to talk with Old Don about this game tonight. Old Don is not well. Age is catching up, but he is still respected. She asked him for permission to play tonight. They want to play pool and gamble without any problem. This would be outside the scope of a family pool hall so it had to be closed. He gave his blessing to this match, understanding many games are played within these walls and the stakes can vary. Old Don knows the nature of high-stakes gambling; that's why he created Carmichaels. Play will be fair, and no one will get killed. Poncho will attend and his men will ensure fairness. Part of the winnings will go to the house. They know Frisk is gone, God rest his soul. What Hector failed to realize is that Frisk has been training Graham and Raff for the last couple of years, longer for Raff. But both sides are strong. You will play until someone loses, a best out of three in straight pool. Each game is a race to three hundred points. Win two games in a row and it is over, but this is difficult pool. Each straight pool game will be a true test. That was the agreement." Ed sipped a beer, listening to Johnny read Tommy the riot act. I seldom see someone so calm as Red Ed, a true inspiration to me.

Johnny gave me the nod and a thumbs-up. "Give 'em shit. I know you can beat this guy." I entered the arena with a calm, open mind. Everything was at stake, and nothing was at stake. One of the lessons the Kid taught me: winning wasn't the point of gambling. Gambling was. It was its own reward, so there was no risk. And that's when the winning happened.

Just then, Lenny and Holly walked in the side door, ordered two beers, and walked back to join us. Lenny already knew the plan to clean out Hector once this started. "Well, boys, how are you all tonight?" A cigarette was lit. They took a nice corner seat at the back. Lenny was sporting the white blazer he picked up in Colombia. Was he sporting dual glock pistols too?

Shanelle and Raff showed up. I knew Raff was on yellow alert, but he hid it well. Between him and Graham, I felt safe and could play my game without duress. Shanelle was there to bet. Raff and Shanelle sat on one side. Graham and I sat on the other side.

I talked with Graham. "I will teach him a new respect. It is a good thing Hector takes his pool seriously. It's the break we need. And fuck yeah, you are right Graham: we have a chance to get his money to. Wow, I wonder how much we can win from him. That will be up to you and Raff and Johnny and Lenny here to manage. Here is the plan. We are playing straight pool, sometimes called forteen-one, which means fourteen balls are sunk at one point each. All balls are called pocket, and when one ball is left on the table, it is used as a break ball. That is, I sink the second last ball in a pocket, and the balls are reracked. The cue ball pockets the last ball, hits the rack, releasing a few balls, and the run continues. This way of playing allows for some very high runs to he had. Each game will be to three hundred points. I will start gambling with Hector at one or two hundred thousand dollars for the first game. It will go up for the next games. There will be many opportunities to make rail bets on games and shots. That is the basic plan. I play my game, and you guys watch my back and bet like hell. This time we win."

It was eight o'clock on Saturday night. They say the hardest games to win are the first and last. I was thinking this while standing outside the back door, enjoying a joint with Lenny. A cold, cruel rain was moving toward Carmichaels. A cool wind bit my face, distracting me. We smoked quietly, enjoying the taste and buzz, when Hunter showed up. "Just in time. Good to see you, Hunter. Come on in." I felt completely calm and in control.

A few cars pulled up and parked across the street. Some people were moving around smoking cigarettes, then entered Carmichaels from the front. They had no idea we were watching them from the far end of the alley. "Fuck you, you thieving monkeys. Tonight you will lose," I said.

Lenny growled under his breath and spoke. "Holy old fuck, Tommy, these are the worst slimy pieces of shit on earth. Man, oh man, Tommy, ain't this something." We finished the joint and went back inside. Graham closed the door and stood by it. Raff and Graham exchanged glances between themselves. Security was doing its job. Carmichaels was quiet, warm. I refocused.

I knew the Colombians were here. It just smelled different. Not bad, just different.

There were a couple of Hector's men standing guard at one end. Hector was talking with them. There would be no fighting tonight. There was no need for anyone to be annihilated.

Hector saw us as the guys who inadvertently uncovered a Colombian drug cartel and threatened its long-term existence at this location. He wanted me gone. I saw Hector as the guy who had a misplaced hate for me and what I stood for. He was also the person who stood between myself and my future. It was my job to convince him otherwise.

Hector was several feet in front of me putting his cue together. There was a rare, simple look about him. I could see Catina in him. I could tell this was a man who was respected and doted upon. He has come here to play pool against a local, against me, for very high stakes.

Walking up to Hector, I spoke. "Around here, they call me the Blue Hand." I figured it was best to tell him up front who I was, to be honest. A little sharking. Graham was towering behind me.

Hector looked up at Graham, saying nothing. Graham looked down on Hector and said sarcastically, "I'd kneel if it wasn't for my trick knee." Fuck me, Graham was bold. He had a short-sleeve shirt on, exposing long, muscular arms. The many bruises and small cuts, from his knuckles to his biceps, intimidated the smaller, clean-cut Colombians.

"I see Frisk in this gringo. Frisk lives here." Was said in Spanish.

We moved around to the far end by the door. Catina was relaxed and sitting by her father.

Leaning over to Graham, I asked him about Jimbo and Dave. "Did you get in touch with Jimbo and Dave?"

Graham pointed at the door as those two walked in smiling, then said, "Tommy, I got in touch with Jimbo and Dave and gave them your special invitation. Must say they were surprised, and it took a few minutes to grasp what I was telling them. Like you wanted, I gave them each ten thousand dollars and told them to be here at this time to bet. I told them to bet on Tommy and if in doubt to check with me, and I would tell who to bet on. I told them it was a chance to make a few extra bucks, as you wanted." They each bought a beer and took a seat.

Poncho, Sylvia, the mayor, and her security came in and sat near the back, close to the door. Before sitting down, she came my way. Sylvia stood behind me for a moment, her perfume alluring. She leaned forward, whispering in my ear, and spoke with a quiet, sexy Russian accent.

"In poker, in blackjack, we say the cards have a past and a future. The cards that are dealt absolutely influence the cards that will be dealt. The game has a memory. You must find a way to make the past work for you."

I thought, *Make the past work for me.* Yes. Every shot I ever made since I started playing this game, with angle and speed control, was available to me. The acid trip opened a chakra where I saw pool balls bouncing for hours. The tens of thousands of shots I had practiced, and would practice, were at my command. The Kid was here with me, in the corner behind Lenny. It was all before me, both past and future. I could see the shots. Visualization was the key.

I stood looking about, assessing the situation. There were a few chairs pushed close for spectators. I looked around. Graham gave a cheerful high-five to everyone. He offered tremendous moral support. Everyone soon had a drink. Holly was drunk but in control. A total professional.

Falcon was now with me. Slowly turning my wrists in opposite directions, the two pieces came together. The joints flowed smoothly into one, and I felt Falcon come to life. Falcon became one. I was armed.

There was a pause. Catina smiled at me and nodded; it was the signal to start. "Let's play some pool," I said calmly. "Today, we play for it all. We settle this little war we have going. You think you can take my patent, my work here? You think you can come to my home and fuck with my life? Well, today you will go down. You will lose. You are a slick little fuck, and you will lose to me. We play straight pool. Best out of three. Each game is first to three hundred points."

Hector was all business. "Do not threaten me, gringo, you Blue Hand. We will play, and you will see who is your master. You have made much money with your hashish and your machine, money that should have been mine. Today, I will take that back when we win from you and your gringos." He motioned his arm about the room. He grinned, smirked, then smiled, almost laughing.

My job was to play pool. *This is a test*, I thought. The universe sent this fucking monkey here to test me to test us. Looking directly at Hector, I told him these words. "You want to risk it all, life and death. You know you are second class, not as good as you think you are. You live on your reputation. Are you afraid?" I was planting seeds of doubt.

Hector spoke. "I have come a long way, gringo. Do not fuck with me. When the heat is on, you will shake, you will miss. I face death daily. I am not afraid of you." In fact, he loathed Tommy.

I was jumping at this chance. "We will never get the job done standing here. Let's fucking play pool. We lag for break."

I felt the Kid with me. He spoke to me. "Tommy, you have done the work. You have a talent for pool. Control your nerves, and luck will be with you."

I was gambling with everyone's share, but I was confident. "Hector, we will play for two hundred thousand dollars for the first game." He nodded. Lenny, Shanelle, Red Ed, and others were taking bets from the crowd. *Holy God*, I thought, *Nailer died for a lot less than this*. It made me laugh. It relaxed me to reflect upon that unholy cremation.

The Kid spoke to me as clear as if we were playing in his private billiard room. Every word meant something to me. "There is energy all around us. Only a few select pool players can separate the positive and negative energies. This separation of energies creates an imbalance, and in the moment the energies come crashing together, you provide release and guidance creating the perfect pool swing. You do not command it; you simply guide it, breath first."

Hector won the lag for break and sat down. It was my break. It is a disadvantage to have the break in straight pool because each shot must be called, including the break shot, and that is very difficult to do. When the rack is open, it becomes easy for your opponent to make a lot of balls. My break shot was hit with easy force. The cue ball touching the corner ball in the rack bounced off two rails before returning to the same end of the table I just broke from, a safety break. And so began the final round of pool I would ever play with Hector.

After a few safeties, I made the first ball of the game. It was the two ball. The cue ball was in the middle of the table. I rubbed my bridge fingers up and down the shaft quickly to make it smooth. I did this lots during the game. Hector was not distracted.

I got to work, slowly working my way around the table. Soon I was up forty points. I got stuck with no shot, so I left him safe against the far rail. We played on. I would play safe when out of line. Hector was frustrated. He didn't expect me to play at this level, and so quickly. He hoped I would soon slow down.

Hector made a good run but missed, leaving the object ball directly in front of the side pocket. I was in trouble. The object ball was left in such a way it could only be shot up the rail into the end pocket, but the angle of the cue ball coming off the shot meant a certain scratch in the side. I bet Hector a thousand bucks I could make it in the corner and not scratch in the side. Rail bets were a lot higher than that.

"Sure," he said.

I lined up behind the cue ball and got the angle to make the nine in the corner with a level cue. The cue ball would deflect directly at the side pocket, there was no getting out of that one. Then I raised the back end of Falcon and played it very hard. The cue ball hit the nine ball, driving it directly into the corner pocket. The cue ball jumped off directly for the side pocket and a little bit in the air, not much. The cue ball hit the back of the pocket a little bit higher than normal, above the spot to put it in the pocket, and with such force it bounced straight back onto the table.

"Thank you for the beer money," I said. Hector was silent.

Many bets were being made on the side, much like that pool hall tent in Colombia. What Hector would soon find out is that I get better as I play. My shots went in automatically, or I was safe. I played at a good pace, with little hesitation. My score was at two hundred and ninety-three to his two hundred and forty when I let him to the table. He ran out and won the first game. I paid him two hundred thousand dollars in cash.

Graham walked over and handed me a cold beer. He said, "Guzzle this beer. Sheer will is your greatest talent. Trust me, I know what I am talking about." I gave him a double look. The only other person to say that was Frisk. It made me smile. Was that cultural expropriation? Graham walked back to his seat. I hammered back most of the beer. It was cold on my front teeth and throat. The foam was on my lips, and my stomach stretched. When I put the mug down, I had put that game behind me and was ready to move on.

"Well, that was the first game," I said under my breath to Lenny. "The first game and the last game are the hardest to win and lose." He told me we were up a lot of cash on side bets. Everything was still on track.

I felt Frisk with me too. He would tell me to keep my opponent a little afraid by being aggressive or fast to raise the bet. "Nice game, Hector. That was good shooting. This time we play for five hundred thousand dollars. I can cover that. Can you?"

Hector smiled and said, "No problem. I have gold against your cash."

We started the second game. I broke leaving Hector a shot. He started to pick it up, making some long shots and banks. He seemed happy for now. I was glad to see this. I believe he was peaking. I needed to just play in my space, in my mind. See the shots, visualize, follow the plan. Clock shots were everywhere.

Hector was a good pool player. He had a rather fast style, but the Kid had taught me well. I noticed how Hector held the cue for different shots, and his posture was always square. Hector could make cross corner shots with uncanny precision. His buddies bragged how he ran racks and how good he was back home. That stuff did not bother me at all. I fed off it. But it was true: he was running balls and racking up the points. Soon, his score was two hundred and one to my sixty-four.

Graham sat by the table, keeping track of the totals. I looked out the side window. It was raining and very dark outside. The clock showed four in the morning, and I was reminded of my days, not so long ago, when I would play at this time because I could not sleep from the speed. Tonight, I felt like the training was paying off. It made the addiction have value, in some strange fucking way. If I did not spend months, up all night and day on speed, practicing by myself, I would never be as good as I am. Whatever rage drove me during that time left me with a valuable gift. I was now playing professional-level pool.

It was a slow and systematic attack. I bore down on Hector. No more holding back. He saw my ability, and he was awed. My shots were amazing. His safety play was weak, allowing me offensive moves to start running balls again. He was being assassinated. I would be remembered for this game.

Then he missed and let me at the table. "So, you let me back at the table. Thank you." This time it was different. I played more consistently, just that much more accurately. My points ran up quickly. Side bets were escalating. Hector looked concerned, he thought he would win this game, but he would not. We played some safeties. Then I got a shot and ran out.

Hector said, "It was now one game each, a tie. This is the final game, the tiebreaker," then paid his debt in cash and gold. "This time, we will play for one million dollars." I was ready to play. The night was wearing on, but I did not really notice. I would sip cold beer for a while. Then a thin line, and off I would go again.

Hector's mood changed from business to family. He moved close to me and spoke like a man with something to lose. "We play for more than three million dollars. We play for our honor—the honor of our women, my daughter, and our families. Yes, there is much on the table. We play this last game. If you beat me, you still will not win." *This guy has a lot on the line*, was my only thought.

Just before we started the tiebreaker, the third and final game, I leaned close to Graham, telling him my thoughts. "I will not be the dead bird, falling from its nest into a cold soup. Nor will I be the half-drowned snake, returning to life only to have my fucking head torn clean off my fucking body and left swinging from the trees. I will be like the Falcon. I will wait, then attack with claws dug so fucking deep, he cannot escape." Graham smiled. We toasted with our beer cans. It was my turn to be called to action.

Hector stayed seated. His men were beside him, smoking thin cigarettes and wearing loose-fitting golf shirts with breast pockets that held packs of smokes. They always looked like they were on their way to a beach party. Their girlfriends were well-dressed and horny. The distraction was good.

Nothing could be better than seeing Catina in a blue top and a real tight skirt, walking toward me. Catina was proud of her intuition. She moved close to me. "Good luck, Tommy. I hope you win." I smiled and watched her as she turned and walked back to sit with Hector.

The last game began. I broke by calling the head ball two rails in the side pocket. I then placed the cue ball near the long rail, hitting it hard against the far back rail. The cue ball bounced fast, hitting the back of the rack hard, sending the first ball two rails and into the side pocket. The rest of the rack broke up nicely. I made one hundred and twenty points, then played safe.

When I got to the table again, Hector had made one hundred and ninety-six points. I got back to the job of making balls and running out the racks. I told Hector, "The high watermark has been reached. The wave will roll back. You are going down." I stood at the table, making shots one at a time. Soon he was only leading by a few points. Then I was winning, and still going.

The winds had changed. He was fucked. I never really looked back after that. I was the tide and the ebb tide. My shots rang true. I banked, double-banked, caromed, and sliced shots with Philippine accuracy. I remember the Kid telling me, "Players from the Philippines cut the ball so well because they eat a lot of worms. Apparently, it helps with their vision."

At one point, the object ball was a couple of inches from the rail near the side pocket. The cue ball was on the opposite rail close to the end pocket. I lined up a ticky shot and pounded the cue ball into the rail just behind the ball. It was an unexpected shot. The cue ball sank deep into the rubber on the rail and came off directly into the back of my ball. It jumped and almost flew across the table, into the opposite side pocket. The cue ball rolled into the middle of the table. I got a few claps for that one.

I chalked my tip by looking directly at it, then painting chalk on in short, quick strokes, like a woman putting on lipstick. I noticed my tip had some roughage sticking out. Instead of using sandpaper to smooth it out, I rolled the cue tip on the edge of the table cloth. This is not something ever done, except to throw a little bit of sharking into the mix. I just kept on going as if it were the usual thing to do.

But the real kicker, the thing that just pissed Hector off, was me making all my shots. I was putting them in left, right, and center. I was running up points one ball at a time. My arm gave true strokes through the cue ball. I lost myself in the game. I was not thinking about anything or anyone. I was just playing. It was a sign I was on my own time. I finished the one rack with two bank shots and a long dead on shot. The last ball was just a few inches left of the new rack, the cue ball sitting close to the side pocket. I lined up the cue ball to hit the object ball directly into the rack, bouncing off and going into the corner pocket. Basically, I banked the ball off the rack into the corner, a very nice shot. My rail birds made money on that one. Jimbo was ear-to-ear smiles, giving me a nonchalant thumbs-up.

Hector was becoming distracted, but he was cool, professional. We were bantering back and forth. It was a lot to have on the line. Unfortunately for Hector, he wasn't trained by the Kid, and he was playing the Blue Hand. My claws were dug in. They were set. He could not win this battle tonight. My bridge hand moved quickly up and down Falcon's shaft. My fingers warmed. The shaft became smooth and slick.

I ordered a beer and sipped it. I ordered a chuck wagon and devoured it. Graham was happy to get me anything I wanted.

Then I got serious. It was time. I beat Hector slowly, my shots going in. I stayed one shot ahead of him. He was frustrated because he was close to tasting victory. He truly believed the odds were in his favor and the pendulum of luck would swing his way. He was wrong.

I shot with a medium stroke, always passing the cue ball through the center of the table, leaving it on the correct side of the next object ball. This made it easy to go from ball to ball. Shots sounded clear and crisp. My run was one hundred for a total of two hundred and sixty points, forty from winning. Graham marked the score. I felt The Kid's approval.

I chalked up and started another run after a miss by Hector. He added too much English on that last shot. Many times, the Kid told me about extra English. "There is a lot of English added by the angles balls sit at and the problem with not hitting the cue ball where you think you will. All this adds up to a miss as the object ball veers just oh so slightly off course and juggles in the pocket." Truer words were never spoken.

Hector got to the table and made sixty eight before missing. I got back and made ten more for a total of two hundred and fifty. Hector was tired. He slowed down, then he played a poor safe. I made balls until I was at two hundred and ninety nine, one ball short of winning then missed. Hector played to two hundred and ninety before playing safe with the cue ball jammed in the corner. The game switched from pool to billiards. Rail bets were out of control high.

I didn't know he could play carom billiards, the game with two cue balls, one object ball and the table has no pockets. The only way to get a point was to have your cue ball touch the other two balls. It required finesse and a very light touch, sometimes only moving the balls an inch or two. I knew billiards also, responding with a short billiard shot, leaving the cue ball and object ball against the long rail, just two inches from the corner pocket. Hector and I battled several more nurse shots, or very soft shots in the corner, not wanting to give up an advantage. Rail bets continued to soar.

Finally, Hector made an incredible shot, leaving the object ball against the long rail, one inch from the end pocket and the cue ball directly in front of the object ball and touching it. *Wow,* I thought, *such a perfect, beautiful configuration, with the two balls square to the rail like that.* I had never seen this shot ever come up in a pool game, but I had practiced it a number of times when I was having fun with trick shots. This shot required banking the object ball that was against the rail into the opposite corner pocket. The cue ball had to be hit at the absolute exact spot directly into the face of the balls. This was not an easy shot. We were down to the last shot at Carmichaels. If I missed, it would leave the table open, and Hector would run out. The rail bets went up, but the real cash was with Hector and me. Almost three million dollars was on the line. All down to one shot.

Hector was in the corner, leaning on his cue with two hands, believing I would miss and he would win. "You are scared, Tommy. Is the Blue Hand going to lose now, and that will be the end of that?" The crowd was quiet.

Light from Sunday morning was trying to get around the shades. The atmosphere was thick. Side bets were finished. Everyone had decided whether I could make this shot or not. Everyone who knew me had made their bets.

Someone in the crowd spoke. "It doesn't look possible. Many players, even pros, can't make that shot."

My words reflected authority and confidence. "Now we play, all in. If I lose, you get it all, everything I have. I will not be worthy, and I will sleep in the streets." No more words were spoken.

A bell tolled twelve times from a local church told everyone it was noon Sunday. We had been playing for sixteen hours straight, and we were basically tied. It would all come down to the next few minutes. Most good people were at church. We were saying our own version of mass. I was the high priest, and these were the followers. Hector was a sheep.

"Fuck this no-good vermin-eating creep. You can beat this little genetic mistake," Graham said quietly and in all seriousness. But he had no answer for this shot. It was all about the moment. I had put my faith in the Kid. I felt his presence. I let him take over. I was granted courage.

I went back to my training. I focused, remembering the Kid's face. The joy of winning was something to experience when you were with the Kid. He forced me to play good technical pool, and to gamble. For that, I am grateful.

I stood before the shot, chalking the end of my cue in slow twisting motions. I lined up behind the cue ball as it totally eclipsed the object ball, the winning ball. I put my right hand on the table, making a high bridge. Falcon rested easily between my thumb and first finger, my left hand elevating the butt end of the cue slightly. I placed the cue tip at the bottom of the cue ball, at that spot where the cue ball touched the felt. The middle of the cue tip lined up with the middle of that spot. Then I slowly moved the cue tip upwards, keeping it in line with the center of the cue ball. When I got to the top half of the cue ball, to that spot two cue tip widths above center. I began to move my left elbow back and forth, directly facing the front of the cue ball, lining up the shot to pass through the tops of both balls and not down into the balls. I was quickly analyzing the shot. It would require one thirty-second of a cue tip of aim into the object ball, just the slightest aim off center. This was a type of Sailor Barge shot. However, the trick to this shot was my left shooting arm. It had to be moved just slightly toward my body. I heard nothing from anyone around me. I was focused.

In the back of my mind, I heard Old Don's words. "Never miss the money ball, never." I was perfectly calm.

The final trick to this shot is to pause the cue at the back of the swing, to stop just for the briefest of moments before stroking, smoothly, straight through the tops of both balls. Then I stroked. The positive and negative energies came together, everything was exact. It was not luck that made the shot go in with power but dead on accuracy, dropping into the middle of the pocket beneath me with a sold sounding *plunk*. It was skill. The game was over. I had won.

"Holy God, Hector, did you see that?" I screamed. Everyone yelled.

In his world, Hector was master, boss, and a killer. In this world, at this moment, he had found his master, and he was not happy. He did not need any more embarrassment. His rage was stronger and more powerful. He would learn nothing from this. In every loss there is a victory, a philosophical truth he was incapable of comprehending.

Hector was beat. He was put down, his spirits dropping. He leaned on his cue stick. It bent, then snapped as he applied more pressure. It broke several inches below the top. Hector gathered the pieces, quickly turning away from the table. He was in a rage.

My character and my soul stood up to the test. I felt Frisk's presence, and he was proud. The crowd had accepted me. Hector, however, would never accept me. There would be no respect between us. He was a full-time loser, and there was just no way he could win this fight.

The time was right for Poncho to talk with Hector. Poncho spoke in Spanish. "Hector, it is time to let this go. Allow me to make you an offer. I have plans to make you stronger here in this country than ever before. You can see I trust Tommy. These people who you fucked with was wrong, but now the air is cleared. You have had your chance, and you lost. Now we work together."

Hector was silent. I am not sure he even heard Poncho. Then he responded, "Fuck you and fuck Tommy. I will kill that cocksucker someday soon."

Poncho was upset and gave Hector a direct order. "Go now. Return home to Colombia. Cool off. We will talk when I return in a week." Poncho walked away from Hector.

Catina came from the crowd. She kissed and hugged me. I held her close and said, "Never a doubt, my love. Never a doubt." People looked me in the eye, shook my hand, and offered to buy me drinks. I accepted, of course.

After a few minutes, Poncho came to see me in the back of Carmichaels. Graham was beside me as he spoke, "I invite you to meet out the back door in two minutes. Please have your people be there too."

I said to Graham quietly, "Go get Lenny, Raff, Hunter, Catina, and Holly." Graham quickly followed orders.

Lenny, Graham, Hunter, Raff, Shanelle, Catina, and Holly were outside now with Poncho and myself.

Standing outside the backdoor at Carmichaels, Poncho surprised us when he fired up a joint and then began talking. "It is called Punta Roja. We have no trouble bringing whatever we want into or out of your country. The embassy never gets searched. We have diplomatic immunity," he said, and he passed me the joint. It looked like a joint—very large and long, with the ends twisted tight. It burned hot, with seeds popping in every direction. This was a fatty. Poncho knew how to roll a joint.

"Thank you," I said. "You are with the embassy too. That helps a lot. Fuck yeah." Without hesitation, I took a big toke. The taste was amazing, easily the best I ever had. There was nothing finer when it came to weed. I breathed in. "Ah, the powerful Sativa you call Punta Roja, but which we like to call Colombian Red. Holy God, this is good pot," I said, passing the joint to Hunter. It was the same weed Holly had in Colombia. More joints were lit. While holding my toke, I told Poncho, "This is the best weed I have ever smoked."

Hunter said, "This is pure Sativa. Amazing, I can taste the mountains, so powerful, ah good shit eh. I am most impressed." Then looking over at Poncho, he said, "Did you know they call Tommy the Blue Hand? Well, they do." I think Hunter was drunk, and now stoned.

Poncho acknowledged Hunter. Looking at Tommy's blue chalk infused hands said, "The Blue Hand is a very good name. Very fitting for a champion pool player."

Hunter had one more bit of information for Poncho. "Did you know Frisk named the valley we grow all this weed in—Val Lenny after Lenny here," he said, pointing at Lenny. Lenny stood tall, acting indifferent.

Poncho bowed his head. For a moment, his son was with him. Then he smiled and spoke. "Yes, that is a fitting name Frisk bestowed upon your valleys. Very wise, 'Val Lenny.' It has much meaning and strength, like the character of the man who found them." Poncho snapped his fingers and a bottle appeared.

Poncho had a bottle of Frisk's favorite Colombian whiskey. Luckily, we all had water glasses. "Only the embassy is allowed to bring this strong whiskey into the country. It is not sold in stores. This was Frisk's favorite drink. He would drink it slowly, passionately at sunset and well into the evening. I make the first toast to Frisk, to my son and missing friend." Proudly, we drank with respect, honor, and dignity to our missing friend, to Frisk.

When the whiskey settled in our stomach, Poncho became serious, all business, then spoke to us, "Tommy, you will be the first cartel leader in this part of the world. I want your team to hear this because they are your family." Poncho looked at Catina. "Catina, your father has become obsessed with jealously. He is dangerous. He cannot continue as cartel leader. I want you to lead your family cartel. Only you know the business and have the ability to be successful."

Lenny briefly spoke. "That is wise, very wise. But what about that fuck, Hector?" Lenny sure had a way to saying what we were thinking.

Poncho continued, "Hector is returning to Colombia, and we will speak when I return. For now, Catina, you must prepare to take over the family duties. Tommy, only you have the capacity to work with Sylvia and Catina and run a world-class hashish manufacturing and distribution business. We will be a powerful family." We stood like soldiers receiving our orders. Poncho relaxed and smiled, his vision shared. Catina and I shared eye contact and smiled.

We finished the whiskey in shots, between lines. We were somber, and in those moments, we bonded.

I was stoned and hyped from the game. I told Poncho how I felt. "I am here to make you stronger. We are together. You help me with seeds and a safe way to get rid of thousands of pounds of hashish, and a family business is born. Yes, I will lead your northern cartel."

Poncho kept his word from the first meeting we had in Colombia. Looking at everyone, he began. "I give you your eternal place in the mountains, that place shall be known as 'Val Lenny.' From my heart, you will have the eternal right to grow Colombian weed in your fields. May you enjoy today and many generations to come. You are very serious and will produce the best hashish. You will help others with your machine, with your inventions. You will have direct access to the source of seeds and weed from my fields forever."

Looking Poncho in the eyes I nodded, again agreeing to the life commitment.

Poncho calmly explained what I already knew, but I always thought it was a good thing to verbalize your thoughts, as I do not read minds. "Your men, Hunter, Lenny, Graham, and Raff, and the women, Catina, Shanelle and Holly, are the best in the world. You know this is true. They are here and with you. You have political influence in Sylvia and with the mayor. We have a very strong team that will make us all many millions. With this, you will have more power, more influence too. May you and your family continue for many years to come. Hunter and Lenny, you will now go with two of my men to collect that which is yours." Poncho waved this arms, and two men stepped forward. No one rushed.

I seized the pause and spoke. "These seeds are the beginning for Val Lenny. You will be very proud of the fields we will grow. I will come visit you in Colombia when this season is over." Poncho acknowledged my vision. I was further grateful to him. "I know Frisk would be very happy you raised him well. You were a good father."

Poncho commented, "You will become very powerful. I like you. It is genius, very wise." We shook hands, smiled, and moved toward the front of Carmichaels. It was a slow walk with Poncho and Holly close beside me. Graham and Raff were in front and to my side.

Hector's men paid me in gold. *Holy God*, I thought. With that, Poncho had done his job, supervising this game to make sure it was fair, and everyone got paid without any fights or bullshit of the likes that started this fucking mess.

The crowd cheered and sulked. Debts were paid in cash and gold, but more importantly, I won my life. Impressed at first, Catina sat back in her seat. Then she grew distant, almost worried. Sylvia and the mayor left immediately. Others left slowly. Hector had already left with his people. Raff stayed close to me, Shanelle just a few feet back, with Holly.

They were most impressed with their winnings. Dave and Jimbo followed the plan and walked out with much more than they started with. They were all grateful.

Hunter and Lenny left to get the weed. They walked out the back door of Carmichaels with a couple of Poncho's men. The door swung shut, locking behind them. At the curb, Lenny's truck was waiting. Poncho's men took them around to the back of a long black limousine. When its trunk opened, five hundred-pound potato sacks packed full of Colombian weed that had gone to seed lay inside. There would be millions of seeds, which meant millions of plants.

They told Hunter and Lenny, "In these bags are many seeds, my friends. Poncho had a feeling it would turn out like this. He had us privately gather these rather large sacks with the best Colombian weed for you. We used the notes Lenny made when he was here. The red bag contains Punta Roja and is from the lower elevations. The gold bag is Colombian Gold, very valuable, from higher elevations. This is our present to you and your reward. Do good things with these plants. You will make Val Lenny plantations of Colombian Rojo Haze and Colombian Gold for many generations to come. The best in all the world. You will make us proud." The bags were moved to Lenny's truck, covered with a tarp, and they were gone, headed for Val Lenny.

My mind drifted. I had to nearly lose my life to gain everything, or maybe it was always meant to be like this: lose to win. Maybe that was the lesson of the bird falling from the nest that autumn day. There would be struggles and loss in my life so other parts of my life could flourish. Weak parts of us would be ripped away, yet we would go on to inherit new, unknown wonders. The weak bird died so the strong would live.

Poncho talked with us. "It was a revelation, Tommy. Your family is strong. I admire that. This year, you brought me much wealth and excitement. I think it was good for you too? You continue to grow the weed and make the hashish, and I will help take it off your hands. My friend Sylvia will be glad to provide any assistance you may need, or anything else." He talked slow and articulated with his arms a lot. *All these fuckers do that, talk with their arms*, I thought.

I said to Poncho, "We will work together. We will work as a family," and I extended my hand in partnership. We shook hands again and moved to leave Carmichaels, to walk out the side door.

Hector was not happy to lose again. His only recourse now to save honor was to kill Tommy. The rage was too strong. Hector could not stop. His honor, his ego, would not allow it. After all he had been through, he was never able to best Tommy, never able to get the advantage. It started with a pool game. It ended with a pool game. The threat of violence is never as strong as violence itself and always at arm's distance, just around the corner.

Graham stood beside me. Raff was outside, waiting by the side of Carmichaels, relaxed, guarding, waiting to walk beside me. I left Carmichaels through the side door with Holly, the side door Frisk, and I left through many times. Poncho was behind me, and his guards were behind him. Graham had held the door open for me and Holly, once outside he walked on my right side.

Graham was tall, looking over me, and Poncho too. Raff was in the middle with Poncho on his left beside Carmichaels. As we stepped around the corner turning to the left, there they were, Hector with a rather large knife in one hand and a pistol in the other hand. The crippled, gimpy bounty hunter beside him held a short sword. Knives and killing were in their blood. The two assassins moved quickly, their attack predetermined. They felt confident now with Frisk gone. They felt safe. It all happened very quickly. Hector wanted to cut me first, then use the pistol in his other hand to machine gun me to death in the street. *Medellin, Colombia, cartel style*, I thought. Poncho was clearly in direct path of any bullets coming this way. He was in harm's way. He was in mortal danger. His guards behind him, the timing was bad. They could not protect him.

Hector's knife came straight at my stomach. The other killer lunged a sword directly at Poncho's heart. Things happened faster than I could see but not for Graham or Raff. Graham stepped forward, grabbing Hector's attack wrist, twisting it violently away from me. The wrist snapped immediately, the knife dropping to the ground, making a short high-note sound as the blade struck concrete. The automatic pistol in his other hand was being raised, ready to fire, to kill. None of us had a chance. At the same time, the gimpy bounty hunter lunged at Poncho. Death was certain.

These were the two people who hated Tommy and Poncho the most, who wanted them dead. Poncho's guards saw the danger. They were unable to intervene quickly enough, but Raff could. Raff spun halfway around backwards, his large foot extending straight out in a near-perfect sidekick, catching the small sword approaching Poncho in the middle, pinning it to the brick wall. The assassin stumbled. Raff lunge-punched him straight below the throat, then in the temple with the other fist. As he went down, he stumbled against the force of his sword being stopped in midthrust. There was no hope for this assassin. The job Frisk started so long ago was about to be finished. He tried to turn away, but it took only one more punch directly to the side of his neck, crushing a critical vertebrae, severing the spinal cord. The body was dead before hitting the ground.

Hector had myself and Poncho in his sights. The pistol was moving upward toward us, it was a machine pistol set to full automatic. Graham stood before Hector, holding his broken wrist tightly. He snap-kicked Hector in the knee, shattering it, sending sheer pain through his body. The gun still raised, Graham was there to protect. Hector started to collapse, a brief smile on his face as he thought for one brief second that he would kill Tommy and Poncho. The feeling was only a moment long. Graham reached over with his right hand, grabbing the gun hand by the butt of the pistol. Graham pulled the gun upwards, away from Poncho and Tommy, taking them out of danger. Extending the arm straight, Graham slowly bent the arm back toward Hector's face, the weapon upside down, approaching his face. The muzzle slowly came in line with Hector's forehead, then his face. Graham squeezed Hector's trigger finger, and Hector shot himself in the face with a machine pistol. As Hector died, so did the psychotic killer. Both landed dead, face first on the street.

Graham walked over to Poncho and looked down at him. Graham raised his fist to Poncho's face, squeezing tightly, his fist nearly the size of Poncho's head. Reciting quietly, with lips drawn back, in a very controlled rage. "Do you want to see how fucking hard I can hit. What if I beat the fuck out of you right now? I could kill you right now. Do you want me to kill you? Right fucking now, I could kill you." Graham was calm, accentuating himself as he spoke, looking directly into Poncho's eyes. Graham was getting everyone on the same page.

Poncho looked him square in the eyes, unflinching, his security moving closer. Then, in an instant, Graham lowered his fist and laughed. Poncho relaxed, making a joke. "For this line of work, I thought you would be a lot bigger." They shared a handshake, a short hug, and a laugh. A new generation of fierce warriors and truth seekers was born in that moment.

Graham turned, looked at me, and said in a calm, reassuring voice, "The war is over Tommy both sides agree. We won."

I spat on the bodies and screamed, "Savage bastards, die." Then I relaxed.

Poncho spoke very quietly, knowing a disease had just been cured. "We never had a chance. We would have died in that moment just then if not for you two, for Graham and Raff. I am so fucking glad you were trained by Frisk. You are masters."

"They are fucking heroes," Holly said as reality sank in. Poncho's men had the bodies cleared quickly and without incident. People from within Carmichaels soon scattered and were not there that day. The lone witness was Carmichaels itself.

It was quiet on this cold Sunday afternoon. There were low, puffy, dark rain clouds in the sky. "Jesus Christ Almighty," I said to Poncho. "How in the fuck do I get into these situations?" I breathed deep. The cold air felt calming on my stomach. There would be no answer.

Poncho moved to Graham and Raff, "Frisk would have been proud, you are well trained, you kill fast, and without hesitation. Fast attack and close combat were Frisk's favorite, He had that Colombian thing for being in your face, he just hated using knives. Today you have graduated, you are truly worthy to protect my fields, your fields, Val Lenny. It is also about leadership, and trust, and taking control." Poncho was grateful, shaking Graham's, and Raff's hand, looking long into the eyes of the men who just saved his life. Poncho got into his vehicle, ready to depart; then spoke, "You are now cartel leader as much as Catina is, let my strength be your strength. We will meet again soon, my friend. I never liked that fucking piece of shit, Hector. Your men did well today Tommy, you did well. Frisk did well. God bless Frisk. He lives strong in you."

"Frisk lives on in us all," I said. Poncho left.

Catina stood in the background through all the violence, she knew Hector would try something. Catina began to speak even as I was moving to her. "I didn't think that would happen. I never thought he would try to kill you Tommy or Poncho. Today, I lost a father, and a short time ago you lost your best friend." Catina cried. I held her. The tide hit the high watermark and was now rolling back. The fire was out yet the fever of life continued to burn. Holly walked over and stood beside us. In that moment Catina, Holly and myself held each other together in a long, heartfelt hug. There were no more words to be said. We survived.

The sun was hot as Holly, Catina, and I slowly walked across the schoolyard back to my place. A spring rain began misting on our faces in a rare afternoon sun shower, and my brain cooled.

# Snooker

THE PREDAWN SUMMER MORNING WAS COLD AND DARK, and I said out loud, "It's fucking great to be alive." There were clouds low in the sky, and I knew it would warm slowly today. My energy was good as I cruised toward Lake Clear. It felt good to be back in the neighborhood. My house in the mountains was becoming a home. The coffee was hot in my mouth and smelt so good. I drove the highway to Lenny's, where Holly and Catina were waiting.

It was a couple weeks now since Hector died. Catina was so very sad to lose her father. She cried and mourned for two days. Then she stopped. Her strength grew. It became her time. Poncho knew she worked very close with her father, that she had grown with the family business and knew it well. He respected her business sense. Her cool head, and most of all her excellent intuition. Catina rose to the top. She would leave here soon to run the family business near Medellin as a cartel leader. It was her right. She had support, respect, and fear. People were afraid of her, and that was OK. It was good. It was their way.

I always wondered why Frisk sent me Falcon, and now I think I know. I came to realize he loved me unconditionally, without judgment, as a true friend. He knew early on we would be lifetime friends, sharing a trust that could not be shattered. He knew someday he would need me to be with him, and I was. I came to see Falcon not just as a gift but as a symbol of our friendship. I will never forget my friend, and part of him will forever be alive through Falcon. Wood never dies.

I am driving the backroads now, watching Venus occult with Jupiter through the clouds. Soon both set on the western horizon. I stopped a few miles from Lenny's to sit on some rocks and watch the day start and reflect. As the planets set, high clouds scattered while a bright sun broke the eastern skyline. It was calming and reminiscent of that Colombian morning in the fields with Frisk and Lenny. It would be a nice day. I breathed deep, sitting, relaxing, meditating.

My mind became very aware of just how close to death I actually came during my activities over the past several months. I did turn things around, but not without severe cost. The loss of Frisk and the loss of a father ran deep, but our spirits are strong.

My eyes closed, and Frisk was there, alive, talking, loving, and very much at home. My heart beat faster. My stomach ached. Thanks to Frisk's hard work and teachings, we now had fields of weed stretching for miles in the middle of a country where no one will find us. We had Val Lenny. The country side was alive with pot in all directions. It was a marvel to behold. Frisk would be proud of this year's crop.

I thought of Catina and Holly and our friendship while hurrying toward Lake Clear again. When I drove up to Lenny's place and pulled in the lane way, I saw a couple of cars and a truck. It was quiet and serene. The lake was calm. There was little wind. It was sunrise on a warm summer day. *They must be playing an all-night card game*, I thought. My mind was going empty as I walked up the few steps and through the front door.

Inside Lenny's kitchen, a new madness was unfolding. A card game ensued. Sitting at the kitchen table were a bunch of rednecks, drinking whiskey and beer while chain-smoking cigarettes. Holly was saving me a seat beside Lenny. Catina was beside Mike. I came over, gave Holly a kiss, and sat down to play a hand or two. The game was seven-card stud. They were all loud and drunk.

Lenny was very good to acknowledge Frisk and the loss of a father. He made a prayer, then lead a moment of silence. "We all truly miss Frisk and support Catina in her time of loss. We also wish Tommy and Catina well on their new path." We all bowed our heads. Soon, we were playing again.

It was a beautiful antique kitchen table we were sitting at. The top was a very dark, thick hardwood with solid legs of intricate design. There was enough room to sit six people without problem. This table came all the way from New York City, strapped to the roof of Lenny's car. Lenny stole it from some poor black family in Harlem. He saw it at the home after doing some carpenter work there. It was midday when Lenny nonchalantly knocked on their door, only to find the place empty. The moment was seized, and the table went missing. He threw it on top of his car, along with everything else he owned, and left in a cloud of blue smoke. A wine bottle could be seen being chucked out the driver's side window, crushing and busting into many small pieces on the sidewalk. No one cared.

We had been playing cards and drinking for the last few hours when Calvin started getting loud and stupid. My moment of bliss was shattered. "He should quit drinking, that fucker," is what I said to Holly.

Calvin started talking about Lenny's kitchen table. He was giving us a seminar on how well it was constructed. First he slapped the table and it did not move. My drink did not ripple one wave. This crazy fucker then jumped up on the table and started to tap dance on top of it, insisting, "With just a few more taps, I will break this fucking table in half."

Lenard was a true example of someone who could switch to action in an instant. "It pays to have a natural rage," I often told people when trying to explain his behavior.

Lenny got up walking purposely toward his gun rack. There was a nice low-caliber rifle, blending in very well with its rack, just lying there waiting. Quickly and without hesitation, Lenny loaded the rifle and told Calvin, "Get the fuck off my table or I will blow you off the fucking table," and fired a shot into the ceiling.

Everyone was sitting and cheering on Calvin until the shot went off, and a shell flew from the chamber, bouncing off the stove. Like a child putting his finger in a light socket for the first time, this crew were instantly shocked. They stood immediately, lifting their hands, stuffing their money in their pockets, begging Lenny not to shot them while backing up slowly, bumping into each other.

Lenny had craziness in his eyes, and mania surrounded us. Both hands held his rifle high, pointing at the ceiling, while all the time staring down Calvin. No one was in danger. Calvin leapt off the table, landing on the floor with a load slap, and quickly moved to the door. The table remained unscathed by the attack, a brother to the one we hid behind in Colombia during that shot out. Cards and cash lay strewn and abandoned everywhere.

The front door of Lenny's burst open, and people started filing out at a good pace. Calvin led the exodus. His arms were up in the air, waving while cursing savagely. His bright red and black lumberjack shirt stood out at me through the window. Immediately behind him were others. As Calvin ran, he bypassed his truck, choosing to vacate the property on foot. The last player outside was Lenny. He appeared in the doorway with his rifle in hand.

Lenny yelled at Calvin not to get mad. "Where are you fucking going? I was only kidding. I wasn't going to shoot you. Come on back." Lenny was trying to calm down the situation, but humility was never part of his being. No one believed him. They were gone for now.

By then Calvin had split in a near gallop. Others drove out rather quickly, kicking up dust and rocks. Lenny was holding an intense stare up the road. I screamed from inside, "What the fuck was going on out there? Are you crazy, waving that gun around?" Lenny walked back inside his home.

Lenny held the rifle now with one arm bent at the elbow and the rifle pointing straight up. It was comfortable in that position. Continuing to hold the gun, he looked over at Catina, Holly, Mike, and me. We were the only ones left sitting at the far side of the kitchen table. I felt safe.

Lenny came over to the table and emptied the weapon. He put the gun back in the rack then opened a beer and sat down. I said to Lenny, "Well, you got good taste in kitchen tables. Do you think you could leave me this in your will?" I said, my hand caressing the top softly, like it was deserved. I didn't see any need to pursue this little drama any further. We sat in comfortable silence.

We drank a beer while Bridget cleaned up. Soon it was time to leave, to head home. Lenny was heading to the race track and reading the sports section with full attention. Holly and Catina said goodbye, and we left.

It was cool inside, but we quickly found the air outside hot. The leaves in the trees made patterns on the ground while sunlight followed the openings. There were a few birds bouncing between branches. We watched the lake during the drive out. It distracted me. I did not slow down as I skidded a ninety-degree right turn onto the next road. The dust from the dirt road was soon behind us. My foot was heavy on the accelerator. It was fun to drive fast. I drove to the maximum I could handle, to my new home on the mountainside.

Soon, we drifted into my long, rising laneway, trees provided shade. I parked beside my home. After getting out, Holly said, "We are tired. Let me give you a hug," and the girls went inside to rest. Catina would be leaving in two days.

I had not been up all night playing cards, so my energy was still good, my thirst for cold beer rising. I kicked the cooler, sitting by the side of the house. It swished about, and when I looked inside, sure enough there was ice and cold beer inside. The water was cold, the beer can numbing my fingers. The air was getting warmer, and I was hungry for chuck wagons, so I threw on some shorts and left for Carmichaels. It was a quick drive, and I parked in front of the high school by my first home. The walk to Carmichaels was enjoyable. It gave me time to think.

I was drinking a beer in a brown paper bag as I walked across the schoolyard. The beer was cold and felt good in my hand. It felt right.

For some reason, the pocket in the shorts had the chalk holder from the crazy British kid I got in a fight with last year when I was sloppy drunk. I always felt sorry about that mess. Funny thing is, I truly do not remember stealing it from their place. I had one of those blackout moments. Not a big blackout, where all of a sudden it's the next day, but a short, drunken black hole of misery. I would not be doing that again. Anyway, I was over it now, still fumbling with the holder. It got warm in my hand.

But it did cause me to reminisce. I thought about the past year again and all that had happened. It was a lot. There were many gifts. Catina's, Holly's, and Shanelle's faces came and went. Frisk, Lenny, and Hunter all made my heart beat a little faster. For brief moments, they were here, and we were together.

I thought of the lesson learned with Hunter at the prison, to stop worrying. That was a very strange and dangerous adventure, but it helped put things in perspective. It was a place to fear, and I bonded with Hunter. I did stop worrying about many things after that. Interesting, I thought, how these memories returned after finding a stolen chalk holder. Who would have guessed?

As I walked across the schoolyard, a guy was walking from the other side toward me. As he approached, we quickly recognized each other. Holy old fuck, it was the punk's father, Al, from that fucked-up house party. Al was the true owner of the chalk holder. I stopped. What was the universe doing now? I pondered. He too stopped.

"Al," I said. He looked like a boxer. I could see the muscle in his shoulders and his short, powerful arms. I did not want to ever get punched by this guy.

I cut to the point. "Al, I know I was drunk that night last year at your house party. I am sorry, and I want to return to you what is yours." I gave him the chalk holder, with the original pink chalk still in it. "I am very sorry and will never act like that again."

He looked shocked and in his British accent quickly said, "Thank you, sir." Then he looked at me for a moment. He paused. His eyes looked in my eyes, and he knew I was sincere. He knew I was sorry. Al did not hesitate to say he understood. We talked for a few moments. A new peace was made. It was a giving. We briefly shook hands before walking off in our own directions.

"Not to worry, lad. I had forgotten all about it. But thank you anyway." The words echoed in my ears. I knew Al had not forgotten, but he did forgive me. I was grateful he understood. Strange how he was there at that time. I wondered what force of nature caused us to walk that route just then. I felt relieved. I walked across the street, ducking into Carmichaels a lighter man. I was a man with one less thing to hide.

Through everything that happened over the last year, I carried the weight of that fucking chalk holder with me. Today, I let it go and the chaos with it. In a way it represented much of the stupidity in my life, my lack of character. But I had learned from the last year. There are things I will do better, and some things I will never do again. Trust is something that can be found, lost, and earned back. I had learned to trust again. I had developed character.

Snooker is my roots, and I felt nostalgic, so I had Johnny give me a set of snooker balls and a couple of beers, and I headed to the back of Carmichaels for some practice. The walk was long. I had nothing but memories and feelings for my friend in my mind and heart. Those days when we would play for hours, laugh, and party together were spent right here. I felt it in the back of my throat. It was hard to swallow. Frisk felt right in front of me and just seconds away. Everything made it real. The tables, the smell of chuck wagons, the lights over the tables, and the back door jammed slightly open. I felt alive in that distant moment of time, and the tightness in my stomach made it real.

There is always a winner and always a loser at a game of pool and this game of life. And every game was a new game. No one knows who will win. We play until we become weak and overtaken by the opponent. Our losses are earthly attachments and must be released quickly so our energy may continue to flow.

People were playing tonight, and that was a good thing. At the back of Carmichaels, I dumped the balls out on the last twelve-foot snooker table and began shooting them, one at a time down to the far end pocket. I would line up a ball, get my stance, take a practice swing or two, and gently roll the ball down the table at pocket speed. It would roll slowly down the table and drop into the pocket.

Sometimes I would miss, the ball juggling in the pocket. No worries. I would take a small sip of beer and keep on going as if nothing had happened. *Keep on going* was the most important thing just now, and forever more. Never to give up while the fever of life burns within me—never.

# The End

# Graham Green

Aug 6th 1991-
Aug 24th 2020

Dear Mr. Green:

First off I'm incredibly sorry for your loss.
Graham was an amazing, one of a
kind person, I miss him more than anything.
He was a huge inspiration to me and
many others, there is a ~~[illegible]~~ whole
generation of drummers out there now that
are all massively inspired by Graham.
thank you for raising such an incredible person,

—ISAAC/Blast Addict

EXPRESSION OF PAIN

1. UNFED
2. INCORRIGIBLE
3. DEMENTIA
4. RETCH
5. ASTRAY
6. DEFICIT
7. LESION
8. DROWN
9. TORSION TRAP
10. CYST
11. GASP
12. EXTIRPATE
13. WRING
14. SCORCHED
15. TRANSGRESSION
16. DETAINED
RECORDED BY SAL DUNCAN IN THE FALL OF 2012 AT THE HIVE IN BURNABY BC.
RE-MIXED AND MASTERED BY JESSE GANDER IN THE WINTER OF 2021 AT RAIN CITY RECORDERS IN VANCOUVER BC.
THANKS TO ISAAC BLAST ADDICT BUBBA FOR THE PHOTOS TOMMY WILSON FOR THE INLAY HELP
KATE LEDUC FOR THE POSTER, ALL OUR FRIENDS AND FAMILY FOR THE ENDLESS SUPPORT
THIS ALBUM IS DEDICATED TO OUR DEAR FRIEND GRAHAM GREEN. WE'LL MISS YOUR WILD SENSE OF HUMOUR, YOUR GENUINE CHARM, AND YOUR RAW TALENT. WE LOVE YOU FOREVER BROTHER, UNTIL WE MEET AGAIN.
GRAHAM - VOCALS
HOOTZ - VOCALS
PHIL - BASS, VOCALS
DAVE - GUITAR
GOAT - DRUMS, VOCALS
103/300

CPSIA information can be obtained
at www.ICGtesting.com
Printed in the USA
BVHW050956240722
642826BV00005B/11/J

9 781665 719575